ATM

The boy who could talk to cash machines

Tom Chaine

2.10.21

Dear Fahima,

As promised. I hope you enjoy. This book is under my author pen name - Tom Claine.

With very best wishes,

Steve

x.

ISBN: 9781916229006

First published 2019

Northmont Publishing

NORTHMONT

To Eric.
A soldier; a father; a good man
who showed me the way.

Contents

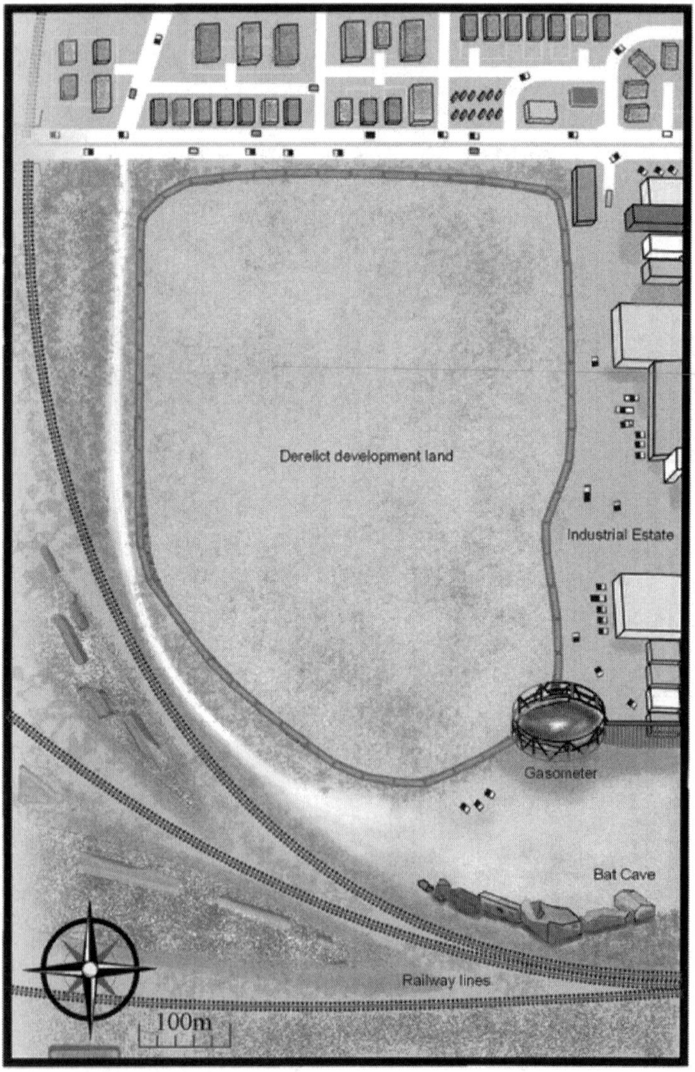
Derelict development land
Industrial Estate
Gasometer
Bat Cave
Railway lines
100m

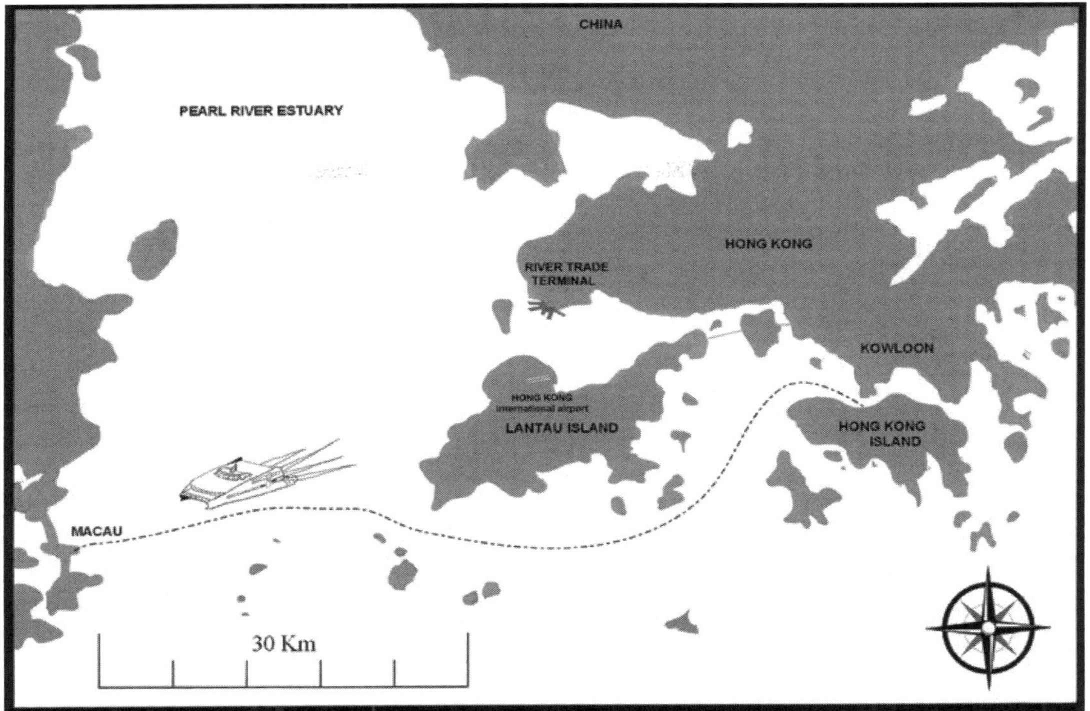
CHINA
PEARL RIVER ESTUARY
HONG KONG
RIVER TRADE
TERMINAL
KOWLOON
HONG KONG
International airport
LANTAU ISLAND
HONG KONG
ISLAND
MACAU
30 Km

ONE

Jace Bonchurch had a problem; a big one, in fact massive. It was money; a ton of it. Crisp bank notes, pink, blue and green stuffed into bulging bin-bags in his locked bedroom. It was way too much. He'd crossed the line. There was no going back. The damage was done and he was scared.

Loads of cash wouldn't be thought by most a problem. But this wasn't just loads; this was a money avalanche filling the back bedroom of the run-down council terrace in the poor postcode that Jace and his widowed mother called home. The thrill had worn off months ago, now there was just the hollow addiction and the weighty consequence of all that money. It was pressing him deep into a dark hole and Jace wasn't sure he could get out.

He didn't even know how much he'd taken. He'd attempted to count it several times but even a single bin-bag contained way too much. Beneath the bed; on top of the wardrobe, propping up his desk, behind the door and climbing the walls, the other bulging plastic bags remained unopened, crowding in on him.

The stupidest thing of all was he couldn't even spend it; well not much of it. Shops, supermarkets, stores would only take cash through the tills up to a small set limit; they certainly wouldn't accept hundreds let alone thousands. On-line it was all credit and debit cards. He couldn't pay the cash into a bank even assuming he had an account, which he didn't. After the London bombings the banks had tightened diligence 'till the pips squeaked. The law now demanded they know everything about customers including their inside leg measurement before even considering accepting large lumps of cash. A random teenager hefting bin-bags full of notes across the counter would have been like a butcher depositing a bucket of fresh offal; bloody messy. Hiding the cash in his room for much longer wasn't an option either. Thankfully his mother was too tired to worry, most of the time working long hours at the care home, but the lock on his door wouldn't last for ever. What he desperately needed was secure storage, but he was seventeen for Gods' sake; too young to sign a lock-up lease or self-store contract, even assuming he could find one that would take payment in cash. It was crazy. Each of those bloody bin-bags had become a ball and chain; heavy as hell and pulling one way only – down. He was fresh out of ideas. There were no more options. What he needed was help and he needed it quick.

TWO

The offices of the grandly named Financial Inter Bank Enforcement and Regulation Authority were housed anonymously behind three floors of mirrored windows fifty feet above Vaughan Way in London's East End; the financial no-man's land between the City and Canary Wharf.

Known to a select few simply as FIBER it was the most important financial authority in the country after the Bank of England. When faced with the catastrophic collapse of the British banking system in 2008 the government had acted. It had injected £500-billion of funds to stabilise the markets and underwrite financial guarantees; a £120-billion of this being paid directly to shore up individual British banks; a staggering mountain of money coming mainly from one source, the British tax payer. The government would never trust the unregulated banks again. Their recklessness had almost brought the country to its knees. It had acted quickly. FIBER was born; its remit simple. Police and protect this vast sum of money at all costs on behalf of the government and the British people.

The agency had lost no time. Quickly, quietly, it recruited the industry's best brains; the best forensic accountants, the best dealers, brokers and analysts and the best financial IT specialists. Also at its immediate disposal, by government special order through the Bank of England, were the entire resources of the nation's Security Services. The banks and the financial industry at large quickly recognised FIBER for what it was, no soft QUANGO but a formidable enforcer with a jaw full of razor-sharp regulatory powers. More to save their own skins than anyone else's the rapacious ranks of financiers had reluctantly fallen into line and slowly the country's financial systems had been pulled from the brink. But the banks could never be trusted again. FIBER was strengthened, given even greater powers. Now, from a position of strength and secrecy FIBER ruled the financial roost. Banks who before had been deemed too big to fail; the whales of the financial seas, now had an Orca in the waters with them and it was hungry.

Raphael G. D'eath stood in his capacious office looking out at the city through the one-way glass. The stuff was meant to be self-cleaning; a miracle of the modern age, but the view remained smeared and dirty. "Like everything else around here," he muttered, "bloody useless".

D'eath, pronounced 'Dee-ath', a legacy of his French birth in Marseilles forty-seven years earlier, cut an imposing silhouette against the wide oblong of grey October window light. Angular and thin, standing six-five in his shoes with olive skin, shaved head, dark suit and even darker eyes, FIBER's first and only Chief Executive exuded authority like rust on wet steel. Never married, childless, reporting solely to the Governor of the Bank of England, he didn't administer FIBER; he ruled it. He wasn't popular and he didn't care. What mattered in his exacting world were results; nothing else. Throughout the three floors of offices it was rumoured his middle initial, a mystery to all but himself and his long dead mother, stood for 'Genghis', as in Khan. D'eath knew the rumour. He liked it.

But times were changing and quickly. Lately D'eath hadn't felt much of a 'Genghis' at all, in fact the opposite. Recent months had brought nothing but failure and frustration for FIBER and by association himself. Feelings of inadequacy were growing and not just inside the organisation. D'eath had built a reputation, an entire career, on enforcing control and along the way had made many enemies; enemies that would now be sensing weakness; a growing vulnerability. He could almost hear the knives being sharpened. And all because of this damn ATM fiasco. It had started as nothing, a mere inconvenience. But it hadn't gone away. It had grown, day-after-day, multiplying, spreading like an aggressive tumour and now if he couldn't finish it, it would likely finish him. But what angered him the most . . . he hadn't even seen it coming.

The intercom startled him. Returning to his desk D'eath jabbed the button on the box.

"What!"

"The disc is here. You wanted to see it straight away." Frobisher's voice, electronic, emotionless, hung in the air.

"Damn right I do. Bring it in and get Carter and Bishop in here too."

The intercom clicked off without acknowledgement. Scowling D'eath sat back heavily into the plush leather behind his desk. His mood was spiteful. If the morning had been a disaster, the afternoon had become a complete train wreck. Last night another cash machine had been stripped, this one in Elephant & Castle. To make matters worse the machine had only been filled the day before. This was the twelfth in the last month, almost three a week, and still everyone remained bloody clueless. D'eath's frustration sat like a stone in his gut. He was the man who got results; the man who got the job done. But there were no results and the job was nowhere near getting done. And worse; others were beginning to know it too.

A few seconds later the wide double doors to his office opened and Frobisher strode in. She crossed the floor imperiously, all five-feet-ten of raven-haired Milanese fashion, seriously heeled, curvaceous, DVD case in hand. D'eath watched her approach. He'd overhead the office speak; a £500 haircut on a £100,000 head. Even at today's rates that was a serious rep. But Lucinda Frobisher was much more than a Prada suit under a Nicky Clarke haircut. She was a pain, a dangerous pain. Officially his personal assistant, it stated as much on her payslip, she was in reality the bank's appointee, not his. She was the Governor's eyes and ears within FIBER, an interloper, the bank's spy and both she and D'eath knew it. Suffering Frobisher had been a condition of his appointment. He'd objected. Was ignored but had still taken the job. He'd regretted it every day since.

Frobisher extended a manicured hand. "The disc . . . sir."

The pause, hardly subtle, didn't go unnoticed by D'eath. Long, immaculately shaped nails, glossed a deep ruby, contrasted with the matt black of the DVD case. For the briefest instant an image sparked in D'eath's shaven head; darkness, a big cat, the red of fresh blood. He blinked, dismissing the thought.

"Where are Carter and Bishop?"

"Here sir!"

Two unlikely-looking men hustled through the double doors.

"Sorry sir. We had a wait for the lift."

The larger of the two, Bishop, florid-faced and balding, stood wheezing heavily. His crumpled ill-fitting suit, creased collar and stained necktie did nothing to rescue an image of a mid-fifties overweight dishevelled lump. But whatever his image Bishop was also FIBER's best CCTV analyst and as such had been at the centre of all the recent ATM theft investigations. The other man, Carter, young enough to be Bishop's son, was straight out of the Cambridge silicon corridor and looked a different species to everyone else in the room. Lean as a whippet, Carter was graffiti in human form. With two sleeves of violently coloured 'tats', a yellow and black peroxided buzz cut, hip-hanging baggies, fluorescent red trainers, multiple piercings and an old Metallica emblazoned 'Tee', Carter was not just a different species he was from a different planet. But he was also a genius programmer and tolerated as possibly the best of FIBER's resident IT specialists. With his dubious hair he was known throughout the company as the 'Geek with the streak'.

D'eath, slotted the DVD into the drive on his desk and spoke without looking up. "Thank you, Frobisher. That will be all."

A long self-conscious moment passed, and another, stretching slowly, like gravity pulling at pegged up pizza dough. D'eath fiddled with the DVD drive. Bishop pursing his lips patted a sweaty forehead with a grimy handkerchief. Carter, head down, just looked at his trainers. At last Frobisher moved. Swivelling abruptly on the thick carpet, she strode out without a word, the double doors closing forcibly behind her.

"I'll be damned if I let the Governor know what we've got before we know ourselves," D'eath muttered to no one in particular as a picture flickered onto the monitor.

THREE

It was getting bloody cold up on the Heath. Daylight was almost gone, and the Dome of St Paul's was just a dirty thumbnail puncturing the city's horizon. Jason gingerly laid his bike on the ground and sat down beside Chris who was trying to fight his way into a bag of bacon-flavoured crisps.

"Supper is it then?"

Jason couldn't resist the jibe knowing Chris' parents had been away for the better part of the week. Apparently short pre-winter breaks right now were cheap as chips.

"Stuffing recession," Chris answered. "I could cop for some sun but no. It's feed the bleedin' cat and look in on yer Nan while we're gone. I'm telling you Jace that cat's getting better grub than me."

"Maybe you should try it then." Jason chuckled. "Likely it'll put some hairs on that parrot cage you call a chest."

In the physical stakes Chris was not one of nature's queue jumpers. Several inches shorter than Jason at five-foot-six, his slight build, pinched face and greasy long dark hair gave him the air of a malnourished apprentice undertaker. All he needed, Jason thought, was a black topper and the bodies would be queuing up. Chris though, was his best mate. Together since pre-school they'd grown up on adjacent streets, been rejected by the same girls, had their ears clipped by the same teachers and, despite looking like a greasy weasel, Jason knew Chris to be a steadfast and loyal friend. Scoffing the last of the crisps Chris lay back against the slope. His nose looked like a beak in the growing shadows. "You know Jace, I'm really pissed off. There's got to be something better than this, mate. Jesus! I'm only seventeen and look at me."

Jason lay beside his friend peering into the not-so-dark city sky. It was getting on for rush-hour and the office hordes would soon be grid locking the streets and turning tube trains into virus-infected sardine cans. It was that time of year.

"You know mate I've been thinking about that," murmured Jason. "Say you suddenly fell into a swimming pool but filled with cash not water. What do you think you'd do?"

"Shit! No problems there, mate. Bring it on. Clothes, girls, cars, you name it."

"But you can't bleedin' drive, you stupid nutter."

"Well I'll polish the stuffin' things then, won't I, or hire a chauffeur. Yeah that's what I'd do; a sexy blond chauffeur; all blond, kinky boots and big knockers, maybe Swedish. Y'know, with the uniform, the cap, the lot."

Jason grinned at the sky.

"Don't ever change, mate. But seriously, if you really did have that sort of money, and I do mean *really*, what would you do?"

"Shit Jace that's a stupid question. You know I'd never get money like that."

THREE

Jason, resting on his elbow, turned towards Chris. The day had stopped and night was now starting.

"You could win the lottery?"

"Yeah and West Ham could win the league."

"Well they might . . . one day."

Chris faced Jason. Their faces were barely discernible now. "Look Jace, mate, stop pissing around you know it's never going to happen."

"What if I told you it already has?"

Chris was silent. Moments passed. The wind on the heath was picking up now.

"Well?" asked Jason.

"Stop shitting me, Jace. All this talk of money, it's not a joke anymore. You've just seen me eat a bag of bloody crisps for supper for Chrisake!"

Jason took a long deep breath.

"Chris, this is serious". "

"Yeah, yeah, whatever."

"No! I bloody mean it. What I'm going to tell you will change your life, mate. But I need you to promise it stays between us, right?"

Chris sat up abruptly. Jason couldn't see his face but in the dark he could sense the sudden tension.

"Shit Jace, don't tell me you're serious?"

"Bloody right I am."

"Well? C'mon mate. I promise it stays with us."

Jason closed his eyes and took another deep breath.

"I'm getting cash, tons of it, from bleedin' cash machines."

"Cash machines?"

"Yeah. Y'know, hole-in-the-wall ATMs."

"What! You stole some poor sod's cash card with the PIN on it?"

"No. That's just it. I don't need a card. I don't need anything."

Jason sensed Chris thinking hard.

"Must be a faulty machine, mate. I'd make the bleeding most of it before it gets fixed."

Jason reached out in the dark gripping his friend's elbow. It felt pointed and bony through the sleeve of his hoody.

"It's all the bleedin' machines, mate. All of 'em. I've been doing it right across London."

"What! And no card or anything?"

"Shit Chris! You need your bloody ears syringed. Haven't you heard what I'm telling you?" Jason's voice was a harsh, piercing whisper. Chris could be bloody stupid.

"Okay mate. Keep yer hair on. I heard you right enough, but you've got to admit it sounds bloody far-fetched."

"What's bloody far-fetched?"

It was Chris's turn to whisper back savagely.

"You, jerkoff! You! That's what. You expect me to believe that you just walk up to any old cash machine in London and it spews out money like duck soup. Not bloody likely mate. You'd better leave that cider alone. It's rotting what's left of your bleedin' brain."

THREE

"Bleedin' brain is it? So I'm guessing that means you don't want a gander at the money then?"

Jason lay against the slope adopting an exaggerated relaxed posture, both hands behind his head. He crossed his legs idly and waited. Chris fidgeted in the dark.

"Well . . . er . . . how much we talkin' Jace? A hundred? Two-hundred?"

"Don't exactly know, mate. I'm guessing nearer three-hundred at least."

"Jeez Jace!" Chris pummelled Jason's shoulder with a fist.

"Three-hundred quid in your pocket and you're letting me survive on bleedin' crisps."

Momentarily, just for an instant, Jason put the burden of all those bulging bin-bags in his bedroom out of his mind. He smiled into the night, He couldn't care if Chris could see or not.

"Not three-hundred quid you moron. Three-hundred-thousand."

FOUR

Raphael D'eath was impressed. The Governor's historic office within the 300-year-old Bank of England was an imposing space. All about him the walls, floor and ceiling screamed opulence with fine Derbyshire limestone, burnished mahogany, polished leather and painstakingly beautiful mosaic floor tiles. The colours were rich and muted and the sense of power permeating the silence, palpable. D'eath sat patiently, listening to his own breathing, waiting for the Governor to finish reading his report. He was restless; uneasy. He wanted to stand, to move, but he daren't. It was as if he was in a vacuum, powerless. It wasn't a feeling he liked. Not a feeling he was used to. Not a feeling he wanted to repeat.

Finally the Governor finished reading. He closed the manila file marked 'Topmost Confidential' and placed the folder carefully on his desk. Steepling his hands under his chin he continued looking at the document as if it reeked of dead fish. Then he spoke. "It appears *you* have a problem Mr D'eath."

The Governor's voice, modulated and soft, was emotionless. He may just as well have been asking his wife what was on TV that night. But D'eath had noted the Governor's words. He was being isolated. Responsibility was going to be his alone. It was going to be his head on the block, no one else's and certainly not the Governor's. He regarded the man sitting opposite him. Immaculate, if slightly corpulent, he thought. Grey Saville Row chalk stripe, light blue Jermyn Street shirt, obviously tailored. Windsor knotted woven navy silk tie, manicured, exfoliated, primped and preened; the whole package bringing to mind an aging pink-faced cherub. The picture would have been complete if it wasn't for the steel rimmed glasses perched on the snub nose and the silvering, well-barbered hair. But D'eath knew appearances could be deceptive and this was especially so in the Governor's case. Here was a formidable survivor, a man of acute and scheming intelligence who had fought his way up the greasy pole from the bottom. His was no mere political appointment. Having joined the bank as a junior forty years earlier he knew better than anyone its intricate workings and, more importantly, where its skeletons were buried. That he remained Governor of the bank following the Armageddon of the 2008 financial meltdown was testament to this. D'eath blinked almost imperceptibly. Sitting opposite him was a man that would have given the legendary Machiavelli a run for his money.

The silence in the cavernous office had become almost unbearable. D'eath waited for the Governor to continue. The silence grew some more. D'eath's attention was drawn weirdly to a tacky plastic desk tidy sitting on the corner of the Governor's desk. A single fluorescent yellow marker pen stood in it. The marker pen and the tacky piece of moulded plastic seemed incongruous. They didn't belong in this fine historical office, amongst the books and panelling. D'eath knew the feeling. Finally the Governor spoke again, still quietly, as if asking a librarian for a book reference.

"Perhaps you would care to enlighten me Mr D'eath as to your proposed plan and solution?"

D'eath replied quickly not about to let the deafening silence encroach again.

"Sir, the problem facing us is without precedent."

"*You,* Mr D'eath."

"Sorry sir?"

"The problem facing *you* is without precedent."

D'eath wanted to swallow hard but he'd be damned if he would give the other man the satisfaction.

"Actually sir the problem is FIBER's". He hoped his voice didn't sound strained.

"Whatever." The Governor's quiet response dismissed D'eath's reply as casually as if he were swatting away a fly.

"However the question remains Mr D'eath. What do *you* propose to do?"

"Sir, we believe these attacks are entirely random. That is, they don't appear coordinated or part of any pattern we can see. We also believe that the perpetrator is the same in every instance."

"You've identified him?"

D'eath shuffled in his chair.

"Not exactly sir but all the CCTV footage indicates it's the same person. Same height and build and the same articles of clothing are repeated over the cycle of attacks. Two types of Hoody, jeans and we think the same pair of Reebok trainers, although with the camera angles it's more difficult to tell about the footwear."

The Governor hadn't moved. Like a seated statue of the Buddha he remained ensconced in his stitched leather chair. He did however sigh quietly.

"Mundane clothing that can be bought at a thousand outlets across London?"

"I'm afraid so, sir."

The Governor changed tack.

"Why do you refer to these episodes as 'attacks' Mr D'eath? My information and your report indicate no evidence of force being used?"

"You are, of course, correct sir…"

The Governor interrupted with another small sigh.

"Really Mr D'eath. That is so reassuring to know."

Bastard, thought D'eath.

"What I mean sir is that we at FIBER deem the scope and extent of these episodes to be an attack on the very system of currency circulation in the public domain."

The Governor's grey eyes widened slightly behind his lenses

"Don't you think that's somewhat alarmist Mr D'eath?

After all we are talking about small hole-in-the-wall cash machines and only in London?" D'eath blinked. Hadn't this idiot just read his report? It was all in there.

"With respect sir, we have no clues as to the perpetrator; worse, we have absolutely no idea how the machines are being stripped. We can't even begin to guess which machines will be hit next and if the raids continue on their present scale they could accumulate into the biggest robbery in British history. Personally sir I think alarmist is an understatement."

D'eath sat back. It was done. He'd said it. If the bastards wanted to crucify him so be it. While D'eath was speaking the Governor hadn't moved. Now he sat studying D'eath the way a toad might study a particularly succulent insect. Then, judging the moment, he spoke.

"It seems Mr D'eath that what you are saying is that FIBER under your leadership is not up to the job? Please correct me if I have misunderstood."

D'eath clenched his fists. This was too much. He strained to keep his voice level.

"I'm sorry if I misled you sir. But yes, you have misunderstood. FIBER is mobilising all its expertise and is targeting these raids as its number one priority. Up to now the perpetrator has had it easy. This is changing today. If the bank gives its authority, we will bring in the organised crime and robbery squads of the Met. together with all their covert surveillance and CCTV assets. We will bring on board GCHQ to monitor terrestrial communication and internet traffic using key words and phrases, we will publish sizeable rewards for the apprehension of the felon or felons involved and we will be implementing increased security for the cash dispensers themselves through urgent liaison with the manufacturers. Of course the authorities and proprietors of all banks, building societies, corner shops, petrol stations, supermarkets, train stations and airports across the capital where ATMs are in use will receive briefings and will be required to increase vigilance and security."

D'eath paused, attempting to gauge the effect of what he'd said on the man facing him. The Governor remained impassive but his eyes never left D'eath's.

"Most comprehensive I grant you Mr D'eath but expensive. Assuming I sign off on what you are proposing how long do you suppose it might be before we have those responsible in custody?" D'eath gambled. Now was not the time to be noncommittal. He needed those resources and the man opposite him held the key.

"From my experience sir and given the immediate release of the resources I have indicated I am confident we will have our man by Christmas."

The Governor's expression hardened. "That's less than twelve weeks Mr D'eath."

"I know that sir but with the resources I have requested and the bank's support, I stand by what I've said."

"If I grant your request Mr D'eath you most certainly will have to. Be sure of that."

FOUR

D'eath sensed cogs turning inside the other man's head as he weighed the options. Finally, reaching a decision, the Governor spoke again. "You will have your warrant to proceed waiting for you at your office when you return Mr D'eath."

"Thank you sir…"

The Governor raised a hand. "It will of course be conditional upon your personally signed statement being on my desk tomorrow morning confirming the details of what you have promised. I assume this is acceptable?"

D'eath was so far down the toilet it didn't matter anymore. Clearly the meeting was at an end. He'd got what he'd come for but it hadn't been easy.

"Perfectly sir. Thank you."

D'eath rose and moved towards the door. He was almost out of the room when the Governor called him back.

"A word of advice Mr D'eath. You wouldn't want to be delayed so avoid taking a taxi. Apparently, the traffic is backed up the length of Threadneedle Street. They're putting in a new water main and of course it will soon be with us won't it?"

D'eath paused in the doorway, perplexed.

"Soon be with us sir? What…the water main?"

"No, no, no Mr D'eath." The Governor smiled benignly. "Christmas."

FIVE

Four-thirty on a wet, bitingly cold morning in the boondocks guaranteed one thing, no bloody people. Well actually that wasn't entirely true. Two darkly hooded exceptions to the rule appeared from a side street and scuttled across an empty car park into the lee of a two-story warehouse building. Here they stopped, huddled against the wall as if seeking some shelter.

"Shit Jace, I'm tellin' you now you'd better be telling the truth. I'm freezing me bloody balls off."

"Keep it down," whispered Jason urgently. "You'll see soon enough. Now pass the bag and keep your bleedin' eyes peeled."

Chris handed Jason a tough black dustbin liner while glancing over his shoulder.

"Quick now the gaffer tape mate."

Chris dutifully handed over a roll of two-inch-wide black tape. Moving with practised speed Jason tore of a strip and used it to tape the mouth of the bin liner over the slot of a cash machine set into the wall of the warehouse. It hung slackly from the slot like a long black tongue.

"Okay mate," whispered Jason, "is the coast clear?"

"You kiddin?" answered Chris, trying for some bravado but failing, "even the bleedin' ducks won't be coming out in this lot."

"Then watch 'n learn Chrissy mate. Watch 'n learn."

Jason placed a hand on the wet glass screen of the ATM machine and closed his eyes. Suddenly the hidden innards of the dispenser whirred into motion. The slithery sound of notes being counted at tremendous speed filled the night and then the bin liner was billowing, filling out as notes poured into it from the cash machine's slot. To anyone who has withdrawn cash from an ATM machine, the action, the sound and the dispensing of cash are as common an experience as, say, brushing one's teeth. But when the action, the sound and the dispensing doesn't stop but just goes on and on and on, the whole experience becomes something totally weird. To Jason it had become commonplace. Chris, on the other hand, was dumbfounded. He stood in the rain, his mouth so wide he was in danger of drowning. The bin-liner, bulging and taut like a great black sausage, was now standing out from the wall and quivering. Finally the tape gave way and the bag clumped weightily to the ground. Bank notes continued to vomit from the machine, scattering into the darkness of wind and rain. At last the dispenser fell silent and Chris put his gaping mouth to use.

"Holy shit! Holy shit! Holy sheeeiiit!"

Jason bent grabbing the mouth of the bin-bag. He smiled remembering his own reaction the first time. It was not dissimilar.

"Shut up moron and grab the other end. The bag weighs a bleedin' ton."

FIVE

That had been three nights ago. Now, early on the fourth evening, the two boys were in the small kitchen of Chris' parents' house. Jason, deep in thought, was peering at the floor. It had been state of the art once. White linoleum. But that had been a long time ago. Now it was a strange blotchy yellow and curling up in the corners like the ends of Ali Baba slippers. On it a large tin bowl occupied a space between an old fridge freezer and a row of chipped melamine cupboards. Under the harsh light of a single fluorescent tube stuck to the grubby ceiling, the bowl looked full of week-old porridge. Little wonder the cat hadn't touched it in days. But Jason wasn't bothered about cat food. His mind was on other things.

The absence of Chris' parents had its advantages. He'd been staying over with Chris to keep him company for the duration. They had stored the bulging bin-liner behind the couch in the small front room. It was as good a place as any and certainly relieved the diminishing space under his bed at home. But it wasn't space, diminishing or otherwise, troubling him. It was his conscience; his conscience and all that money.

He should never have taken the stuff. He'd known from the start, clear as day, but it hadn't stopped him. What was worse, he'd kept on taking it, for months now, stealing like a thief in the night. There were no justifications, no excuses. He'd taken because he could; because no one seemed to care, no one was being hurt and, in the end, because it was so bloody easy. It had been exciting in the beginning. Like a drug high; a sense of euphoria and power driving him on. His addiction supressing any fear of getting caught. But when nothing had happened and it had dawned that there was little he could do with all that money anyway, excitement had quickly evaporated. That's when he should have stopped. But like a prat he hadn't. Out of habit and just plain boredom he'd continued. Filling his bedroom week after week with bin-bags, deluding himself it was all just a game; a game played with paper money, most of which he would never be able to spend.

But as his bedroom filled, seeds of anxiety had begun to grow. Then one day he'd woken up and it wasn't a game anymore. Somewhere along the way he'd crossed a line. He'd painted himself into a corner with a mountain of bin-bags and he was stuck solid. That's when the first worm of fear had come sneaking back. And then yesterday, for the first time, he'd seen the poster. It had come like a stomach punch. Rewards were being posted; big ones. Suddenly the uniforms and suits *did* care. They were looking for the thief hard, all over London, and unless he could somehow 'disappear' a bedroom bursting with bin-bagged cash, it would only be a matter of time before they found him.

His first panicked thought had been to come clean; to give the money back. Most of it was untouched. He could make up a story. He was only a kid after all. The authorities would understand. Or would they? They would demand to know how he'd done it. But he didn't know. He wouldn't be able to tell them and then where would that lead? And it wasn't just about him. His mum was sleeping not ten-feet away from all that bin-bagged money. No way would they believe she wasn't implicated. And finally, like a bloody idiot, he'd just gone and put Chris up front and centre too. He should have known better. Just because Chris had wanted to see was no excuse for stupidly showing him. But it was too late now.

The loud belch made Jason look up. Stuffing his mouth with the last of the chicken whopper Chris took a swig of coke and belched again.

Jason winced.

"Has anyone ever told you you're a bleedin' pig Hutchins?"

Chris tilted back on his chair.

"Tell you the truth, mate, since getting that money I couldn't give a flying stuff."

"Well you'd better give a flying stuff, Chris, because as of yesterday reward notices are being posted. I saw one in the newsagents. They're offering a hundred-thousand quid for chrissake! People round here sell their own grandmothers for that kind of money."

Chris, apparently unconcerned, belched again.

"Look mate it's not that bad. I've bin thinkin' about what you said. Y'know 'bout what to do next. And I've got an idea 'bout storing and washing the stuff."

"Laundering," muttered Jason.

"What?"

"The correct term is laundering."

"Yeah? Well whatever, I've got an idea. I've got this cousin Davey see. He's me mum's brother's son and is a really good bloke. He's much older than me, in his thirties now I reckon, but when we were younger we were really good mates. Whenever I was in the shit it was always Davey Boy there pulling me out. Me mum thinks the bloody sun shines out his arse and you know what Jace? She's not wrong. Davey Boy will know what to do. He'll help. I'm sure of it mate."

Jason furrowed his eyebrows.

"Your cousin? Wasn't he something in the army?"

Chris nodded, half of Burger King still running down his chin.

"That's him. He was out in Afghanistan."

Jason nodded. "So where's Davey Boy now then? Still running up mountains after mad mullahs?"

Chris finally wiped his mouth with a paper napkin.

"No. That's just it, Jace. Dave's out the army now. He's working up in the City; somethin' in security."

Jason exploded.

"Security! For chrissake Chris you got a bloody screw loose or what? Half of London after us and you want to cough to a cousin in security. Why the hell don't you just walk up Wandsworth road knock on the prison door and ask to be let in. Sloppin' out at six in the morning might knock some sense into you."

Chris glared back defiantly.

"I'm tellin' you Jace, Davey is family. I don't know what

that means to you but around here it stands for summit. The Hutchinses are no bleedin' grasses."

"He's not a bloody Hutchins Chris," Jason was not letting up, "unless you're telling me your mum just happened to marry a bloke with her same maiden name."

Chris paused, confused.

"You know what I bleedin' mean Jace. What I'm sayin' is family. We all stick together 'round 'ere and Davey Boy is salt of the earth mate. Salt of the bleedin' earth and anyway I don't see you coming up with any better ideas."

This threw Jason. Chris was right. All he'd done recently was to sink further and further into a soup of fear, apathy and self-pity. It wasn't like him. No one had twisted his arm up his back and forced him to strip the machines. He'd got himself into this mess and now he'd drawn in Chris too, although Chris was still too high to realise it. The whole thing had turned into a pot of shit. But something had to happen soon. He couldn't stay put doing nothing. Maybe bringing in a third person, a family member, older, wiser, with experience, with connections, might be the answer? It had to be better than waiting for a knock on the door or pitching up in the local cop shop alone with his hands in the air. Chris had a point.

"Okay okay, you might be right mate." Jason's voice softened. "It's not like we're surrounded with bleedin' options."

He thought some more, looking idly at the tin bowl of cat food. It looked exactly like he felt. Jason swallowed, took a long breath and exhaled.

"Okay Chris, go for it. Make the intros and let's give Davey Boy a spin, but for chrissake, promise me one thing, leave the talking to me.

SIX

Carter studied the glowing characters and digits scrolling across his thirty-inch PC screen. They constituted the programme log of the latest stripped ATM machine. The attack had occurred the previous night at a warehouse complex down by the river in Wandsworth. Carter had uploaded the data from the machine's solid-state management chip as soon as notification had reached him. It was past midnight, his workstation the single oasis of dim light in the otherwise dark FIBER office. He swallowed another mouthful of lukewarm coffee. It tasted bitter but at least it was keeping him awake. The story unfolding on his computer display was the same. He had become used to it. What he hadn't become used to was his feeling of complete inadequacy. He had never seen anything like it before. For months now it had had him stumped. Carter buried his face in his hands and bowed his head tiredly. It was crazy. It went against all computerised logic and computerised logic was something Carter understood very well indeed. He knew it should have been simple. Every time a cash machine is used a formidable array of security technology is automatically employed to protect the data being passed from the ATM to the bank's computers. At the heart of this process are the cryptoprocessors. The black boxes that scramble the information punched into the ATM so it cannot be intercepted and manipulated as it travels along the wires. These black boxes also scramble the program that the receiving bank's computers run to check the validity of the input PIN number. The cryptoprocessors should have been impregnable with their strong physical construction and inbuilt self-destruct programme to counter any physical tampering. But from what Carter could ascertain, in every case so far, these black boxes had simply been by-passed as if they didn't exist. That, according to the well-thumbed pile of ATM design manuals littering his desk, just couldn't happen.

"This is some crazy shit man," he murmured into the shadows.

"The programme activates like it's meant to but where's the bloody instruction?"

Speaking to himself had become habit. In the past it had helped formulate his thoughts; leading him always to an acceptable solution. But that wasn't happening here. His investigations had confirmed that virtually all modern ATMs were now designed around the Microsoft Windows Operating System. This enabled remote diagnosis and repair. But like all computer programs the operating system was based on the founding principle of the BIOS; the Basic Input Output Systematic flow of information. To get something out one had to put something in. This could be by way of a mouse or keyboard or even a pre-loaded hard memory programme that activated when the power switched on. The latest cash machines used the glass touch screen on the terminal as their input interface but whatever the mode any input was bound to leave a trace, a footprint of code in the activity log, something. Carter's problem was simple. Despite close study of all the activity logs of all the raided ATMs he couldn't find in any of them a record of the input instruction that emptied the machine. It wasn't as if it had been hidden, corrupted or disguised. It just didn't exist. There was no card input. No PIN input and the cryptoprocessors hadn't been tampered with or compromised in any way he could see. There had been rumours in the industry that the encryption keys in the black boxes could be compromised when the cryptoprocessors were interfacing with other programs in the system to disseminate information. But even if this unlikely event had happened it would only reveal the single PIN for the compromised transaction and given that every PIN had a withdrawal limit that would be insufficient to completely empty the dispenser of all its cash in one go. The more Carter pondered the more his head ached. There was no credible answer. It was as if each machine had just suddenly started up and emptied itself. As far as Carter could see the dispensing programme in each case had simply initiated and run until there was nothing left to dispense. This couldn't happen. The machines were doing something that all logic, programming and design were telling him couldn't be done. Gulping down the last dregs of the coffee Carter spun around on his chair and looked out into the darkness. He'd checked, double checked and triple checked. There was nothing for him to miss. If this was a sci-fi movie the solution would have been simple. The machines were alive and acting under some form of artificial intelligence. But this wasn't a sci-fi flick. The machines in all other respects remained lumps of alloyed metal, circuitry, electric motors, plastic and glass. There was no way they would be ripping themselves out of walls and marching on Downing Street saying take me to your leader. It was a damn mystery. Carter yawned deeply and started typing out his report for D'eath. Genghis wanted it on his desk by morning but at least that wouldn't be a problem, apart from the date, time, location and amount the report would be a copy of the last one and the one before that. In the dim light Carter's peroxided head nodded over the keyboard like a badger's. He'd leave the finished report on Frobisher's desk for the following morning. Let her be the one to give it to the boss. Of one thing Carter was sure. He didn't want to be around when D'eath read it.

SEVEN

Chris' kitchen hadn't changed. The linoleum remained a sickly curdle of yellowy white; the same tired cabinets exhibited the same chipped melamine and the old fridge freezer still puttered in the corner. At least the cat food was new. Dave Gilroy surveyed the room and its two occupants over the rim of a mug of instant coffee. It wasn't a pretty sight. A dry sink stacked with dishes growing mushrooms and a corner waste bin overflowing with the detritus of a dozen take-aways, didn't help.

"Shit Chris, how long have your folks been away?"

Chris grimaced, failing in his attempt at an ingratiating smile.

"Comin' on a week now Davey and not even a bleedin' postcard."

"Well a word to the wise young Chrissy." Dave Gilroy put down his mug. A single swallow of the stuff had been enough. "If you don't want to end up like that cat food, you'd best get this place sorted before they get back."

Jason hadn't spoken since Chris' cousin had arrived. He sat regarding the man quietly. Would he be the answer to their problems? He'd certainly responded quickly enough to Chris' phone call. Jason's mind was not made up, though encouragingly Dave Gilroy certainly looked the part. Jason judged him to be about two inches taller than himself, somewhere over a lean and fit looking six foot he reckoned. His dark two-piece suit appeared immaculate and expensive as did the gleaming black leather of his belt and shoes. Davey Boy wasn't wearing a tie, his plain navy shirt, open by a single button at the neck lending him an informal, relaxed look; a look straight out of a magazine advert for Dunhill or Hugo Boss. It was a look Jason wanted. Understated, expensive, stylish but, most of all, assured. That was it, assured.

"So what's this all about then Chrissy," continued Davey Boy, "and who's your mate?"

Davey Boy casually switched his attention while speaking. His pale grey eyes now fixed on Jason.

"I'm Jason Bonchurch, Mr Gilroy." Jason did his best to sound assertive, but it was difficult under the calm unblinking scrutiny of those eyes. He had heard of the thousand-yard stare; had seen it portrayed in films, but this was the real thing. He felt like a specimen under a microscope and not a particularly good specimen at that.

"Jason is it?" Davey Boy smiled easily. Thick dark hair curling just off his collar, white even teeth, tanned, chiselled. It was a look that could probably unsnap a bra strap at thirty feet, thought Jason, if it wasn't for that unsettling stare and a livid four-inch scar cutting across Davey Boy's right cheek. Davey Boy pushed away the cooling mug of coffee but remained seated.

SEVEN

"As happy as I am to see Chris again why is it, I'm thinking this is all about you Jason?" Again those pale grey eyes.

Chris tried to interject but Jason flashed him a look.

"Chris is my best mate Mr Gilroy, and I don't want to put him in it but, to tell the truth, I'm in a helluva of a jam and Chris thinks you might be able to help."

"He does, does he?"

Davey Boy shifted forward, placing both elbows carefully on the table. The Rolex chronograph on his wrist rode up from beneath the shirt cuff; a steel and sapphire glass manacle. It looked heavy, expensive.

"Did Chris tell you what I do?" Davey Boy's eyes were unwavering. Jason responded.

"He mentioned the army and that now you're in security or something." Davey Boy smiled again, this time back towards Chris.

"Security or something? My young cousin always did have trouble with specifics. Right Chrissy?"

Chris shrugged an inane smile but otherwise kept quiet.

The smile left Davey Boy's face. "Suppose you tell me about this helluva jam, Jason, and I'll see what I can do. I'm assuming you haven't murdered anyone?"

Jason emitted a hollow laugh. It sounded contrived, even to him, but he needed time. Right now his options could be counted on the finger of one hand. Could he trust Davey Boy or not? Once the cat was out of the bag there'd be no putting it back.

"I'm sorry to disappoint Mr Gilroy but no, I haven't murdered anyone recently."

"Well that's a start at least." The smile had returned, but Davey Boy's eyes remained pale, implacable. Jason felt their scrutiny burning into him. There was just something about that look. Jason made up his mind.

"Okay Mr Gilroy. Here's the deal. I guess you're not going to believe this but . . . " Jason paused, swallowing hard. This was it. There would be no going back afterwards. The cat wouldn't just be out of the bag it would be so far down the road it'd be halfway to Peckham.

"I've been emptying cash machines for months; right across London. I haven't hurt anyone, and Chris isn't involved. He didn't even have a clue 'till a few nights ago but now the authorities are after me and I'm . . . " Again Jason paused, the piercing eyes of Davey Boy never leaving his face. "Well to tell the truth Mr Gilroy I'm bloody scared."

Jason stopped speaking but Davey Boy didn't stop staring.

Silence.

Chris shuffled in his chair. Jason waited, hardly breathing. The smell of cat food filled the small kitchen. More silence. Sod this, thought Jason. He stood, pushing his chair back abruptly.

"Okay Mr Gilroy. That's it. I haven't murdered anyone but I'm in the shit just the same. I've trusted you but if you can't help fair enough. I guess what happens now is up to you."

Davey Boy's stare didn't alter but for the first time he pursed his lips, as if thinking. Jason snatched a look over to Chris. Taking his cue Chris spoke up.

SEVEN

"C'mon Davey. You've heard Jace. He really needs your help and that part 'bout me not being involved, well that's a load of shit. It was me that helped him unload the last machine so if he's in trouble then I'm in it too. C'mon Davey, please, you've just gotta help."

Yet more silence.

Chris looked anxiously at Jason who returned his worried look. This was getting crazy. Chris was at the point of pleading again when Davey Boy at last raised a hand.

"Life," he said quietly.

"What?"

"It never fails to amaze me," murmured Davey Boy, as if to himself, his gaze leaving Jason and playing idly across the kitchen.

"Only yesterday I'm reading a confidential communique raising hell. Months of raids against cash machines right across the capital; the entire city's currency circulation system under threat, the Met involved, GCHQ, the Bank of England, all leave cancelled, the works."

Davey Boy paused, his stare refocussing on Jason.

"And here I am less than twenty-four hours later listening to this."

He stopped speaking. Jason and Chris sat open-mouthed, stunned, trying to assimilate Davey Boy's words. Even if he was only half right, they were screwed and totally. Davey Boy stood up.

"Okay Jason, before I walk out of here and forget all this shit what have you got to prove this isn't just a mess of crap, cat food and cold coffee?" Jason felt stung. Gathering his thoughts he stood, motioning Davey Boy to follow him. Together they walked silently into the front room. It wasn't much better than the kitchen. Grey once-white nets across the low window; a flying formation of china ducks going nowhere on woodchip wallpaper and a much-trodden carpet of vivid flowery swirls. Pulling forward the mock leather settee Jason dragged the lumpy black bin-liner from behind it. Maybe he hadn't expected Davey Boy to believe him, but the arrogance of the man had him steaming.

"You might think this crap or cat food Mr Gilroy, but others wouldn't." Jason's words came out harsher than he had meant. He was having difficulty controlling the emotions boiling just below his skin. Davey Boy, appearing not to notice, knelt and opened the bulging black sack. Bank notes have a unique smell. Maybe it's the ink or the paper or maybe it's the collective sheaves of closely packed notes; but whatever its source, that unique financial incense flowed up from the opened mouth of the bag, filling the room. Davey Boy sat back on his haunches. He peered at the densely packed notes. He rummaged his hand deep into the bag like a child at a lucky dip striving for the bottom-most present. He clutched and pulled up a handful from the bottom of the bag, all twenties. Then he stood up, the bin-liner at his feet, and looked across at Jason and then Chris, who had followed them into the room. His face was a picture of incredulity.

SEVEN

"Okay Jason, I'll give it to you." He looked at the notes clutched in his fist. "Definitely not crap or cat food." Davey Boy dropped the notes back into the bin-liner.

"So is this it?"

"Shit no Davey," blurted Chris. "Jace reckons he's got a bedroom full of bags back at his."

"You're taking the piss, right?" Disbelief grew across Davey Boy's face. Jason's returned a stony look.

"I'm not taking a thing Mr Gilroy. For once Chris is dead right. Now do you believe me?"

Davey Boy turned and sat down heavily on the cheap settee. Cupping his chin he peered into the vulgar flowery swirls of the carpet, thinking hard. Jason and Chris stood together silently, their hearts hammering, like defendants in the box awaiting the jury's verdict.

"Damn it!" exhaled Davey Boy after a long moment. It was the first sign of real emotion he had given since arriving at the house.

"It's got to be you two. There's no other answer. Shit! What a mess."

He looked up at the two boys. Jason returned his stare defiantly. Chris, on the other hand, looked like he was about to pee his pants. Then Davey Boy uttered the understatement of the year.

"This is not good," he said.

EIGHT

"Okay the two of you," Davey Boy gesticulated at two ropey armchairs each occupying an opposite corner of the small front room. "Sit down and give me the whole story."

Slumping into one of the armchairs Jason felt terrible but he also felt a twinge of relief. It appeared Davey Boy wasn't about to shop them out of hand, well not yet at least.

"Where do you want me to begin Mr Gilroy," he said.

"From the start Jason and you'd better get used to calling me Davey. I think you can safely say we're well past any point of formality."

Jason, back under that piercing stare, felt more like a microscope specimen than ever. He steadied himself, taking a deep breath.

"Well I don't know when it started exactly Mr . . . er, Davey. But I guess it must have been around March, about eight months ago."

Davey Boy remained silent. Jason collecting his thoughts continued, straining to keep his voice steady.

"I remember because I'd just royally screwed my mocks and dreaded mum finding out. She's always been drumming on about me getting ahead, going to university, getting something better out of life and I knew my screwing up the exams, even mocks, would devastate her. She's always sacrificed everything for me, my mum. There's never been much money. She's a carer down the council and I help with a few odd jobs here and there in the holidays but everything she does she does for me."

"What about your dad?"

"Never knew him. Mum says he died just before I was born. She showed me photos. He worked overseas; in a jungle someplace. Mum says he was a brilliant engineer. I'm meant to look a lot like him."

"An engineer in a jungle, it sounds dangerous?"

Jason shrugged away Davey Boy's remark.

"Don't know about that. Mum was about to have me. He flew back for the big day. Apparently, he'd been pretty sick for a while. He just got worse and died in the same hospital."

"I'm sorry," said Davey Boy quietly.

"No need. I never knew him but that's what I'm saying. It's just been mum and me for years. Anyway, there I am, a lad no different to a hundred others round here, waiting for the bus outside Lloyds on the High Street. You probably drove past it on the way here?"

Davey Boy nodded.

"So there I am. Standing up against the wall next to the bank's ATM. No money in my pockets, thinking about mum, about how upset she's going to be, about what she's going to say and I'm getting really worked up; y'know, angry at myself for letting her down so badly, then suddenly . . . it starts. It's not even cold but I begin to shiver. The hairs on the back of my neck and on my arms are quivering. I feel pressure changing around me; my ears popping. I sense a massive energy; a kind of magnetic energy and it's drawing me, somehow, towards the bank's cash machine. In front of it there're still a few people in a queue so I wait with the energy building, humming, crackling. The people seem oblivious. Then the queue clears and I'm right in front of the machine reaching out. I haven't a clue what I'm doing. My fingers connect with the machine's surface and instantly everything changes. I feel as if a part of me has somehow been injected inside the machine. I sense it around me, surrounding me, trapping me. Then the worse part happens."

Jason stood up and started pacing. Putting into words the fear he had felt that very first time had made it all come rushing back. He was feeling it again; the sweat, his pounding pulse, hands trembling. He continued with difficulty, both Chris and Davey Boy hanging on every word.

"It suddenly hits me. What I'm in isn't a machine, it's a coffin. A coffin of metal and cables and it's shrinking around me. I scream but there is just silence. The solid steel walls of the machine are like industrial presses. They close on me. There's no room to move. I can't squirm. I can't scream. Still those steel walls are pressing in. Then they are crushing me; splitting my skull, grinding my bones to dust, popping my eyes like grapes under a car tyre. I feel the crunch of my collapsing ribcage, the bursting of my heart and lungs. And still those steel walls press in on all sides. I know I should be dead but somehow . . . I'm not. There's no pain either; just the terrible sensation of my body being pulverised to blood and paste. The steel walls come together at last and I am just a formless sludge between them; a soup of what had once been me." Jason slumped into the armchair. Everything else in the room remained as motionless as the china ducks stuck to the wall.

"You can't imagine that first time," Jason mumbled. "Words can't describe it; the fear; the terror, the isolation, the loneliness."

"What do you mean, Loneliness?" Davey Boy's voice was calm, probing. Jason rubbed his eyes.

"You're not there anymore, don't you see? You've melted into the machine. You've been absorbed. You don't exist. But then suddenly you realise you're still conscious, still thinking. It's as if you've been somehow reborn, but now as part of the machine." Jason fixed Davey Boy with a penetrating stare of his own, searching for the right words. "No! Not *part* of the machine. You *are* the machine. Suddenly it's just you fixed in the wall. You can feel the cement, the bricks. Panic wells up. You want to scream, to claw your way out of the wall and back into yourself but it's impossible. There is nothing you can do. Everything has become a terrible nightmare and you can't wake up."

"Jesus Jace!" Chris' face was rapt with horrific fascination. "You're not saying all this was going through you the other night when we did that ATM are you?"

EIGHT

Jason shrugged ruefully. "I'm talking about the first time Chris, the baptism of fire if you like. It gets easier when you become used to it, when you know what's going to be happening."

"Do you need a drink Jason? We can take a break if you like."

Jason welcomed Davey Boy's solicitous tone. It was a marked improvement on his previous sarcastic arrogance.

"No that's okay, Davey. I'm on a run and may as well get it out of the system. In fact it feels good putting it into words. I've never spoken about it before."

Davey Boy nodded, appearing to understand.

"Okay Jason, so you're trapped in this terrible nightmare but then what happens?"

"Then you wake up." Jason's voice was a bare whisper in the small room. "What I mean is . . . the panic, the fear, somehow it isn't so bad anymore. You can sense your new body, feel its circuitry, manipulate its switches, its relays. You don't have to learn it. It's suddenly all so natural; as normal as breathing, as automatic as blinking. You are in control and with the control comes realisation. The machine is you and you are the machine and you can do whatever you want because . . . it's just you." Jason stopped speaking and looked up at both Davey Boy and Chris. "Am I making any kind of sense?"

"I don't know Jason," responded Davey boy honestly. "To tell the truth it all sounds like something out of the 'Twilight Zone, but don't stop."

Jason nodded, marshalling his thoughts, searching for the right words. "Then you become aware of something inside you, something separate, something not a part of you."

"The money," said Davey Boy.

"Exactly!" Jason nodded. "It's there in your system, just an indigestible lump. It's foreign and irritating, an inert mass at the core of your being and you just want rid of it."

Chris snickered involuntarily. "Jeez Jace I've never heard money described that way before".

"As I said Chris, it was the first time. That's what I felt. The stuff just didn't have any value for me, in fact the opposite. It was . . . well, like something dirty, something unnatural, blocking up my insides."

"So you ejected it?"

Jason nodded sheepishly. "All of it. It was pretty easy to do really."

"And then you felt better?"

Jason looked surprised. "How did you guess that?"

Davey Boy allowed himself a brief smile, "Oh let's just say there've been a few times when ejecting an 'inert mass' as you put it, has made me feel a lot better too."

Jason smiled, getting the message. "Well that's about it. The weird thing is once the money had gone things immediately felt different. Somehow it wasn't just me anymore. It was me and then the machine; like I'd somehow separated back out from it. I was trapped in that coffin again, just like in the beginning, but this time the walls were reversing out giving me space to move and there was light in the dark. I could see the void left by the money and I felt myself pouring into it, filling it, overflowing from it, following the path of the money towards the light and then . . . I was out."

"Whad'ya mean out?" Chris' voice filled with incredulity. Jason stood up again. He felt miles better now. Sharing his feelings like this for the first time had seemed to lift a burden from his shoulders.

"Out! Y'know? Back on the street; normal again." Jason chuckled. "Well normal apart from all that dosh scattered everywhere. By the time I came around to myself it was a real free for all with half the high street on their knees scrabbling around. As for me, I was so happy to be alive and myself again I just legged it."

"Idiot!" Chris grinned, relieved at his friend's new buoyant mood. "Typical. Knee deep in cash and Jacey's away on his toes without so much as a handful."

Davey Boy wasn't picking up on the jovial mood.

"I wouldn't worry Chris. It seems Jason has more than made up for that since."

As he spoke Davey Boy pulled out a slim leather notebook from his inside jacket pocket. Plucking an expensive-looking pen from another pocket he began to make notes.

"Okay Jason, I won't lie to you. If it wasn't for the money here," Davey Boy kicked the bulging bin-liner at his feet, "I would be calling the guys in the white coats to come pick you up right now. I might even put you in the straightjacket myself.

Maybe there's a mad scientist somewhere that can explain it all or maybe there isn't, either way that's got to be the weirdest shit I've ever heard. But it's what we do from this point forward that's important. We've got to figure out where we go from here. I take it all the money is stored just like this?" Davey Boy nodded towards the bag of notes on the floor.

Jason nodded.

"How many bags in all including this one"?

Jason screwed his eyes upwards, making a mental calculation. Davey Boy waited; pen poised.

"Eight months, roughly three a week; I reckon around a hundred bags including this one."

Davey Boy emitted a low whistle as he jotted the figure down.

"And they're all stored back at your house?"

Jason nodded again. "In my bedroom."

"A hundred bin-bags! In your bedroom?" Davey Boy looked totally perplexed. This really was the bloody Twilight Zone.

"How the hell do you sleep and what about your mum?"

Jason shrugged, holding out a key.

"Mum works long hours and sleeps most of the rest and I'm able to keep my room locked".

"But it must have been a slog getting the bags back?"

"It depends. Sometimes I use my skateboard, or the cross-bar of my bike. A few times I've even used a Tesco trolley. I can only take one bag but that's enough."

EIGHT

"And no one notices anything?"

"I guess it's dark, it's late and it's London."

"London?"

Jason shrugged. "Most people just keep their heads down and pass by on the other side. They probably see a kid with a bin-bag and think homeless, a rough sleeper. I don't know."

Davey Boy closed his notebook. Shaking his head in disbelief he sat back into the sofa with a loud exhalation. It was all totally crazy. If the situation wasn't so damned serious it would have been laughable. But it was serious; more than serious and Dave Gilroy was struggling. Time was not on his side. Knowing Chris and now having met and listened to Jason he had to decide; a decision that would impact all their lives. The two boys opposite had placed their trust in him. They looked frightened, little more than kids, and he knew more than most about the nature and extent of the forces marshalling to catch them. Alone they wouldn't last past the end of the year. The net was closing. They would be caught and caught soon; of that he was certain. Dave Gilroy was the best at his job, and it was his job to know such things. And when that happened, given Jason's strange ability, he knew the boys would simply disappear; one into the confines of a secure military laboratory to suffer the horrors of the scientists and doctors, the other, simply knowing too much, into a maximum-security isolation unit. And those were the optimistic options. Either way the boys would never see the outside world again. Yes, they were thieves; they'd broken the law, stolen God knows how much but did they deserve such a fate? No one had been hurt; the banks were heavily insured, individuals hadn't been robbed, the government could easily print more money. The law may be the law, but Dave Gilroy was under no illusions. He had seen it first-hand. If the authorities discovered what Jason was capable of one could forget any due process. The law would be forgotten. All bets would be off. It would be open season.

In the diminishing late afternoon light the small north-facing front room had become a gloomy sepulchre. Soon the streetlamps that still worked would blink on, the night of early winter not far away. Dave Gilroy sighed heavily. Jason and Chris sat expectantly. Each a still shape growing from a shadowy armchair. The boys had placed their trust in him. They depended on him. Without his help they would be lost. Really there had been no decision to make. Slipping the slim leather notebook back inside his jacket he spoke quietly, his scar a mere smudge on his face in the darkening room.

"Okay Lads. Listen up and listen up carefully. This is what we're going to do."

NINE

"I wouldn't call it a breakthrough sir but it gives us the clearest indication yet of what appears to be happening."

Bishop, flushed, dishevelled, addressed the small of D'eath's back. His boss stood peering out into a manky dusk obscuring much of the east London skyline. D'eath turned away from the bank of windows. The view remained depressing, like everything else at FIBER in recent days.

"Run through it," he said tiredly returning to the relative comfort of his desk, slumping in his chair.

"Well sir I believe you've seen Carter's latest report?"

"What of it, man?"

"It's virtually identical to all other recent reports sir."

"I *know that* Bishop." D'eath's knuckles clenched forming fists on the mahogany desktop. Why were the gods suffering these cretins on him?

"It's just that the identical nature of Carter's reports establishes that it's the same modus operandi being used on each of the raided machines sir and for the first time we have image capture that's visually excellent and clearly shows us just what that modus operandi is."

D'eath propelled upright in his chair, fixing Bishop with a mongoose stare. This was better news, much better.

"Well what is it man? Come on. This could be the key!"

"Well that's just it, sir," whispered Bishop. "We don't know."

It was six weeks to Christmas. London, like D'eath, had been gloomy, cold and bloody miserable for days. Little if any change was forecast. The only luck to be had was bad and the pain in D'eath's head penetrated like a nail.

"You don't bloody know!" D'eath exploded. He railed into a cringing Bishop.

"You said the image capture was visually excellent. Do we have clear vid of the perp's tampering or not?"

"Er . . . both . . . sir."

"Both!" spat the boss of FIBER.

Bishop wanted to self-combust and the ashes blow away.

"We have a clear video of the perp . . . er perps, sir, but there was no tampering. No tampering at all."

"Perps? What? Now you're telling me we have more than one?" D'eath cupped his face in his hands.

"For the first time sir," Bishop whispered. "We've got two of them on camera; young, still teens. I'd bank on it. One is our old friend the other we've never seen before."

"Faces?"

"Hoodies again I'm afraid sir."

"And what was that about no tampering? Surely, they must have had equipment, tools, something?"

NINE

If it were possible Bishop's whisper sunk even lower.

"They had a bin-liner sir."

The boss of FIBER erupted into choking manic laughter. He just couldn't help himself.

"A bin-liner!" he chortled. "Of course! Just what every twenty-first century crook needs to assault a supposedly impregnable computer-controlled security machine - a bloody bin-liner!"

FIBER's investigation was turning into a farce worthy of the Keystone Cops. Thank God Frobisher had left early.

D'eath shook his head still chuckling at the inanity of it all. Bishop looked devastated. FIBER's boss didn't care. Bishop's mental wellbeing could go to hell in a handbag as far as he was concerned. Time was running out. He needed answers and would have happily water-boarded the hapless Bishop himself if he thought it would provide any.

"You said the CCTV capture gives a clear picture of what is happening?" D'eath's eyes, fixed on Bishop, were hard, unblinking. Bishop couldn't meet the stare but he could speak, which he did, falteringly.

"Yes sir. Previous footage was from angles that prevented us seeing actual 'hands on' contact with the machine. The camera units were just in the wrong places. In all these cases we could see elements of the perpetrator but not what he was actually doing to the machine."

"But now we can?"

"Yes sir. We struck lucky. A perimeter security camera on a lamp post in the car parking area captured a perfect view."

Why hadn't the idiot Bishop said this at the start?

"But what we see sir makes no sense. No sense at all. The perpetrator doesn't do a thing wrong. He simply puts an empty hand on the ATM screen, the machine starts up and the cash is ejected into the bin-liner." *Ah ha,* thought D'eath, the ubiquitous bin liner. Was it really that simple? "What about fingerprints? There must be fingerprints. It's a glass screen?"

"Unfortunately that's a problem sir. There are just too many prints; hundreds, layered over each other by a multitude of users and all smudged to hell by rain, grease and whatever else over time. The screen is just a mess sir; forensics confirm."

Death frowned, his initial hopes sinking.

"So what you're telling me is all we've got is some kind of superman who can control the ATM at will with his bare hands?"

"I don't know about a superman, but bare hands, yes sir".

"Are you absolutely sure of this Bishop?" D'eath watched his CCTV expert closely. Bishop's reply was quiet but for once unfaltering. "Absolutely sir, we've scrutinised the sequence minutely, digital frame by digital frame. There's no sleight of hand or jiggery pokery going on. An empty open hand is placed on the flat screen of the ATM and less than two seconds later it starts issuing the money."

Bishop was a poor excuse for many things but evaluating CCTV footage wasn't one of them. He was an acknowledged expert in the field and D'eath had to be satisfied. But the bold, stark, fact remained. What Bishop had described; what he had seen on CCTV, was patently impossible. It couldn't happen. But it had.

Dismissing Bishop with a curt nod, D'eath swivelled his chair reaching urgently for the desk phone. The CCTV man's discovery had just injected a startling new dimension into the investigation. It was incredible; a game changer. Suddenly it wasn't about the money anymore. A whole new ball game had hit town and a superman had just torn up the rule book.

TEN

Cloudless blue sky, bright wintery sunshine, long sharp shadows. A coat and scarf day at sea level, maybe a pair of gloves, but at three-thousand feet of altitude, it was icy cold. Ensconced within the comfortable pressurised cabin of the Sikorsky S76C the boss of FIBER wasn't worried about the external temperature. He had other far more pressing matters on his mind. D'eath, the sole passenger in the helicopter's luxurious eight seat VIP cabin, stretched his long lean frame. Through the plexi-glass he looked down on Wiltshire far below; a drab green-brown-ochre carpet, its far-off edges dissolved in late November haze, patch-worked with lanes, villages, fields, hedgerows, spires and plains. On another day in a different mood it might have been a pretty sight. They'd been airborne for forty minutes. The flight time from London City Airport should have been thirty minutes but they'd been re-routed mid-flight. Instead of a direct line the aircraft had been looped northwest away from their destination but thankfully it had now been cleared to land and was returning back on a south easterly course, descending rapidly. The delay frustrated the hell out of D'eath. If what he was daring to think could possibly be true, he couldn't afford to lose one minute let alone ten. A crackling through the cabin's speakers interrupted his mood.

"Out of the left side window, Mr D'eath there's a wonderful view of Stonehenge." The pilot sounded vaguely American. D'eath didn't care, either about the voice or the five-thousand-year-old stones it referred to. Just get me on the damned ground he thought.

A few minutes later and that's where they were. D'eath, coated and belted, leather portfolio under his arm, ran in an awkward crouch from beneath the slowing rotor blades. The aircraft would wait to ferry the boss of FIBER back to London once he was done. Patterson was waiting just beyond the circumference of the rotors' downdraft. He shouted hard to be heard over the now slowing turbines.

"Welcome to DSTL Mr D'eath!"

Between the idyllic villages of Gomeldon and Idmiston, innocently sprawling across acres of pretty Wiltshire farmland high on the chalk uplands of Southern England, is a Pandora's Box of terrifying capacity. Manufactured and stored within its secretive reinforced walls are some of the most heinous weapons ever known to mankind; lethal viruses, deadly toxins, nerve gasses and disease spreading pathogens. All refined for maximum lethality; all capable of ravaging humanity across the globe if ever unleashed. At the very heart of this modern day Pandora's Box, the infamous British Ministry of Defence Establishment Porton Down, is the United Kingdom's most controversial and secretive military research facility, The Defence Science and Technology Laboratory, and it was here, to DSTL, on this fine late November day that Raphael G. D'eath had come.

The men and lone woman, some wearing white coats, looked expectantly at their unusual visitor. His arrival had been unscheduled and for most of them it was an unwelcome interruption. They sat in steel government-issue chairs around a steel government-issue table. The oblong table filled most of the floor space. On it in front of each occupant was a notepad, a pen, a disposable paper cup and a small plastic bottle of water. The conference room was windowless; the walls a peppermint green, the floor polished concrete. A single heavy steel door with a rubber seal was both entrance and exit; two parallel rows of halogen spots let into the concrete ceiling provided ambient light. A large dark video screen was set flush in the centre of one wall, high in a corner of another, an air-conditioning grill. It could be day or night and you wouldn't know down here, thought D'eath. Thank God he wasn't claustrophobic. He sat alone at one end of the long table. Facing him at the other end stood Patterson, DSTL's Director of Research. Patterson finished a brief introduction and sat. It was time for FIBER's boss.

"Thank you, Director. And thank you all for assembling at such short notice. I know you're all busy, so I'll get right to the point."

D'eath stood, pushing back his chair. He'd come to rely on his height and appearance injecting a good dose of authority and gravitas when speaking. A wiry, olive skinned, six-and-a-half footer with a shaven head and dark eyes he could do that particularly well, especially when attired in his habitual tailored three-piece with button down, tie and silk pocket square, all in matching shades of dark midnight.

"First and foremost everything said here today remains topmost secret. Given where I am, I don't think that will cause anyone any problems." Polite laughter rippled around the table. The boss of FIBER didn't smile. "I am here today with government authority through the Bank of England. My authority and credentials have been confirmed with your director."

At the far end of the table Patterson nodded.

"In short we seek your assistance with a situation that has developed over the past months in London. A situation that my colleagues and I believe is possibly without precedent. If you can dim the lights please, I would like you to watch the following CCTV footage on screen."

D'eath had handed Patterson the DVD on arrival. It had been prepared and on his prompt the room dimmed, and images filled the large wall screen. The show only lasted a few minutes.

"Lights please," instructed D'eath.

The conference room brightened. Faces around the table looked at one another bemused. There were a few coughs, some shuffling, the scrape of a steel chair leg on concrete. D'eath still standing, continued.

"What you have seen has been independently verified. I can promise you the images are genuine. To avoid any doubt, let me be clear. The CCTV images you have seen show what we believe to be a boy, a youth, removing all the cash, and I do mean *all,* from an ATM simply by touching the screen. We further believe he has done the same with a variety of other cash machines right across London in recent months. I can tell you we have exhaustedly checked every suspect machine. In every case the computer processes and machine integrity prove faultless. There have been no compromises. This is a phenomenon like none we have come across before. I'm not here to ask *if* this is possible. Clearly it is. I'm here to ask *how* it's possible? How can this boy or anyone, empty money from secure machines at will simply by touch?"

D'eath stopped speaking. The room fell silent. The faces around the table looked at each other. D'eath looked at the faces. It was the woman who spoke first.

"Astonishing! The amplitude is an order of magnitude *years* away from what we've been able to achieve."

D'eath arched his eyebrows. "I'm sorry? You are?"

"Audrey Pinkus. *Doctor* Audrey Pinkus. I'm head of Biomedicine here at DSTL". Her voice carried a light lilt. The Scottish Borders or maybe the Western Isles, thought D'eath. Plump, grey-haired, permed, glasses around her neck on a cord, sensible leather flats under the table; Pinkus looked more a kindly grandmother lost on the way to Sunday services than a scientist at Britain's most secret military research laboratory.

D'eath sat back down. The woman's comments seemed encouraging. He'd talked enough now he would do some listening; maybe even start getting some answers.

"You have an idea about this, Doctor?"

"Well it is rather obvious isn't it?"

Audrey Pinkus polished the lenses of her spectacles with a tissue, smiling benignly at D'eath.

"We know nothing about the boy, but we do know rather a lot about the cash machine. We know the only force that can operate the ATM is electrical power. If there's a power outage; a cable cut, a blown fuse, the machine is dead; no electricity, no power, no power, no ATM."

"So you're saying this boy must be generating electrical power?"

"Of course he is. We all are. But what's exciting, as I said, is the order of magnitude of that power. "

"I don't understand."

Pinkus smiled patiently.

"All of us generate and store electrical power. We need it to function; for our brains to work, for our nervous systems to operate. Many of the minerals and elements our bodies need such as calcium, sodium, potassium, magnesium, have electrically charged ions. Put very simply the cells in our bodies are able to manipulate these ions to produce electrical current."

"But not enough to power up an ATM?"

"No, no, no," laughed Pinkus, "not nearly enough."

She had delicately placed her glasses on the bridge of her nose while talking, her eyes smiling at him through the lenses.

"A healthy person produces in a day about a hundred watts of power. I don't know the power requirements of a standard cash machine offhand, it's not my field I'm afraid, but I'm sure it must be a great deal more."

"About fifty times more," interjected a new voice.

D'eath switched his gaze down one side of the table. The new voice was attached to a younger man, slim, untidy, stained off-white lab coat, acne and a hat of unruly black hair.

"Apologies sir. Samuel Morgenstern; team leader, Mechanical Sciences".

"Thank you, Morgenstern. So, if I heard right, you're saying our boy would need to generate fifty times more electrical power than the average person to have any hope of powering up an ATM machine?"

"Yes sir, five-and-a-half kilowatts at the very least. That's five-thousand five-hundred watts, sir"

"I see. And there's no way his average power output could be increased?"

This is crazy, thought D'eath. I'm talking about this kid like he's Battersea Power Station.

"It's possible," said Morgenstern. "An ATM is essentially a big block of insulated steel. Assuming the boy's insulated when he touches the machine, wearing rubber soled trainers for example, his capacitance, his electrical charge, would certainly increase."

"But not enough?"

"Not by fifty times sir."

D'eath looked around the table.

"So there needs to be something else, something extra. If Doctor Pinkus is right our boy is getting one hell of an electrical boost from somewhere and he's not getting killed in the process. So . . . ideas? Anyone?"

The faces around the table looked at one another. Silence. Then the oldest man in the room spoke. Over the years Hollywood central casting has had many ideas of what a 'scientist' should look like. The man who spoke, his voice deep if a little ponderous, was a distillation of them all. A head of silvered hair thinning into a deep widow's peak; pale inquisitive eyes behind tortoise shelled John Lennons, their lenses glinting in the artificial overhead light. A silk bow tie of outrageous proportions and even a serrated row of requisite pens clipped into the breast pocket of a Harris tweed, it's worn elbows patched with leather. He wasn't wearing his lab coat. That was draped carefully across the back of his government-issue steel chair. It looked freshly laundered; unmarked, a pristine white.

He does know he's a caricature, doesn't he? thought D'eath. Maybe that was the intention.

"Franklin Benjamin," declared the older man with a challenging look; "Professor, Human Biological Sciences."

D'eath struggled to keep a straight face. The older man

knew his name was a joke; a scientific pun played by long-dead parents. Not great for growing up in the schoolyard but the man was old enough now not to care and if the professor didn't care, D'eath decided, he wouldn't either.

"Yes Professor?"

"Have you considered an extraordinary microbiome?"

"I'm sorry, a what?"

The aged professor sighed, his eyes rolling upwards behind the John Lennons.

"You do know of course that a human body is actually only partly human."

D'eath didn't know but kept quiet.

"The rest, the other much larger part, is the microbiome; a unique personalised mix of bacteria, fungi, protozoans and other micro-organisms all inhabiting the human body. We're talking trillions of microscopic hitchhikers all along for the ride. They outnumber the body's own cells three-to-one. On occasions some of them turn nasty, suicidal, killing us off along with themselves, but mostly they're the good guys keeping out the bad guys. Without them humanity as a species couldn't exist."

"And you think these . . . 'good guys' might hold an answer?"

"My recent research indicates some of them might, particularly the bacteria. They make up the biggest slice of the human microbiome; about a hundred-trillion. Imagine a horde of that size in every living person."

"And what makes you think these bacteria are something special?"

Benjamin folded his arms, leaning back heavily. The sudden movement grinding his steel chair legs into the concrete. This was becoming tiresome. Long ago as a much younger man he had developed a serious dislike for arrogant authority. He wasn't about to change today for this ignorant interrogator no matter how tall, how important or how dark his suit.

"Oh I don't really know. Probably the fact they can produce something called electricity, certain tropical strains at least."

D'eath ignored the sarcasm in the older man's voice. He was too busy thinking.

"Currently my team are examining two previously unknown strains recently discovered in the Far East," the professor continued, "not at all pleasant unfortunately. In some respects very similar to the bacterium that causes botulism, but apparently with greater lethality. But what's really interesting is we've discovered their ability to coordinate their metabolic activity when combined to produce electricity, under laboratory conditions of course. Who knows Mr Bank Man, if you catch your boy they might even name these bugs after you."

D'eath, deep in thought, was oblivious to the comment.

The professor carried on.

"Theoretically, if just ten percent of the boy's bacteria had a similar capability, it would be the equivalent of . . . "

"Ten trillion microscopic batteries," mused D'eath

"You *have* been listening."

"That would be one hell of an electrical boost."

"Indeed . . . theoretically," Benjamin nodded.

"But a charge like that would kill him?"

The professor sighed heavily again.

"Would you be here if it had?"

The uneasy developing deadlock between the two men was broken by young Morgenstern.

"Not necessarily," he interjected. "If this boy has become a bacterium powered battery, he will be producing direct electrical current, not alternating. The current would flow in one direction only, away from the source. This could be what's protecting the boy. Of course without tests it's just pure speculation."

For long minutes now D'eath's thoughts had been in overdrive; attempting to assimilate information, to construct coherent patterns, questions fizzing in his mind like bottle rockets. Now he loosed them off into the room.

"What are the prospects of a London teenager getting such bacteria into his system? Would it not kill him? Wouldn't his body's immune system be compromised? Assuming he survived the bacterial infection and developed the necessary electrical power how the hell does he use it to *control* a machine's functions? Bombarding it with blasts of electricity would just fry its circuits. Is this boy an anomaly, a freak of nature? Is he the only one? Are there others out there? What the hell are we dealing with?"

At last the boss of FIBER stopped talking. He pushed back his chair from the table and looked around the silent room. Why the hell had some idiot painted it peppermint green? The doctors, the scientists, looked back at him. D'eath knew the look well. There had been little else on the faces of his own staff for months. He had even coined a name for it; complex, crazy and clueless, the three Cs. But he hadn't expected to see it here.

Patterson, DSTL's Director of Research, had been quiet, listening silently since making the meeting's introductions. Now he stood, clearing his throat. At D'eath's request he had agreed to keep the boss of FIBER's name confidential. Patterson twisted open a bottle and poured a little water into a paper cup. He took a sip. D'eath sat back in his chair. He sensed a speech coming on.

"Sir, without the boy, without being able to test and evaluate physical evidence, this meeting was always going to generate more questions than answers. My team and I here at DSTL can offer opinions, theories and speculate on possibilities all day. What you've just heard is only the tip of a very deep iceberg. We could say the boy inherited a 'unique' microbiome from one or both of his parents. Because it grew with him in the womb and as an infant there would be no rejection, no attack by his immune system. We could theorise that rapid hormonal production during puberty might have caused that unique microbiome to develop, maybe to mutate, into something else; in the way that chicken pox, a mere inconvenience to a child, develops into something much more serious for an adult. We could hypothesise a bacterial battery within a mutated microbiome boosting human electrical power to unknown levels. We could even speculate about an extraordinary microbiome being able to establish some kind of organic neural net in and around the cortex of the human brain. Physical brain implants are a fact of modern medicine. Research shows patients with such implants, remotely connecting with computers; playing space invaders, operating flight simulation games, with just their minds. Research on the next step; replacement of a physical implant with one developed internally, organically, is well advanced by certain agencies. In short, sir, we can say many things; we can hypothesise, speculate, theorise and in the end just simply guess but, without this boy in front of us, I'm afraid that's all it will ever be. I am sorry."

D'eath lowered his eyes. He looked along the middle of the long table, thinking. Then he stood, buttoning his suit jacket expertly with one hand. The meeting was at an end.

"That's quite a speech Director Patterson. Easier said than done in respect of the boy unfortunately but know we will be trying. You can be sure of that."

D'eath turned a final time to the faces around the table.

"Professor, Doctor Pinkus, Morgenstern, gentlemen. Thank you. I appreciate your time and your assistance. It's certainly been . . . interesting."

Picking up his portfolio from beside his chair the boss of FIBER moved towards the single steel door. It could be sun, rain, night or day up on the Wiltshire fields above his head; and he would never know but escaping this sealed underworld crypt to find out wouldn't be the worst thing he could do today. D'eath reached for the heavy steel door handle.

"There is one final thing to keep in mind, sir."

D'eath looked over his shoulder. Patterson was still standing.

"This boy may well be the next evolutionary leap for humankind; a pinnacle of defence and technology capabilities that are beyond revolutionary. You came to DSTL today seeking answers. You could well be leaving seeking the holy grail of human advancement."

D'eath pulled the heavy door from its rubber seals and stepped into the reinforced concrete corridor.

"Well in that case Patterson you'd best hope I do a better job than Arthur and his bloody knights."

The door closed with a weighty hiss. He'd had his fill of white coats and theories for one day.

ELEVEN

This was the life! Jason sank into luxurious leather as the Uber XL Mercedes purred through the sparse South Circular traffic. He could barely conceal the boyish grin threatening to erupt over his face as he pulled today's burner from inside his jacket. Jabbing dial buttons he waited for connection.

"Shit Jace this suit is the business."

Jason looked at Chris sitting next to him. He had to admit it was an improvement. His friend's makeover would have made any TV reality programme proud. Chris beamed back, rightly so. A facial; manicure, haircut and a dark Boss single breasted suit had turned the undertaker's apprentice into a gentleman playboy of the western world, or an approximation of one at least. The manners, speech and sophistication would need to come later if they arrived at all. Before Jason could think of a suitably denigrating retort Davey Boy answered his call.

"How's it going?"

Davey Boy's voice still resonated with the assurance and confidence of their first meeting almost three weeks previously.

"We're on our way in. We should be with you by eight, in about twenty minutes. Is everything okay?"

Davey's metallic voice echoed confirmation.

"Great! Look forward to seeing you then. Keep the coffee hot."

Jason replaced the burner in his jacket with a flourish while checking the steel Rolex on his wrist. It was pre-owned; a gift from Davey Boy. He'd told his mum it was a fake off a man down the market. It was still early days and following Davey Boy's instructions he'd kept his mum in the dark as had Chris with his parents. Any decent purchases had variously fallen off the back of a truck; been fakes or bought from some bloke behind a pub. Hopefully there would be a time to come clean, but that time was some way off. Right now the watchwords emphasised by Davey Boy were secrecy, secrecy and more secrecy. Their combined futures depended on it. Glancing across at Chris he answered his friend's enormous grin with one of his own. How the hell had it come to this, and so quickly?

There was no denying Davey Boy, he was a bloody marvel. A few days after the meeting in Chris' kitchen he had turned up in his new guise as a man with a van. A long white panel van to be exact. With Jason's mum at the care home the three of them had removed eight months' worth of bulging bin-bags from his fit to bursting bedroom in a single afternoon. They had driven the load several miles away to an old railway services warehouse on the edge of what, a century before, would have been marshalling yards of the Great Eastern Railway. Any rolling stock was long gone; the land zoned for urban renewal. The future promised a shopping centre, offices and affordable housing but for now it remained boarded acres of rusting switch points, graffiti tagged sidings and weedy scrub.

Davey Boy had sublet the building from a struggling joinery company, paying cash. Tucked away in the shadow of an old gasometer it looked decrepit; an ageing wreck. But Davey Boy had scoped it well. Solid walls of soot blackened Victorian brick under a roof of pitched iron trusses and thick Welsh slate. Importantly the entire building had only three apertures. All let into its front wall. The recent addition of a secure steel roller shuttered door filled the largest; the smaller two, above head height on either side, held the original heavily barred windows, their fire-wired glass panes dirty, but unbroken. Small by modern standards the warehouse was big enough to garage Davey Boy's large panel van and came with three internal walls of floor-to-ceiling industrial shelving. It was dry and secure, with power and water laid on. In the back it even had an ancient washroom and kitchenette, though one wouldn't want to spend much time in either. Stored inside awaiting the arrival of the bin-bags had been a plethora of equipment and furniture previously delivered by Davey Boy; a couple of old but serviceable Safescan banknote counters, several large collapsible tables, some chairs, portable lighting, coffee machine, microwave, industrial space heater; a box of electrical cable extension reels, a couple of lap-tops, colour printer, a small camping stove with several cardboard trays of bullet shaped gas canisters and even a flat-screen TV with DVD player. Seeing it all for the first time Chris had half-joked he wanted to move in, but Davey Boy was having none of it. "No changes Chrissy. We agreed. Everything continues the same way. When a pattern changes, that's when people notice."

The bin-bags had moved on a Saturday. On the Sunday the boys' education had started. As a teacher Davey Boy knew his stuff. Jason could remember that first day like it was yesterday. A large white board had been propped on an easel alongside a trestle table covered with a blanket. The panel van, still warm, was parked up in the rear of the building.

"Get some coffee down your necks lads and pay attention."

"My first time in Sunday School," sniggered Chris, "this should be interesting."

"Muppet," murmured Jason.

Davey Boy picked up a thick felt-tip and stood in front of the white board. He scribbled fast; just four words, capital letters, jagged and black on the shiny white surface.

Danger!

Secrecy!

Discipline!

Concentration!

The end of each word was a vicious down stroke and stab exclamation mark. Silence filled the large space. Even Chris had quietened.

"Let's cut to the chase," said Davey Boy. "I'm not going to sugar coat it, lads. Right now we, all of us, are at maximum risk. We are being hunted by dangerous people whose sole expertise in life is to hunt. One mistake, one instant of carelessness, and we're done like kebabs on a spike. I shit you not."

Chris swallowed hard, his Adam's apple bobbing like a fishing float. Jason recognised his friend's apprehension. He felt it too.

The felt-tip was a dagger in Davey Boy's hand. He swiped it again and again, underlining each word as if filleting a fish.

"*Secrecy* is our protection, *discipline* our armour, *concentration* our friend. Are we clear?" Jason and Chris nodded silently.

"Good!" Davey Boy smiled, instantly changing the mood.

"It's frightening as hell lads. I know. But do exactly what I tell you and trust me we'll get through it."

The boys nodded again, cautiously, unsure if they were buying what Davey Boy was selling, not yet at least.

"Talking of secrecy these will help."

Davey Boy carefully rolled the blanket away from the surface of the table. Revealed underneath were mobile phones. Three long rows of small black plastic cases, each with a screen no bigger than half a playing card.

"These are cheap throwaway phones, 'burners' in the trade and no merry quips please, Chrissy. The sims are prepaid; use and dispose, one a day, smash and into the river. These are the only phones we use to contact each other from now on. Never use names, never talk specifics and never anything about this business over the airwaves. Am I clear?"

Again a double nod.

"Good! Keep everything simple; a secret amongst us and we'll be fine. For now the important thing is to keep our minds focused and on the job."

Davey Boy nodded towards the panel van.

"Jason you'll find aluminium ladders, brooms and packing materials in the back of the van. You and Chrissy stack the materials and get a ladder up on the windows, smear them over. You'll find rags and a six pack of windolene in the van. The windows are high but better safe than sorry. The last things we need at this point are prying eyes. Then get all this bloody sawdust swept up into the corners. We need clean space to work in. I told the joiners I wanted it gone before I moved in; so much for bloody promises, the lazy tykes. In the meantime I'll get the Safescans working. We need to unbag the cash, separate the denominations, count them into thousand-pound bundles and shrink wrap the bundles into bales of no more than a hundred-thousand pounds each. It will take some mixing and matching but try to keep the bales roughly the same size. Any bigger than about two cubic feet and they will be difficult to manhandle."

"Then what?"

"One step at a time, Jason. Get this place sorted. Get the cash baled. Then we'll see."

Over the following weeks every moment they could snatch away from home and school had seen Jason and Chris at the warehouse. By now, of course, it had been nicknamed the 'bat cave'. Bin-bag-by-bin-bag the money had been emptied, sorted, counted, banded, wrapped and stored into closely packed mixed bales of fives, tens, twenties and fifties. The emptiness they had unlocked on that first day was long gone; just a memory. In its place, populating the shelving around the walls now, were shiny shrink wrapped blocks of multi-coloured green, pink and blue.

On the financial front it had been Davey Boy from the start. His cash had acquired the short-term rental of the bat cave; the second-hand panel van off a forecourt somewhere, the old surplus Safescan counters and all the other equipment and furniture. One of his credit cards had paid for Jason's Rolex, another for Chris' attempt at sartorial elegance; although with the latter he was thinking of asking for his money back. He'd also subbed both boys with a working cash float. Jason and Chris had protested. They were surrounded with the stuff. They didn't need his. But Davey Boy had insisted. "We don't touch a single note of this cash 'till it's clean lads. If it makes you feel any better, I'm no charity. Don't worry. You'll be paying me back big time and then some when this is over. Until then we keep our heads down and do it my way."

That had been three weeks back. Three weeks of counting, baling and shelving, of smashing and drowning used burners, of looking over shoulders, of varying routes to and from the bat cave, of lying to parents. Three weeks of entering each day's count into the bookkeeping programme Davey Boy had downloaded onto one of the laptops. Three weeks of trepidation, excitement, sleepless nights and anxiety. But today, in the rear of a Mercedes arrowing through dark early morning traffic, Jason knew things were about to change. Last night the final bale had been hefted onto its shelf; the last count entered into the lap-top, the final balance recorded on its hard drive. Davey Boy had punched the sum key. A number had appeared in the totals box, hard to read, too many commas and zeroes.

"One million nine hundred and twenty thousand pounds," Davey Boy had said quietly. "About twenty K per ATM I reckon."

It was a beaming Chris who'd best summed it up.

"Eight months and two million quid tax free. Not too shabby, not too shabby at all," he'd said with a grin a yard wide.

TWELVE

Jason and Chris walked the last half-mile to the bat cave from the Uber drop off point. Street Craft Davey Boy called it. Keep alert; be watchful, a different drop off point each day, walk the rest, even if it's raining. The early morning was bitterly cold, Christmas was on the way. Chris had covered his suit with a drab green parka, hood up. Jason walked beside him in a quarter-length woollen pea coat and beanie. Skirting familiar weather boarded hoardings with nailed on signs about demolition, trespass and fly tipping they arrived in front of the bat cave's roller shuttered door. The design provided for a smaller 'wicket' door to be let into the surrounding shuttering. This smaller door was open.

"You call this twenty minutes?" asked a smiling Davey Boy.

The ex-military man was bareheaded in an old padded camo jacket, jeans and muddy Hunters. On the ground next to him was a two-gallon plastic bucket slopping at the brim with what looked like more mud. Davey Boy looked pointedly at Chris' suit under the flapping parka.

"You here for a job interview Chrissy?"

"Aw give over Davey. Last night you said tomorrow was going to be a big day. I just thought . . . "

"There's the problem right there Chrissy; you and thinking. Anyway no matter, lads let's get inside. It's bloody monkeys out here."

Three large mugs of hot coffee later with the door closed and locked Davey Boy had to raise his voice to be heard above the roar of the space heater.

"While you lads were counting and stacking shelves these past weeks, I'm guessing you were wondering where I was, what I was up to?"

"We assumed you were working," offered Jason, "at your job in an office somewhere."

"Half right, about the job at least. Keeping up appearances, maintaining a routine, is vital. It's when a pattern . . . "

" . . . changes that people notice," finished Chris.

Davey Boy smiled.

"Exactly! But importantly it also allowed me to keep tabs on the ongoing investigation, on the guys looking for you, looking for us."

"And are they?" asked Jason.

"Affirmative. In fact things are ramping up like I've rarely seen."

Jason suddenly felt uncomfortable. He was getting overly warm and it wasn't all to do with the space heater.

"But I've also been making enquiries off the record and calling in some favours," Davey Boy continued. "And I think I've nailed a way forward."

He walked to the white board. It was still on its easel in a corner; its surface wiped and clean. He put down the coffee mug and picked up a felt-tip. With a jerk of his elbow he scrawled a wobbly circle roughly in the middle of the board.

"This, gentlemen, represents almost two-million stolen pounds of Her Majesty's legal tender." He drew a question mark inside the circle. "But what are we going to do with it?"

"We agreed." Jason shrugged. "We launder it".

"Exactly, but how? It's easy to say, not so easy to do. Especially given the amount, the way it was stolen and the calibre of people after us."

"But it's not that much Davey," Chris chipped in, "drug cartels and terrorists launder tons more. There was a programme on the box about it only the other night."

"But their money didn't lead back to a 'Jason'. To a goose laying golden eggs, did it Chrissy?"

Davey Boy placed a hand on Jason's shoulder. He squeezed gently.

"Truth is Jason I've seen the latest communiques. The money has become secondary. I'm afraid what they're really hot for now is you."

Jason felt as if a doctor had just given him a terminal diagnosis. He slumped in the chair, head in his hands.

"I knew it, Davey. I bloody knew it! I could have stopped ages ago. I just kept putting it off. It was too easy. I kept kidding myself it didn't matter; that nobody was getting hurt, that no one cared a shit. Now I'm screwed. And all because of a cheap bloody thrill and a few lousy bin-bags of cash. Shit! Davey, what am I going to do? What am I going to tell my mum when they come?"

Davey Boy tightened his grip. Jason felt the pain in his shoulder.

"Snap out of it, Jason. Can this self-pity bullshit and stick to the game plan. Okay, so they're looking. What the hell did you expect? But it's my job to make sure they find squat. And that's *all* they're going to find. Why else do you think we're doing all this?"

Bent over, head still in his hands, Jason was silent.

"Look Jason. I know what I'm doing. I'm cut from the same cloth as these guys. I know how they operate. They're not going to find you and that's a promise, okay?"

Jason was silent.

"Okay!"

Emotional, eyes reddened, Jason looked up, nodding. "Sorry Davey".

Davey Boy nodded, patting Jason reassuringly on the back.

"That's it! Keep that mind-set, you too, Chrissy. Remember we talked about concentration? About discipline? This is where it comes in. We focus, we keep to the rules and we see this through."

Davey Boy paused, allowing a long moment for what he'd said to sink in. But it was just a moment.

"Okay, now it's important you both hear me out."

TWELVE

Keeping the momentum Davey Boy drew a series of thick lines on the white board all coming out of the wobbly circle in different directions. It looked like a five-year-old had drawn a picture of the sun.

"Right lads, these lines represent some of the usual money laundering techniques."

He used the felt-tip as a pointer.

"We have diamonds; over-and-under invoicing, dodgy corporate investments, property deals and Smurfs."

Davey Boy waited. Chris didn't disappoint.

"C'mon Davey, really? Smurfs? You have got to be kidding. I wouldn't touch those little blue buggers with a barge pole. I don't know where you got your recommendation but I'm telling you Davey, Smurfs are total tossers. Wobbling around farting smurfberries all day. If you want the real deal, we'd be far better off asking SpongeBob Square Pants."

"Have you finished, Chrissy?"

"Well I've got SpongeBob on fast dial, just give the word."

Davey Boy sighed heavily.

"Sharing DNA with you, Chrissy, scares the crap out of me. We're not using SpongeBob and a Smurf is just a term for an ordinary person; small job, low profile. The money is split up with a little going regularly to lots of different 'Smurfs'. They pay it into their bank accounts keep a small cut and pay back the balance in instalments over time as clean funds."

Chris shrugged.

"If you say so, Davey. You're the expert. I'll pass SpongeBob the news. It's a crying shame but I guess it can't be helped."

Davey Boy looked at Jason, rolled his eyes, and pressed on.

"But none of these methods will work for us. Either they take way too long, have third party security risks or involve too much exposure of the cash on home soil where the ongoing search is strongest."

Davey Boy used his thumb to erase all the sun's rays but one. He pointed at it with the felt-tip.

"So I've settled on Macau!"

"What's that?" Jason was confused.

Chris wasn't. "It's when you drop a burger on your foot, idiot!"

Davey Boy's patience was on empty.

"It's a place, guys, out in China. It's where we're going to ship the money to."

Jason and Chris, totally bewildered, looked at each other. It was Jason who grasped the nettle.

"Sorry Davey but that doesn't sound right. If we ship the money isn't there a good chance customs will just pick it up and track it back? It seems one helluva risk. You said it yourself, it's me they're really after and they're looking bloody hard. To be honest I'm not sure I want to risk it. If that's your best idea maybe we should just try and give it back or burn or bury the stuff?"

TWELVE

Davey Boy dropped the felt-tip back on the table, picked up his mug and moved towards the coffee machine. He waited for the Americano to brim before speaking.

"Give back what? They want you Jason, not the money and the time for burning or burying was months ago. We're way past that. You came to me, you and Chrissy. You involved me, not the other way around. God knows I understand you're afraid but, believe me, pushing ahead now is not only the *right* thing to do, it's the *only* thing to do. Look, I'll make it simple. These guys, the authorities, they aren't going to stop even if you do. If you hand the money back they'll keep coming. If you burn or bury it, they'll keep coming. This money is all you've got to protect yourself. And once it's clean and untraceable that's just what you'll be doing. You've just go to trust me on this Jason. This is what I do for living. Believe me, there are no other options."

Jason looked at Chris who had been unnaturally quiet throughout the conversation.

"What do you think Chris?"

"I'm sorry, Jace. I'll support you whatever mate but this one's between you and Davey."

Jason sat back in the chair. He folded his arms across his chest and looked around. The bat cave had never looked better. The panel van; the easel and white board, the computers, printer, coffee machine and all the other equipment, furniture, burners and assorted paraphernalia were neatly in their allotted places. Outside the cold grey light of early morning had brightened, hard and flat. Inside, muted by smeared windowpanes, the light was opaque, soft. It played across the clean stone floor and the bales of multi-coloured pink, green and blue amongst the shelving racks. Everything ordered; everything complete. They'd done it all, reflected Jason. It hadn't been easy. It was their effort; their achievement, it was real, something to be proud of. He glanced at Chris, seeing the mixture of eagerness and anxiety etched in his friend's face. He thought of his mum; the long hours she worked, the sacrifices she'd made and was continuing to make. He heard Davey Boy's words again in his head, words from a man risking everything to help two boys, one he didn't even know. Their efforts, the risks, the sacrifice, it was all about hope. Hope for a better life, for the future, for friendship, for family. How could he even think about burning or burying that? Jason stood, squared his shoulders and smiled at Chris. He shifted his gaze away from Chris and looked straight into the eyes of Davey Boy. It was time to start paying back some of the faith others had placed in him. Simply put it was time to step up to the plate and grow a pair.

"He who dares? Right Davey?"

"Damn right, Jason"

"So we're good to go?"

"We're good to go" affirmed Davey Boy.

"Then let's do this."

"Yes!" With a savage whisper Chris punched the air.

THIRTEEN

Bishop was having a bad, bad day. Everything at FIBER was going down the toilet. The investigation of the ATM thefts had been stalled for weeks. D'eath, that bastard, was treating him like something he'd found on the bottom of his shoe and to cap it all he'd woken up flat stony broke; his last thousand disappearing into a fixed odds betting machine the night before, quicker than wet shit off a shovel. It wasn't a surprise. It wasn't even unusual. Bishop was an addict. He lived with his addiction every day, close up and dirty under his shirt like a disease. He was a gambler; worse he was a gambler who couldn't win. A wretched combination that had ruined his life and now looked like ending it, altogether. Sandwiched and terrified between two thugs in the back of a Range Rover, Bishop was staring at rock bottom. He was being taken to McGimlet and even he wouldn't accept a bet on his coming back.

Bishop wasn't a small man but he looked it, squashed and dishevelled between his two leather jacketed minders in the back seat of the vehicle. The driver was smaller, much smaller, more a ferret against the bears of his colleagues. But strangely they were all brothers. Bishop knew this because he'd had the displeasure of having painfully met them all before, several times. The brothers Vostok; Demitri, Vladimir and ruthless little Nikoli; they were McGimlet's personal enforcers. But this was the first time they'd taken him off the street in broad daylight. It was only a hundred yards of pavement between the tube station and the office door dammit! What was the country coming to? The Range Rover hooked a right, another right then a left finding rat runs through the traffic clog of early rush hour London. Bishop had no clue where he was being taken. McGimlet didn't have an office. He had rooms. Rooms scattered around South East London like confetti; rooms where he conducted his affairs, affairs of money and pain. And as South London's most reviled and powerful loan shark McGimlet was cruelly adept at dispensing both.

Within fifteen minutes the Range Rover was parked, and Bishop perched awkwardly on a wooden stool. It was a tiny stool, painful for a man of his size and weight, but standing wasn't an option. The brothers Grimm had made that clear. Minutes passed. Bishop's knees, up by his chin, were numb and he could no longer feel his lower legs. He would need help to stand if he was ever to get out of this damned room. Apart from the stool the room held no furniture. No pictures on the walls; no windows, only bare floorboards and a low-watt bulb dangling on a ceiling flex. The ferret stood to Bishop's front absentmindedly running a comb through a headful of black brilliantined hair. His brothers didn't need combs, their twin shaven bullet heads gleaming dully in the poor bulb light. Perhaps the ferret could tell them apart but Bishop couldn't. Ominous black-clad book ends they looked down on him from left and right; solid as teak, each as wide as a fridge. One wore a weighty gold cross hanging off a gold rapper's chain. The cross was Russian Orthodox, hooped and heavy. It glinted in the dim room.

At last footsteps; a door opening, closing, more footsteps, heavier now, a final door and McGimlet entered the room. Bishop couldn't see him at first, crouched on the tiny stool surrounded by the phalanx of brothers, but he could smell him; whiskey, tobacco and lavender. It was pretty much McGimlet's trademark and his taste wasn't cheap; Jameson's Gold, Cuban Montecristo and Aqua di Parma Lavanda. It was a smell Bishop associated with abuse, debasement and pain and he despised it. If he ever got out of this mess, he hoped never to smell it again.

"Well, well, well big fella. We meet again, do we not?"

McGimlet's accent was straight off Belfast's Falls Road. Born into the skulduggery of the post-war black markets he was an old man; a criminal dinosaur; a villain of the old school from the gold fob chain across his waistcoat to the flat nasal style of his brogue.

"Will yer be lookin' at me now when I'm speakin' to yer."

Bishop raised his forehead off his knees and met McGimlet's gaze. The Irishman's face was lined and heavily bearded. He'd kept his hair but the fiery red of his youth had bleached through age to a pale straw and he wore it like a mane, swept back off his broad forehead, long over the ears and down on the collar. Big and bluff he stood menacing over the bent Bishop like an old bull.

"How long has it been eh Mr Bishop? And here's me thinking yer'd have been knockin' on my door long before now with what yer owe. But there's been not a word Mr Bishop. Not a word. What do yer have to say about that eh?"

Bishop cringed silently.

"How much is it Niki?

The ferret's comb had quickly disappeared back into a pocket the moment McGimlet had entered the room and now he stood to attention, small beside the looming figure of his old boss.

"Wid interest, tirty-five-tousand."

"Never!" squealed a sweating Bishop. "You only gave me ten and I paid off five of that the last time. Surely you remember?"

"I remember well enough big fella but aren't yer about forgetting something?"

Bishop turned his stare back into the floorboards. He knew what was coming.

"Yer were overdue, yer tried to run. The five was fer you avoidin' a knee capping so it was. Now yer overdue again big fella but this time it's not goin' to be yer knees."

The ferret spoke, his accent shrill.

"E's never goin' to pay boss. Look at 'im. E's avin' nothing. I cut 'im deep. As example."

McGimlet snorted.

"Yer may be good at cuttin' Niki but yer bloody awful when it comes to the English. But I'm thinkin' yer may be right. Too much time to be sure has been spent on Mr Bishop here and me a busy man. What say you to that eh Mr Bishop? Is it time to have done with you big fella?"

The bookends hadn't moved an inch since McGimlet's arrival. They remained threateningly close. Bishop had a card; only one and in desperation he played it.

"I've got information, Mr McGimlet. It's easy money, lots of it." He strained to keep his voice steady. "I was coming to you with it when you snatched me."

"Were yer now?" McGimlet smiled at the ferret. "Did yer hear Niki? Mr Bishop was coming to see us so he was."

"I can prove it. Just check my coat for God's sake. There's a DVD case in the inside pocket."

McGimlet gestured and the ferret moved in bending over the half-crouching, half-squatting Bishop; a moment later he stood, a thin dark matt DVD case in his hand. He handed the case to McGimlet who regarded it with curiosity.

"So yer man thinks this is goin' to save him now, does he? What do you think, Niki? Is this I'm holdin' goin' to be worth thirty-five thousand do you think?"

"I cut 'im anyway boss."

McGimlet waved the thin case like a Chinese fan.

"If there's cutting to be done Niki yer'll be doing it soon enough."

He threw a cruel thin smile in Bishop's direction.

"But just for now I fancy a little taste of what the big fella's brought us."

The nearest DVD player was in the Range Rover; integrated into the front monitor system, along with the satnav, audio and vehicle control systems. The small screen, the size of a paperback, required McGimlet and Bishop to occupy the driver and front passenger seats. Bishop's legs had cramped up badly. The bookends had to physically carry him to the vehicle, stuffing him into the passenger seat like a sack of potatoes. They were now squeezed up in back either side of the ferret who had a seven-inch knife up against Bishop's ear. It had taken several minutes of curses and jabbing at the touch screen but finally the DVD images were playing. Bishop started to speak. McGimlet, watching the screen intently silenced him with a raised finger. Bishop held his breath, ferret's blade cold against his neck. The sequence played out. The screen went black.

The Range Rover was parked askew down a long narrow cul-de-sac; half up on the pavement, half on a lane of irregular stone sets. Back a hundred yards the alley opened onto a glimpse of noisy high street normality; shops, traffic, commuters, pedestrians. Twenty yards to the front, cast iron bollards in front of dark brick brought the alley to a dead end. Close on either side, tall walls of encroaching buildings, featureless apart from the single door they had just exited. If Bishop had landed on a distant planet, he couldn't have felt more vulnerable and alone.

McGimlet twisted in the driver's seat, his eyes less than a foot from Bishop's, his smell in Bishop's throat.

"Yer better be up to explaining this and quick. Niki's not used to waiting, are yer Niki?"

The blade against Bishop's ear twitched launching him into a stuttering commentary.

"It's, it's this kid, the one on the DVD. He's a freak. He's got some kind of power. He can empty cash machines just by touching the bloody things. You've just seen him doing it."

McGimlet was dismissive.

"Pah! Parlour tricks. Slick I grant yer but bloody parlour tricks all the same. Don't insult my intelligence son. I've been round the block a few more times than most I can tell yer. If this is all yer've got I'm not interested. Niki take this eejit out of my sight and I'll not be wanting to see him again if yer understand me."

"No! No! Please!" blurted Bishop. "It's totally true. You must've read the papers; listened to the news, the TV, all those raids on cash machines for months and months. Hundreds of thousands stolen; this is that kid. He's the one doing it all. He's been robbing dozens and dozens of cash machines all across London, just for fun."

McGimlet stayed ferret with a raised hand.

"The cash machines again, is it?" he said wearily. "The bastard police were all over me and my associates for weeks about yer bloody cash machines. The scum tore our places apart. They enjoyed it, the bastards. They found nothing so they did but I'm not about inviting them back for more."

Bishop pressed his palms together as if praying.

"You see. It *must* be true. The police were hammering all the villains on their books not just you. Why else would they do that? I'm telling you Mr McGimlet, this is big, really big."

McGimlet's eyes narrowed.

"Are yer saying I'm a villain, Bishop?"

Bishop stopped in his tracks. "Err . . . umm . . . I . . . I wouldn't personally go that far Mr McGimlet. Er . . . perhaps just a person of interest as the police might say."

McGimlet emitted a scoffing laugh.

"Person of interest! Yer know why I don't like yer Bishop?"

"Er . . . because . . . er . . . I haven't paid back your money?" Bishop winced.

"Really? That's yer reason? Yer poor misguided bastard. If people owe, they pay. If they don't Niki and his brothers make sure they learn the error of their ways. But it's just business. It's not personal. But what turns my stomach about yer Bishop is yer snivelling. Yer two-faced toadying. Thirty seconds ago I was orderin' yer dead. Now if that doesn't make me a bleedin' villain what does yer soft gobshite? Get some grit in yer man." McGimlet suddenly grabbed the grubby lapels of Bishop's jacket. He yanked him viciously to within an inch of his sneering face, the smell making Bishop gag.

THIRTEEN

"Of course I'm a bloody villain! I'm the nastiest oldest piece of crooked shit south of Wapping. And do yer know why?"

Bishop mutely shook his head.

"Because I eat bastards like yer fer breakfast."

McGimlet slammed Bishop back into his seat with a force belying his age. "But also because I know how to stay ahead; how to grab an opportunity if it comes knockin'. So, fer the final time of asking big fella, if this is the opportunity yer say it is yer'd better be about sellin' it to me better than yer have been."

The frayed collar of Bishop's shirt was sodden through; his pulse just one shuddering palpitation. The sweat was heavy; wet, under his arms, his groin, the small of his back. Bishop was a gambler but this was his life, not a month's wages down the bookies. There wouldn't be a second chance. Bishop inhaled deep, steadying himself. He could almost feel the pumping adrenaline.

"I work for the government's top financial enforcement authority. Check if you don't believe me. My team is in charge of catching this kid. He's a danger to the whole financial system. It's not a trick. We've got scientists, doctors, security experts, the police, the lot, all after this kid and the net is closing. We're close to catching him. No doubt. But what if, along the way . . . "

"Yer deliver him up to me," concluded McGimlet.

Bishop nodded.

"And yer can do this?"

"I can," Bishop lied.

"I'm central to the core investigation team. No one moves on this without our authority. We will have the heads up before anyone. Once we have the information, I can slip you the nod and you're in and out with the kid before anyone knows different."

McGimlet ran thick yellowed fingers through his beard, thinking.

"How long before yer know the kid's location?"

"I can't say for sure. But we're going to be all over him like a rash. Trust me. A couple of months and I can get this done. There'll never be a better opportunity. You've seen the news; TV, the papers. All I need is the room to move and your guarantee that we'll all be good after you get the kid. Think of it, Mr McGimlet. This kid in your pocket would be better than a lottery ticket; thousands and thousands free at the touch of a hand and I can deliver him straight to you. Maybe it might even be worth a small percentage finder's fee?"

Bishop held his breath. He'd said it the best way he knew how. The next seconds would decide. Face down in the Thames or free and clear with maybe a little money in his pocket. As for locating the kid, let that calculating bastard D'eath do *him* a favour for a change.

The old Irishman's thought processes didn't take long.

"If I get the kid and he turns out the way yer say then the slate is clean. But there'll be no percentages. Yer'll take what I give yer, if I give it to yer, and be bloody grateful."

THIRTEEN

McGimlet retrieved the DVD disc and pocketed it.

"Yer have three months".

"Boss!" yelped the ferret alarmed.

McGimlet raised a hand. "There's plenty will need cutting Niki. Bide yer time. Yer'll be busy soon enough."

He turned back to Bishop.

"Niki will come home with yer. Give him yer passport and he'll give yer a phone. Use it when yer know the kid's location. Niki and the lads will do the rest. Be clear, any shenanigans and it's the end for yer big fella. Know we'll be watching. Are yer understanding me?"

Bishop retrieved his grimy handkerchief. It had been in a pocket since he'd been snatched. He held it to the sweat on his flushed face, nodding. "Thank you Mr McGimlet. I won't let you down."

"If yer do big fella it'll be the last thing yer do. Now sod off and take young Niki with yer."

McGimlet watched the incongruous pair walk back up the alley towards the bustling noise and activity of the High Street; Bishop hobbling, rubbing his thighs. He could understand Niki's objections, but this was business and he was a businessman; thirty-five grand against untold wealth if the kid was the real deal. He'd take that bet every day of the week. He'd seen the news reports; he knew where Bishop worked, the man couldn't have known he was about to be snatched and yet the DVD was in his pocket. Could it all be true? It would be worth the slack he'd cut the man to find out. The stakes couldn't be higher. Of one thing though McGimlet was very sure. This was one gamble Bishop didn't need to be worrying over. When this was ended, no matter the roll of the dice, he wouldn't be seeing Bishop again. No one would.

FOURTEEN

As Bishop and the ferret emerged from the alley, several miles to the southeast a meeting was continuing in the bat cave.

"So this is how it's going to work."

Davey Boy sat at a trestle table. It was the same table on which he had revealed the burners. Only now its Formica surface was bare. Chris and Jason sat opposite him. The light through the bat cave's windows; still soft, still opaque, had become a little brighter with the morning's advance.

"I have a friend who runs security for a new casino in downtown Macau. We're going to buy gambling chips, play a little, lose a little and cash out with clean money; US Dollars. We'll even have a receipt from the casino. Those dollars are then going for a ride on a carousel. For a fee there's a lawyer in Hong Kong who's the best in the business at financial fairground rides. After that, in a couple of months, we should be set up free and clear."

"So where the hell is this place Macau?" Chris looked blank.

"South coast of China," said Davey Boy. "It used to be a Portuguese colony in the same way Hong Kong was British.

The best part is it's the gambling capital of the entire bloody world. The Chinese love gambling more than their own grandmothers and there's a billion of 'em."

"A billion grandmothers?" Chris looked shocked.

"*Chinese* you spanner." Davey Boy grimaced.

"In terms of gambling revenue Macau makes Las Vegas look like Southend in February. Our two-million wouldn't even be a drop in the ocean to them. Tracing it would be like trying to find a microscopic needle in the world's biggest haystack; a haystack importantly six-thousand miles away from here".

"But what about your friend? You trust him?" Chris was dubious.

"About as much as you can trust anyone, Chrissy. We did three tours together in 'stan. Brother officers in the regiment. We ended up saving each other's lives more than once."

"So he's going to provide us with gambling chips in return for the money?"

"Not directly. He needed to know how much is involved so he could entice a junket onto the hook, but he doesn't know much else. He will act as our go-between with the junket."

The look on Chris' face said it all.

"Smurfs are one thing Davey, but what the hell is a Junket when it's at home?"

Davey Boy's smile turned into a chuckle

"It's just another term for a local agent Chrissy, a mainland Chinese gambling facilitator. We turn up to the tables with two-million quid and a big red balloon goes up; we turn up with a bag full of casino chips no one blinks an eye."

"But isn't that going to cost?"

"About twenty percent but it'll be worth it. The junket provides the chips and our ATM cash disappears into the local system forever. We'll still be over a million-and-a-half to the good."

"But what about your mate? He'll be wanting some too."

"And he'll be getting some. We have an agreement; ten percent of the cleaned net."

"The pie is shrinking pretty fast Davey, is he really worth it?"

"Think of it as an investment in our financial wellbeing, Chrissy. He has local security; connections, the inside track with the junket and one hundred-and-fifty-thousand good reasons to make it happen."

Jason had listened long enough.

"Sorry about busting up the family meeting guys but am I the only one not missing the point here? It all sounds very impressive but how the hell are we going to get the money to Macau in the first place?"

Davey Boy beefed up his morning caffeine with another slurp from his mug.

"We're going to ship it there Jason, just like I said."

"I know what you said Davey but it can't be that easy."

"Who said anything about easy? You two will be hefting and packing and I'm going to be driving all over half of England. And we start today."

"Today!"

"Check the van Jason. In the back there's a large roll of butyl lining."

"What?"

"Industrial strength rubber liner. It's nonporous; air, gas and watertight. It makes the DIY stuff in garden goldfish ponds look like the skin off a rice pudding."

"But what do we do with it?"

"Build some bleedin' ponds I guess." quipped Chris.

Davey Boy rolled his eyes.

"You two dipsticks will cut it into squares; each square big enough to completely wrap a bale of cash. You make sure all the joints and seams are sealed with self-adhesive butyl tape. There are rolls of the stuff in the van. But make sure only one of you handles the bale while the other one wraps and seals."

"Why's that?" enquired Jason.

"It's a precaution. Customs has dogs and other kit than can 'smell' money. Well not actually the money but the printing ink. The bales are made up of both plastic and paper notes so it could be an issue. We don't want to risk transferring even a molecule of 'smell' to the outside of the butyl wrapping. It could compromise the whole operation. Clear?" The boys nodded, as Chris desperately tried to figure out which job option was the easiest, hefting or wrapping.

"Given the bales are wrapped and sealed, then what?" asked Jason.

Davey Boy looked at the date on his watch.

"Over the next few days I'll be bringing in some large shipping cartons, tri-walls, plastic lined, along with a banding machine some wooden pallets and dried milk powder."

FOURTEEN

"But I thought you take your coffee black?" grinned Chris.

Davey Boy looked up into the roof trusses with a deep sigh. "*Sacks* of milk powder. The Chinese are mad for it. They can't get enough of the stuff for some reason. We conceal each wrapped bale in a lined tri-wall under layers of loose milk powder. We band each tri-wall on a pallet; address it with shipping marks provided by the junket and deliver as loose cargo to container consolidation depots in Southampton, Tilbury, London Gateway and Felixstowe. All together we prepare about twenty identical consignments with each tri-wall worth around one-hundred-thousand pounds. The van holds four tri-walls; one to each consolidation depot. As soon as the first four are packed I'll start delivering. It should take me a couple of days. Then we wait. All being well the junket should confirm successful receipt through coded communication with my mate in about four weeks. If everything is well, we go again. The important thing is not to have all our eggs in one basket. If a shipment doesn't get through, we change the strategy. Any questions?"

"Just a few," said Jason trying to get his head around Davey Boy's plan. "What's to stop this junket fellow from running off with our money? How do we load the van? The tri-walls are going to weigh a ton and I don't see any forklifts lurking nearby and how about the docks? We can't just pitch up and say stuff these boxes into a container for Hong Kong, there's a good chap."

Davey Boy smiled wryly.

"I'm glad to see you thinking Jason. We load the empty tri-walls from inside the van. There's enough room, I've checked. As for the docks you're absolutely right. Each tri-wall will have different consignee and consignor details on the shipping instructions. The booking will be made on-line out of an internet café using a made-up Hotmail account. Freight and handling charges will be payable upon collection at destination. The junket's got his connections and will add the costs to his percentage. As for the shipping docs, we clone any small freight company off the net and use their details. It's amazing what you can do with photo-shop and a decent printer these days."

Davey Boy took another swallow of coffee.

"Remember, this is a shoot and scoot strategy. Once a tri-wall is delivered to the docks, it's gone. If we don't get a coded safe receipt from HK, we're not about to go looking for it. As for the junket; well he'll be playing ball for the oldest reason in the world. Greed! He's been led to believe there's a helluva lot more money coming down the pipeline. He isn't going to jeopardise that by stealing away the first two mill."

Jason had been listening intently. It seemed Davey Boy had thought of everything but he wasn't done yet.

"Don't these container depots all have CCTV where you deliver?"

"They do." Davey Boy nodded.

"So what if they check a tri-wall after delivery, find the money and trace it back to you and the van?"

FOURTEEN

“Fair point but that’s why I’ll be wearing a wig and hat for each delivery. That, plus glasses and some concealer for the scar and trust me I could be any Joe Soap delivery driver.”

Chris wasn’t about to be left out.

“You haven’t thought about the van? The registration plate. That’s sure to be picked up on CCTV.”

“Do you know how many white nine-year-old panel vans of this model are out there, Chrissy? Thousands. I’ve made up plates from a photo I’ve seen of a similar van for sale on-line. Not professional mind, just painted plywood with black electrical taped numbers, but they’ll do a job in passing. If anyone runs the numbers, they’ll expect to see a white panel van and that’s exactly what they’ll get, except of course it won’t be ours”.

“But up close won’t they see the plates are just made up?”

Davey Boy smiled.

“It’s winter. The weather is shit. The plates, wheels, bumpers, door sills, the lot, will all be covered in mud. It will be virtually impossible to see anything.”

“But you can’t know that Davey?”

“Can’t I? When you arrived this morning, tell me, what do you think was in the bloody bucket?”

FIFTEEN

As usual the bookies had cleaned up. London sprawled grey, wet and miserable on both sides of its great river, very little moving under darkening slate skies. Boats were moored; the underground barred, stations deserted, roads and rail tracks empty. In huge transport sheds tall ranks of double-deckers stood empty, red and silent. Shops were shut; banks locked; supermarkets closed. A bitter westerly, sharp, cold, moaned between buildings, through branches and hoardings, kicking up litter and leaves, chasing remaining pedestrians home off sludgy puddled streets, their umbrellas harried by squalls of low scudding rain. As far from a pretty postcard as it was possible to be and without a snowflake in sight, London welcomed Christmas Day.

Christmas Day: For many the most anticipated day of the year. A day of festivities and celebration; of faith and prayer, of togetherness, of family and friends, of decorations, presents under the tree, food, drink, gifts and excited children. But for Raphael D'eath the day held none of these things. Frustrated and angry he indicated right guiding the beamer off the A3 up onto Kingston Hill. The road was empty. Switching to cruise control he could have been the last person on the planet. The tempo of the wipers, set on automatic, quickened as the rain intensified. The weather had worsened through the day. It was mid-afternoon but almost dark. He needed the halogens, their twin beams probing up the gradient as the car passed the narrow entrance to a university campus.

On either side a quarter mile of wet larch-wood fencing held back tall banks of indistinct jungled shrubbery, evergreen and drenched, split through with gnarled tree trunks, their dark overhanging boughs and bare tangled branches rattling above the road in invisible gusts. It all looked like D'eath felt; dismal, miserable, forbidding. He'd been summoned. On Christmas Day for God's sake! The Governor was waiting. His home, a grand six bedroomed pile amidst half an acre of ancient oaks and rhododendrons, was just a half-mile away. D'eath knew what was coming. There could be no other reason for the summons. Today of all days was meant to be one of friendship and understanding. He doubted his destination would be offering either. He slowed, indicating again, and turned the car off the main road onto a narrower lane. A wooden sign in the headlights, white and sculpted, announced the entrance to a private residential estate. The trees seemed bigger here, spearing up behind tall stone walls and fenced manicured hedges pierced every so often with wide gates in wrought iron and varnished timber. He drove on slowly down the dark lane, the car lurching over unseen speed bumps. The residents had probably been given a choice, he thought; streetlamps, gates or road markings? It was clear what they'd chosen. Five large gates later he saw it. A brass plaque set into a brick gatepost, the metal gleaming gold in the halogens. 'Highclere'. One leaf of the double gate stood open. He was expected. D'eath manoeuvred the car carefully through the gap and drove slowly up a gravel drive. Ahead through the bushes he could see light, warm, bright, spilling out of leaded windows. It wouldn't be long now. He parked and walked the last few metres; wet gravel crunching underfoot, the rain cold on his bared head. The heavy door didn't have a buzzer or a knocker. It had a bell pull. He pulled it and waited.

For Jason and Chris the day was all about celebration. The kitchen table, covered with a paper cloth patterned with holly berries and candles, had been moved into the Hutchins' front room. It was loaded with bowls of cabbage, brussels, carrots and roasties. After ten days away, grilling in winter sun, Chris' parents had returned with tans as orange as some of the swirls in the multi-coloured carpet. They bustled busily between steamy kitchen and table, the boys helping with plates, glasses and cutlery. Jason's mum, petite and thin, sat quietly, legs together on one of the black mock leather armchairs sipping a small sherry. Founded on the boys' friendship it had become something of a tradition for the single mum and her son to spend Christmas with the Hutchinses, the dinner always being the centrepiece of the day.

Joan Hutchins entered through the doorway carrying a large oval dish. Following behind in his wife's ample wake, Jack Hutchins held a gravy boat in one hand and a carving knife and fork in the other. On his head a creased red paper crown.

"Here we are everyone," she announced triumphantly, "I hope you're all hungry".

"Indeed! Merry Christmas everybody," grinned her husband with a toothy beer-infused smile.

Humped on the dish the turkey looked heavy, more than enough for the five of them. Straight from the oven it should have looked almost the same colour as the cook. It didn't. But that was no surprise. Despite her enthusiasm, Chris' mum was well known for her spectacular lack of culinary skills. The family normally survived on pre-packaged microwave offerings, take-outs and maybe a pub lunch on Sundays, but once a year Mrs H. cast chance to the wind and really tried to row the boat out. Inevitably it would sink and today was to be no different.

The small group crowded around the table on mismatched chairs. "Thanks Mrs H.," mumbled Jason as his plate was heaped with shards of dry turkey flesh, bullet hard potatoes and mushy brussels.

Jason glanced askance at Chris who like a condemned man was waiting for his own plate to be loaded. He returned Jason a swift look of mock horror. Jason's mum, noticing, smiled but kept quiet. Both the older Hutchins appeared oblivious.

"Jace is thinking of becoming a vegetarian, Mum," declared Chris with a twinkle in his eye.

"Oh surely not," she replied, looking concernedly at Jason. "And miss all this lovely turkey next Christmas?"

Jason grinned sheepishly, chewing manically, jaws aching. There were five birds in the small front room and the one on the table was no more palatable than the four nailed to the woodchip. Chris meanwhile was attempting to smuggle a few of his slices down the side of a leg to the cat but the cat was having none of it. Finally Jason swallowed his mouthful.

"Don't believe it, Mrs H. Chris couldn't tell a vegetarian from a post box."

"Well mind you talk to your mum Jason before doing anything. I always say, a growing lad needs his meat and gravy."

"Oh Joan, don't listen." Jason's mother had cut the turkey into meticulous miniature slices and was now dousing them in thick lumpy gravy.

"You'll have more chance of winning the lottery than tearing Jason away from his full English and hamburgers."

"Nice one, Mum." Jason grinned across at his mother. With a shy smile she patted his shoulder affectionately.

Mr H. smacked his lips. He was done carving for the moment but the doom of 'seconds' was never far away.

"Well, whatever anyone says Joaney," he beamed around the small table, "this is one beautiful bit of turk."

Mrs H., hand on ample breast, smiled happily.

"Oh I'm so pleased. Really it's nothing special."

Around the table the boys rocked silently on their chairs. Susan Bonchurch, eyes locked on the cabbage bowl, buried her nose in a paper napkin, while Mr H., bemused, shovelled another slice of petrified bird into his mouth. Cue another bout of silent shoulder trembling around the table. It was Chris who finally stifled enough silent laughter to change tack.

"Wishbone!" he yelped excitedly, waving the thin angle of bone like a trophy.

"C'mon Jace, grab an end. We've got a wish to make."

He threw his friend a big pantomime wink. Jason caught on and grabbed the loose end of the spindly slippery piece of bone. Next Christmas would be different. His mum deserved better. They all did. The first four tri-walls had shipped without incident. It was looking good. Others would follow as soon as Davey Boy received word. Fingers crossed; better times lay ahead. Jason grinned at Chris and returned the wink in style. He smiled over at his mum. She smiled back. Gripping the bone he closed his eyes and pulled.

It wasn't a day of celebration for Dave Gilroy. He had his own tradition; his own unique ritual of replenishment and renewal. Entrusted with the keys he stood quietly in the central hall of the empty Dojo. Usually it would be filled with sounds of exertion; grunts, exhalations, bare soles rasping over tatami mats, the same mats breaking the slapping fall of thrown bodies. Today there was only silence. Davey was bare footed, wearing a cotton singlet and loose tracksuit bottoms. He was alone. There was no need for either Aikidogi or Hakama and in truth he preferred the freedom without the thickly woven judo pyjamas and black trouser skirt. Dave Gilroy was Aikidoka, an exponent of the fighting art of Aikido. He had been introduced to the martial art as a young teenager, long before he had joined the military. At first, like most young men, he had just wanted to strut his stuff, boast and kick ass but the more his Sensei taught the more he became attracted to the calmness and flexibility of the discipline; a discipline that had at its core the blending with and controlling of attacking energy. He had learnt well; his disposition and natural athleticism finding an easy balance with the philosophy of the teaching. Over the years his dedication, training and skill had been rewarded. He had been conferred 'Shihan', Master Instructor, upon reaching the rank of sixth Dan and now, several years later, he had attained the rank of seventh Dan; one of the highest ranks of skill degree outside of Japan. For the last six years, army tours allowing, he had stood alone in this Dojo on Christmas Day. It was an important moment; a moment of silence, a moment to put aside past efforts, disappointments and achievements in preparation for the new. The slate wiped clean. This year, more than any before it, he sensed the magnitude of the coming challenges. Clearing his mind he emptied himself, feeling the energy in the quiet space. He bowed slowly, deliberately, to the front of the Dojo, the shomen, respecting the space and all those aikidoka who had passed through it before him and who would pass through it after him, then a pause, a breath and suddenly, erupting across the tatami with fast fluid movements, he commenced the ritual of his seventh Christmas kata.

Bishop had no tradition; he had no ritual and celebrating was the last thing on his mind. He looked around the small, cheap bed sit. It was cold. The catalogue-purchased fan heater made more noise than warmth. He was still in his dressing gown. There'd be no visitors today. He never had any visitors. Unwashed clothes littered the unmade single bed. Three neckties, one heavily soiled, hung over the opened door of an ancient wardrobe. Next to it, in an alcove masquerading as a kitchenette, a grungy Baby Belling grill oven still held the tinfoil remnants of a congealed turkey dinner. Opposite, in little more than a broom cupboard, a grimy plastic shower enclosure jostled for space with a sink and chain pull toilet.

In an attempt at cosy lighting Bishop had covered the bedside lampshade with an old pillowslip. It just made the room dim and shadowy. Outside the weather was darker still; filthy with cold wet winds buffeting the old timber sash, rattling the single panes. A tea towel stuffed into the frame was sodden, useless. Bishop could feel the draft across the room. He sat on the bed his head in his hands. Christmas Day in the midst of eight-million souls and no one cared if he lived or died, except maybe McGimlet and Bishop harboured no illusions about his preference.

But it hadn't always been so. He'd had a wife once, a pleasant apartment with a view, its own parking space and a decent car to put in it. The gambling had put paid to it all. He'd heard it described as a cancer. It wasn't. It was a black hole. It had swallowed everything; car, savings, apartment, relationship and now it was intent on taking the rest; his career and maybe even his life.

He had no one to blame but himself. But he was still breathing. He was still good at his job and McGimlet, the bastard, had thrown him a lifeline. But that lifeline was getting shorter every day. There had been no further ATM raids and there had been no sight or sign of the kid in weeks. Maybe he'd gone on holiday? Maybe he'd fallen off the end of the world? But the money, nearly two million quid of it, was still out there somewhere. The strategy, always the same, was find the money and follow it back. But so far there was no money and the clock was running. If D'eath couldn't nail the little bastard's location soon it would be too late. There wouldn't be a second chance. He would have to pick a date, pack in his job and run for it with nothing in his pockets. He doubted he would last long. The approaching New Year held little for him, least of all time and that was running out fast. Maybe it was McGimlet or perhaps the corner shop turkey dinner but either way, as Christmas Day began to dwindle under dark storm-strewn skies, Bishop, alone in his small bed sit and not for the first time that day, bent over and was sick to his stomach.

SIXTEEN

The Governor's wife Henrietta, Henny to her friends, answered the bell. She was not a happy woman. If her cultivated position in society had given her any sense of privilege or manners, it wasn't showing.

"Mr D'eath?"

"Ma'am."

"Mr D'eath, my husband arranged this meeting against my wishes. This is Christmas Day. This is my family's home, not an office. I object in the strongest terms to you being here and I want you to know that."

Wet and cold D'eath looked down impassively.

"I totally agree. I would rather be elsewhere too. I suppose we both have the Governor to thank for our misfortunes."

This was not quite the reply the lady of the house was expecting from one of her husband's employees. The tall, dark-suited stranger looked down at her, the eyes in his shaven head unmoving. She suddenly felt uneasy, cold in the rain and wind coming through the open door.

"Well as you're here you may as well come in."

She ushered D'eath into the hallway and then into a dimly lit drawing room.

"You may wait here," she said stiffly, pointing to a large sofa.

"Pour yourself a drink if you must. My husband will be with you shortly."

"Thank you that won't be necessary. I'm wet enough as it is, but I'll try not to drip too much over your fine furniture and carpets."

The woman started to reply but thought better of it. With a face like a rusted vice, she turned quickly back into the hall, shutting the double doors abruptly behind her.

So much for 'goodwill to all men' murmured the boss of FIBER. Alone, he looked about him, dabbing what moisture he could off his head and face with his silk pocket square. With the hallway doors firmly shut and the heavy curtains drawn against the weather, much of the room was in shadow. Firelight threw changing shapes across the ceiling, climbing walls, playing amongst corners while matching table lamps illuminated each end of the sofa with twin pools of dim light. Long and dimpled the sofa looked as comfortable as an ironing board. It was a classic Chesterfield; a massive slab of buttoned and nailed leather. Burgundy in the firelight, it set the tone for the whole room. A tone of cut crystal, darkly gleaming parquet flooring, polished mahogany, and thick velvet drapes. D'eath moved towards the warmth of the fire. Embered logs crackled and spat, flaming behind a woven copper fire screen. The fireplace was deep and wide; engineered brick above a broad stone hearth, its polished mantle of heavy oak covered in two yards of colourful Christmas cards. Above the cards a lone schooner battled the elements on a foam-flecked ocean, sails billowing under menacing thunder clouds. The dramatic oil, the size of a door, filled the entire chimney breast. D'eath, his gaze wandering, stood in front of the fire, he extended his arms towards the grate, palms open, feeling the warmth.

On each side of the fireplace was another Chesterfield, these were smaller, leather buttoned tubs, facing the matching sofa. In a far corner a tall long cased clock all walnut and etched brass. There were family photos, grouped in silver frames, rugs of silk and fine wool, gilt-framed oils on wooden panelling, rosewood, teak and satinwood softened with seasonal vases of ivy, mistletoe and scarlet poinsettia. It was a handsome room, a room of evident cultivation, a room designed to impress and D'eath had to admit it did its job well. But there was no Christmas tree. He was disappointed. Probably in another room he thought; a more informal family room. A shame though, a few seasonal twinkles might have helped to brighten his mood.

D'eath returned to the sofa. His clothes were still uncomfortably damp. He sat carefully, straight-backed, at one end. It *was* hard; as hard as the stone hearth. What was the point of that? A seat you could hardly sit on. All show, no go, a theme uncomfortably familiar to FIBER's boss over recent months. Thankfully the fire had been well stoked, and he faced its warmth gratefully. The minutes passed. He stared into the flames. He checked his watch and then looked across at the long case. The old clock was running fast. He stood to relieve his aching backside. His trousers, still damp, held the marks of the hard-quilted leather. He checked his watch again.

The Governor's wife had said shortly. But she was wrong. It was nearer half an hour before the double doors opened again. By now D'eath, a little warmer and drier, was standing, his back to the fire.

The Governor entered carrying two fingers of brandy in a crystal balloon. Behind him, delicately holding a similar glass was a wide ruby smile.

Attached to the smile was a little black dress with sparkling diamond accoutrements and inside the dress, with hair dark, soft and Audrey Hepburn high, was Frobisher. *Shit!*

"Merry Christmas, Raphael. Thank you so much for coming." The Governor smiled.

As if I had a choice, D'eath thought.

He had only ever seen the Governor in business suits. Upstairs hanging in some cavernous wardrobe, this was their day off. The Governor wore a plush velvet jacket in navy held over a bulging mid-rift with matching buttons. Clearly someone had enjoyed their Christmas dinner. It was a holiday for neckties too. The jacket had an Indian Nero collar. Trousers and suede loafers in the same colour as the jacket completed the ensemble. D'eath guessed the Governor's wife had selected the outfit to make her husband look casually sophisticated for the special day. If so, it was a mistake. The man looked absurd, like a velvety blue saveloy. But D'eath wasn't about to tell him.

SIXTEEN

"Merry Christmas to you too, sir. I'm sorry to disturb your Christmas dinner."

"Not at all Raphael, not at all. We were through to the brandy when you arrived, so no damage done eh."

The Governor had never used his first name before. D'eath sensed a precipice forming beneath his feet. Behind the Governor, Frobisher remained silent, still smiling like a TV toothpaste advert.

"Let's get comfortable, shall we?" The Governor motioned for D'eath to sit back on the sofa. He took one of the fireplace tubs, Frobisher the other. In one smooth movement D'eath found himself pinned like an insect on the sharp point of a Frobisher-Governor triangle.

"I trust you have no reservations about Lucinda being present?"

So, it's Lucinda now is it?

"Well, actually sir, I don't believe it is appropriate given what we need to discuss."

"Really?" The Governor feigned surprise.

"Come now, Raphael, if it wasn't for Lucinda here, I would still be totally in the dark over this ATM fiasco. It's not as if your own reports have been regularly forthcoming. You must agree?"

No I bloody don't, thought D'eath, noting first name number three.

"May I speak frankly sir?"

"You may."

"With respect sir, the FIBER team and our associated agencies have been working around the clock for the last three months. The scope of the investigation is massive and expanding all the time. I had to make a choice. I took the decision that action was more important than report writing. If in hindsight that decision was wrong, then I am sorry."

The Governor held the brandy balloon up to his nose, inhaling an aroma that had been eighteen years in the making. He studied FIBER's boss across the crystal rim, his gaze implacable.

"What do you think, Lucinda? A good decision?"

"No sir, not even close I'm afraid."

Frobisher was indulging herself, loving the parlour game. D'eath could see she and the Governor had done their planning long before his arrival. She continued to smile sweetly as she stuck in the knife.

"Mr D'eath had, *has*, an obligation to report all crucial information pertaining to his investigation. An investigation only possible because of the resources he persuaded you to authorise, sir. Clearly, he hasn't done so, and I think we can all see why."

D'eath's jaw tightened. He had anticipated the course of the meeting as soon as the summons had hit his inbox. What he hadn't known about, what had completely blindsided him, was Frobisher's involvement. He could take shit from the Governor. That pecking order came with the job. But not from a bloody PA stooge like Frobisher! He countered, ignoring the smiling Frobisher, straining to appear outwardly calm.

SIXTEEN

"Have there been any further ATM thefts?" D'eath knew the answer.

"It seems not," said the Governor.

"Exactly sir, there have been zero ATM thefts since I ramped up the investigation with your authority. The efforts of my team under my direct supervision have limited the money stolen to less than two-million pounds. And as I'm sure Ms Frobisher will be able to confirm; we continue vigorously investigating all avenues in pursuit of the perpetrators."

D'eath could feel the fire's heat in his eyes.

"Sir we have been busting a gut, twenty-four seven for the past three months working this case. We are not letting up. The thefts have stopped and the breakthrough is going to happen very soon. I can feel it."

Clearly the plan was for the Governor to keep his powder dry. Frobisher would be the haute couture attack dog. No wonder the man had survived atop the greasy pole for so long. Frobisher placed her empty glass carefully on the hearth. She sat back, crossing one lithe, stilettoed leg over the other, a shark smile on her face. Her dark hair was piled on top of her head and her diamond earrings sparkled in the firelight. She cleared her throat, the smile unrelenting.

Here it comes, thought D'eath. *Nail down the lid time.*

"Mr D'eath, if we wanted a gut busted, we would have hired a butcher. Your job was to deliver results. Something you have singularly been unable to do."

Expressionless, D'eath sat rigid, looking between Frobisher and the Governor into the flames of the fire.

"Further, you persuaded the Governor to authorise substantial sums of taxpayers' money on a promise; a fabricated promise on which you have woefully been unable to deliver, a promise documented and signed in your own hand."

Tell me about it, thought D'eath.

"The fact is you are a loner Mr D'eath, a maverick. You have concealed information, failed to deliver results and exhausted significant assets pursuing nothing more than your own ego."

Frobisher moved imperceptibly, leaning forward, the smile was gone now.

"In short, Mr D'eath, you have presided over an unmitigated and expensive shambles. A fiasco! You have delivered nothing but failure, Mr D'eath, and I'm here to tell you it ends now! Here! Tonight!"

Brownnosing bitch! D'eath remained motionless, outwardly a neutral expression on a passive face. He was damned if he would give these two shits the satisfaction of a meltdown. Job done, Frobisher looked towards the Governor, her mouth morphing between smile-sneer-smile. D'eath turned away. So that was it. No discussion, no argument. So be it. He was done here.

He addressed the Governor quietly.

"You will have my written resignation delivered to your office the day after Boxing Day. If there's nothing else I have other matters to attend to and quite frankly I would prefer to be elsewhere."

D'eath began to stand.

"Sit down!"

D'eath paused, surprised at the tone in the Governor's voice. Slowly he sat back onto the Chesterfield.

"I'm not interested in your broken promises, D'eath. You're human. You took a risk. You failed. It happens. It's on your head and you have accepted the consequences. All very excellent, except you are not resigning."

"I'm sorry?"

"Do you seriously think, even for a moment, I would ruin my family's Christmas Day by summoning you to my house on matters of your incompetence and a trifling two-million pounds?"

D'eath stared at the Governor.

"No Mr D'eath. We are here because a person or persons unknown appear to possess powers sufficient to render our banking security measures in London and probably across the country, totally redundant. And you know all about that don't you D'eath?"

D'eath clenched his teeth. *Bishop! That stupid imbecile.* He should have known the man couldn't keep his mouth shut. Frobisher must have wheedled it out of him. Probably only took that bloody smile. *Shit!*

"So, when were you intending to share this rather vital information with me, D'eath?"

Draining the last of his brandy the Governor carefully placed the empty glass next to Frobisher's on the hearth and fixed D'eath with an unblinking stare.

With nothing to lose D'eath hit back hard.

"When there was a modicum of half-decent evidence. That's when. We don't know what's happening. All we have are some half-brained theories and speculation based on some inconclusive digital CCTV footage. If I were to bring you everything like this that passed over my desk you wouldn't get out of your office for a month."

D'eath had dropped the 'sir'. He didn't know if he was still employed or what the hell was happening. At least Frobisher had stopped smiling. Thank God.

The Governor sighed heavily.

"You signed the official secrets act when you were appointed to FIBER. You're bound by the terms of at least two clauses concerning national security. Our masters have deemed this *is* a matter of national security; a most urgent matter, and that you Mr D'eath are the best placed with your accumulated knowledge to bring it to a satisfactory conclusion. As such you will continue in your post doing everything in your power to catch the persons responsible and resolve this unsettling matter and in so doing you will report to Ms Frobisher who will account for your work directly to me. You will be under her direct supervision until this matter has been ended. Are we clear?"

"And if I refuse?"

"That matter will be out of my hands, I'm afraid, but I believe the general protocol is that you will be arrested and locked up, Mr D'eath."

Frobisher interjected. She was smiling again.

"Don't be too despondent, Mr D'eath. You're close to a breakthrough. You said so yourself. It shouldn't take long. For the time being you will retain your office and your privileges. Well most of them. I will be supervising your budget and overseeing expenses. I am sure we will make a fine team."

Resplendent in navy velvet the Governor stood, extracting himself from the leather tub with some difficulty.

"Good. I'm glad that's settled then. I will leave you with Ms Frobisher to sort the details. You must now please excuse me. I have family issues to attend to. It is Christmas Day, after all."

Giving D'eath a sallow smile the Governor opened the double doors and disappeared into the hall.

Frobisher was standing too, no sign of a smile now. D'eath turned to her. Before he could speak Frobisher put a finger up to her lipsticked mouth motioning D'eath to follow her into the hall. They moved towards the front door. Indistinct voices, raised, a man and a woman, were coming from somewhere in a nearby room.

"Check your inbox," she spoke quietly.

"Within the next twenty-four hours you will receive a bullet-point memorandum detailing my operational requirements.

Essentially you report everything to me; you check everything with me, any requests and requirements go through me. You have freedom to continue pursuing your investigations subject to my approval. The rest of the detail will be in documents delivered to you tomorrow."

She held open the front door. The wind and rain had increased substantially since D'eath's arrival. He turned up the collar of his jacket and reached in his pocket for the Beamer's key. He would have to make a dash for it. He set himself on the threshold key in hand just as Frobisher leaned in.

"Payback's a bitch, isn't it?" she whispered.

D'eath hesitated. They were alone in the empty hallway. Over the threshold the night was wet, wild and dark. He bent to her diamond-decorated ear.

"Crow all you want but you'd better pray I break this case and quick. You think you've got what you wanted? You've just put your name on the list above mine, you stupid cow!"

With that the ex-boss of FIBER strode out into the night.

SEVENTEEN

Huang Fu stood on the edge of jetty four of Hong Kong's River Trade Terminal. He was looking northwest across the bay, towards the wide waters of the Pearl River estuary. He knew little of the great river's origins save what he had learned in school. It was the third longest in China after the great Yangtze and Yellow Rivers and it was known as the Nile of South China, whatever that meant. But aside from those two nuggets Huang remained ignorant and disinterested. At forty-one he'd been out of school more years than he could remember. He had cared little back then and today he didn't care at all. All that mattered was the river and its massive estuary being there in front of him. It had always been there and doubtless it would remain there long after he was gone. But in the meantime, it was his highway; a wide, far-reaching highway carrying his illicit contraband smoothly and undetected into and out of the far reaches of the wealthy South China interior. That was all that mattered to Huang Fu. And he hadn't been taught that in school.

Turning up the collar of his cashmere Huang flicked a half-smoked cigarette out over the black waters and checked his watch. The night, already cool, was turning cold with a stiff wet breeze blowing onshore amongst the gantry cranes and container stacks. It was well past midnight but all forty-nine jetties along the south quay were noisy with activity. Here time was money; lots of it.

From where he stood on jetty four, he could see the end of the quay two-hundred yards south. Beyond it, three miles across the channel, the blinking lights of aircraft departing and arriving Hong Kong International Airport. Back along the quay to the north he could only see the length of a football field before his view became obscured. Wherever he looked up and down the quay ships were at berth; loading, unloading, others departing, others at anchorage waiting to dock; the waters between them churning with tugs, lighters, barges and the smaller motor vessels of the pilot and customs services. Up and down the docks massive eight wheeled Straddle Carriers trundled between the crowded jetties underslung with twenty and forty-foot steel containers. Above the noise, lights everywhere, white and multi-coloured, fixed and blinking, shivering on the oily, dark waters, gleaming statically off wet concrete. Where the machines couldn't work crews of high vizzed stevedores in crush boots and hard hats clambered on decks, gantries and amongst netted cargo piled on the quayside; calling, shouting, gesticulating above the incessant din of engines, forklifts, conveyor belt loaders and pallet stackers.

A million containers a year pass through the RTT. It is the bi-directional valve in the Pearl River's billion-dollar pipeline. Break-bulk cargoes from oceangoing container giants unloaded in Hong Kong's deep water Kwai Tsing docks going into South China; domestic goods for international export coming out with a thousand square miles of the majestic Pearl River delta as the revolving doorway.

Huang had long settled on the RTT's forty-nine jetties and one-hundred-and-sixty acres of bustling activity as the perfect matrix within which to conduct his lucrative smuggling operations. Like a few grains in a sack of rice his containers mixed with the three-thousand transported daily into and out of the wealthy South China interior. Drugs and contraband went in; profits came out, laundered through a web of small mainland banks to fuel his expanding enterprises in protection, gambling and prostitution. It was the way Huang liked it. It was the way he intended to keep it.

Huang was cold and getting wet. He hadn't been to the docks in months. But the promise had been easy money, lots of it, and he needed to make sure for himself. He wasn't about to wait any longer. It was time. Huang Fu turned away from the jetty's edge towards the parked Mercedes. His driver opened a rear door. Huang shook his head preferring to walk the fifty yards to the warehouse. Facing the jetty square-on the building resembled an aircraft hangar, large, open portal steel construction with a steel sliding door wide enough to park a bus against. In the space between the top of the door and the roof a ten-foot-high blocky number was painted in red. Number four. No chance of picking the wrong warehouse. South quay, number four, one a.m., the message had read.

The money he paid ensured such messages were rarely wrong. The sliding steel door was four feet shy of being closed. Light spilled out. Huang, turning his shoulder, moved through the gap. It wasn't a coincidence the warehouse resembled an aircraft hangar. The brightly lit interior could have accommodated a Boeing 737 easily. But it didn't. What it did accommodate was shipping cargo; lots of it. Crates in steel and timber; wired panniers, cartons, drums, barrels, bales, casks, assorted packages and three exotic low-slung fluorescent coloured sports cars.

The floor of the hangar/warehouse was smooth concrete over-painted with geometric yellow lines. The lines marked out the floor into twenty-six wide sections, each section stencilled with a letter of the alphabet. Space between the sections had been left for the access of forklifts and pallet stackers. Section 'Z' filled the left backmost corner of the building. Section 'A' nearest the door. Various assortments of the break-bulk filled Section 'Z' and all the other lettered sections across and down the building through to and including section 'C'. Section 'B' was filled with the parked supercars. Section 'A' had no break-bulk in it. It did have four men, one Hilux crew cab and four palleted tri-walls. Huang walked towards the men. Three were his. The fourth, standing apart, was the assistant deputy director of Port Customs; the man who had sent him the message. Approaching the group he called out in Cantonese.

"Any problems?"

"Seems good but we haven't checked the boxes yet."

SEVENTEEN

"Well get to it we haven't got all night."

His three men commenced tackling the banding around the four tri-walls with long-handled bolt cutters. The uniformed customs official stood to one side clearly nervous. Huang looked at him.

"You worry too much."

The man didn't reply. Banding cut and removed it was the lids next. The milk powder had compacted during the voyage but still almost filled the tri-wall. His men looked to Huang for direction.

"You will need to dig." He gestured a shovelling motion.

His men had come prepared. With two foldup entrenching tools taken from the back of the Hilux, surface milk powder was shovelled into a clean, empty carton Twenty seconds of effort revealed the first rubbery package buried halfway down inside the tri-wall. It took two to remove it. The displaced milk powder was returned, patted down, smoothed over. The remaining three tri-walls received the same treatment under Huang's watchful gaze. Finally, lids replaced, the four tri-walls were re-secured on their pallets with new polyprop banding. Huang regarded the four rubber bales on the floor. Like giant kids' bricks; two columns, one brick on another, with a dusting of flour or icing sugar. He turned to the fidgeting customs officer.

"You can go."

The official nodded thankfully. Pulling his cap down over his face he scurried out the way Huang had entered. Huang looked around. Apart from himself and his men the warehouse was empty. Bending he took a switchblade from his coat pocket. He flicked it open, scoring the nearest topmost bale. He pulled the slit apart. Bundles of notes densely packed in shiny shrink wrap reflected the overhead light. He allowed himself a brief smile. He looked up.

"Get them loaded."

"What about the milk powder?" enquired Kai.

Money motivated and meticulous, Huang Fu's lieutenant, like his boss, despised loose ends.

"Milk powder is not cheap. The cartons are clean now. Collect them in the morning and find a buyer".

Kai nodded.

The four rubber wrapped bundles were hefted onto the Hilux's flatbed along with the folded entrenching tools, bolt cutters and banding machine. The tailgate was chained up and a hinged steel cover, an after-sale add-on, was locked down tight over the top. Huang gestured at the vehicle's tailgate.

"You know what to do. Phone me the numbers. They'll be waiting on confirmation so be quick".

Kai nodded again.

The sound of three doors slamming and the Hilux starting up was startlingly loud in the cavernous space. Huang walked back to the wide steel door and pushed a red plastic mushroom sticking out of the wall. A motor whined and the wide, steel door started to move back. Five-foot. Seven-foot. Eight-foot. At ten-foot the Hilux accelerated through the widening gap, turned sharply and disappeared up the quay. Huang punched the mushroom again. The door stopped opening and started to close. Eight-foot. Six-foot. Huang looked around. The four tri-walls were pushed back against the wall. They looked as if they belonged. Everything else looked as it should; a standard shipping warehouse full of break-bulk cargo and three exotic sports cars. Four-foot. Three-foot. Huang slipped through the narrowing gap of bright light into the night, the wide steel door settling shut just behind him. He walked towards the open door of his Mercedes, stepping lightly around the black pools of oily water dotting the jetty. He felt good. It had been a good night's work. Four-hundred-thousand in the back of the Hilux on its way to Kowloon with more promised. Huang lit a cigarette, smiling. And the stupid Gweilos expected most of it back. Idiots! No one got rich giving money back. Welcome to Hong Kong.

EIGHTEEN

"Thank God that's over with for another year", said Chris.

"What? Christmas?" Jason was confused.

"Not Christmas. Pillock! You know, the doom and gloom stuff after."

"Your mum's food wasn't that bad, Chris. C'mon, credit where credit's due. The brussels were almost edible."

"Edible! I was farting for a week. No what I'm getting at Jace is one minute you're looking forward to everything, you know, the holiday, the partying, presents and stuff then it's come 'n gone just like that. School starts up, it's back to early rises, the mornin's as black as Darth Vader's hat, everyone's cold and bloody miserable with no money and nothing to look forward to. Like I said, just bloody doom n' gloom. Then, a few weeks after New Year's, it kind of gets back to normal with things settlin' down. Some good stuff starts on the box and people begin lookin' forward to Easter and their summer hols. That kind of stuff. That's what I was getting at."

"Bloody hell Chris, I never took you for a bleedin' philosopher."

Jason stepped across the path dipping his shoulder into his friend's, barging him down off the shallow bank.

"Oi! You bloody plonka!"

Chris looked at his shoes in the mud.

"Very clever Bonchurch. You Pratt!"

Jason hauled Chris up out of the ditch and back on to the cambered path.

"Cheer up, Chrissy. Another few weeks mate and you can buy the bleedin' shoe shop if you want."

"I'll believe it when I see it, Jace. It's been weeks since we heard from Davey."

"You've got to give it time, mate. Macau's the other side of the planet."

"We've given it time Jace. Davey said a month and that's been and gone and we still haven't heard dick shit. I dunno, mate. I'm getting a bad feeling."

"What? You think Davey's scarpered with the money?"

"I'm not saying that Jace. I . . . I dunno. It's just all this waitin'. It's doin' my head in, mate."

"Yeah. I know where you're comin' from but think about it. We're only a few days past the month. Anything could have happened. Storms at sea; port delays. I dunno, maybe the bleedin' propeller dropped off. All I'm saying is we've trusted Davey up to now and we'll know one way or another soon enough. A few more days isn't going to make any difference."

Chris picked up a spindly fallen branch and speared it into the ditch with venom.

"But we should have heard *something* Jace. We never even got a 'Merry Christmas' or 'Happy New Year' out of him."

EIGHTEEN

"Look Chris. He's your cousin. You know him better than me. All I know is he told us both to keep shtum. Act normal. Enjoy Christmas and the New Year and he would contact us when he gets the confirmation from his mate. And you know what? I reckon that should be about any time now."

"I hope you're right, Jace. I just hope to God you're right mate."

It was Sunday, the end of the third week of January. The weeks of Christmas and New Year had been grey and miserable with almost constant rain, gusting cold winds and some hail thrown in. This was the first good day for some time; cold but dry and crispy bright. Jason and Chris had been at the bat cave since early on. With nothing better to do they'd lain around the whole morning drinking coffee, eating toast and playing computer games. By mid-day boredom had called them out. The sun was as elevated as it was going to get. The sky was blue and the air after the weeks of rain had a gin-like clarity. If it wasn't for the mud, bare boned branches and the cold, one could have been conned spring was around the corner. They'd edged through a gap in the hoarding opposite the Cave and were out across the development site just walking, aimlessly kicking cans and joshing.

Trudging the muddy remains of a narrow path towards the middle of the forty-acre site, the boys approached the old railway siding platforms. All that remained now amongst the weeds were graffiti-daubed rotting concrete footings pierced here and there with rusting and twisted iron rebar. Arriving together the boys gingerly stepped up two feet onto the concrete outcroppings and looked around. Any standing buildings on the site had been long demolished and timber hoardings had been erected around the perimeter. But apart from that the site had been left raw and desolate for two winters. The twelve-foot-high plywood hoardings showed it. Their paint was blistered, the panels warped and the joints in the wood rotten and swollen. But apart from one or two hidden gaps, like the one they had edged through, the barrier had somehow survived the winds and weather and, for the time being at least, fulfilled the function of keeping the site secure. The only official way in or out was four-hundred-and-fifty yards away on the northeast perimeter; a gate made of two hinged hoarding panels secured with a heavy chain and padlock. It hadn't been used for months. To the west and south, near to where the bat cave stood, the site was bordered by curving railway lines set down deep behind raised and fenced off banking; to the north, the dual carriageway, and to the east, beyond the old gasometer, a trading estate of low modern warehousing. The nearest buildings tall enough to overlook the hoardings were a pair of seventies council tower blocks. But they were over half a mile away and only eight storeys high. Effectively the land within the hoardings was a walled oasis; a muddy, derelict wasteland of an oasis but an oasis just the same. And the boys were standing alone in the middle of it.

EIGHTEEN

Chris perched carefully on a bar-free corner of the outcropping. "You know, Jace, I've got to admit you're pretty damn special."

"Thanks mate. I think you're pretty cool too . . . most of the time."

Chris sniggered.

"Thanks, I think. But that's not what I meant. I'm talking about that weird shit with the cash machines. I mean that's pretty freaky stuff."

"Yeah. I know. I try not to think about it too much."

Chris paused, fidgeting for a more comfortable perch.

"Well that's just it, mate. I think you should."

"Should what?"

"Think about it. I mean if you can do that shit to cash machines what other stuff might you be able to do?"

Jason looked at his friend. He saw the waiting had worn at him. Chris hadn't been in his suit since the day he'd first worn it to the bat cave and his hair was growing out; getting greasy again. The undertaker's apprentice wasn't far beneath the surface. What Chris needed, more than a wash, cut and blow dry, was a big dose of reassurance. Jason had had his wobble when Davey Boy had first outlined his plan to ship the money to Macau; when the realisation had hit that people were after him, not the money. It seemed Chris was having his now.

"I'm listening, Chrissy".

"Well, what if you experiment a bit? I dunno. Maybe try what you do to ATMs on other stuff."

"What do you suggest?"

"I was thinking you could start say with a TV?"

"So if I can get money out of a cash machine, you're thinking I can start up and change the channels on a TV?"

"Why not, mate? Both have glass screens. Both run on electricity."

"Great! So why hasn't it happened already? I watch enough of the bloody thing."

"I don't know Jace. But isn't that the point of experimenting? To find out?"

By now Chris was perking up, smiling. He hadn't done much of that since Christmas. Jason noticed. Maybe it wasn't such a bad idea. He stood looking out across the site. Despite the cold, the sun was warm on his shoulders and the back of his neck.

"Okay, I'm up for giving it a go Chrissy, but just for you mate. If I disappear in a bang and puff of smoke, you make sure you remember that."

Chris stood with a grin. Punching Jason lightly in the shoulder he made to jump off the rubble of concrete.

"Whoa! I'm not walking back to the bat cave. We've only just got here and I want to sit in the sun for a bit. We haven't seen it for weeks."

Chris paused looking around, thinking. Suddenly he snapped his fingers. "The phones, mate. The burners. They're electric. They have screens. We can try it right here. See if you can make a call or summit without turning it on."

EIGHTEEN

"You're a nutter, Chris. How the hell am I going to do that?"

Chris was really excited now.

"I don't know. Try holding it or looking at it. Just do what you do with the ATMs and see what happens."

"I'm not bloody using mine. Davey could be calling on it any minute."

Chris was unperturbed.

"No worries mate, here."

Reaching around under his coat he slipped his burner out of the back pocket of his jeans and offered it.

"Davey never phones me, anyway. Go on, give it a try."

Jason took the small plastic case as if it was infected. He cupped it in both hands at arm's length. He looked at Chris.

"Now what?"

"I dunno. Stare at it. Will it to switch on or something. Just do what you usually do."

Jason glared at his friend.

"Haven't you got it yet? Hasn't it sunk in? I don't know what I usually bloody do. It just happens."

"Okay, keep your hair on, mate. I get it. Just try and see."

Jason looked at the small inert plastic case. Inside it had a lithium battery, a printed circuit board, some LEDs, a SIM card and a miniscule microphone and speaker. In his hands it looked cheap and innocuous. He focused on the phone. He concentrated. He focused some more. He went cross-eyed looking at the bloody thing. But nothing. It remained a plastic case of cheap electronic components.

"This is stupid, Chris. Nothing's happening. I feel like a bloody prat."

"Okay, Okay, maybe you need to . . . "

Chris went silent, rubbing his chin for some seconds, thinking. Then he spoke again.

"You know what, Jace? I haven't got a bleedin' clue."

"Join the club, dipshit. What have I been telling you for the last ten minutes?"

"The only thing I can think of is for you to put the phone down and try from a distance," said Chris. "Maybe you shouldn't be holding it. With the ATMs you told me it all kicks off even before you put a hand on the things. Maybe that's the trick?"

Jason considered for a moment then bent down placing the small plastic phone on the rubble, propping it against a six-inch length of old rebar pushing through the concrete. He stepped back a couple of paces and held out both arms.

"Okay here goes," he murmured.

Wincing, Chris involuntarily stepped back a few paces too. Again Jason trained both eyes, wide and focused, on the small, dark, plastic box propped on a sunlit piece of crumbling concrete. He force-stretched both his arms out as far as his shoulder sockets allowed; his palms and fingers trembling, his face one big grimace.

"Come on you bastard! C'mon! C'mon!" he yelled.

The plastic case lay peacefully in the sun.

"Try just pointing one hand," suggested Chris softly.

EIGHTEEN

"Who the hell do you think I am, Chris? Harry bloody Potter?"

Chris shrugged.

"Just try it, Jace. You never know with this kind of stuff".

Jason was getting exasperated big time now.

"Since when are you the world's expert? And shut the crap up telling me what to do. I'm only trying this to cheer you up."

"Well it's not bloody working Jace and if you're goin' to be like this about it let's just knock it on the head and go get fish and chips or summit."

Jason was having none of it.

"You started this, Chris. I'm goin' to finish it. I'm supposed to be the freakin' special one. The one everyone's after, right? So get the hell out of my way and let me get this done."

Chris jumped off the low outcropping on to the long black mat of his own shadow. The sun wouldn't be long above the horizon now. He hadn't wanted or expected Jason to get so wound up. It was just meant to be an experiment; a bit of a laugh. But there was no laughing now.

Jason adjusted the small plastic box on the concrete. He stepped back along the crumbling footings until he couldn't reverse any further. The phone was about ten feet away and level with his feet. Jason set himself. Braced his feet; right knee bent forward, left leg straight behind, supporting. He looked at the shitty, little, cheap phone. It was as offensive as hell. He hated it. Jason extended a single arm, right palm up as if stopping traffic. He focused. Ten feet forward, five feet down.

Okay you piece of shit. You or me! He leaned forward as if into a strong wind. Eyes focusing; ten feet forward, five feet down. Summoning all his will power; dredging it up, concentrating it, centralising it, willing it through the conduit of his arm at the phone. Ten feet forward, five feet down. He strained, his breath stuck in his chest, his eyes mere slits. Nothing existed but the phone now, nothing. His legs ached; his arm, back, neck and shoulders ached. The seconds accumulated. His vision blurred and re-focused, blurred and re-focused. Ten feet forward, five feet down. Nothing! The phone lay where he had placed it, ten feet forward and five feet down. A stupid piece of inert plastic that didn't even know he was there. Jason moved his head. The sun glared an instant off the miniature glass screen. *It was winking at him.* Anger boiled, rising in his belly. If that cheap piece of shit wouldn't turn on for him, he'd make damn sure it never turned on again. And he didn't need any so-called special powers for that. With a jerk of his head Jason broke his stare, casting around for a suitable lump of rock. Then, in the middle of the wasteland, under the limitless blue, with the sun warm on his neck and on his back, the shivering began.

As anger flooded through Jason's brain the switches activated. Neurotransmitters opened fire; surging cocktails of adrenalin, noradrenaline and testosterone through his young body. Jason gasped; his muscles tensing, his heart rate and blood pressure rocketing. Avalanching through his body the hormonal messengers did what six million years of human evolution had programmed them to do; heightening senses, strengthening muscle, seeking out threat. But then they went and did something else. As if a completely different switch had been flicked on, trillions of dormant bacteria that had no business being where they were, suddenly activated in the catalytic hormonal flood. Interacting frenetically like rice grains in boiling soup, the bacterium roiled, quivering, metabolising electrical energy; infinitesimal, incalculably tiny amounts of electrical energy. But there were trillions of them; trillions of microscopic batteries acting as a single power source. Jason felt the familiar quivering of the hairs on his body; the pressure building in his ears, the sense of energy increasing within him. Then, for the first time, came a glow. At the end of his arm, around the extremities of his hand; a pulsing blue glow in the bright sunlight. He heard a low hum; the air smelling sharp, clean, almost like bleach. Then a millisecond of nothing as trillions of bacteria reached their maximum collective voltage and discharged. A surge of power rushed down the conduit of Jason's arm, leaping from his hand in a fizzing, cracking arc of plasma energy. There was a deafening staccato crack, a flash of blinding light, and then, nothing.

"Holy shit Jace. Are you okay?"

Chris jumped up on to the outcropping. Jason was lying flat on his back. The smell of bleach was still strong in the air.

"Not sure mate" came Jason's groggy response, "Think I'm winded. I need to catch a breath."

Chris hooked an arm under Jason's and together they staggered upright.

"What the hell was that!?" Chris was incredulous but Jason seemed strangely unfazed.

"That Chrissy is how you kick the shit out of a ten-quid burner."

He pointed. What had been the phone was a scorched congealed mess lying yards away from the outcropping. It looked as if it had been dropped out of a tenth-floor window and the remains collected up and stuffed into a pizza oven.

Chris smiled with relief.

"Anymore experimenting, mate, and I think we'd better have a fire extinguisher handy."

Jason appeared a bit dazed. All his previous anger had disappeared. He looked like he'd just gotten out of bed having forgotten to set the alarm. He sat on a shard of concrete. Bemused, he looked at his right hand. He wriggled his fingers. His hand appeared unmarked, unharmed.

"I don't feel too bad Chris." He yawned widely. "Tired and a bit lightheaded but that's about all."

Tired and lightheaded were off Chris' radar. In excited overdrive he was launching big time in the opposite direction.

"Jace! What the hell was *that!?* It was 'effing amazing, mate! Off the bleedin' charts."

His voice was a high-pitched torrent of disbelief.

"I've never, ever, seen anything like it. Seriously! God's own truth, mate. I thought the shit with the ATMs was crazy but *lightning bolts!* Man I'm so totally freaked. And did you see that blue glow coming out of your hand? Shit! I'm tellin' you, Jace. You looked like a superhero or something."

EIGHTEEN

Jason sat tired but happy letting Chris babble his adrenalin out. Finally he ran out of steam and sat next to Jason on the concrete; two lads silently looking out across the deserted site. Nothing seemed to have changed apart from the lengthening shadows. The sun was low down over the railway tracks now and it had turned a lot colder.

Chris broke the silence

"Have you any idea what just happened Jace?"

Jason ran a tired hand through a mop of dusty hair.

"I'm not really sure, Chris, to tell the truth. I know I was really pissed off. I don't know why. It was only a bloody phone. But I got so angry all I wanted to do was smash it. Do you think maybe that's got something to do with it?"

"What? Like the Incredible Hulk or something?"

Jason laughed. Although drained he was feeling better now. Much better; better than he'd felt for months.

"Well I'm not green and I'm not bare-assed naked so probably not."

"Well I wouldn't want to test it, mate. I don't think I'd like to be around the next time you get pissed."

A trilling suddenly started up in Jason's coat pocket. He pulled out a phone identical to its recently deceased brother. He jabbed a button.

"Hello?"

He listened, Chris looking at him attentively.

"Great! Yes, he's here. I'll tell him. See you tomorrow then, usual place, usual time."

He jabbed another button and replaced the phone in his coat pocket. Impatience was all across Chris' face.

"Well?"

For a moment Jason's grin banished his tiredness.

"It's Davey. In not so many words he's got the confirmation. The first four boxes made it through."

"Yes!" Chris punched the air.

"And he asked me to pass on something else."

"To me?"

Jason nodded.

"He says sorry it's late but . . . Happy New Year."

NINETEEN

Spring washed in on a wave of enthusiasm. The January consignments had paved the way. The February, March and April shipments had quickly followed. A small fortune along with enough powdered milk to lighten a lake of coffee had been safely delivered to Hong Kong. Davey Boy's plan was working. They were making it work.

And now, with the arrival of May and the security services still chasing shadows, the end was in sight. The last bundle had been wrapped, the last sack of milk powder split and shovelled, the final tri-wall packed. The van had made the last of its long round-robin motorway journeys and in the docks, boxed and anonymous, the final four-hundred-thousand pounds was warehoused awaiting despatch. The export documents were cut; the voyages booked and in little over a month, with a fair wind, Jason, Chris and Davey Boy would be home free.

D'eath had absolutely no desire to answer the warbling telephone. It had been twenty weeks of nothingness since his demotion; in his eyes emasculation, and he had little desire to do much of anything. He didn't want to be here, but the Governor's masters had forced the issue. This was no longer about money. It was a matter of national security. His choice had been stark; FIBER under Frobisher or prison under the Official Secrets Act. He had opted for FIBER and Frobisher had been rubbing his face in it ever since.

Through the wide-open double doors he saw her. *The bitch.* She was on the phone, her back to him, head bobbing animatedly. The double doors remained open all the time now, effectively making his office and Frobisher's one large manageable space; manageable by Frobisher, that was.

The phone on his desk continued to warble. *Persistent bastard.*

It kept warbling. Putting himself out of his misery he finally picked it up.

"What?" he said tiredly.

"It's Carter. You won't believe it but something's breaking on the ATM case. Can I come up?"

D'eath looked through the doors. Frobisher's head was still bobbing.

"Er, no, no. I was actually in the process of leaving. I'll come to you. It's a floor down isn't it?"

"Nope. I've moved. Two floors down. Room thirteen but don't let that worry you."

Spare me, thought D'eath. Carter's strong points might just about stretch to filling a very short list, but subordination, deference and protocol wouldn't be on it. The Geek with the streak lived by his own rules.

"I'm coming down."

NINETEEN

The label on the door said, 'Room 13', but it was little more than a cubicle. A cubicle stuffed full of garish heavy metal posters, painted fantasy figurines, concert flyers, piles of skateboard and gaming mags, an astronomical wall map of some sky at night and at the centre of it all a maxed-out 18-core Xeon iMac Pro computer.

Kicking back, hands behind his head, the Geek looked totally at home in front of the computer's wide screen. His hair had grown out of the buzz cut but the streak was still there, peroxided and bright.

"Come on in boss. Sorry it's a little tight. Hold on a mo."

With a flourish of a densely illustrated forearm a pile of skateboard magazines hit the deck revealing the seat of a second, smaller, chair. "There you go. Pull up a pew."

D'eath looked around the cubicle. It didn't take long.

"Are you sure you've got the room?"

"Always room for the boss," quipped Carter.

"Thank you."

D'eath squeezed his long frame carefully into a chair.

"Weren't you operating out of the open plan up on the next floor?"

"Too much going on up there, boss, too many eyes. I prefer it down here. It's small, granted, but I don't need much."

"Apparently."

D'eath moved his shoes trying to find some carpet between the shiny magazines scattered on the floor.

"So Carter, what's this about the ATM case? You said you have breaking news? ".

"Damn right! Can you Adam and Eve it? Months with nothing and now they've intercepted a pile of cash."

"Who, where, and how much?" D'eath was cautious. He'd been promised breakthroughs before and been let down.

"UK Customs. Tilbury docks, en route to Hong Kong in a box full of milk powder. About a hundred grand. Apparently, a forklift speared the box while loading it into the container. What are the chances, eh?"

"And the serial numbers check out?"

"Yep. Some of the packaged notes were new with sequential serial number groupings. It was easy for customs to upload the data as part of their initial in-house report. All I did was run a number comparison with our records. It's definitely part of the ATM thefts."

"Shit!"

"Damn right again!"

D'eath was thinking quickly. "Who else has this information?"

"Right now just customs. I've been piggy backing their in-house systems since the investigation started. I put in flags on some key words and hey-ho! Even they don't know what they've got yet."

"Let's work to keep it that way. What does their report say?"

Carter nimbly clicked a few keys. The iMac's screen changed. He peered at it.

NINETEEN

"A single tri-wall, I think that's a kind of big cardboard carton. Anyway, it was delivered in by a company called Pan Freight Services. They have an address near Ipswich. It was booked in on the twenty-eighth of April."

He clicked another key and a calendar popped up on the screen.

"That was last Tuesday."

"Okay. So we have a company, an address, and a date. Do we have any pictures?"

The peroxide streak shook.

"Nope. Sorry boss. Nada. This is just a text data report."

"I don't give a damn what it is. We need pictures. Can you access their systems?"

"It'll be tricky. There's a ton of data to sift through."

"Do it. I'll authorise the overtime. We need those CCTV images. When you get them call in Bishop for analysis but force it down his throat, this is on a strictly need-to-know basis between the three of us. No one else. Clear?"

The streak bobbed.

"Good. Now tell me about the Hong Kong connection. I assume you have the consignee details and shipping marks from the customs report?"

The streak nodded.

"The consignment is addressed to a company in South China via some place called the River Trading Terminal in Hong Kong."

"Okay. Dig up the info on this terminal place. They could have more of these tri-walls in transit and where there's cargo there's a customs office. Get the contact details and route them a request for assistance. Make it look like a formal message from UK Customs. Put them on alert to search and seize any cargo transiting through their hub to this company in South China; especially any cargo manifested as containing milk powder. It's a long bloody shot but we're due some luck."

"What about this company in China? Should I request them to investigate?"

"Don't bother. It will be outside their jurisdiction. And if the money's already transited Hong Kong it's gone for good."

D'eath extricated himself from the chair, stepping over the magazines. "Carter, this is the closest we've been to catching the bastards. Don't screw it up. Whoever delivered that money I want their balls in a vice. And remember, this stays between you, me and Bishop."

D'eath palmed a card from his pocket.

"This is my personal cell. When you have the data call me direct, any time, twenty-four seven. Time is against us. Customs won't be staying dumb for long. They'll be alerting the police and security service as soon as they make the connection and then it'll be out of our hands."

D'eath paused in the doorway.

"Do this right Carter and there's a big bonus with your name on it."

He turned away into the corridor, closing the door marked 'Room 13' behind him.

As the door shut Carter swivelled back to the computer screen.

Overtime and bonus!

He smiled flexing his fingers. He laid them lightly on the keyboard.

Okay Genghis, you want some balls in a vice. Let me find you some.

D'eath walked back to the lift and took it down. He needed to walk; to think. He could feel his nervous energy building. It would only be a matter of hours before the information leaked. He knew this as surely as he hated that bitch Frobisher. This case had started on his watch. He would be damned if he let it finish on Frobisher's. Once the data was out it would be a straight race. Her against him. He had a head start but she had the establishment. It would be a tight finish. But as he exited the building something else was gnawing away in the back of his mind. Something about the Customs report. He couldn't put a finger on it, but it was there all the same. Maybe the walk would clear his mind. He pushed through the vestibule doors out into the cold.

While Carter worked the early hours slicing and dicing the Tilbury port firewalls, on the other side of the world another hectic business day had already dawned in Hong Kong.

The customs administration building had not been built

to look pretty. A formidable four-square block of white cement it stood fifty metres inland from jetty twenty-four, facing out over the channel, halfway along the north-south quay of the River Trading Terminal. With its looming authority, angular whitewashed walls and its cohorts of uniformed customs enforcers it was known ironically by all in the docks as the 'sugar cube'.

The office of the Assistant Deputy Director of Port Customs was on the fourth floor of the sugar cube, directly overlooking jetty twenty-four. It was a not unpleasant office but the ADDPC hated it. To him it felt like a slap in the face every day. Only a few years from retirement and the best they thought of him was a fourth-floor broom cupboard. The insult ached like a bad tooth. He was halfway through his third cup of morning coffee when he was interrupted with a quiet knocking at the door.

"Come!"

The door opened and a female customs officer entered. Fresh out of training school in Kwai Tsing, she was young and pretty in her new uniform. The ADDPC had had his eye on the girl since her transfer. It was a little early in the game for his usual approach. She needed time to understand the status quo. The type of ship the ADDPC ran; the 'personal' services he expected in return for favours granted. But the time for that private little 'chat' wasn't far off.

The pretty uniform held a flimsy paper print-out.

"Sir a message from Tilbury Customs in London."

NINETEEN

The ADDPC looked up at the government issue clock on the wall and then at the watch on his wrist. He frowned.

"Strange? Are you sure? It's the early hours back in London."

The pretty uniform nodded.

"Maybe it was queued to be sent automatically. We can do that with our own systems here."

The ADDPC nodded. It seemed a reasonable explanation.

"So what does it say, this message?"

"They are alerting us to contraband currency from the United Kingdom transiting through our hub here. They seek our collaboration and assistance. They ask that we urgently identify any cargo transiting RTT addressed to a company in Guangzhou, especially any cargo with milk powder on the manifest. They ask us to hold it pending a joint investigation"

The ADDPC put down his cup.

"That's a lot of seeking and asking. What is the value of this currency they have intercepted?"

The pretty uniform glanced at the paper.

"About a million Hong Kong dollars sir. One hundred-thousand British pounds."

"One hundred-thousand pounds!"

The ADDPC was indignant.

"They do know this is *Hong Kong*. My teams handle over a million containers a year with a throughput of six-billion dollars and they want us to redeploy our limited resources based on one hundred-thousand British pounds!"

He moved to the window. The sun off the distant waters narrowed his eyes. Somewhere out there in the morning glare was Lantau Island.

"No. I'm afraid it would be irresponsible of me to waste the RTT Custom's resources looking for not much more than petty change."

The ADDPC turned back from the window.

"Of course we cannot say this to London. It would not be seemly. There is such a thing as professional courtesy. But as it is my decision it is also my responsibility, please do not worry. Kindly leave this information with me and I will respond to London myself."

"Yes sir. Thank you."

Relieved the pretty uniform handed the printout to the ADDPC and left smiling shyly.

The ADDPC scanned the details on the printout, swallowed the last of his coffee, gathered up his cap and sunglasses and left the office. Down in the lift, exiting the sugar cube, he walked up the quay to jetty eighteen's large hangar/ warehouse. He ducked inside. The interior was cool and dim. He could see the profiles of stacked cargo all around but no people. He moved between the stacks pulling out a phone.

'Idiot!' He returned the phone to a trouser pocket and pulled another from inside his jacket. This was the one. It was bulkier than the first. He jabbed a speed dial button and waited. Moments later Huang Fu answered. There was no ceremony.

"Yes?"

NINETEEN

"They've discovered one of the milk powder shipments in London. You know the consignee. The British are asking us to search for further consignments involving milk powder. I thought it important you be informed."

"Indeed. You know what to do?"

"Of course. The usual response will be sent shortly."

"Good."

There was a click and the phone went dead. Conversation terminated. The phone was encrypted and had been supplied by Huang Fu especially for this type of conversation. The ADDPC returned it to his inside pocket and sidled back out on to the bright quayside. He was feeling good. Another easy tick in the box with Huang. Another pay day. He put on his sunglasses, adjusted the peak of his cap and looked around the bustling quay side. Everything was normal; if frenetic noise and chaos could be called normal. He glanced at his watch. First, he deserved another coffee then he would send London the 'usual' reply. Then maybe the time had come to ask the pretty uniform in for that 'chat'. With a spring in his step he set off back towards the sugar cube, square, white and gleaming in the morning sunshine.

Huang put down the phone and rubbed his chin reflexively. There would be no investigations in Hong Kong. The money he paid would ensure that. He wasn't worried about the consignee in Guangzhou. It was a shell company that would not lead back to him. But whoever had sent the money would be coming now and soon. The money supply wouldn't continue under the British customs investigation. The authorities had been alerted. It would be too dangerous. So the flow of money would stop, and they would be coming; expecting to get back the money they had left in his care. Huang allowed himself a small smile. He was unworried. This was his town. Let them come.

Working through the night Carter had drilled down through Tilbury's data banks and located the image files well before the sun broke the east London skyline. The key had been the milk powder. It was like a waving flag. There had been seven separate deliveries of the stuff into Tilbury during the time window. Six were described as palletised polythene sacks; one as a palletised tri-wall carton. The sacks were of no consequence. However the tri-wall details matched the seizure report so closely it could have been cut and pasted. In fact it probably had been. The booking in sheet had two pieces of data missing from the seizure report; a specific delivered in time on April the twenty-eighth and a specified delivery gate in the terminal. The missing information Carter needed to interrogate Tilbury's digital imaging database. Within minutes he had located the digital files. They were good. He downloaded copies and logged out leaving Tilbury none the wiser. Carter locked the door marked 'Room 13' and took the lift down to the vending machine in the empty reception for a long cardboard coffee. Nearly an hour of overtime later it was time. He couldn't delay any longer. As FIBER's resident IT genius he had a reputation to protect. Back behind his computer he checked the number on Genghis' card. The print was small. He had to hold it up to the desk lamp. He pushed the buttons slowly in sequence. The boss answered within two rings sounding fresh and determined. He gave the message. Then he phoned Bishop. This was easier. The number was on FIBER's database requiring just one click of the mouse. The man was half asleep, confused and groggy. He took several minutes just to understand an Uber was coming for him. Then with calls made and the data prepared Carter put the computer to sleep, locked the door and went out for a walk.

Forty minutes later with the sun still to break over Hackney Marshes everyone had arrived. Carter unlocked the door. He followed D'eath and Bishop inside. There would have been more space if the meeting had been convened in a phone box. He edged between the two men and pushed a button. The computer screen lit up. He typed a quick password. D'eath and Bishop crowded around peering over his shoulder. A bunch of icons appeared. Different shapes, different colours. One was a mpeg video file. Carter clicked on it. The screen filled with movement. There wasn't any sound but there was colour and an old white van delivering a very expensive carton of milk powder.

TWENTY

The three men crowded around the screen. D'eath spoke first.

"Okay so what can you tell me?"

Bishop exhaled, still bent over the screen. He was befuddled and well out of his comfort zone. He was still half-asleep.

"Well it's a long wheelbase, so slightly out of the ordinary. No markings. Definitely not new but don't ask me a year with all that crap over the plates."

"But isn't that unusual?" D'eath pressed. "The mud? It doesn't look that kind of day on the images."

"I can check." Carter pushed between the two bigger men and tapped the keyboard. The rear three-quarter view of the long white van; blue palisade gates, a skyline of cranes, container tops and shed roofs, all shrank into a small window on the computer's desktop. He tapped a flurry of other keys and a series of solid yellow circles appeared.

"Bright dry and sunny all day on the twenty eighth and the three days before," Carter announced.

"So, either they're lazy bastards who don't give a shit about keeping their delivery vehicle clean or the mud is there deliberately."

D'eath looked at Bishop.

"So which is it?"

Bishop cleared his throat.

"If pushed I would have to say the spray pattern tends towards the unnatural."

"Meaning?"

"Meaning it probably *is* man-made."

"Why the hell didn't you say that in the first place?" D'eath's eyes rolled. "Okay. Can we get a front-on view?"

Carter tapped a key closing the video file. The screen reverted to the desktop. It was difficult operating between Bishop and D'eath at arm's length. He moved the mouse over another mpeg icon and clicked. The new image file opened. The van appeared again. This time it faced the camera with a view behind of roadway, bridges and waiting trucks. "Oops!" exclaimed Bishop. "Not such a good job with the front plate. They must have driven through a puddle or something. We have the first letter and most of the parts of the last two. R, U and I think an . . . S."

"That's enough." Carter interjected quickly. "I've got an algorithm that can run the plate. All I need is to access the DVLA database."

D'eath's pulse quickened. "Can you do it?"

"Is a duck's arse watertight? I reckon twenty minutes tops, but I'll need the room."

D'eath nodded. He motioned to Bishop who had his nose virtually up against the screen staring at the van's front plate.

TWENTY

"We'll go get a coffee. Back in fifteen."

The door marked 'Room 13' closed behind them and Carter, relieved to be back in his seat, got to work.

D'eath stood by the vending machine with a cardboard coffee in his hand. Bishop, deep in thought, wasn't interested in coffee. Apart from two uniformed security commissionaires behind a counter by the door, the reception area was empty. Outside it may have been spring, but it still looked cold and dark. There was no sign yet of the dawn, but it wouldn't be long in coming. D'eath looked at his watch.

"That's time enough. Come on."

He threw the cardboard cup with what was left of the coffee into a bin by the vending machine and walked back towards the lift. Bishop, his mind elsewhere, followed along behind.

Carter stood as the two men re-entered the cubicle.

"Got it! The number's registered to a white Iveco Daily 35s XLWB, whatever the hell that is."

"I'm guessing it's an extra-long wheelbase white van," said D'eath dourly.

"Who would've thought it?" Carter gave a cheesy grin. "Anyway the registered owners are, and get this, a private school in Buckinghamshire."

D'eath frowned. "Are you sure?"

"Absolutely!"

"That can't be right."

"It isn't," said Bishop.

Both D'eath and Carter looked at the dishevelled CCTV expert in surprise.

"Blow up the number plate on the screen and I'll show you."

Carter's finger jabbed at a single key several times. Each time the front of the van expanded until just the mud splattered registration plate with its R, U and S filled the screen. The picture was grainy, but the definition hadn't suffered.

"Bloody good cameras on the docks these days," muttered Carter as he dragged the plate centre screen.

Bishop put the forefinger of his right hand lightly on the screen. He traced each of the discernible letters in turn.

"We're lucky with the letters. Look at the 'R'. See the stem and the tail, the two straight lines? No problem there. But look at the bowl, the enclosed curved line joining them. Can you see? It's not right. The same goes for the arching shoulder of the 'U' and the spine of the 'S'. These letters are handmade, probably painted or taped."

D'eath looked at Carter and raised his eyebrows. At magnified resolution they could see it. Bishop, the scruffy old buffoon, was right.

"Clever," said Carter, impressed.

"A double bluff," acknowledged D'eath. "Conceal false plates and we reasonably assume they're legit if we uncover them. A team of armed officers storming a school would be something of an embarrassment. Zoom in on the cab. I want to see what these clever bastards look like."

TWENTY

Carter jabbed at the keys again. The number plate shrank revealing the front of the van. He moved the mouse over the windscreen.

"Just one guy. The driver. What do you think?"

D'eath and Carter both looked at Bishop. He had suddenly acquired an air of importance in the small room.

"Definitely not one of the perps from the ATM digital. This guy's bigger and from what I can see of the facial structure, a lot older."

"And he's a ginger," added Carter.

"No he's not," responded Bishop wearily.

"It's clearly a wig. You can't see the hairline because of the hat but look at the neck. See how the hair curls up of the nape in a little curlicue. Sure sign of a wig, a cheap one at that."

"So if we can't ID the driver and the van's a red herring then we've got nothing. We're back to square one," said D'eath.

"We've got back the hundred-thousand found by customs," offered Carter.

D'eath glowered.

"I doubt the perps will miss it. They stole nearly two million."

He slumped back against the map of the night sky. *God he was tired.* He motioned at the computer.

"Close it down. I need to think."

Carter clicked and the windscreen with Ginger at the wheel turned into a desktop of icons again. D'eath closed his eyes, forehead furrowed. Bishop looked at Carter who just looked back and shrugged. Then D'eath's eyes snapped open and he came back off the wall.

"I knew it! It was there in the customs report all the time. I just couldn't put my finger on it. The clever bastards! They've been . . . "

The door marked 'Room 13' opened abruptly. Carter hadn't thought to lock it. Why would he? Bright artificial light spilled in from the corridor. The five-foot ten-inch silhouette of Frobisher filled the doorway, behind her were the head of FIBER's security and the two uniformed commissionaires from reception. For a moment there was absolute silence. It didn't last long.

Frobisher's voice was sharp and hard.

"Good evening gentlemen, or is it good morning? I didn't know a meeting had been scheduled. I trust I'm not late."

D'eath momentarily closed his eyes. He pictured it; the phone call in the middle of the night, water over the face, clothes hurriedly thrown on, the urgent call to security from the car; driving in fast and direct through empty streets. The commissionaires must have made the call. They would have been briefed. Another thing he hadn't seen coming. He had to admit Frobisher did look good. There must be a skill to throwing on clothes; tight jeans, zipped ankle boots, dark turtleneck and supple black leathered biker jacket. It was open, a gleam of a silver oval at the waist. He had only ever seen Frobisher with her hair up and officed. This morning there'd been no time and it was loose about her shoulders, dark and soft; the opposite to her eyes.

Assessing the situation Frobisher turned back into the corridor.

"Thanks Daniel, Stan, George. Your support as always has been magnificent, but I can take it from here. Thank you so much."

The corridor emptied behind her. It would be all over the building by breakfast. A drama exaggerated to titillating proportions. Secret meetings in the middle of the night; Genghis caught with his trousers down, security in attendance. There would be whispers and conspiratorial smiles, maybe even an office sweep on how long he'd last. But for now it was just the three of them in a cubicle the size of news kiosk with Frobisher in the doorway.

Frobisher turned back from the corridor and looked around the small room. It didn't take long. Then she looked at Carter and Bishop. That took longer. Then finally she looked at D'eath. That took longest of all. The looks were all ugly.

"The last time I checked, secret midnight trysts weren't a part of FIBER's mission statement so there had better be one hell of a good reason for this one."

Silence filled the small space. Then D'eath, standing nonchalantly with his hands in his jacket pockets spoke.

"A hundred-thousand reasons actually."

"What!"

"Customs unknowingly uncovered a cache of money from the ATM thefts. It was on its way to Hong Kong. One-hundred-thousand pounds. Carter picked up on it. He called up but you were busy. I came down to check the details. We've had a lot of dead ends in this case. I needed to be sure this wasn't another."

"In the middle of the night!"

At five-ten, Frobisher's eyes were only level with D'eath's chin. He looked down into her face.

"This all happened before close of play yesterday. We needed more details. I authorised Carter to work through the night. We all know how important this is. I told him to call me as soon as he could verify the information. He did and that's why I'm here. I would have informed you first thing of course. But I needed to see the details for myself."

"You would have informed me?"

Frobisher sneered.

"Of course, as I said, first thing in the morning."

"Pull the other one, D'eath. And if Carter is doing the work why the hell is Bishop here?"

D'eath was practiced. No need to lie when the truth would do.

"I asked Carter to call him in. That's right isn't it, Bishop?"

Bishop nodded mutely, not knowing what the hell was going on.

"Carter told me he might be able to get some CCTV footage of the cash being delivered. I wanted Bishop on hand to analyse it just in case."

"Just in case?"

"Yes. Just in case."

Frobisher pursed her lips. "So did you get any footage?"

D'eath looked hard at Carter and then Bishop. He took the chance. "Regrettably no. Carter did his best, but the dock databases were locked down tight."

D'eath's delivery was smooth, confident. He looked knowingly at Carter. Inside Carter was squirming but he said nothing. Bishop, not knowing what the hell was going on, kept quiet too. He had enough trouble of his own to start stirring up more.

"So what *do* you have Carter?"

Frobisher looked at him directly.

"The in-house customs report. They don't know I've got it and as I said to the boss, they don't know the significance of what they've found yet."

"Show me."

Carter turned, reaching over to the iMac he moved the mouse and clicked. A document file opened. He did a control P on the keyboard. It took just seconds. Whisper quiet, pages started pushing out from a laser printer. He handed the loose A4 pages to Frobisher. She scanned quickly, moving pages from her right hand to her left.

"And customs don't know we have this?"

Carter nodded.

"And this report is all we have. Nothing else?"

This time D'eath nodded, glancing quickly at the two men.

Frobisher pulled an iPhone from inside the biker jacket. It had a matte gold protective cover. She looked at her watch. It was white, ceramic, strangely at odds with her dark attire. Reaching a decision she pushed a button on the phone and held it up to her ear. It rang for long seconds then picked up.

"Good morning, sir. Yes, I'm sorry. I know it's early, but I wanted you to know immediately."

She paused, listening.

"Yes sir. It is very important."

Frobisher looked hard at the three men in the cubicle.

"I've got my hands on a confidential report from UK Customs. Yesterday they seized a hundred-thousand pounds in London docks, Tilbury en route to Hong Kong. I've checked sir and it's definitely cash from the ATM thefts."

Frobisher paused again.

"Thank you, sir, that's very kind of you to say."

She hesitated again; the phone pressed to the side of her head.

"I know sir. I totally agree. I have him here with me now. Sorry sir? What now? Yes of course. Just hold please."

Frobisher held her phone out, screen side up.

"The Governor wants it on loudspeaker."

D'eath saw the Governor's name on the screen above a green circle. Frobisher raised her voice.

"Okay sir, please go ahead. I have D'eath and two of his team with me."

The Governor's voice sounded flat and tinny.

TWENTY

"Good morning gentlemen. So it looks like change could finally be bearing fruit?"

"Good morning sir," chorused Carter and Bishop.

D'eath kept quiet.

"Now you have me on the line what do you propose, Lucinda? I assume time is of the essence? "

"Thank you, sir, indeed it is. According to the report the cash was delivered to Tilbury docks just a few days ago, on the twenty-eighth. It was very-well concealed. It was only discovered by a freak accident. I'm guessing the perpetrators don't know their money has been found. If we move fast sir, I believe we can apprehend them."

Frobisher sounded assertive, confident.

"You have a location?"

"We do sir. Ipswich. It appears to be a freight forwarding company. Even if they aren't directly involved, they'll have records we'll be able to follow to source. I need your authority to act, sir. If we don't, customs will. Can I have your permission to proceed?"

There followed a pause. Clearly the Governor was thinking.

"What does Mr D'eath have to say about this?"

Frobisher extended the phone a little farther towards D'eath.

"Er, hello sir. D'eath here. I appreciate what Ms Frobisher is saying but I really do have to advise utmost caution against rushing in. This is all very new, and we need much more information before launching any precipitous action."

Frobisher glared ferociously at D'eath.

"With respect, sir, this is exactly what I have come to expect from Mr D'eath over recent months. He has contributed nothing to the investigation. If anything he's become a hindrance and a liability. If we don't act now, today, customs will. We know how important this has become, sir. It's not just about the money anymore. You know this better than anyone. We have the chance to be the agency that ends this once and for all. Please sir, speed is of the essence. May I have your permission to proceed?"

Carter looked at Bishop and they glanced at D'eath. He turned away from Frobisher. She couldn't see his face. He winked at the two men. The Governor's tinny voice came again.

"You *are* sure of this, Lucinda?"

"Absolutely sir, I'm holding the customs report in my hand as I speak."

"Very well, you have my authority. Proceed as you think fit and the very best of luck. Heaven knows we all want an end to this matter."

D'eath's dramatic interjection would have made a soap star blush.

"Sir! A knee jerk reaction like this when we have limited information is risky in the extreme. I ask you please to reconsider. Ms Frobisher is inexperienced. This is reckless opportunism on her behalf, believe me."

There was a pause before the Governor's voice sounded again.

"That's just it, Mr D'eath. I don't believe you and I'm afraid that's your problem, not mine. Please go ahead, Lucinda."

"Thank you, sir, I will get things moving immediately and will keep you informed".

Before Frobisher could sever the connection D'eath timed a parting flourish.

"Sir, I require my objections to be put on the formal record with immediate effect."

Frobisher terminated the connection before the Governor could reply. She looked at D'eath with contempt.

"Months of failure and now I know why. You're a weak, insipid coward D'eath. Now keep out of my way until this is done. I'll deal with you then."

With that Frobisher turned about and marched off down the corridor to the lifts. As she walked away, the three men could hear her connecting a call to the security liaison officer at the Met.

D'eath waited. The lift doors closed behind her. She was gone. He pulled his own phone from his jacket pocket. The screen was blank except for four large digits in black counting up on a white background. He stopped the count at 03:38. He tapped the screen. The digits reverted to zero and then he tapped again.

Frobisher's voice sounded flat but unmistakeable through the small speakers:

We have the chance to be the agency that ends this once and for all. Please sir, speed is of the essence. May I have your permission to proceed?

D'eath swiped his finger across the screen and tapped again. This time he heard his own voice emanating from the phone:

Ms Frobisher is inexperienced. This is reckless opportunism on her behalf, believe me.

He swiped and tapped one more time and the Governor's unmistakeable voice echoed electronically in the small room:

That's just it, Mr D'eath. I don't believe you and I'm afraid that's your problem, not mine. Please go ahead, Lucinda.

D'eath tapped the screen a final time. The voice recording became a saved digital file in the phone's 64 gigabyte memory. He smiled.

"You recorded the conversation?" said Carter looking bewildered.

"When she was talking to her goons. The chance was there. I took it. I didn't know it would end up with a call to the Governor. That's blind stupid luck for you."

"But why?"

"I would have thought that was obvious."

"To you maybe."

D'eath sighed. Carter could be a dense lump when he wanted to be.

"Look, you heard her. Right about now she's authorising an armed police raid on some location in Ipswich. She hasn't a clue what she's getting into. She's out of control and she's taken the Governor along with her. She won't find any criminals and there will be no records to trace back. At best it's going to be one hell of an embarrassing cockup. At worst someone could get seriously hurt. The recording gives us protection. It sets the record straight about our position in all this mess. You heard me. I tried my best to warn them. But if they are both hell bent on holding hands all the way to the crapper and then around the 'U' bend what can anyone do?"

Carter looked uncertain.

"But you can't know for sure it's going to be a cockup. She could be on to something."

"Come on, Carter. You've seen the CCTV. You've read the report. The whole thing's a set up. If you can't see it, I'll show you but first you need to delete all traces of your computer work last night and this morning; the images, the hacks, footprints, everything."

"Why should I do that?"

"Big bonuses and untarnished reputations should be pretty convincing. If that doesn't work, try the avoidance of any aiding and abetting charges should that computer data ever see the light of day."

Carter looked at Bishop, whose mouth resembled an open flytrap.

"Okay. So I delete everything but how do you know it's still all going to go tits up?"

D'eath smiled.

"Interesting use of language given Ms Frobisher's central involvement but it's really very simple. Look, these guys are clever right? I mean smart like a fox clever. The mud, the fake plates, plates referring to the same type of van mark you, the driver in disguise. They are going to a helluva lot of effort to hide their tracks. Do you think these are the type of smarts that would put all that at risk by making a booking through a freight forwarder? No way. This freight forwarder, assuming such a company even exists, has never touched this money. They know nothing about it. Never did. Never will. Whoever booked that ATM money into the docks just used a name and address as a convenient smokescreen."

Carter was unconvinced.

"You're guessing. You can't know that for sure."

D'eath smiled. He seemed to be smiling an awful lot all of a sudden. "Normally you'd be right, Carter. The mud, the plates, the disguise, all just circumstantial but then there was the final giveaway. It tied everything together. I couldn't grasp it at first, but it was in the customs report all along. It came to me just before her ladyship bust in."

Carter was intrigued.

"What final giveaway?"

"An Ipswich freight company booking cargo through Tilbury, sixty-five miles south, when Felixstowe, the UK's biggest container port with hundreds of voyages direct to Hong Kong, is only twenty minutes up the road. I don't think so."

Carter stopped, he thought for a moment.

"Shit!"

"Exactly! We've all been played big time. Something Lucinda Frobisher and the Governor are about to find out. But it's not our ball game to worry about anymore, at least for now."

"How do you mean, sir?" It was the first time Bishop had spoken since Frobisher's entrance.

"Well when the shit hits the fan this little beauty," D'eath patted his phone, "will make sure we three are well in the clear. I don't plan on hanging around for too long afterwards, just long enough to get reinstated and authorise hefty bonuses for the two of you. I happen to think you both deserve it, even you Bishop."

D'eath looked around. He needed to get out of this small stuffy room. Outside would be a beautiful day whatever the weather and he needed to be in it. His tiredness had suddenly evaporated. He felt edgy, good and . . . ravenous.

"So, thank you Mr Carter, Mr Bishop. I appreciate everything you have done over the past few hours more than you know. I assure you it will not be forgotten. Take Ubers home on the company, both of you. You've more than earned it."

D'eath walked into the corridor.

"But what about you, boss?" Carter called after him.

"Me? Don't worry about me, Carter. I'm off to find the one thing you Brits do better than anyone else in the world."

"Sir?"

D'eath had to raise his voice for it to carry back down the corridor.

"A full English Mr Carter, maybe even two."

He arrived at the lifts. He reached out with a smile and pressed the button marked down.

TWENTY-ONE

The freight forwarding company was not the modern shipping and logistics operation its advertising suggested. There was no warehouse; no transport fleet, no smart brick and glass offices, no expansive loading yards and virtually no staff. It did, though, have a sign. A four-foot square of thin painted metal. Faded letters, green on a once white background. The sign was nailed to the centre of a five-bar timbered gate. Both had been there a long time. The wood weathered and grey, the sign bleeding rust from iron nails. The gate stood across a narrow lane, a single vehicle track between tall hedges running back straight as a die through a quarter-mile of winter barley. The track ended in the bricked yard of what had once been a working farm. It wasn't working anymore. On three sides of the yard were the buildings; the farmhouse itself, one black corrugated iron barn, the remains of a long, low milking shed and a few decrepit outbuildings. But there was some continuity. The sign on the five-bar gate had a twin. Equally faded, equally weathered. The sign writer had given a discount for two. It was fixed to the side of the barn. *'Pan Freight Services'*. It too looked like it was bleeding.

The signs; the gate, the rutted lane, the yard and the surrounding buildings were owned by Ridley Brown. Apart from the clothes on his back they were the only things he still owned. Everything else had gone. If Suffolk farming had been in his father's blood it had been leached out of Ridley's. He had tried. He had toiled with the best of them. But it hadn't happened. Harvests had failed; debts had mounted, loans had been called in. Three generations of his family had lived off the land. It was his fate to be the last. He thanked God his father hadn't been alive to see it. The land and livestock had gone to meet the debts and he had started the freight company with the little savings he had left. With Felixstowe port expanding and the barn and outbuildings providing storage it had seemed like a good idea. It wasn't. He hadn't reckoned with competition and the farm's remoteness. And this time there had been no land or livestock to sell. The failure of the farm had been difficult to swallow, the failure of the freight company, impossible. Reduced to a world of benefit hand-outs in an isolation of hard winters and guilt, it hadn't taken long. The bottle had been dangled and like a goat at the tit Ridley had grabbed and not let go. To make matters worse he was a nasty drunk; abusive and belligerent. Life had kicked him in the head so many times he didn't care anymore. Twice his wife had tried to leave with Reg. On the second attempt a brain haemorrhage had intervened before she could even pack her bags. Now it was just him and Reg at the end of the quarter-mile track.

TWENTY-ONE

Reg was twenty-four and a child. Acute learning disabilities the doctors had said. It didn't matter now but back then it had shattered his world. Ridley loved his only child, but the boy was next to useless; just another failure in a litany of failures. Wife, money, self-respect, even hope, all were long gone. What were left were the burdens of guilt and failure and no one would be taking those off him.

High above the moss-stained roof slates the DJI Phantom 4 was oblivious to Ridley's car crash of a life. It wasn't designed to see or record any of it. What it did see and was recording from three-hundred feet up was the decrepit square of farmyard buildings; the yard, the narrow track back through fields and in the distance the gate and a small portion of the minor B road running alongside it. The drone was a new idea. Twenty-first century policing the Chief Constable had called it. She had only signed off SUSA, the Small Unmanned Surveillance Aircraft unit, a few months earlier. Operated by two-man teams of pilot and camera operator an inaugural three drones had been acquired for shared use across Suffolk's emergency and rescue services. This morning, high above Ridley Brown's farmhouse, this one was under police control.

"Lima one, Lima one. Receiving Foxtrot. Over."

"Receiving Foxtrot. Go ahead. Over."

"Lima one. We are not receiving images. Over."

Superintendent Jack Farthing, head of Suffolk Constabulary's Specialist Operations Department couldn't see shit. The monitor blinked with a green LED, but the screen remained stubbornly dark.

He was Gold Commander. TFU team Amber were deployed past Somersham in the boondocks waiting for his call. But how the hell could he devise a plan if he couldn't see anything?

The shout from Division had come in early. It had Home Office authority all over it. The chief had called and he'd acted. There were four Tactical Firearms Unit teams in the Suffolk force. He had deployed team Amber.

Silver Commander on the ground was Tom Lewins, call sign Lima One, one of the most experienced Chief Inspectors in the TFU. Leading the assault force was Bronze Commander, Sergeant Andy Waterman, call sign Whisky One. The assault force itself was a stick of six AFOs and three SFOs all Kevlared up, primed, fully loaded and ready to go. Command and Control would be his out of Force HQ in Martlesham Heath. It was all standard operational procedure and they were all well practiced.

The mission brief was a simple one. Secure all personnel and facilities of an entity called Pan Freight Services. The address put it out somewhere in rural Suffolk, about seven miles northwest of Ipswich. The mission threat level had been marked high; a matter of National Security. The threat was not perceived as terror related but other than that no information had been forthcoming as to the 'why' or the 'what'. As Gold Commander he was in charge of the 'how'. But for that he needed information and for that he needed to see.

"Foxtrot, Foxtrot, this is Lima One. The glitch is our end. You will have images momentarily. Over."

A moment passed and the monitor flickered into life displaying a high definition bird's eye view of farmyard buildings and barley fields. The picture froze, stuttered back to life, dissolved into blocks of warped colour and then reappeared, shivering disjointedly up and down the screen.

"Lima One. Negative. I say again Negative. Imaging is bad. What the hell is going on? Over."

"I think I can answer that, sir."

Farthing turned away from the monitor and looked at his ICT Director. The man was in a suit. No uniform. No rank. The Information and Communication Technology Department had no need of either. Farthing turned back to the microphone.

"Lima One. Lima One. This is Foxtrot. Hold one. Over." He turned back to the suit.

"It's TETRA sir. It's old technology. It can't handle the amount of mobile data coming off the drone's HD video feed."

"Can you fix it?"

"Sorry sir. It can't be done."

"What!"

"It's old kit sir, running at seven kilobytes a second. The drone's video feed is a hundred Megs a second. It's just not possible."

Farthing scowled.

"Why the hell did we get the drones if they won't work with TETRA?"

The suit was unperturbed.

"They work perfectly well with direct video feed on the ground sir."

"You mean Silver can see everything and I can't?"

The suit nodded.

"So this," Farthing gestured dismissively at the monitor, "is all I'm going to get?"

"Afraid so sir."

Farthing swallowed an expletive and spoke into the microphone.

"Lima One. Lima One. Receiving Foxtrot. Over."

"Receiving Foxtrot. Go ahead. Over."

"Lima One. The image feed is bad. I say again, image feed is bad. Sorry Tom I'm going to need your eyes on this one. Over."

Static hissed through the Command Centre speakers. It dipped and Tom Lewins' voice sounded, small and far off.

"Received Foxtrot. Understood. Stand by four. Over."

Gentle static once again filled the room.

Nineteen miles to the west of the Martlesham Heath Command Centre Tom Lewins depressed the comms button and looked at his Bronze Commander. There wasn't a lot of room in the back of the converted LDV van. All he could see of Waterman were his eyes, clear, unblinking, through the letterbox of his balaclava hood.

"You heard all that?"

Andy Waterman nodded. Like the rest of the TFU team he was uniformed in black Nomex from head to boot top. His goggles were around his neck so as not to foul the small video cam fixed to the side of his MICH 2000 helmet. With his ballistic vest; headset, ear protectors and comms array he looked like something out of a science fiction movie; Darth Vader without the cloak. Who needed a light sabre when a Glock 17 was holstered on your hip; your webbing was festooned with stun and CS gas grenades and you were hefting an MP5SF Semi-Automatic 9mm carbine with thirty rounds in the mag.

"It was always going to come down to MK1 eyeball boss. Best I take three up the lane. The hawthorn will shield us until the edge of the yard. I suggest splitting the remainder; two squads of three, flanking left and right out through the barley."

Lewins frowned.

"Gold needs our data. We can't keep him dark on this."

Waterman tapped his helmet.

"Relay the feedback from the helmet cams boss and you do the talk over. Should be good enough?"

"It'll have to be. It's all we've got. Okay get set up to move on my mark. I'll brief Gold."

It had taken fifteen minutes. Gold had issued the 'good to go' and the teams were in position. Throughout Lewins had sat in the back of the LDV van. His cap off, his headset on. In front of him were two video monitors and a bank of comms equipment. It was a tight space with the drone's pilot and camera operator alongside him. Neither were small men. Monitor one displayed feed from the drone cam high overhead. On it he could see the police TFU vehicles; small toys on a miniature ribbon of road. One Volvo V70 Armed Response Vehicle blocked the road two-hundred metres east of the five-bar gate; another did the same job two-hundred metres west. In between, a hundred metres from the gate, he saw a third next to the mobile Command Centre van. The van he was in. The blocked road wouldn't be much of an inconvenience. Traffic was normally light and mainly agricultural. He hoped it would stay that way. Several minutes earlier the same monitor had shown the three TFU teams snaking out from behind the five-bar gate like the prongs of Neptune's trident. Bronze up the middle along the track, between the hedgerows; Alpha team looping waist high through barley to the left, Bravo to the right. Small figures. Black. Scuttling like insects. Immediately alongside the drone monitor another screen displayed bronze leader's helmet feed. The video picture rising, falling, jerky and erratic as the team moved quickly up the track.

Lewins thumbed the comms button.

"Foxtrot, Foxtrot. Receiving Lima One. Over."

"Receiving Lima One. Go ahead, Over."

TWENTY-ONE

Lewins peered at the pair of monitors in front of him.

"Teams in position. Whisky One at point. Alpha perimeter west. Bravo perimeter east. Patching in Whisky One's feed. Standby one."

He flicked a switch on the console and green LED blinked.

Nineteen miles to the east a similar LED flashed on a monitor in the Martlesham Heath Command Centre.

"Foxtrot. Foxtrot you should now be receiving live feed from Whisky One. Over."

"Affirmative Lima One. We confirm live feed. Advise sitrep Over."

Lewins was glued to the monitors. In the air the pilot had moved the Phantom 4 up higher over the farm buildings. On the ground Waterman's helmet cam scanned the bricked yard. Nothing moved anywhere.

"No movement on the ground, Foxtrot. No movement observed since TFU deployment Over."

There was a pause before Gold's voice sounded again.

"Lima One. We have two adult males registered at the property. Both IC1. A Ridley and Reginald Brown. Acknowledge. Over."

"Acknowledged Foxtrot. Waiting on your order. Over."

Lewins pushed a button on his headset activating the TFU only comms channel.

"Whisky One. Whisky One. Receiving Lima One. Over."

"Receiving Lima One. Go ahead. Over."

"Whisky One. Gold has your cam feed. Acknowledge. Over".

“Acknowledged Lima One. Awaiting instructions. Over.”

“Whisky One. Gold confirms two adult males IC1 registered at property. Have you any sign? Over.”

“Negative Lima One. No movement. Nothing observed. Over.”

“Acknowledged Whisky One. Hold positions and await further instruction. Over.”

Lewins, an experienced silver commander, knew too well his crucial link in the command chain. While strategy was laid down at HQ it was up to him on the ground to decide the tactics. Sometimes as the game unfolded the playbook had to be thrown away and you had to play what was in your face. As bronze leader Waterman would be waiting on that call.

A tap on his shoulder and Lewins turned. It was the drone pilot.

“Sorry sir,” the man pointed at his wrist, “we need to swap out the battery.”

Lewins nodded. The drone had done its job. They had the physical layout scoped, fields of approach, fences, walls, obstacles. The rest would be up to the TFU team on the ground. What was new?

Nineteen miles to the east in the command centre the constable moved to tap the super on the shoulder but thought better of it.

“Excuse me sir you’re wanted on the phone. They say it’s urgent.”

TWENTY-ONE

Jack Farthing kept his face to the monitor. His eyes on the screen. The feed from Whisky One's cam was not much better than the drone's. Every few seconds a broad black band descended the screen wiping the image away like a rubber squeegee; as the band dropped it pulled a fresh image down behind it.

"The call. Is it op related?"

"She says so sir."

She? Keeping his eyes on the monitor Farthing held out a hand. The constable filled it with a cordless phone.

"Superintendent Jack Farthing speaking."

"Good morning, Superintendent."

The voice was deep but feminine; the accent cut glass, the tone confident, assured.

"I am Lucinda Frobisher acting head of FIBER in the City of London. As Gold Commander Superintendent you should know you are prosecuting the Pan Freight operation on our behalf."

Farthing stiffened.

"Good morning, ma'am. I assume this call has been cleared with the Chief Constable?"

"Indeed it has, Superintendent."

"Ma'am we are in the middle of an operation. It is not appropriate…." Frobisher's voice hardened subtly.

"Superintendent let's agree not to waste each other's time. Kindly nominate an officer to provide me the ongoing situation report updates and I won't bother you further."

"Ma'am I'm afraid…."

"Perhaps I haven't made myself clear, Superintendent, this is not a request. I want the situation updates *now.* Check with your Chief Constable if you must but a word of warning, do it quickly."

Farthing mentally stepped back. This Frobisher woman had come through on a secured line. He didn't doubt what she was saying. It was time to tack. Maybe he could learn something to his advantage.

"FIBER? That's financial isn't it? City bank stuff?"

"You've been doing your reading, Superintendent."

"So how come you people can suddenly initiate police operations flagged at maximum threat level? Do you know what we are facing out there?"

"Friends in very high places, Superintendent, and no we don't. Now are you or are you not going to provide me with the updates?"

The impatience was clear in Frobisher's voice. The door to command and control opened and the Chief Constable entered. She looked inquisitively at Farthing.

"Is that the Frobisher woman?"

Farthing nodded.

"Give her what she wants, Jack."

"But Ma'am . . . "

"Jack!"

Farthing took his hand away from the phone's mouthpiece.

"Ms Frobisher?"

TWENTY-ONE

"I'm here, Superintendent."

Farthing swallowed his reluctance with a deep breath.

"Ma'am, the current sitrep is as follows; TFU team amber under command of Chief Inspector Tom Lewins are in position as of five minutes ago. We have not engaged. The site is quiet with no sign of target personnel. The site is registered to a Ridley Brown. We believe another adult, possibly a relative, resides on site also."

"Resides? What kind of site is this?"

Frobisher's voice sounded suddenly uncertain.

"It's a farm, or it was. It's remote, out in arable country, northwest of Ipswich."

"A farm?"

"Affirmative."

"Not a freight company?"

"There's a sign on the gate. 'Pan Freight Services'. But it's old. Our initial observations indicate there hasn't been any commercial activity on site for some time,"

"How much time?"

"Difficult to say but likely years rather than months."

This wasn't what Frobisher wanted to hear. Farthing could hear it in her voice. It made him feel a little better but with Waterman and his team still in the field on a mission flagged 'threat high', he wouldn't be smiling yet.

Frobisher wasn't done.

"Superintendent, it is imperative you secure the site intact and undamaged along with all personnel unharmed. Is that absolutely clear?"

Before Farthing could reply she continued. "Once cleared the site must be placed in lockdown. No one in, no one out and that includes SOCO. Any personnel found on site are to be secured and held separately. They must not be allowed to communicate between themselves or with anyone else in any way. Your chief has a number. Call it and I will arrange immediate secure onward transportation. Am I clear?"

"Yes Ms Frobisher. You are very clear."

"Good! I will be waiting for that call. Good luck, Superintendent."

The phone clicked off. Farthing pulled it away from the side of his head and lobbed it back to the constable who had remained standing nearby.

"Get rid of it. No more calls. I'm trying to run a bloody operation here." He turned back to the monitors just in time to see another broad black band make its way down the screen.

Andy Waterman was not impatient, but it wasn't like Silver to keep them waiting without some form of info update. The teams had been in position now for approaching ten minutes. There had been no movement in the farmhouse or in any of the other buildings around the yard. It was a bright late-spring morning in the countryside. Shades of burgeoning green everywhere. The ten nomexed TFU officers stood out like crows in a snowdrift. Big ones. Exposure was vulnerability. He wasn't happy. They needed to move.

TWENTY-ONE

Farthing ran a hand over his short, silvered hair.

"Lima One. Lima One. Receiving Foxtrot. Over."

"Receiving Foxtrot. Go ahead. Over."

"Lima One. Sitrep please. Over".

"As you were, Foxtrot. No change. Teams in position. All quiet. No subject movement. We are good to go. Over."

"Acknowledged Lima One. Rules of engagement apply. No lethal force to be used unless there is a clear and present threat to life. Objective is to secure subjects without harm. Over."

"Received and understood Foxtrot. Briefing Amber team on channel two now. Standing ready. Over."

Jack Farthing leant forward in his chair. The mission critical point had been reached. There was nothing more he could do from Martlesham HQ. On the monitor the black band appeared and disappeared.

"Lima One. Lima One. Receiving Foxtrot. Over."

"Receiving Foxtrot. Go ahead. Over."

"Lima One. Control is yours. Over".

"Acknowledged Foxtrot. Control is mine. Proceeding. Over."

Jack Farthing stood, looking around the darkened command room.

"Bring it home Tom," he whispered.

Inside the farmhouse Ridley Brown was through the first bottle of the morning. There was minimal effect. The shakes had stopped but the pain was still there. It was always there.

Sometimes viciously sharp, like a spike through the ribs, other times, if he had drunk enough, just a dull gut ache. He bellowed up the stairs. There was no response. Where the hell had the boy got to? He knew there were more bottles in the kitchen. At this rate he would have to go himself.

"Lima One. Lima One. Receiving Whiskey One. Over."

"Receiving Whiskey One. Over."

"Lima One. Sounds from the house. Shouting. A single male. Over."

"Understood Whisky One. Standby."

Ridley Brown lumbered to his feet, the old ladder-backed chair toppling over. He was a big man. Strong back in the day when hefting bales of winter feed miles out into the snows was just a daily chore. He shouted again; listened, nothing. Bloody kid! He meandered through the doorway along the dim flagged hallway and into a sunless filthy kitchen. Where were the bloody bottles? He started banging cupboard doors.

In the back of the van Tom Lewins felt it. The moment. It was down to him now. The door cracked open. The drone pilot gave him a thumbs up. Lewins nodded back and the pilot disappeared. It would take just a minute to get the Phantom 4 back above the mission area. It was a bonus. He would wait. One could never have enough information.

TWENTY-ONE

"Whiskey One. Alpha. Bravo. Receiving Lima One. Sequence Acknowledge. Over."

"Whiskey One. Receiving. Over"

"Alpha. Receiving. Over."

"Bravo. Receiving. Over."

Images appeared on the screen of the drone monitor. The Phantom 4 was back on station high above the farm buildings. Lewins looked at the screen. Except for the three groupings of small black insect figures nothing much had changed. At ground level on the helmet cam screen the farmyard remained deserted.

Okay. This was it. Lewins took a breath. It was time to conduct the orchestra. Pressing the boom mike closer to his mouth he spoke.

On the screen of the drone monitor the insects moved, quickly and efficiently. Three from the west; into and through the black barn, passing the 'Pan Freight Services' sign. Three from the east; into and through the dilapidated outbuildings and old milking shed. Radio speak was quick and brief now.

"Alpha clear."

"Bravo clear."

All that was left was the farmhouse. Inside there was at least one man. An angry man if the shouting was anything to go by.

The only team that had not moved was Waterman's. As Bronze commander he'd kept station in front of the farmhouse behind a low wall at the edge of the yard. He checked his team. Eyes hidden behind wide goggles; fingers on trigger guards, safeties off. One officer was armed like himself, the second with a Remington 870 twelve gauge, the third, McLellan, had drawn the short straw with the L104A1, its 37mm barrel looking like eighteen inches of sawn-off drainpipe. It was time.

Alpha, having cleared their outbuildings proceeded to the rear of the farmhouse. Bravo team, similarly, to the east where two large sash windows were let low down into the wall.

"Whisky One. Whisky One. Receiving Lima One. Over."

"Lima One. Receiving Over."

"All ready and in position. Over"

"Acknowledged Whisky One. EXECUTE! EXECUTE! Over.

Waterman looked at his team. He held four gloved fingers together across his forearm and then raised them to point to the front of the farmhouse. They would go in across the yard together. He held up a finger, then another, then a third. They moved as one on the third finger.

Lewins, back in the van, saw four black figures scuttle across the yard to press up against the front wall of the farmhouse, either side of its main door. Three walls of the farmhouse; the front, back and the east, now had black insect figures pressed up against them.

TWENTY-ONE

Waterman held up a clenched gloved fist. His team froze. Keeping his body concealed by brickwork he reached an arm out across the door to the handle. It was old and crusted with years of paint. He twisted slowly. It was open. No need to blow the slab off its hinges with the Remington. They were too close to the target for speech now. Waterman thumbed his radio switch twice. The twin squelches of static were answered by Alpha and Bravo. They were ready. Three seconds. Again Waterman held up a finger, then another, then a third. Again they moved as one. Waterman was point. He clattered the door back, charged into a small vestibule and burst through the interior door into the main living area. Behind, on his shoulder came the rest of his team, quickly fanning out, their weapons high in the shoulder, barrels panning the room. It was empty. Waterman could hear Alpha and Bravo entering. It sounded like a herd of cattle. Waterman motioned and his team followed him out into a gloomy hallway. It was stone flagged and smelt of something unpleasant. Alpha and Bravo appeared into the hall from different doors. They were back on the radio now.

"Alpha. CLEAR."

"Bravo. CLEAR"

"Whisky One. CLEAR."

There were only two ways left to go. At the end of the hallway was another door. Likely the kitchen. To the side were the stairs. One short flight to a quarter landing then another flight at right angles up into the house somewhere. Waterman gestured. Alpha and Bravo took the stairs. With his three men he reached the end of the hall and burst through the last door. He'd been right it was the kitchen. It was empty.

Tom Lewins watched the action unfold on his screen in the van. The helmet cam was jerky and juddering, but the focus was clear and the definition sharp. The voices, even through the balaclavas, were unmistakable. So far so good.

Farther east Jack Farthing was having difficulty. The operation had started with him not being able to see shit and it looked like ending that way. The helmet cam feed was difficult to see. The speed of movement was bleeding, smearing the video picture while the black bar marched ever downwards over the screen. He knew better than to cross comms with Lewins now. All of Silver Commander's focus would be on the unfolding operation.

"Alpha. Receiving Whiskey One. One subject. Male C1 in custody. No other subjects found. All upper rooms cleared. Over."

"Whiskey One acknowledged. Over.

Waterman winced. At least the teams he had sent to the top of the house had lucked out. They had the shouter.

He turned back towards the hall, dropping radio protocol in the adrenalin after rush.

"Good job lads. Copy book. Make sure we leave nothing behind. Debrief in fifteen."

TWENTY-ONE

Behind him a concealed larder door smashed back against the wall and sixteen stones of Ridley Brown came rushing out of cold darkness screaming obscenities. He swung a large arm towards the back of Waterman's head. At the end of the arm was a hand the size of a dinner plate. In it was something hard, reflective; something with four inches of narrow tube protruding. It was McLellan who reacted. Grabbing Waterman's chest webbing with his left he yanked the man hard towards him away from the charging Ridley. With his right hand he pulled up on the L104A1 from where it dangled down his thigh, barrel to the floor. No way would he make it to the shoulder. It would have to be a hip shot. Training kicked in. Centre mass. But the barrel was coming up too slowly. Like pulling through treacle; his gloved finger on the trigger. Ridley, screaming, Waterman, turning, half crouched.

In the confines of the mobile command van Lewins saw what those caught up in the kitchen maelstrom couldn't. Waterman turning; the assailant berserk with rage; McLellan's barrel; like a short length of drainpipe, swinging up. He shouted hard, almost a shriek, his voice reverberating inside the steel box. *"Don't shoot!"*

If Lewins and the Amber team had been using walkie-talkies the command would have been received instantly. But they were using TETRA, an old system long overdue for replacement. Terrestrial Trunked Radio, halfway between a walkie-talkie and a mobile telephone.

When Lewins shouted, an app fired up making an IP connection and then the communication started. It wasn't instant. There was a micro delay. The experts called it latency. In the fraction of a second it took for the app to fire and connect *'Don't'* didn't make it into the message.

The drainpipe was horizontal now and still moving up. Centre mass. Like an old movie gunfighter McLellan thumbed the hammer back; the breech of the weapon against his right hip, the spindly pole stock protruding away behind him. Centre mass. He pulled the trigger.

TWENTY-TWO

The call over the burner was clipped, urgent, Davey Boy's voice terse. "No questions. Get to the bat cave for six."

The call had come to Jason. He'd alerted Chris. And they'd got their skates on. They had arrived at 5:45. A coffee each and now it was just a waiting game.

"Whatdya think Jace? It's gotta be bad news?"

"No shit Sherlock."

Jason was as nervous as Chris. In the back of the Uber their conversation had been stilted, frustrating. But on the walk in they'd had free reign. Ships sinking; containers washed overboard, warehouse fires, crooked Chinese, Davey Boy found out, a list as big as their imaginations. Jason swallowed a mouthful of coffee. It was as bitter as hell. He looked again at his Rolex. It seemed he'd been doing nothing else since Davey Boy's call.

"Well it's almost six, mate. Not long now."

Minutes later the small wicket door in the large expanse of entrance shuttering opened and Davey Boy stepped through. As usual he looked like he'd just come from a meeting with his bank manager; dark suit, navy shirt, patterned silk tie, all under a mid-length tailored shower proof. He appeared calm, business-like.

"Thanks for being prompt, lads. Appreciate it. Get me one of those will you, Chrissy?" He pointed at the coffee mugs. While Chris did the business Davey Boy took off the coat and looked around. Now that the last of the money had been shipped, the bat cave looked empty; tired, surplus to requirements. The boys had swept the mess of dried milk powder back into the corners where it mingled with the previously swept sawdust. The piles looked greyish, mottled, dirty; the air tasting gritty with invisible particles. Chris handed him a mug of hot black.

"Well it's happened, lads. It was always a possibility. They've intercepted at least one of the last shipments."

Jason and Chris looked at each other.

"The important thing is we planned for it. It can't be tracked back. I need you to understand that, okay?" The boys nodded.

"So what happened Davey?" asked Jason.

"We were called in to an emergency briefing this morning."

Davey Boy took a gulp of coffee.

"It seems customs discovered the Tilbury box by accident a couple days ago. Somehow the financial authorities got wind of it. They've always been the ones pushing hardest. They tracked the shipping documents back and ordered a raid. Local plod was given the job and by all accounts they really ballsed it up. It's all over the news. Some poor bugger was batoned almost to death on a farm in the middle of nowhere. They thought he had a gun. It turned out to be a bottle of cheap scotch. Another guy, his son they think, was thrown into solitary. They say he's got the mental age of a young kid. Of course nothing was found. Customs are pissed their operation was hijacked; there are half a dozen agencies all screaming blue murder. Plod is blaming the finance guys. The finance guys blaming plod. The papers are having a field day; police brutality, child cruelty, abuse of human rights. You name it. It's a bloody mess."

He paused, taking another deep swig. For once Chrissy had done a half decent job.

"Batoned? Shit Davey. What did the poor bastard do to deserve that?"

Jason felt unavoidable guilt. Admittedly, it wasn't their fault, not directly at least. They couldn't have known the consequences of pin-pricking an address out of a commercial shipping directory.

"Well they weren't gathered round beating the poor sod with clubs if that's what you mean. He was hit once in the chest with an AEP. He's lucky to be alive. It was virtually point-blank range."

"An AEP?"

"Attenuating Energy Projectile, Chrissy. A baton round. You'll probably know it better as a rubber bullet."

"But he should be okay? He should make it?"

"We can hope, Jason, but there's no guarantee. Chest trauma. Point blank. It's not pretty."

Jason nodded. There wasn't much else he could do.

"But at least it's made the decision for us," said Davey Boy. "It's time to put a shift on out to Hong Kong. I'll phone in a sicky tomorrow. With luck I'll be back by the weekend, job done. In the meantime you lads batten down the hatches and lay low."

"What about the other three consignments?" said Chris.

Jason looked up into the roof space. Some poor bloke fighting for life in a hospital somewhere and all Chrissy could ask about was the money.

"I won't know that 'till I get to Hong Kong. I'm not about to raise any flags by asking around. We keep fingers crossed and hope for the best. We'll know soon enough."

Six o'clock seemed to be the pick of the day for meetings. Once again D'eath found himself within the panelled splendour of the Bank of England. This time there was no nervous apprehension; no sense of being in a vacuum, of being powerless, in fact the opposite. The game was on and he was savouring every minute of it. The Governor, stony faced, implacable, sat behind his desk. For most of the day he'd been through the Whitehall ministerial mill and it showed.

"I assume you know why you're here D'eath? Because of you a lot of very important people have been put through a very difficult day." D'eath, feigned animated exasperation.

"A difficult day! It was an absolute disaster. I've never seen such blinding incompetence. Heads will roll for this one and deservedly so."

The Governor's eyes widened. The fool was making this easy.

"Indeed Mr D'eath. Roll they certainly will with yours first amongst them."

"What!"

"Of course! What did you expect? As head of FIBER, as the head of the organisation that primed the Home Office and instructed the police in this sorry affair, I think we can safely say that not only is your head firmly on the block but it's probably half way into the basket"

"But what about Frobisher?"

"What about her?" The Governor's face was expressionless.

"You appointed her over me. She was running FIBER with your authority. The raid was her decision with your support. This shit storm is down to both of you, not me."

"I have no idea what you're talking about D'eath." The Governor's face remained expressionless.

"Then why don't we ask Frobisher."

"Impossible I'm afraid. She's no longer with the bank. She left to travel the world. Something about finding herself, I think. It looks like she'll be gone indefinitely."

"But the three of us talked on the phone just two days ago; you, me and Frobisher. She pressed you to authorise police interdiction. I counselled against it. You backed her against my protests. I told you she was leading FIBER into harm's way. You ignored me."

The Governor smiled, chuckling.

"Come now, Mr D'eath. Please. I know you must be desperate but let's try and keep to a modicum of truth."

D'eath grew a smile of his own.

"That's what I thought you'd say you snivelling little toad." The Governor started. His smile vanished. The light in his eyes changed. "So I recorded the conversation. Here is a copy for you to play back at your leisure. It may serve to remind you what a modicum of truth actually is."

D'eath took a small flash drive from his pocket and threw it nonchalantly on the Governor's broad desktop. It hit the wood with a plasticky click and lay there like a small pebble.

"Oh! And don't worry, Governor. That's just one of many copies. That's the wonder of digital."

The Governor's face was turning hue. He still hadn't spoken.

"I hope the recording matches what you told the minister. It wouldn't be clever for the Governor of the Bank of England to be caught lying. Apart from anything else just think what the wife would say?"

D'eath stopped speaking. The room was totally silent. Across the desk the Governor sat motionless. Behind his pink well-scrubbed facade cogs turned; a complex game of mental chess playing out. It didn't matter. Every move had the same outcome – checkmate. The Governor came to the same conclusion. It had taken him less than fifteen seconds.

"So what are you proposing, Mr D'eath?"

"Not much really."

D'eath reached inside his jacket. He retrieved a small square of yellow paper. He put it on the desk. He made a show of unfolding it; one way, two ways, three ways. After each operation he painstakingly ironed out the creases with the ball of a thumb. Finally he had a single page of lined lawyer's foolscap unfolded on the desk facing him. The Governor could see seven lines of upside down writing on it. Scrawled with a fountain pen each line started with a bulbous bullet point of ink.

"As you can see, I made a bit of a list."

D'eath studied the paper as if refreshing his memory. It was all an act. He knew his demands off pat.

"Now that Frobisher is off, so conveniently inspecting her naval on the other side of the planet, I think it's time for some changes, don't you? Now, let's see, oh yes, number one. You will reinstate me as head of FIBER with immediate effect. I expect full attendant privileges and pension rights, of course. Number two. I require full autonomy to pursue this case without let or hindrance, especially from the likes of you or anyone else within the bank. Number three. I will not be writing any damned reports for you or anyone else. Number four. I will require double the current operational budget."

"Double! That's a significant sum of money Mr D'eath."

"I have some significant disbursements to make."

"But it may be difficult to sway..."

"You are the *Bank of England*. Sort it!"

D'eath was in no mood and the Governor knew it. He nodded.

"Anything else?"

"Yes. Number five. I find my own people from now on. No more appointees brought in over my head. Number six. I am neither a traitor nor a spy and will not be treated like one. Disappear that Official Secrets document. It was never signed. And I am not under threat of incarceration. Are we clear!"

The Governor nodded.

"That's only six. There are seven bullet points on your paper."

"Oh yes." D'eath smiled. "I only intend to stay around this festering tip long enough to close this case. Put it down to professional integrity if you like; something your sort wouldn't know if it bit you in the arse. Then I'll go. At which point you will provide me with your finest, most glowing, reference. For those who don't know the truth the Bank of England still stands for something out there."

D'eath stopped talking. He neatly re-folded the paper and put it in his pocket. He sat back in his chair and looked around. He had to admire the man opposite him. He had staged his little show for reaction; he wanted the Governor crawling up the walls, pleading, pulling hair, gnashing teeth but it wasn't going to happen. Throughout the charade the man hadn't moved or shown a flicker of emotion.

The Governor broke the silence.

"Assuming I accept your terms. How do I know this," he pointed at the small plastic hard drive on the desk, "won't find its way into the public domain anyway?"

"I guess you don't. But look at it another way. What choice do you have?

You and Frobisher set me up to protect yourselves. By pure stupid luck the tables turned. As long as you remain Governor, I get everything I want. Why would I put all that in jeopardy by going public? No Governor, it's very simple. You deliver what I have demanded, and you secure your future. You don't and I have nothing to lose in releasing the recording. It's your choice."

The Governor considered. This time it took a lot less than fifteen seconds.

As D'eath happily walked out of the Governor's office, Bishop was attending a very different meeting of his own. He had no piece of yellow paper; no demands. The options he faced made falling foul of the Official Secrets Act look like a visit to a Butlins holiday camp. There would be no second chances for him and he knew it. He had called the ferret on the phone he had been given. The black Range Rover had picked him up off a street corner and now for the first time since McGimlet had taken the ATM disc he was in front of the big old Irishman again.

"My patience's about worn through. Yer'd better not be here disappointing me again Bishop."

McGimlet looked tired. He was an old man but now a touch of frailty, just a touch, seemed to hover about him. His posture seemed a little more stooped; hair a little thinner, movements a shade slower. But with the ferret and the bookends close by he still presented a formidable figure. This time the meeting felt different. Before, it had been Bishop snatched off the street. Now he was the one doing the convening. It was a subtle distinction, an important one, but not without risk.

Back in December McGimlet had thrown him a lifeline. But that time had gone. Bishop needed more. The Ipswich debacle could buy him more.

"I'm not here to disappoint, Mr McGimlet. I take it you have seen the press?"

"What?"

"The police raid that went bad in Ipswich a couple of days back."

"What of it?"

"That was our boy. Well not *our boy* but to do with him."

The wrinkles about McGimlet's face cut into a scowl.

"Will yer speak plainly, man!"

Bishop pulled several folded sheets of typed notepaper from his coat. Each sheet was stamped with FIBER's letterhead.

"This is a copy of the official report. I'm leaving it with you."

Bishop started to hand McGimlet the papers but the old man waved them away.

"Tell me."

Bishop stopped. He looked at the ferret, then the bookends. They stared back without expression.

"Well, ah, the essence of it is UK Customs discovered a shipment of cash being smuggled out of Tilbury for Hong Kong. The serial numbers matched some of the money taken from the ATMs. From the shipping documents and the CCTV in the docks we traced the money back to a farmhouse near Ipswich. The police went in and found nothing. But the point is it didn't matter."

McGimlet frowned. "Didn't matter?"

"No. I'd already noticed something from the CCTV that no one else had picked up on. It's what I do you see. It's what I'm good at; my job, analysing digital imagery."

"So what was it you noticed?" McGimlet sniffed.

"The consignment was delivered in a van. It was the driver. His face seemed familiar. I should have alerted my team, but I wasn't sure. I needed to check."

"And I'm guessing yer did just that?"

"I did. I had to keep the search off the books, so it took longer than I wanted. I called up all the police booking photographs we had in the database and did a run through."

"Booking photographs?"

"Mugshots."

"Ah." McGimlet nodded. "And so yer found him and now yer here."

"Er, yes. Exactly. I found him, his photo anyway. In a bunch of past case files. No doubt about it. His name is Peter Levine; a company director done for financial fraud around the middle of last year. You see? I knew I was right. Faces and images. It's what I do."

"Good! So let's go get this Mr Levine."

"No, No, no. It's not that simple, Mr McGimlet. I've made some enquiries, under the radar of course. It appears

Mr Levine is not in the country. He is overseas with his family. Hong Kong I'm told. Not surprisingly the same destination as the seized money."

McGimlet closed his eyes.

"Where's the good in any of this fer me? This is goin' nowhere and if yer think I'm about goin' to Hong Kong yer can forget it, Bishop."

Bishop had always known this would be the hard part. Two for one, added discount or bargain basement, whichever, Bishop had to make the Irishman buy.

"But you don't have to go anywhere Mr McGimlet. Levine will be coming back."

"So yer have a crystal ball too do yer?"

"Not a crystal ball, Mr McGimlet. A Bar Mitzvah. Eight weeks from now. North London. It's his only son. Levine will be as good as on a plate. The authorities won't have a clue. It's just two months Mr McGimlet."

McGimlet's rheumy eyes looked unfocused into the middle distance. Throughout the duration of the meeting the ferret and the bookends had stood apart silently. Bishop sensed they too could see the gathering tiredness; the ebbing strength of the old man.

"Ah well. We've come this far, Bishop. If another two months will see an end to it then another two months it is. But this is not a reprieve, big fella. No way. We have a deal you and me. A deal that's goin' to end in one of only two ways and don't yer be about forgettin' that."

TWENTY-TWO

A Range Rover had brought Bishop but it was a long walk and two buses taking him back. The return to his cheap bedsit had taken nearly two hours but it didn't matter. Bishop wasn't happy. That would be asking too much. But there was relief. He'd done it. He'd sold the old Irishman a man that didn't exist; a figment of his imagination, a figment that had just bought him another two months. Something would break in that time. It would have to, surely.

TWENTY-THREE

The flight out of London, almost twelve hours of it, had been uneventful. Davey Boy had slept most of the way. Business class in the Boeing 777-300ER wasn't the best he had experienced but at least the fold down seat-bed had been long enough, just.

It was nearing eight in the morning local time when he exited customs into the cavernous arrivals hall of terminal one, Hong Kong International Airport. Wheels down to arrivals hall had taken under an hour. It helped he was toting only a carry-on. With luck he'd be done in twenty-four hours and on his way home.

He took up position in front of pillar six; one of eight standing in a row. They weren't really pillars but he supposed they had to call them something. Take an empty blue plastic shoebox. Feed it some steroids, stretch it twelve feet high, stick a number on the top and a few LEDs and you had a pillar. But together with its seven replicates it provided some rearward security as he stood looking out into the vast hall, scanning, assessing, evaluating, he wondered where the hell Archie was? He had promised to be here. Exit A. Pick Up Point Pillar Six. But he wasn't.

His phone pinged. The text displayed a welcome to Hong Kong message. Roaming charges would be five-and-a-half Hong Kong dollars per minute or part thereof. Great! Just what he needed to know. He deleted the message.

Almost immediately the phone sounded again. This time it was his ring tone. He held it up to his ear.

"Archie mate where the hell are you? I'm standing here like a dipstick."

Archie's voice sounded reassuringly close, but it wasn't.

"Shit Davey I'm so sorry mate but there's been a change of plans. You're not going to believe it, but I've done my leg in. Broken it. Two places mate. I'm done up like a kipper. I'm calling directly from the hospital now."

Davey Boy's stomach sank.

"I'm sorry Bro but that kind of leaves me up the shitter."

"I know Davey. What can I say? I'm sorry as hell man but I have a plan B. My man Chang should be with you anytime now. You'll see him. A cool-looking dude in a red jacket. A flair for the ostentatious has our Chang. Anyway, he's a really good bloke Davey and he'll drive you into town. I've got you holed up in the Renaissance Harbour View."

"Whoa! Hold on Archie. I wanted in and out as fast as possible. Get the stuff, do the necessary and get out. What's with the hotel?"

Far out on the periphery of Davey Boy's vision a small dab of bright strawberry appeared. Archie's voice continued in his ear.

TWENTY-THREE

"Hotel Foxtrot can't see you until this evening. It can't be helped. He's out in the New Territories. He'll be back at nine. His offices are downtown Island side. The hotel is just two clicks from the ferry terminal and his office is in between. Chang will take you there. The last cat to Macau isn't until eleven-thirty, mate. Nothing sleeps on the strip so you should be able to do your business and be out first thing in the morning."

The dab of bright strawberry was getting larger.

"I'm not happy, Archie. You should have told me."

"You were in the air, mate. It came out the blue. What could I do? The leg didn't bloody help. Three tours of Helmand and I slip on a bar of bloody soap. Trust me, this is the best I can do Davey and, like I said, you'll be back on track in the morning."

"I hope you're right Archie Anyway, I can see your guy now, so we'll catch up later. You take care and get yourself fixed up, okay mate."

"Sure thing Davey and . . . thanks for understanding."

Archie's voice disappeared. Davey Boy pocketed the phone. The bright strawberry was no longer a dab. It was a jacket.

"Mr Chang?"

"Mr Gilroy! It's a pleasure to meet you sir."

The idiom and accent took Davey Boy by surprise. Chang's style-sense would have been a surprise too if it hadn't been for the fifty acclimatising yards of his approach through the terminal. The jacket was bespoke; tailored linen. Not pink. Not red. Somewhere in between. Everything else was immaculately white; loafers, jeans, belt, open-necked shirt. There were no socks. Chang looked no more than twenty-three or four. Tall for a Chinese, about five-ten, his hair, styled long, danced with highlights of hazel and brown in a thick fringe above pale eyes and a quick smile.

"You're not quite what I expected Mr Chang."

"Just Chang, sir. Is that all you have?"

Davey Boy hefted the carry-on.

"Travelling light, Chang. In and out. I guess you have a room for me in the Renaissance?"

"You guess right, sir. And I also have a car waiting if you would like to come this way."

Like Chang, the car was a standout too. An immaculate 66 Jaguar MK2, midnight blue; bright chrome work, cream leather. It gleamed an invitation in the morning sun, 'drive me'. And they did. Route Eight out onto the North Lantau Highway. It could have been a late spring day back home, bright, cool, with sparse clouds high up against the blue.

Clear of the airport approaches, traffic settled. Chang dropped a gear and accelerated hard. The throaty guttering of the 3.8 engine rose to a reverberating roar. He grinned wide and slowed the speed.

"Some noise, eh?"

Davey Boy smiled,

"There can't be many of these old beasts still around in Hong Kong."

"A few but the import costs are through the roof. They're pricing older vehicles off the road; too dirty and inefficient. Archie keeps this one around for the high spenders who want something a little different. He thought you might appreciate it."

The car pulled well, Chang driving with assurance. Davey Boy sat back into aged leather and stretched his legs.

"Talking about Archie, how did you two end up together?"

Chang flicked down a gear and accelerated out from behind a bus bedecked with advertisements.

"You could say he's a friend of the family, or my mother's to be precise. They met through the golf club some years back when I was overseas."

"Overseas?"

"School. In the States. East Coast. My mother's alma mater."

"So your mother's American?"

"Boston Irish. She married Dad about thirty years back. She was travelling around Asia, they met, married, and I guess I'm the result."

"I assume he's Chinese?"

Chang nodded.

"Hong Kong through and through."

"Any brothers, sisters?"

"No. Only child. Attention seeker. That's me. I guess you can tell."

Davey Boy smiled.

"So you work in the casino?"

"Not directly. Archie needed a translator. I was at a loose end, kicking my heels back home. Mom put us together. It's been a couple of years now. We get on well enough and it seems to work."

The Jag was through the tolls now and well up along the Lantau Link Way, the traffic still moving easily.

"What about yourself Mr Gilroy? If you don't mind my asking."

"It's Davey, Chang but there's not much to say really. I'm in security in London. Archie and I go back a ways. We were muckers in the Regiment."

"Muckers?"

"We served together in the British Army. Now we're both in mufti. Him out here with the casino, me back in London."

"Mufti?"

Davey Boy laughed.

"Sorry Chang. It's soldier slang for no longer in uniform. If you like we're both back in civilian life. Out of the service."

Chang grinned.

"Mufti! Cool. I'll have to remember that."

A gap opened in the traffic and the Jag quickened. The road, three lanes each way, rose up onto a cabled bridge taking the Jaguar high out above the water. To the right small islands dotted a sea widening to a distant horizon. To the left the water extended less than two kilometres. Then there were hills rising behind tall buildings indistinct in the bright morning haze.

TWENTY-THREE

"The Tsing Ma Bridge," said Chang. "Spectacular, isn't it?"

Davey Boy nodded.

"It looks like the Golden Gate in San Francisco."

"That's sixty years older and about three-hundred feet shorter," said Chang. "I do a bit of tour-guiding for some of Archie's casino VIPs and it helps to know some of that stuff."

They came off the bridge at Tsing Yi and swung south, still on Route Eight. Hong Kong was getting close. By now the traffic was thickening, carrying them up onto another high bridge. The roadway hanging between soaring twin towers on a spider's web of cables.

"Stonecutters," announced Chang, his tour guide hat firmly in place. Seventy metres below acres of container yards, docks and oil storage terminals splayed left and right cut through by wide shipping channels; flocks of white Egrets skimming the waters.

Then down off the bridge and another two kilometres of curving auto route into a massive gyratory of intersecting highways. Chang pulled right amidst a cacophony of horns. For the first time since the airport they were no longer on Eight. Heavy traffic pulled them down a wide boulevard. Three congested lanes either side flanked by tall buildings; shopping esplanades, the central reservation full of palm trees.

"So you'll drop me off and come back later?" asked Davey Boy.

Chang nodded. "Your meeting is set for nine. I'll pick you up at 8:45. It's just a short drive. Huang's office is in the 'Center'. Archie has asked me to tag along. You might need a translator."

The boulevard was gradually descending now but widening massively with multi lanes expanding on each side. The traffic was slowing to a crawl. Ahead, beyond a wide stretch of toll booths, Davey Boy could see the small black letterbox slots of twin tunnel entrances. The Jag crept forward in a line with hundreds of other vehicles, the letterbox slots getting bigger.

"West Harbour Crossing," said Chang, "time for the lights."

Through the tolls the multiple lanes funnelled to just three and filtering forward they entered the left-hand tunnel disappearing under the bay.

Twenty minutes later they emerged out of the ground blinking into Hong Kong Island daylight. Nearly nine in the morning, traffic crawling bumper-to-bumper. The mercury rising. To the left the waters of Victoria Harbour gleamed in the May sunshine, to the right skyscrapers, forests of them in every size and shape pushed down the hillside to crowd in along the highway. And everywhere people; throngs of scurrying humanity. Coughed up onto streets from the MTR; disgorging from buses, cars, taxis, alighting from ferries and trams, jostling, shoving, barging, jay walking, hands glued to phones, eyes to screens, heads to earphones. Davey Boy thought of one of his father's favourite expressions, 'The Great Unwashed'. Perhaps 'automatons' should be added as an appropriate twenty-first century suffix. The Jaguar edged along, carried within the flow of traffic. Chang motioned with his hand. "See those two buildings to the left. The ones looking like house bricks stood on their ends?"

Davey Boy looked. "The ones with the red bands round them?"

Chang nodded. "Right between them on the harbour side is the ferry terminal to Macau."

Davey Boy made a mental note. The Jag moved slowly on; the water temperature needle on the dash dialling towards ninety degrees.

"And there on the right is the 'Center'. That's where we'll be tonight; up on the forty-third floor."

Davey Boy cranked his neck against the window glass to look. The slim mirrored tower seemed to rise up forever.

"I hope to hell they've got fast lifts."

Chang grinned.

"Didn't you know? In Hong Kong everything is fast!"

"They should have told the traffic," murmured Davey Boy.

The road and traffic looped away from the waterfront into the forest of tall buildings then came back on itself. The Jag carried along like a boat in a slow current.

"So tell me about this Huang we're meeting tonight?" asked Davey Boy.

"Not much to say really. He's a businessman. The commercial directory says mainly shipping, warehouse storage and some property developments on the mainland. Not much in Hong Kong. But that's all for public consumption. One never really knows. But he's got to be pretty successful. He's one of the whales at the casino. That's where Archie came to know him."

"Whales?"

"Big spenders. He lays a lot through the tables. Not just ours. Roulette mainly."

Davey Boy nodded. "So he's pretty mainstream then?"

Chang laughed. "Mainstream! What does *that* mean? This is Hong Kong."

At long last traffic freed up a little. Hopefully it wouldn't be long now. They'd been in the car for over an hour.

"So has Archie said anything about why I'm here?"

"A little." Chang looked across and winked. "Let's just say you're here to grease the commercial wheels a little and do a spot of gambling. And if Archie is happy with that then so am I."

Davey Boy sat back in the seat with a wry smile.

Three sets of traffic lights and another fifteen minutes and Chang pulled on the wheel taking the Jaguar off the main drag onto a narrow slip lane. "The Renaissance" he announced.

Finally, thought Davey Boy. The airport was thirty-eight kilometres away and the drive had taken nearly an hour and a half. Welcome to Hong Kong. Chang manoeuvred the car under a massive corner overhang of silvered glass and concrete. The structure looked as welcoming as a cold war bunker.

TWENTY-THREE

"Everything's taken care of, Davey. The reservation's in your name. It's on the casino's account so no worries. Talking of names, you are going to be 'Mr Smith' for tonight. Archie thought it best."

"Top marks for imagination," said Davey Boy drily.

Chang grinned. "I'll be back to pick you up at 8:45 this evening. Any issues give me a call."

Chang offered a printed card. It was quality; bleached woven vellum with gold edging. Black copperplate filled the centre, 'New Era Hotel and Casino', underneath in the same font but smaller, 'A.T. Chang – Executive'. Davey Boy was curious.

"What's the A.T stand for?"

Chang laughed.

"That's between me and my birth certificate, Davey. Trust me. You wouldn't want to know."

TWENTY-FOUR

Davey Boy had slept on the plane and then again in the hotel room. It was a military thing. Sleep when you can, you might not be able to sleep when you want. It helped that the view from his room was down onto the roof of the Hong Kong Convention and Exhibition Centre. It looked like the back of a dead Armadillo and about as interesting. It had been dark two hours when Chang rang through on the room phone. Davey Boy, dressed and ready, turned away from the window. While he slept the outside world had changed. A cosmic bucketful of twinkling gems had been upended over Kowloon. Rubies, emeralds, sapphires, diamonds; all glowing, sparkling, flickering and gleaming. Incandescent light was everywhere, cascading down buildings, overflowing streets and shimmering on dark waters in all the colours of an electric neon rainbow. Hong Kong at night. It was as good a backdrop as any. He was good to go.

Davey Boy took the elevator down. If everything went to plan, he wouldn't be coming back. He wore the same dark suit from the plane, but the shirt was a fresh white open neck. He had one more in the carry-on. Twenty-four hours and home.

That was the plan. Chang met him in the lobby. Strawberry and white had been day issue. Now it was black leather, charcoal and a gleaming yellow jacket. Linen was out but socks were back in.

"You could have warned me," grinned Davey Boy, "I've packed my sunglasses."

Chang smiled back. "No worries. I've got spares. Are you ready?"

"Ready as I'm ever going to be. Let's get this show on the road."

The Jag was retired for the night. In its place Chang had arranged a Mercedes and driver. The Mercedes deposited them barely a kilometre from the hotel, back along the way they had driven in the morning. The 'Center', all seventy-three floors of it, rose up above them into the night sky, its upper mirrored extremities fluorescing in changing bands of bright neon colour. Davey Boy was impressed. They stepped from the kerb, fifty metres across a plaza planted with small ornamental trees, and into the building itself. The entrance was no less impressive. A greenhouse of sparkling glass panels on a matrix of stainless-steel rods rising into a glass cupola forty feet above a floor of polished granite. Davey Boy wondered how much window cleaners got paid in Hong Kong. Three escalators took them up onto a marbled mezzanine, Chang leading the way. The elevators were grouped in different banks, separated off to the left and right sides of the building, servicing different chunks of floors. They went right.

TWENTY-FOUR

Nine p.m.; forty-three floors in twenty-five seconds, ears popping all the way. They stepped out into a vestibule. Chang knew where he was going. Davey Boy followed along, the carry-on over his shoulder.

The double doors at the end of the corridor were glass, heavy and opaque. A sign was at head height on the wall next to them. 'Heavenly Luck Trading Enterprises'. Three-dimensional brass letters on a five-foot plank of polished rosewood. Appropriate thought Davey Boy. Each door sprouted a handle of chromed steel. Chang put his hand on the nearest and pushed. Then he pulled. One glass leaf opened towards them. They went inside.

Davey Boy was surprised. He'd expected a spectacular view but that would have needed windows, and there were none. The room, lit with bright ceiling diffusers, was partitioned as an internal lobby, a lobby panelled in rosewood and not much else. The plank of the outside sign was probably a creative left-over. They crossed the cream carpet to a single desk, rosewood again, like the walls. What was it about rosewood? Behind the desk sat a middle-aged Chinese woman in a black pantsuit. Behind her, up on the wall, was a painting. Interior design fodder, six feet across and full of abstract reds, oranges and golds.

The woman stood as they approached. Chang spoke to her in Cantonese. Smiling, she nodded and turned pushing at a portion of panelling to the side of the painting. It swung inward revealing a corridor. She didn't speak but gestured for them to follow her. Davey Boy put the carry-on down by the desk and this time he walked ahead of Chang.

The corridor was nondescript and short. The woman knocked lightly and held open a door and they left her into an altogether different space. The room was more penthouse apartment than office and it was spectacular. The light didn't come flat and bright from ceiling diffusers here. It collected in pools beneath silk-shaded table lamps, mellow and intimate, spreading on richly designed rugs of hand knotted wool from Tientsin and shimmering Shanghai silk. It gleamed off the ebony corners of exquisite Chinese cabinetry and cast shadows amongst an oasis of greenly variegated plants growing luxuriantly from low carved containers of wood and stone. Davey Boy took a step and stopped, Chang butting up behind him. So, this is where the view had got to. Huang's office/penthouse filled a corner slot on the tower giving it two external walls. Both were just frameless slabs of photochromic glass. And through them, to the north, east and west, from the forty-third floor, glittered the bejewelled entirety of Victoria Harbour and Kowloon Bay.

It was like looking from a darkened room into a brightly lit aquarium. Fluorescing scintillating movement was everywhere but in miniature; tiny boats twinkling on the bay, beads of bright traffic on intersecting necklaces of highway, neon logos and advertising slogans, as small as headed note paper, blinking, glaring, strobing. And the buildings; like blocks of children's bricks, edges gilded, flanks glistening with a million blazing scales. The entire collective sparkling against the dark backdrop of Tai Mo Shan and Kowloon Peak like diamonds scattered on a jeweller's velvet and all silent, noiseless, through thick slabs of glass forty-three floors up.

"Is nice yes?"

Davey Boy turned away from the view. Across the room in a far corner figures sat around a low table.

"Very," he said.

One of the figures stood with a hand outstretched in greeting.

"Welcome Hong Kong Mr Smith. Sorry Mr Huang for keep you waiting."

Davey Boy walked over and clasped the hand. The grip was unusually strong, almost aggressive. He tensed his own hand to match it then stopped. Instead he conceded a small grimace of pain allowing his own grasp to dissolve weakly in the other man's grip. He looked into the face attached to the hand. It was level with his own. The mouth in the face was smiling. The eyes, dark and hard, weren't. The man looked fit like a gym animal, his dark two-button suit tailored wide over the shoulders, lean around the hips and stomach. Long jet-black hair, pulled away from his face, hung a foot down his back in an oiled ponytail.

"Mr Huang?

The man chuckled mechanically, the ponytail dancing.

"Mr Huang assistant."

Ponytail's hand released Davey Boy's and swept back as if opening an invisible door.

"*This* Mr Huang Fu, man you come meet."

A second man rose from the group. He was cream-suited and slim to the point of skinniness and a foot shorter than Ponytail. Davey Boy put him somewhere in his late forties, early fifties, but age with Chinese was notoriously difficult. Ponytail had at least attempted a smile. Huang didn't even try. His look was one of pure disdain. Davey Boy started to offer his hand and then thought better of it. He inclined his head in a small bow. Huang sat back down, still silent. The remaining three figures at the low table, all younger men, followed his example. Davey Boy clearing his throat spoke in a slow clear voice.

"May I introduce my associate, Mr Chang. He is with me tonight representing Mr Bell."

"Yes," said Ponytail, "Mr Bell say us his accident. We hope for him recover soon."

Davey Boy acknowledged the sentiment with a nod. In the grandeur and sophistication of Huang's penthouse/office Ponytail's broken English jarred. Like a street hawker who had taken the wrong turn at the lifts. But the gist was clear enough, so far at least, and it was a hell of a lot better than his Cantonese.

"We thank Mr Huang for his help," started Davey Boy, "and for his confirmation that the first sixteen consignments have all been safely secured."

There was no response. Huang and his group looked at Davey Boy the way they might look at paint drying on a wall. Davey Boy's antennae started to twitch.

TWENTY-FOUR

"As Mr Huang knows, these are just the first of many shipments. Another four are already sailing to Hong Kong as I speak."

Ponytail held up a hand stopping Davey Boy, he spoke to Huang in Cantonese. He seemed to say a lot more than Davey Boy had. The group around the low table remained silent. Ponytail motioned for Davey Boy to continue.

"And so we extend our hand of friendship and cooperation to Mr Huang and wish to inform him we are moving to increase both the volume and frequency of future shipments to the benefit of us all."

Davey Boy stopped and bobbed his head towards Huang. Ponytail translated. Davey Boy felt like a prat. He'd never spoken to anyone like that. He hoped most of the cack he'd just spoken would improve in translation. He glanced at Chang and received a raised eyebrow back. Silence turned to stillness, building uncomfortably in the dimly lit room. Then Huang spoke. What he said in Cantonese was a mystery to Davey Boy but the manner in which he said it wasn't. His voice was animated and coarse and a gold tooth glinted in his mouth. Ponytail listened until Huang had finished then he spoke.

"Mr Huang no more want business with you Mr Smith. No friendship. No more help. You liar. You no tell police take money. Danger for everybody."

Davey Boy feigned astonishment. Huang finding out about the customs seizure was always a possibility but getting caught in a lie and admitting it were two different things, especially six-thousand miles from home.

"I am sorry," he said, looking at Huang. "I was not aware any money had been found by the authorities. I would have, of course, informed you immediately if I had known this. It is an unfortunate misunderstanding but that is all. I can assure Mr Huang that there is no danger. Our security remains unbroken. Mr Huang knows there are many means we can use to continue moving these consignments if he will reconsider?"

The tone of Davey Boy's voice and his gesturing didn't need translating. Huang barked at Ponytail who barked back at Davey Boy.

"No. No more. Finished!"

Davey Boy looked embarrassed and disappointed, but he couldn't care less. He was going through the motions. For good or bad the last shipments were already on the way. There would be no more whatever happened. Davey Boy bowed his head ingratiatingly in Huang's direction. "I know that this must have caused Mr Huang great concern. Please tell him that my associates and I are truly sorry."

A smile played around Huang's thin mouth as Ponytail finished relaying Davey Boy's words. He summoned the big man over and stood speaking quietly at his shoulder. Ponytail turned back to Davey Boy. His mouth had become as hard as his eyes.

"You take now and you go."

With that he walked to a beautiful carved wooden bureau and bending down opened a deep bottom drawer. He withdrew what looked like a silvered attaché case. He walked back and gave the case to Huang. Huang dropped it on to the low table and pushed it contemptuously in Davey Boy's direction. Chang went forward and picked it up. He walked back past Davey Boy.

"This shit's a snake" he murmured.

Chang moved to another table on the far side of the room. He placed the case down and flipped two locks. By the time Davey Boy reached him he was already peering at the contents. The case was ribbed aluminium; about eighteen inches long and a foot wide. The upper lid filled with black foam. More of the same filled the body but this foam had shapes cut into it. And stuffed into the shapes were gambling chips; ceramic discs, compressed together like coins stacked on edge. The discs were identical; cream with orange edges, centres inlaid with white foil. The printing on the foil was clear and sharp; a stylised logo above the legend Wynn Macau, and below this the figure fifty-thousand followed by HKD. In the centre of the case, nestled between the columns of discs were two cut-outs, one above the other, each the size, shape and depth of a pack of playing cards. Each cut-out filled with a stack of clay plaques, like fat oversized credit cards. In the top cut-out they were mottled cream and gold and imprinted with the same logo but with a printed figure of five-hundred-thousand followed by HKD. In the bottom the plaques were mottled black and silver with an imprinted figure of one-hundred-thousand HKD. Davey Boy ran his fingers up the columns mentally counting the discs. Six columns, seventeen discs in each at fifty-thousand per disc. He took out his phone and fired up the calculator app. Five-million, one-hundred-thousand Hong Kong dollars. He hefted the plaques. There were ten of each. Another six-million Hong Kong dollars. The case contained over eleven-million Hong Kong dollars in casino chips. Davey Boy jabbed at his phone screen. One-point-one-million sterling. He frowned. He turned and walked back across the room. "There seems to be some mistake. The chips are short."

Ponytail smiled coldly. "No short."

Davey Boy shook his head.

"Sixteen consignments, not counting the ones on the sea. That's one-point-six-million pounds. That's the equivalent of sixteen-million Hong Kong. Allowing for your fees there should be nearly thirteen-million in that case. There isn't. You've seen me count it. We're light more than one-and-a-half million Hong Kong."

"No short," repeated Ponytail menacingly.

Davey Boy turned to Chang. "Can you sort this mess out?"

In a flurry of Cantonese Chang let loose at Ponytail. Ponytail let loose back. The look on Chang's face said it all

"It's no mistake Davey. Huang has upped his commission to thirty percent."

"Thirty! Archie said it was agreed at twenty."

"That's not all." Chang was seething.

"They're keeping the cash that's on the sea."

"What! That's three-hundred-thousand pounds!"

"Whatever it is, the bastards are keeping it."

"Shit!"

TWENTY-FOUR

Before Davey Boy could think Chang had started in on Huang directly, his voice rising, speaking rapidly in Cantonese. Davey Boy saw Huang's eyes narrow and the shoulders of his companions stiffen. He tensed. The atmosphere in the room was suddenly like a pressure cooker. Then Huang released the valve. Flipping a wrist dismissively, as if backhanding a fly, Huang spoke; his voice, hard, arrogant and rising in crescendo. Davey Boy had no idea what he was saying but the message was clear enough. Their time on the forty-third floor was up. Davey Boy walked back across the room, snapped shut the case, picked it up, took one last look at the magnificent view, nodded at Chang and together they moved towards the door. They didn't give Ponytail or the four figures around the low table a backward glance.

TWENTY-FIVE

The lift down seemed to take an age. Davey Boy stood smouldering all the way, a case of casino chips in his hand, carry-on over his shoulder.

He'd thought about it hard. Kicking Huang's balls into the top of his sneering little skull, but it was always a no go. It was Huang's turf, he was well thugged up and the outcome would have been as messy as it was uncertain. The consignments on the sea were gone. There was nothing to be done about them, but the case in his hand contained north of eleven-million and he wasn't about to put that at risk.

Next to him Chang had been on the phone since the lift doors had closed. With a grim look he passed the phone to Davey Boy.

"Archie wants to speak with you."

"I bet he does." Davey Boy pressed the phone to his ear and spoke hard and abrupt.

"Archie! What the hell just happened? This Huang bastard has just stiffed us a million-and-a-half dollars and he's thieving all the consignments in transit. That's another three-hundred-thousand quid! He was your guy Archie. You vouched for him and he's screwed us."

"Chang's told me Davey. I don't know what to say. I'm as shocked as you. Believe me."

"Anyone else Archie and I would know they were in on it with that slitty eyed piece of rat shit. But you can forget the deal we made. What's happened is on you Archie, no one else. You should have seen it coming."

Archie's voice was defiant.

"Screw the money Davey. I wouldn't have taken it anyway. Not after this. Listen. This shit Huang has tasted blood. What's to stop him wanting it all? Look, just get yourself over here pronto. To the Taipa terminal; my men will be waiting. Once here you'll be safe, mate. I just hope to hell the little shit is stupid enough to follow you over. The bastard won't be going back if he does and that's a promise."

"Yeah, well I'm not there yet so watch this space. I'm handing you back to Chang."

The lift doors opened, and they retraced their steps; mezzanine, escalators, greenhouse, plaza, kerb. They came out fast. Chang hadn't just been on the phone to Archie. He had the Mercedes waiting for them.

From up on the forty-third floor, traffic had twinkled like beads of light, silent and pretty. But at ground level it was a blaring gas belching bumper-to-bumper mess and going nowhere.

"On foot," said Davey Boy.

Chang nodded. He bent by the car's window and signalled with walking fingers to the driver. Davey Boy kept the case.

TWENTY-FIVE

Chang took the carry-on. Then they set off, filtering into a great flow of bikes, cycles, scooters and pedestrians heading west. The twin buildings marking the entrance to the ferry terminal stood opposite the Sheung Wan MTR station, just a few hundred yards distant. The wind was picking up, the temperature dropping. In the bay, over towards Kowloon, waves were building, their tops white against the dark water. They hurried along in a half-jog, half-fast walk, pushing past slower individuals, stepping out into the road to skirt the bigger groups. Davey Boy glanced at his watch. 10:15. With luck he would make the 10:30 ferry, then fifty minutes to Taipa where Archie had his men waiting. He looked over his shoulder. If Huang and his thugs were back there he'd never know. The traffic and crowds were a moving circus of halogen glare, shapes and shadows. He turned to Chang moving easily at his elbow.

"So what do you reckon?"

"I think he's coming." Chang's breath came as rapid as his steps.

"He missed a trick not taking us in his office. Maybe it was too close to home. Maybe he didn't want blood on his carpets. Maybe he just wanted to get a 'feel' before he decided. Who knows. But if it was me, I'd be coming. It's just too much money."

Davey Boy looked at Chang. There was a steely focused quality to the young man he hadn't seen before.

"I hope to hell you're wrong," said Davey Boy, dodging around a trio of chattering girls who had suddenly stopped to take selfies against the neon skyline. "But if you're not we're going to need a game plan. Did you recognise any of the others in the room apart from Huang?"

"Only Kai, the ponytail guy. I've seen him with Huang in the casino. I think he's close protection or security. The other three I've never seen before. I think they're just goons."

They kept moving. Ahead the twin buildings loomed - each like a pair of giant Rubik cubes stacked one on another, faceted with squares of light. It started to rain. Cold fat drops at first, like a five second warning, then the main event, carried in from the bay on strengthening winds. Umbrellas sprouted, crowds quickened, walkways gleaming wetly under their feet. Just in time, Davey Boy and Chang peeled off between the Rubiks and passed in under the sheltering roof of the ferry terminal complex.

Up on the forty-third floor Huang disconnected the call and placed the phone carefully on the low table in front of him. He'd planned for profit and the evening hadn't disappointed, but there was more to be had, much more. He just needed to be patient a little while longer. He could have acted earlier but that would have been imprudent, risky even. He'd been sorely tempted but he needed distance between himself and the Gweilo. If anyone came asking questions it was all about deniability. But the night was young. Time was on his side and Macau was sixty kilometres away across the Pearl River Estuary. Before sun up he would have his eleven-million back and the hide of that half-breed pup nailed to a wall.

Kai observed his boss from across the room. He and his three wise monkeys waited by the door. Time was wasting. They needed to go. Outside it had started to rain. He could just hear the faint pattering against the huge glass exterior walls. Water ran in rivulets down the glass, smearing the view into an abstract mess.

Huang broke the silence.

"No sign of them yet but the manager is ready. He knows what to do."

"And the vessel?"

"All in hand. The captain's not happy but he will do as required."

"You're paying him to follow instructions," said Kai, "not to be happy."

Huang fixed his security enforcer with a piercing stare.

"Like I'm paying you to get that case back."

"Of course." Kai met Huang's gaze directly, a small smile curling at his mouth. He gestured at the glass walls.

"It might get a little damp, but it won't be difficult. We should be back before midnight."

"And no loose ends."

"And no loose ends," echoed Kai ominously, following his three men out into the corridor, the door closing behind them.

The ferry terminal wasn't as crowded and chaotic as it could have been. Maybe the late evening sailing or the worsening weather had something to do with it. Chang threaded his way through the main ground floor concourse, Davey Boy tagging along behind. The terminal resembled the inside of a small municipal airport. Open plan, long, rectangular, the walls lined with brightly lit shops, cafes, boutiques, travel bureaus and ticket offices above a shiny sealed floor. Chang knew where he wanted to go and quickened his pace towards a long counter garishly framed in blue halfway down the concourse hall.

"This is the one," said Chang. "Cotai Water Jet. Last sailing 11:30 and straight into Taipa."

They joined the small queue in front of the counter and stood fidgeting impatiently. Davey Boy checked his watch again. He was going to be late. No way would he make the 10:30 waiting for tickets.

"Excuse me. Mr Chang? Mr Smith?"

Chang and Davey Boy turned abruptly.

"So sorry sirs if I startled you."

A small rotund Chinese man had appeared out of the crowd. Middle aged and balding, he looked dapper in dark trousers, powder blue blazer, matching tie and white shirt.

"Who are you?" asked Davey Boy.

The man gestured at an oblong badge pinned to the top of the blazer's breast pocket.

"Edward Tan. Cotai Water Jet. Duty Manager."

"Great!" interjected Chang. "Can you help us? We need two singles on the next sailing to Taipa."

TWENTY-FIVE

"We?" Davey Boy looked at Chang. "I assumed you would be staying back here."

Chang shrugged. "Little choice Davey. After what I said to our host earlier, the sooner I get back to my patch the better."

"Yeah I was wondering about that. I thought Huang was going to blow a gasket. What the hell did you say?"

"Just the normal stuff. You know. A turd is still a turd even when it's up on the forty-third floor. That type of thing."

Davey Boy chuckled darkly. "I guess you'd better come aboard."

Edward Tan, in his powder blues, had stood obligingly to one side smiling politely. Now he spoke again.

"Gentlemen, there is no need for concern. Ticketing arrangements have already been made by Mr Bell. Please follow me and have your passports ready."

Chang grinned. Davey Boy, relieved, smiled back.

"About time the bugger did something right. Lead on Mr Tan."

They followed Tan into a wide corridor marked 'Departures'. Ahead were immigration counters manned by tired-looking uniforms. Passengers were being processed through the checks quickly; virtually being waved through. They filled in immigration cards, presented the documents and Tan ushered them through. They were out of time but if they shifted they might just make the sailing. Davey Boy called to Chang to run when Tan held out an arm.

"Gentlemen please there is no need to hurry. The 10:30 sailing has been delayed; an electrical issue. It appears to be nothing serious and we should be departing very soon but it means we are able to get you aboard as late passengers."

Relieved, Davey Boy put down the case, took off his jacket, draped it over his arm and retrieved the case. Despite the air-con he could feel the sweat; under his arms, in his hairline, in the small of his back. Chang seemed unaffected. I'm getting too bloody old for this nonsense, he thought. They walked quickly past an almost-empty waiting room. Walls of glass and banks of metal chairs bolted through concrete, then on down a covered walkway bridging out over the water. Towards the end of the walkway it changed. Solid walls gave way, morphing into thin arches of yellow steel supporting panels of curved Perspex. They continued on under the canopy, the clear plastic thrumming under the impact of heavy rain, and out onto the quayside. The night was filthy. Either side, haloed in spray, lines of lamps, left and right, marked the pier going off into darkness. Davey Boy glimpsed long aerodynamic shapes, red and blue, rising and falling against the concrete piers in a wet salt wind. Heads down, they scuttled through gusting rain the last few metres to the ferry. Davey Boy regretted removing his jacket. It had only taken a moment but already his shirt was sodden and cold. A wide doorway let into a blue expanse of hull beckoned. The door itself lowered onto the lip of the jetty like a small drawbridge. It rose and fell with the strength of the swell as they passed over it into the shelter of the lower deck area. Davey Boy went to move on into the vast cabin but Tan grasped him lightly by a damp arm.

"Mr Bell has booked you both Cotai VIP so we hope that the short delay will not be uncomfortable. This way please."

They followed the powder blue blazer a little way into the economy cabin. It was big and open plan. Almost the size of a pair of tennis courts end-on-end. The space filled with rank upon rank of aircraft seats bolted to the floor. At a glance the seats were about a third full; maybe a hundred-and-twenty passengers. They turned right and followed Tan up a wide flight of internal steps to the first-class upper deck. It was as wide as the deck below but nowhere near as long. It was still filled with aircraft seats but these were wider and plusher and they were set on squares of patterned carpet. Up here the passengers could be counted on two hands. Off the stairs they turned and walked back between the seat rows. Tan opened a door in a partition. It was a private cabin. Two large windows on the outer bulkhead; two fixed tables side by side, eight large reclining seats, four to a table.

"Welcome to VIP Cotai class," said Tan, ushering them into the room.

Davey Boy looked around the cabin appreciatively.

"Thank you Mr Tan, you've been most helpful. Unfortunately we have a very urgent appointment in Macau and we are trying to make up time. I trust we will be departing soon?"

"I believe so sir. Let me get an update from the captain. In the meantime may I offer you some refreshments?"

Chang hoisted the carry-on off his shoulder onto one of the seats. "Thank you. Just some bottled water."

"Make that two and a towel," added Davey Boy, picking at his wet shirt.

Tan nodded and left, closing the door softly behind him. Davey Boy placed the case of chips on the table in front of him. Unzipping the carry-on he took out his last clean shirt. Chang went to the rain smeared window. He stood feet apart feeling the rise and fall of the deck, his yellow jacket the only reflection in the black glass.

"I can't see shit out there Davey. We must be at the back of the boat."

"Hang on."

Davey Boy removed a laminated brochure from a holder on the side of his seat. The front cover was a full-page photo of a bright blue futuristic wedge slicing through sea at speed, behind it a turbulent wake of white water. It was taken from above, probably by a drone or helicopter. Unfortunately some corporate type had had the bright idea of emblazoning the side of the vessel with painted motifs, stars and 'whoosh' go-faster graffiti. Added to this brash decoration in big bold white lettering covering a third of the streamlined hull was the legend 'Cotai Strip'. Good move thought Davey Boy. A vessel with all the potential to be a Lamborghini of the oceans had ended up looking like a seagoing sandwich board.

TWENTY-FIVE

"The Cotai Water Jet," Davey Boy read aloud, for his own benefit rather than Chang's who probably knew the stuff already.

"Twin catamaran hulls; forty-eight metres long, eleven metre beam, seventy tons and a speed of over forty knots with a capacity of four hundred plus passengers, Hong Kong to Macau in fifty minutes."

"Not tonight, Josephine. Not in this weather," said Chang, his finger drawing a smiley face on the dark glass. Davey Boy continued examining the brochure.

"We *are* at the back of the boat."

He held up the brochure. A detailed schematic of the vessel filled the back page in plan form. Apart from a small section at the stern, above the engines, the main deck, full of economy seating, ran the length of the hull. Tiered above it was a shorter quarter deck with first class seating and forward of this, a little higher still, a streamlined command bridge. Emergency exits were marked as were amenities, toilets and staff areas. There were two identical VIP cabins on the vessel. Both were at the very rear of the upper first class deck; one port side, one starboard. Tan had put them port side. The cabins were separated by a short access corridor leading back out onto a small exposed viewing deck at the rear of the ferry above the engine rooms. Chang peered at the plan. He held Davey Boy's wrist to steady it.

"Mmm, Most interesting, most interesting indeed."

"What is?"

"The location of the toilets," said Chang. "I need to take a piss."

When Tan left the VIP cabin he did not go to get an update from the captain. Instead he quickly retraced his steps back onto the quayside, into the Perspex tunnel and back up into the main concourse building. Kai and three men were waiting impatiently at the Cotai Water Jet counter.

"You took your time. Are they on board?"

Tan nodded. "Upper deck, Port VIP cabin. They have the case with them."

Tan was not a bad man. He just happened to be in a very bad place. Huang's money was his chance to get out of it.

"You've got the passes for us?"

Tan nodded again.

"And the captain knows what to do?" Kai looked closely into the duty manager's face.

Tan hesitated but only for a moment.

"Yes. When I give the word, he will find further electrical issues with the vessel and will have to return to Hong Kong immediately."

"Good! And how are you planning to give this word?" asked Kai.

"By radio when you phone me from on board. We've agreed a code."

"Not good enough. Not on a night like this. You are coming with us."

TWENTY-FIVE

While Chang was off acquainting himself with the plumbing Davey Boy changed his shirt. He'd given up on the towel. He'd just put his jacket back on when the vibrations started. First, just a quiver in the floor, then up though his seat; then spreading to the walls, tables and windows. The engines were firing up. He heard/felt the thrum of the four MTU diesels building and sensed the motion in the deck/floor changing. He got up and looked through the window. Chang was right. There wasn't much to see. The roof of the jetty was too close to the side of the vessel but there was a gap and down through it he could see the hull's angle with the pier below. It was widening. They were nosing out from the quayside. They were getting underway.

Davey Boy pulled out his phone. The battery was seriously down but there was enough juice to make the call. The phone picked up on the fifth ring.

"Archie! We're on the ferry mate. The 10:30. We're just pulling away from the terminal now."

On board the noise and vibration were increasing and some sort of tinny announcement was coming out of a ceiling speaker. Davey Boy plugged one ear with a finger and winced trying to make out his friend's reply. "What? No, there was a delay. Chang's coming over with me. He'll explain later. Just make sure your guys are there to meet us. It looks like it's going to be a hell of a crossing. Oh, and thanks for the booking mate. It was a life saver."

The announcement had stopped but now a rendition of Mozart's fortieth warbled from the grill in the ceiling. The vessel was picking up speed; the basso hum of the engines deepening, the glittering Kowloon waterfront starting to feed across the rain streaked window glass. "What? Say again. You didn't make any booking?"

Davey Boy stiffened.

"Did you speak to Edward Tan?" He already knew the answer before he asked the question.

"Shit Archie! They're going to try and take us on the ferry."

TWENTY-SIX

The ferry was well underway but the sea wasn't making it easy. Minutes out from the shelter of the terminal and the wind had seriously strengthened. Gusting heavily with rain at thirty knots it hammered wave after wave eastward into the path of the oncoming vessel. The ferry, essentially a seventy-ton speedboat, hadn't been designed for such seas. It battled windward with all the grace of a bicycle crossing a ploughed field. Passengers hadn't been designed for such seas either. The farther the ferry sailed into the night the greater their unease and growing anxiety. Jarred, jolted, thrown and buffeted, the reassuring lights of Hong Kong disappearing into darkness, this wasn't the ride promised in the brochure.

Edward Tan was neither uneasy nor anxious. He was just plain scared. Bone scared. The deal was to provide the passes, arrange the clearances and then send a coded radio signal from the comfort of his office when the job was done. That was the deal. What wasn't the deal was to be out on a rain lashed two metre sea in the dark with four men about to kill two others. But he was here. It was about to happen. And there was nothing he could do about it.

"How many up top?" Kai, like the passengers, was not enjoying himself. The sooner he was back on the solid land of Hong Kong island the better. Tan had got them aboard under the guise of a work assessment inspection team ordered by the company. Laminated IDs had sealed the pretence and with the captain on side there had been no questions.

"Ten in first along with Chang and Smith in the left VIP cabin," Tan said.

The deck rose, hung for an instant, then dropped like an anvil. Kai winced. Was it imagination or were the bastard waves getting bigger?

"How long 'till we're south of Lantau Island?"

Tan spoke into his Motorola handset then listened. It was his on-board hot line to the bridge.

"Another fifteen minutes at least."

Kai made up his mind. The weather was deteriorating. He couldn't wait. Already turning back would be a task. Much farther out in the worsening seas and maybe they wouldn't be able to turn at all. It had been a wise move dragging Tan along. The original plan had been for the captain to brief the crew and authorise permissions for Kai and his team of plastic IDs to get the job done quietly and quickly. But with the captain up on the bridge the job had become a whole lot easier with the familiar face of the duty manager at his elbow. Tan had squealed like a pig but he'd ignored the little shit's protests. The man had taken the money fast enough. Now he was going to find out what earning it meant, the hard way.

TWENTY-SIX

"Okay, I'm bringing the operation forward. Get the ten down here now and move them up front with the others. Baggage stays where it is. Tell them whatever you like, safety procedure, bad weather, whatever, but get the upper deck cleared."

Tan blanched and swallowed. Discussion wasn't an option. The head of the cabin crew was an earnest looking thirty something. Tan waving his handset summoned him over.

"Message from the bridge. Radar has a storm front north-east beyond Lantau. It looks like it's coming our way. They need us to consolidate all top-deck passengers down here. I want you and one more with me. Keep everyone calm. Leave the baggage where it is. Emphasise this is purely a precautionary measure that will be over very soon. Once they come down make sure everyone moves up front with the other passengers. We need to keep everyone together. Okay?"

The head of the cabin crew nodded seriously. He waved over another crew member and briefed him quickly.

"Ready?" Tan asked.

The two cabin crew nodded.

"Good." Tan put his arm out and waited. The deck juddered, lifted then fell heavily. Tan dropped his arm.

"Go!"

The three blazers disappeared unsteadily up the stairs.

Kai, back in his aisle seat, turned to his team. They filled the front row of a central column of seating in the rear of the cabin immediately in front of the stairs. They were the only passengers back here. The better seats were all up front well forward of the stairwell. The three wise monkeys were not happy, but they didn't show it. Expressionless, they waited for instructions. There was a job to do and the sooner it was done the sooner they would be off this godforsaken boat. Kai had to raise his voice over the incessant throbbing of the engines.

"The top deck is being cleared of eyes. Tan will ensure Chang and Smith are left behind in the VIP cabin on the left-hand side. You know the plan. We go on my signal, take them out, retrieve the case, weight the bodies, lose them over the side and get home. In this weather no one will even notice. The chains are on the outside deck, in the side bins as arranged. Huang wants the boy played with for a while but this is not the night, so quiet and quick for both, okay?"

The three men nodded. They knew the job inside out. One way or another they'd done it a dozen times. This was just one more time to add to all the others.

First-class passengers started appearing on the stairs. Moaning and muttering they descended gingerly, led by the junior cabin crew. Kai waited, counting heads and anxious faces. Finally Tan and the head of the cabin crew appeared. Tan was the last off the staircase. He looked ashen. Giving Kai a small nod he ushered the last of the first-class passengers into the forward cabin area. It was time. Kai looked at his team and then jerked his head towards the stairs. They rose as one, crabbed carefully across the moving deck and began to climb.

TWENTY-SIX

The first-class cabin ran about a third of the length of the lower economy cabin. Apart from a scattering of bags, cases, coffee cups and magazines it was empty. Up here the oscillations of the vessel were markedly increased and they had to steady themselves on the seat backs, hand over hand, as they moved cautiously towards the rear VIP cabins. Two of the team had drawn knives, wicked looking stiletto blades, held unobtrusively down alongside their thighs. Kai had a weapon but there would be no need of it here. He had his pride and his reputation. He would take care of both the Gweilo and the boy with his bare hands. They were weak, especially the scar-faced Gweilo. He had felt it in him the moment they'd met.

The group reached the port VIP cabin. Kai motioned with his hand. His three men took up position around him on the moving deck.

"Ready?"

He took a firm hold on the door handle and pulled hard. The door swung back and Kai delivered the line he had been rehearsing all evening.

"Mr Smith, how nice to . . . "

The cabin was empty. Smith and Chang had gone.

Shit! Kai thought quickly. "Check the other cabin; the toilets, between the seat rows, up in the overhead lockers. Do it now!"

The search took less than a minute. If Smith and Chang were still inside on the top deck, they had become invisible. Kai scowled angrily. They weren't invisible; they were outside. They had to be. There was nowhere else they could be. They were outside on the viewing deck in the dark, in the sheeting rain, the spray and wind. And he would have to go out after them. *Bastards!*

Outside was a black maelstrom of wind and water. Lit dimly through the rear windows of the two VIP cabins the viewing deck rolled and heaved in the heavy seas. Within five seconds Kai and his men were as wet as if they had jumped overboard. Buffeted and shivering they clung to steel buttresses either side of the cabin housing door. In front of them the viewing deck sloped away towards the stern like a three-sided metal tray; slippery white painted steel, open at the end, water cascading over its wide lip into the night. Apart from the spray, the rain, the wind and four very wet and pissed off Chinamen, the deck was empty.

"Check the storage bins." Kai had to scream, his voice almost unintelligible in the timpani of wind, waves and rain. Grimacing through blinding spray he pointed at the metal bunkers flanking the cabin housing. His men fumbled at the latches. It was stupid. The bins wouldn't hide a dwarf but there was nowhere else. Or was there? He looked up behind him, rain rodding down into his face.

"The roof! Up on the roof!"

TWENTY-SIX

The ferry's roof, steel like the viewing deck, was flat, wide and some fifty feet long. The first third of the roof, overlooking the viewing deck, had some side protection. Triangular scallops of sheet steel on either side protruding like fins on an old Cadillac. Only a couple of feet high, they were more design indulgence than anything else. There were no access steps or ladders from the viewing deck. The only way up was by climbing onto the bulkhead bins flanking either side of the wide deck, standing, reaching up, gripping the roof's flat edge and doing a 'pull up and leg over' manoeuvre. It would have been difficult for a fit man with the ferry moored to a quayside. On a slippery black night with steepling waves it was just plain dangerous. Kai pointed at one of his bedraggled men, the tallest. The man, lean, wiry, supported by the other two clambered up on to the top of the port side bin where he crouched, arms out like a skateboarder. The twin hulls juddered into another wave and he stood abruptly, arms up, grabbing onto the lip of the roof above his head. Now he paused, feet anchored by the two men on the deck, arms extended, hands gripping the edge of the roof. He felt the momentum, the hulls dipping into the sea, gathering and then rising with the wave. He went with it, springing from his knees, pulling with his arms, his head and face coming up over the lip.

Invisible from the viewing deck Davey Boy lay prone. He was on his back, feet just short of the roof's edge, his right side pressed into the vertical angle of the port side Cadillac fin. The aluminium case clasped to his chest. He'd been waiting, face to the rain, back pressed hard into the steel roof, his mind focused, counting down the minutes. Twenty since his phone call to Archie. Fifteen since the urgent and revelatory skull session with Chang, ten since the first class cabin started to empty, five since he'd glimpsed Kai and his thugs through the glazed panel in the viewing deck door; three since he and Chang had scrambled up on to the only place left to go, the roof.

For the last two he'd lain still, under the lashing rain, ignoring the wet, the cold, waiting, listening for the inevitable; for Kai to come out onto the viewing deck, to realise and to look up. But Kai wouldn't be able to see beyond the roof's edge. He couldn't be sure what was up there. He would need to check and there would be doubt in his mind. They would have to come up over the bulkhead bins; it was the only way, either on the starboard side forty feet away where Chang waited or up in front of him. It would be a coin toss.

Davey Boy saw the hands first. *Heads I win.* Hands were good. They didn't have eyes and between them they marked a space just above the roof's edge, where a face would be appearing. Davey Boy brought his right knee to his chest. One hand came off the case and under his thigh, gripping, he pulled his leg farther back still, like a bow string, steadying it, holding the tension.

The face came up over the edge exactly where the hands had predicted. A curtain of wet black hair, squinting eyes, effort etched across a sour mouth. Davey Boy launched the kick viciously. The science was simple. It was the timing that was critical; thirty-seven pounds of leg, two pounds of shoe, thirty-six feet a second, seven-hundred-and fifty-foot pounds of impact. Less than a 357 Magnum, more than a Colt 45.

The heel of Davey Boy's shoe met the eyes in the face mid-blink and kept going. He'd aimed for the back of the man's head, not the front. The damage was terminal and instant. The front of the man's head wasn't a face anymore it was a four-minute egg that had been hit hard with a spoon. Shattered eye sockets, smashed teeth, splintered cheek bones and what had been a nose, back in mangled sinuses somewhere between the ears. Soundlessly the man dropped, hit the top of the gunwale, bounced sideways like he was filled with rubber and disappeared overboard into the night. Kai and his two remaining men stood momentarily bewildered. They assumed a horrible accident, a slip on wet metal, a handhold missed. The assumption lasted only a second as Davey Boy followed his kick over the edge of the roof; a dark shape against a black sky, falling with the rain eight feet into the upturned faces of the two men below. The Regiment's HALO instructor would have been proud. Case clasped to chest, feet together in a leg chute, knees slightly bent. He took out one thug with gravity alone. It wasn't a kill. The man or the deck or both, moved. Missing the head strike Davey Boy went second best. Two hundred and ten pounds, heels locked, thirty-two feet per second per second into the angle between neck and shoulder; the man's collar bone, sternum and upper ribs snapping and cracking like twigs on a campfire. They fell the last five feet together; Davey Boy on top, the man underneath, screaming like an infant. They hit hard. Bone against steel deck plate – no contest. Davey Boy rolled off the broken body onto his knees. The man was still screaming. He lifted the aluminium case and punched the riveted corner down through the man's face. The screaming stopped. Two down, two to go. Where was Chang?

Kai was moving. Vital seconds had him mired in disbelief. He'd come aboard intent on two men dying, but not his own. Smith wasn't weak. He was dangerous. He'd underestimated the man. It was a huge mistake. One he wouldn't make again. Forget bare hands. He pulled the Makarov from under his arm. Like most thugs Kai was not a marksman. He could hit a door if he was standing in front of it; if the room was well lit, if the floor wasn't pitching around, if the gun wasn't a sixty-year-old design with a double action trigger pull so heavy that it compromised first shot accuracy. But it was dark and the sea was rough. The trigger pull was heavy, and Davey Boy wasn't a door. He was a moving target on a moving deck fifteen feet away in the wind and rain. Lining up the barrel Kai tried to aim. Bladed foresight, notched rear sight, both gunmetal black on a rain filled night on a slippery pitching deck in the middle of the sea. Then he gave up. He just pointed and pulled the trigger.

With more chance of killing an unlucky fish than damaging Davey Boy the 9mm round disappeared unseen into the wind and rain, high and wide, out over the South China Sea.

TWENTY-SIX

Davey Boy turned, startled. Kai was crouched in the spray and wind, gun in hand, edging cautiously closer over the slippery deck. Much closer and Davey Boy would be that door in a well-lit room that Kai couldn't miss. But first Davey Boy had a problem with the knife waving in his face. A slim needle pointed nine-inch blade in the hand of Kai's remaining thug. The man was swinging it like an orchestra conductor. *Idiot!* If you want to fight like someone directing traffic, get an edged blade, Moron! Davey Boy dropped the case, blocking the dull edge of the blade easily on his forearm. It would leave a nasty bruise but not as nasty as the mark it would leave on the orchestra conductor. Blade blocked, he grasped up behind the hand holding the knife, applying the wrist lock. Tenkai-Kote-Hineri. Now it was a done deal. He swung the man's arm down then high up away from the body. He twisted under it a hundred-and-eighty degrees bringing the arm back down in a fluid movement behind the man's back, doubling him over in pain. Taking the knife was easy, like pulling up weeds. Giving it back was equally easy. He thrust the sharp tip down into the back of the man's exposed neck. An inch above the collar maybe a little more, his weight above the blade, forcing the needle point all the way through with the heel of his hand. *That's how to use a stiletto fool!*

Then there was one.

But Kai had a gun and now was as close as he needed to be.

The Makarov, tried, tested, reliable, wasn't the easiest handgun in the world to shoot well. Curving towards eight on a clock face the double action trigger needed a firm pull past six-thirty to make things happen. Kai, grinning like a madman, had the gun centred on Davey Boy's chest. He was five feet away. As good as in front of a door in a well-lit room. He was pulling the trigger hard through six forty-five when Chang hit him.

The yellow jacket was gone. Now it was just charcoal and black on a dark night with Kai looking the other way. The kidney punch, short and straight, was right out of a boxing gym. A body shot. The type a fighter throws into the heavy bag; leaning in, forehead close, feet anchored, elbow bent, waist and shoulder driving momentum through a straight forearm. But Chang wasn't in a gym. The smooth soles of his Italian leathers weren't anchored in spit and sawdust. They were sliding on wet slippery steel. The floor was moving and Kai was built like a tank. In another environment Kai would have gone down. But the timing was a second off; the momentum a fraction less than it should have been and Kai's obliques were like a pair of oven pans. Davey Boy stared, momentarily transfixed; Kai hunching over, stumbling, almost to his knees, then somehow standing and twisting in one jerky movement, swinging the Makarov like a knuckle duster into the side of Chang's head. Davey Boy was already moving. Five feet was all it would take.

Then the granddaddy of all the night's waves hit.

The deck tipped back savagely. There was no horizon. No

point of reference. No warning. Just black sky; black sea, black rain, an avalanche of foaming black water, the cold taste of salt and a tumbling, slithering, watery darkness.

TWENTY-SEVEN

Davey Boy was on his back halfway down the viewing deck. He felt light rain on his face, or was it spray? Dazed he opened his eyes. Pain sparked in the back of his head. Had Kai fired? He hadn't heard it. He turned slowly on to his knees. Measured, cautious movements; testing, feeling things out. Nothing appeared broken. Everything seemed connected, working.

He looked up. Light from the two VIP cabin windows reflected wetly off the white deck. In front of him the shape and bulk of a body lay contorted caught up against the starboard gunwale, a knife in its neck. He turned his head. Twenty feet beyond the black puddle of his own shadow was another body. Face down splayed near the lip of the viewing deck. It was Chang. He wasn't moving. Between him and Chang, Kai was clambering unsteadily to his feet. His hands were empty. The rain had stopped. It must have been spray on his face. The wind too seemed to be lessening. Davey Boy filled his lungs with wet salt air and risked standing. So far so good. He scanned the deck. The body of the second thug was gone. He looked for the Makarov. He looked for the aluminium case. They were gone too. Apart from Chang, Kai, the corpse and himself, the deck was empty. Scoured clean. Then the laughing started.

Kai had tried to stand but had slipped and fallen back down on his pants. He sat, legs splayed in front of him, like a child sent to the naughty corner. He was looking into the sky, arms held up wide, laughing like a crazy man. Then he stopped. He tried standing again and this time he made it. He looked at Davey Boy. There were maybe ten feet between them on the shifting deck. He smiled. It was a grim, careless, fatalistic smile. He looked to where Davey Boy had looked; past Davey Boy's shoulder at the corpse with a knife in its neck, back over his own shoulder at Chang, around the otherwise empty deck as big as a badminton court, shifting in shadow, wind and spray. He seemed not to care about the aluminium case or the Makarov. Still with the smile he stretched out an arm towards Davey Boy, a broad index finger pointing. It was a pretentious, almost theatrical gesture.

"You, me, Smith. You, me. I kill you now."

The ponytail had gone. Kai's hair, shiny like wet leather, plastered about his face and thick neck. His sodden cotton suit, still double-buttoned, clung wetly, sculpting, defining his powerful physique.

"Well you got the first part right," said Davey Boy coldly.

The easing of the wind had lessened the swell. Feeling the undulations under him Davey Boy stepped forward across the wet chequer plate.

Two feet, three feet, the wind ruffling his hair, arms loose by his side, hands open. Four feet, five feet, easy strides, controlled, balanced.

TWENTY-SEVEN

Six feet, seven feet, Kai's dark eyes widening, smile gone.

Eight feet, Kai's left arm and shoulder dropping minutely, a hint of back swivel in his left hip, all signalling the beginning of the right footed kick. Nine feet, the kick, on its way, fast, hard, chest high.

Ten feet, contact!

But not as Kai expected.

Davey Boy's walk to Kai across the deck had been straight and direct; always the shortest distance between two points, his stride regular, pace constant. Kai had looked down that line. He'd focused down that line. He'd adjusted speed of approach down that line. He'd planned down that line and at the end he sent his kick down that line. Bad move. Davey Boy wasn't on that line anymore and his speed was up big time from constant. Stepping in from the left, Kai still on one leg like an oriental Heron, he hit hard where the beak would have been. Not with a fist. That was for amateurs; too many small fragile bones. But with a length of human two-by-four - a forearm; two rods of bone wrapped tight with tendons and compacted muscle. A man on two legs would have had difficulty standing with a broken face. Kai, on one leg, had no chance. *In through the front door out through the back.* Kai collapsed like a sink hole in a California road, Davey Boy following the body down to the chequer plate. *No respite.* Grabbing a foot of wet black hair, better than rope, he lifted Kai's smashed and bleeding face off the deck. Then he let go and helped gravity with the bottom of his shoe, stamping Kai's head back into the steel chequer plate.

Rinse and repeat. He did it a second time to make sure; a third for Chang, a fourth for the money and a fifth just because it made him feel better. Then there were none.

Davey Boy sat on the wet deck feeling the movement of the waves under him. He looked back off the stern. The wake, fifteen feet below, churned a wide dirty white trail thirty feet before the dark swallowed it. His head ached, his right arm hurt like hell, he was wet to his bones, he was cold and his white shirt wasn't white anymore. He breathed deep, slowly, letting the cortisol and adrenaline ebb, his heart rate slow. The weather had broken. The ferry seemed smoother, quicker or was it imagination? He needed to check Chang. He stood, stepping over Kai's pulpy misshapen head. It lay on the chequer plate like a spoiled English breakfast; red, white, black, unguent and oozing. *You me Smith. You, me. Yeah? Well not anymore.*

Before Davey Boy could reach him, Chang moved, emitting a groan.

"Shit. I feel sick."

"Easy mate. Keep still. It's a concussion. You've been hit in the head. But it's over now. Just take your time."

Davey Boy, kneeling, gingerly turned Chang's head. A livid swelling had closed his right eye. His left was blackened and an ugly lumpy contusion filled the space between his right ear and cheek bone.

"Messy huh?"

TWENTY-SEVEN

Davey Boy smiled in the dark, relieved. Black humour was a good sign.

"I've seen a helluva lot worse. Just hold off getting a passport photo anytime soon."

Chang winced and slowly sat up. He raised a hand and cautiously felt his face.

"Shit. I'm really screwed.

"Forget it, lady killer. Two weeks tops and you'll be back to normal. Can you try and stand?"

Slowly Chang levered his feet under himself and stood shakily with Davey Boy's arm under his. They started an awkward shuffle back towards the upper deck door.

"Shit Davey I'm sorry I messed up."

"Can it, Chang. No one messed up. Certainly not you."

"I didn't hit him hard enough."

"Hard enough? You hit the bastard hard enough to save my life, mate. I think that's plenty hard enough. Don't you?"

They made the last few steps to the door, when Chang paused.

"What about the others? I saw you jump. I came down off the roof as quick as I could. That's when I saw that bastard Kai with the gun. I should have taken him out Davey, collegiate champion, two years. I should have taken him."

"Yeah? Well the bastard was a tough cookie. Not any more though. Same as the other three shits. Anyway enough of that we need to get you inside and warmed up."

Davey Boy felt the warmth and brightness as they entered the cabin, his spirits lifting.

"Right mate. You sit here, warm up and rest. I need to go back out and tidy up. Shouldn't take more than a couple of minutes then I'll go and sort out that weasel, Tan. I reckon we should be almost to Macau by now then we'll get you properly taken care of."

Chang nodded, slumping back into the first-class seat and closing his eyes. Davey Boy walked back to the viewing deck door. Steeling himself he opened it quickly and stepped out a second time into the wet, cold, darkness. There were only two; knife-in-the-neck man and Kai. Knife-in-the-neck man was closest. It took longer than a few minutes. Heavy bastards even without the chains he'd conveniently found in the starboard bunker bins. Finally with a lot of dragging, lifting and pushing, they were gone; job done, over the side to their just deserts, whatever that meant. Davey Boy retreated thankfully to the light and warmth of the first-class cabin. Chang seemed a little better. His breathing less laboured. He still looked like the elephant man but that would pass. Davey Boy let him sleep and quietly padded down the stairs to the deck below. He saw Tan immediately. The fat little twat was skulking no doubt waiting for Kai's return. Tan saw him too. He turned pale, a look of pure shock on his pudding of a face. He didn't move as Davey Boy walked straight up to him and grasped him hard by the shoulder.

TWENTY-SEVEN

"You never came back with the towel Tan. You promised. But you never did. Now look at me."

Tan swallowed, panic in his face.

"Now this is what I need you to do Tan. And I need you to do it right now. Do you understand?"

Eyes wide Tan nodded.

"My friend has had a bad fall upstairs. He needs immediate medical attention. I need dry towels, as many as you can get. I don't care. I want a thermos of hot coffee, plenty of sugar in it and two mugs. I want whatever hot food you have available. Just bring it up whatever you have. I want your cell phone too. I need to make some calls and I want you to make sure this ferry docks in Taipa terminal Macau in the next fifteen minutes. Did you get all of that, Mr Tan?"

Tan kept looking over Davey Boy's shoulder towards the stairs. Davey Boy caught the look and bent to Tan's ear.

"Kai and his men are gone you little shit. As far as my friend and I are concerned we never saw them. We never even knew they were on the ferry. It is best you do the same. Do we understand each other?"

Handing over his phone Tan nodded silently. Then he turned and almost ran back to the galley.

Davey Boy squelched his way back up the stairs. Whatever Tan was involved in was finished. The man was clearly petrified but he almost seemed relieved too.

Chang was back awake. Davey Boy smiled.

"Medical attention is on the way along with hot food and drink. Mind you on this tub don't expect more than a few paracetamols. Also some dry towels. I'm going to phone ahead and brief Archie. We need to get you to hospital and I need dry clothes."

Chang listened. He seemed to be perkier by the minute but with shock and concussion one never knew. Davey Boy's main concern was the lad's skull. A fracture or a bleed was always a possibility.

"But what about the chips, Davey? Where's the case? I haven't seen it." Chang peered at him through the ring blackening his one good eye.

"The case disappeared overboard when the wave hit. I guess it's at the bottom of sea. It's got some company at least."

Davey Boy started walking away down the aisle between the seats.

"Shit Davey. That was *everything*. That's what we risked everything for. I can't believe it."

The anguish in Chang's voice was painful.

Davey Boy stopped, reached up, cracked an overhead locker and took down the carry-on.

"Yeah. It's a helluva shame. It was a damn fine case."

He shook the carry-on vigorously. It rattled like a bag of buttons.

"But I wouldn't lose any sleep over it, especially with what's in here."

Shocked, elated, Chang tried to laugh. It was the wrong move. He winced in pain.

"You switched the chips."

Davey Boy walked back with the carry-on smiling. There were footsteps on the stairs, and he smelled hot coffee.

"Well what else did you expect me to do while you were off pissing all over your shoes?"

TWENTY-EIGHT

Using a heavy tablespoon, Chris stirred milk into a chipped mug of coffee. It sounded like he was ringing a bell. Done, he hurled the spoon across the table. It skidded on the Formica, kept going, and hit the stone floor. No chimes this time, just a flat metallic clatter. The spoon lay on a powdery film of dried milk and sawdust like an accusation. For days he'd swept that bloody floor. He'd swept it 'till the bristles dropped off the brush. And every morning it was the same; another grotty film of grainy powder on every flat surface. Since Davey had buggered off to the other side of the planet he'd given up. He hadn't swept at all. Let that lazy sod Jason take a turn on the broom for once. But he never had. So now the stuff was everywhere. He could even see his own footprints in it. But so what! He didn't give a shit anymore.

Chris was sick and he was angry. His throat was sore, his body ached, the pain behind his eyes throbbed like a mother and his head was so blocked it hurt. He'd unlocked the door of the bat cave at eight. It was now past ten. It was Monday morning; grey, wet, miserable and he'd been sitting looking at the floor, drinking bad coffee and stoking the hormones for more than two hours. He lifted the mug and took a swig. The nut-brown liquid was hot but that was all. He put the mug on the table and held his face in his hands. Self-pity welled up in him like an overflowing toilet. He felt awful; bloody useless, a total waste of space. Good for a joke or two and to sweep the bloody floor but not much else. Well he was pig sick of it all. They could all bloody stuff it; the bleedin' lot of 'em.

A phone trilled. The sound was sudden and startling in the empty space. Chris took the burner out of his pocket. He put it on the table and let it ring. He couldn't be bothered. After a dozen trills it went silent. Thank God for that. He took another mouthful of coffee. It tasted like shit. His headache was worse and the pain behind his eyes hammering. What the hell was he doing sitting huddled in the bloody bat cave? He should be home in bed for God's sake. But then he would have to put up with the bickering and the nagging.

The burner trilled again. He looked at it on the table. It kept ringing like it wasn't going to stop this time. *Shit!* He picked it up.

"What!" His voice came out as a rasping croak.

"Are you okay, mate? I missed you this morning." Jason sounded concerned.

"What the hell do you care?"

"Well . . . we're mates, and I just thought, you know, it would be good to check you're okay?"

"Well I'm not, so now you know."

"Yeah, you sound pretty rough. Have you come down with something?"

Chris didn't answer.

"So where are you?"

"Where the bloody hell do you think I am? Cleaning up after you, that's where."

"Jesus Christ! There's no need to get your knickers in a twist. I just wanted to know you were okay is all."

"Yeah I bet. More likely checking to see what I've screwed up this time."

There was a moment's silence at Jason's end. Then he spoke again, irritation in his voice.

"What the hell's got into you? If you're feeling like shit I get it. But there's no need to get the hump with me mate."

"Just piss off and leave me alone."

The line disconnected. Chris hadn't expected it. He looked at the phone in his hand. Three bars. A strong signal.

Jason had put the bloody phone down on him.

Bastard! He threw the mug of coffee.

Jason sat at the back of the class thinking, but not about the lesson. Chrissy had sounded in a bad way but that was no excuse for acting like an arsehole. He knew his friend. Most of the time a comic, a jokester, but when he got into one of his occasional black dog strops the best thing was to leave him well alone. He usually came out of it after a couple of days. But Davey Boy was due back anytime now. They didn't have a couple of days. And whichever way he looked at it, Chrissy needed to be dosed up back home in bed not hanging around an empty bat cave feeling sorry for himself. He would try again in the lunch break.

A trilling phone broke the silence of the bat cave a third time. It was 12:45. This time Chris didn't wait. He was aching, blocked, suffering with the mother of all headaches and he was ready. Over the airwaves his voice sounded glottal and thick.

"Hanging me out to dry gives you a cheap thrill does it?"

"Bloody hell, you told me to piss off. So I did."

"Yeah? Always someone else to blame with you."

Jason was exasperated; his patience fraying.

"I don't know what you want me to say. I think you need to get home. You sound like shit."

"Piss off tellin' me what to do. If it wasn't for me you'd still be sat on all those bloody bin-bags like a prize dick or more likely locked up by now."

"Shut up you idiot!

"Idiot? Yeah! That's me alright. A prize bloody idiot. Packing money and sweeping milk powder for days while you sit around on your arse drinking coffee. Well I'm done. You can sod off and find some other poor bugger to do your dirty work. See how they like it."

Chris hadn't heard the line go dead. Jason had disconnected again. How long had he been ranting to himself? He sneered at the phone. Bloody typical! He switched it off and hurled it into a far brick corner of the bat cave. He heard the smash and the clatter of breaking plastic. Jason wasn't the only one who could destroy tacky plastic telephones. It didn't make him feel any better. It was past one. He walked across his own powdery footprints to the door. He stepped out, slammed the door behind him and walked off, then stopped. *Shit for brains.* He walked back to the door and locked it. Then he turned and sloped off. He was going to bed and no one had better be stopping him on the way.

TWENTY-NINE

Thirty-five-thousand feet above the Indian Ocean, the Airbus A380 chased the dawn towards London. Cossetted in the forward compartment Davey Boy sat back and watched the bubbles rise. The champagne wasn't vintage but it didn't need to be. It was chilled, the colour of freshly cut straw and delicious. Sleep was out. He'd tried but it wasn't working; too much nervous energy in the system. He would sleep when he got back. His bruises ached. His head was sore, and his forearm carried a welt six inches long. But he'd had worse. In the carry-on in a clear plastic file was what he'd come for; a sheaf of documents needing only to be signed and sealed. The best thing of all though was Chang. The diagnosis had been straightforward enough; concussion. No bleeding, no bones broken. He was young and fit. A week of bed rest and the doctors predicted a complete recovery. There wouldn't even be a scar. The ferry company had wanted to know what the hell he'd been doing on an outside deck at night in a rainstorm halfway to Macau. But Chang, sticking to the story, couldn't remember and anyway 'shouldn't the door to the outside deck have been locked'? Very quickly there'd been no more questions.

Adjusting his position in the wide seat, Davey Boy took another sip of champagne. He tried to let his mind slide back over the past two days. It wasn't easy. Nestled in comfort high above a darkened earth he felt separate, insulated from events that had happened far below. They felt unreal now, hazy, indistinct. Davey Boy knew the symptoms well. He wished he didn't. Mission fatigue syndrome. Events and details blurring into one another like the disjointed clips of a surreal film spliced together by a stranger. The answer was always focus. Training helped. Pain helped even more. He looked at his reflection in the black well of the window. Distorted, tired, gaunt. Not pretty. He closed his eyes against the blackness. Thoughts, emotions and memories of the past forty-two hours swirling and agitating in his mind like the bubbles in his glass. *Focus*. Sighing he dug the edge of a fingernail hard into the red welt on his forearm and let the film play again.

The sleek blue ferry burbled up alongside Taipa's concrete quay nearly twenty minutes late. The weather had been a bitch, but it was beginning to break with a promise of calming seas and clearing skies. Davey Boy and Chang were the last passengers off. They waited for the crowds to clear then together walked slowly away from the sea up a gentle ramp into the arrivals section of the Macau ferry terminal. There was only a slight delay at immigration. The official grimaced at Chang's face but a hard fall in rough seas was no crime. It was late. The official was tired and he waved them through.

TWENTY-NINE

Landside Archie was waiting, six men with him. All dark suited with curly cords in their ears. They looked smart and hard. Archie, his pale freckled face a mixture of concern, anger and embarrassment, looked anything but. Swinging lankily between crutches with a stuck-out leg plastered to mid-thigh he looked like a blue-eyed, ginger-bearded, Ahab searching for a whale. Davey Boy dropped the carry-on, cautiously navigated the stuck-out leg and embraced his friend.

"Bloody hell, Davey. I'm so sorry. Is Chang okay?"

"Hit in the head. He needs medical treatment."

"It's covered. There's an ambulance outside. What about you?"

"Nothing a cold beer, a hot shower and some dry clothes won't fix."

"That I can handle. Okay, let's get out of here. No need to talk, too many ears. You can bring me up to speed when we get to the hotel."

Taipa terminal was done for the night. The weather had seen to that. No more sailings in or out until first light. The group moved across the emptying hall towards the exit. Two men helping Chang, the other four alert on the flanks. Archie's ambulance was a private ride from the Kiang Wu hospital. It was parked outside in a drop-off zone by the terminal's main entrance. With a weak smile, a thumbs up and two curly cords riding shotgun Chang went one way. Davey Boy, in a dark Mercedes people carrier with Archie, the four remaining men and the carry-on, went the other.

The boutique's manager was a trier. He was pushing the silk as hard as he could. A paisley patterned tie and matching pocket square. Davey Boy was having none of it. He looked at himself in the full-length mirror; light weight grey suit, navy shirt, shoes, alligator belt, even new socks and underwear. Apart from his tousled hair still damp from the shower he could have been selling upmarket insurance.

"This'll do," he murmured at himself.

Archie nodded at the manager.

"Write it up. Invoice the cashiers in the morning. Add the same again for your time and inconvenience. The hotel will pay."

The boutique manager, driven in at an ungodly hour to unlock his shop in the hotel's foyer, went home a whole lot happier than he'd arrived.

The room in the New Era was much like the rest of the hotel; rectangular, sharp angles, tinted glass, pale carpet, blond wood. It could have been a management office in a Scandinavian office block. Albeit an office block with seven floors of mirrored lifts, piped muzak and pop-art crystal light fitments. The effect was clean, comfortable and slick but ultimately boring. It had been contrived at great expense to be just that. Guests could sleep, shit and screw in their scandi-minimalist boxes but for everything else the management wanted them out and next door where the real action was; the casino.

TWENTY-NINE

Davey Boy had seen it on the run in. A windowless, ground-floor, single-story block bolted on to the side of the hotel. Small by Macau standards, it could have covered half a football field. The main entrance was through a scaled-down fibreglass Greek Parthenon stuck on the front. Along the top of the fake temple, about where the Elgin marbles would have been if they hadn't been thieved, bright blue neon announced in a flowing brush stroke script 'The New Era Hotel and Casino'. *Where real money is separated from real fools,* thought Davey Boy. But that part wasn't written in neon. It wasn't written anywhere.

"Bloody hell Davey you totalled all four."

It was a statement, not a question. Archie sitting awkwardly on the low king-size bed was fiddling with the locks on an empty black leather briefcase.

"Had to, Arch. No choice."

"Well you haven't lost your touch, buddy."

"Touch? It was plain stupid luck. They underestimated. One gun and a bunch of knives. The other way around and it would have been goodnight Vienna."

"Yeah? Well luck will only take you so far mate. Sometimes you need a bit of something extra to get the job done. You know that. You taught me."

Davey Boy hid the beginnings of a tired smile in the hotel towel.

"Maybe when we were young and invincible Arch; not anymore. The blunt truth of it, I just wasn't quick enough. By rights it should be me at the bottom of the South China, not that ponytailed idiot, and it would have been if not for Chang. Believe me. Most would have bottled it. He didn't. He's a helluva kid. You were right about that. I only hope he's okay."

"The kid's half Irish, Davey. Doesn't look it but he's tough as three-dollar steak. He'll be okay."

"Yeah. Well I hope so. I owe him big time."

Dispensing with the towel, Davey Boy threw it into a corner of the room.

"What about Huang?" asked Archie. "Do you think there'll be any comeback?"

"I'm not sure of squat right now, Arch. But I shouldn't think so. Not directly anyway. Huang's a mother sized shit but he's not stupid. You know too much about each other. He's ahead of the game financially so unless Ponytail was his brother or something I think it's pretty much a stalemate."

Archie pushed the briefcase aside.

"Yeah, you're probably right. But I'm keeping the guard up for a while yet. If Huang wants a fight he knows where to come. Otherwise he can just piss off and find another casino to gamble in. Shit! I can't believe I made such a mistake about the bastard."

"It happens Arch. Don't sweat it."

Davey Boy took off the jacket and trousers, put them on a hangar and sat down in shirt, shorts and socks next to Archie on the bed.

"Sorry mate but I need a kip. Just forty minutes. Then I need to get across to the Wynn. Can you spare some men?"

TWENTY-NINE

"Same ones do? The lads that met you off the ferry?"

"Works for me. Thanks Arch."

"I'd come myself but . . . " Archie gestured towards his crutches propped up against the bedhead.

Davey Boy smiled.

"Old school, mate. What you need is a wheeled Zimmer frame with go-faster stripes."

"And what you need apart from a new arsehole is a decent case for the chips." Archie pushed the briefcase he'd been fiddling with to Davey Boy.

"You can't go waltzing into the Wynn with that duffel over your shoulder. I've arranged a high-stakes table and you'll look more like a prize prick than you usually do."

Davey Boy took the case and slid it over the carpet with his foot to nestle up alongside the carry-on.

"Thanks. And talking about prize pricks have you sorted the lawyer for the morning?"

"Booked for ten here in the hotel. He's coming over on the eight-thirty. I've given him an outline briefing, but he sounded confident. It shouldn't be a problem."

"It sure as hell shouldn't. He's getting paid enough. But my main concern is time. I can't be hanging around. I need to get back."

"Roger that. As I said, I've briefed him, he's bringing paperwork, an assistant and I've put the hotel's business bureau at his disposal. It's all good, mate. Now just get your head down and I'll check back in forty." Archie stood with some difficulty, hopping on one leg, reaching for the crutches.

"One more thing Arch. Can you check out flight connections back to London avoiding Hong Kong? Any time after mid-afternoon would be good. I want to check in with Chang before I leave."

Archie pivoted towards the door, all blond wood and steel fittings.

"No problem oh master. Now get your bloody head down."

Unlike the New Era, the Wynn didn't have a Parthenon. It was bigger and older; a sprawling mass in downtown Macau. Set behind pools and fountains it was fronted by a curving twenty-two story façade of coppery glass. Inside nineteenth century aristocratic Parisian brothel met gilded Sultanic Palace in a gambler's paradise. Sistined ceilings, brocaded drapes, crystal chandeliers, half a mile of woven motif-filled carpets, acres of cream, ivory and red in rich textured hues and enough gold leaf to cover a forest of spring oak. Overkill clearly wasn't a word in the Wynn's lexicon.

The plan itself was simple; Roulette, American rules, private high stakes room, betting red or black. It needed to look good. Thirty minutes at the table or a stop-loss at three-hundred-thousand. Bailing at whichever came first. Then cash out and back to the New Era, escort in tow, with the Wynn's receipt in his pocket. The casino would wire the money to Archie's account across town. Clean money, good to go. It was a simple plan; a good plan, a plan Davey Boy could follow in his sleep. If it was working.

TWENTY-NINE

But it wasn't.

Not by a long way.

A working plan would have had Davey Boy losing. But he wasn't even close; three reds, a black, another three reds, another black. He hadn't been wrong once. And he was letting the winnings ride; his stake doubling with each bet. Why not? All he was risking was the first fifty-thousand-dollar chip he'd thrown on the table. Black wins again! Two in a row. Not possible, surely. But it was. His first bet on the table had doubled his money. He'd doubled it up nine successive times since. Davey Boy looked at his Rolex. He'd been betting nearly an hour. If his commitment to the tables didn't look good by now it never would. His body ached and he needed at least five good hours sleep before the lawyer in the morning. What the hell. One more spin and home. Double or nothing. He bet black again. It couldn't be three in a row, could it?

THIRTY

"So run it by me again," said Davey Boy.

He'd slept five hours solid. Like a dead man. It had done him better than good. Fifteen lengths of the New Era's pool, a hot shower, breakfast and he'd risen like Lazarus. Fit for purpose and good to go. Even with the bumps and bruises.

"It's simple really," said the international legal financial specialist from Hong Kong.

It wasn't.

Immaculately suited, whip-smart and slicker than Teflon the specialist explained patiently one more time.

"Anonymity is the objective. To achieve this, funds you allocate will need to be wired across multiple international borders. With your agreement I propose to set up a Singapore trust managed by a shell company in the Seychelles. The shell company will be owned by another trust set up in Luxembourg managing bank accounts in Ras Al Khaima. The trustees appointed will manage the funds and any assets acquired by the trusts for the nominated beneficiaries, in this case . . .," Teflon man glanced down at his notes, ". . . your two young nephews."

"I see," said Davey Boy. He didn't. It was all smoke and mirrors. But he guessed that was the point.

"And what are the costs involved in all of this?"

Teflon man didn't blink.

"Two trusts, the Seychelles incorporation, the Arab bank accounts, four nominee trustees, all-in-all seven-hundred-thousand in set up fees and two-hundred-and-fifty-thousand Hong Kong per year afterwards for maintenance and provision of service."

Davey Boy steepled fingers together under his chin and let loose the thousand-yard stare. The costs were way over market. But the specialist was up there with the best. It was also the last piece of the jigsaw and time was against him.

"That's a lot of bills," he said.

"It buys a lot of anonymity," replied Teflon man.

"How soon to get it up and running?"

"The details you've given are all we need. It should be possible to get everything set up and ready for signatures in a week."

"Do it," said Davey Boy. "And I want all documents with me before I leave tonight. Communicate with me via this." He handed over an innocuous-looking smart phone. At Davey Boy's request Archie had delivered three of the devices with the breakfast orange juice.

"It's military grade security. Encrypted end-to-end. Use it just like your own hand-held."

Teflon man took the device and looked at it with interest before popping it in his pilot briefcase.

"And you have something else for me?"

THIRTY

"I'm sorry?"

"The funds?"

Davey Boy fixed Teflon man with a cold stare.

"Mr Bell has the funds. On my authority he will transfer instalments to your client account. Please liaise with him before you leave."

Teflon man nodded, replacing folders back into the pilot case.

"I will, of course, need to know the amounts."

Davey Boy picked up a paper coaster and scribed a series of numbers on it in biro. Leaning over the low table he offered the circle of paper. "Instalment number one", he said.

"There will be further instalments when arrangements have proved themselves."

Teflon man took the coaster, looked at it, and looked back at Davey Boy. The expression in his eyes had changed.

"It's going to be a great pleasure doing business with you Mr Gilroy," he said smiling.

Immediately after the meeting Teflon man met with Archie. The two men had agreed a plan and things were moving. The first transfer would be made later that day. Davey Boy gave the third encrypted handset to Archie. He didn't need to be told how to use it. There was just one more thing Davey Boy needed to do and it was at the Kiang Wu hospital. Archie and two of his smart hard men had accompanied him.

Davey Boy smiled inwardly remembering Chang in the hospital bed, the nurses fawning over him like a lost puppy; a lost puppy lapping it up. He and Archie stayed an hour spinning the breeze and when he got up to leave, he'd given the young man an envelope. Inside was a cheap postcard from the New Era showing the fibreglass Parthenon in all its neon glory. He'd scrawled a message on the back:

Chang,

Something for the wardrobe.

I owe you mate, big time.

Yours,

Davey

Taped under the scrawl were two $500,000 gambling plaques from the Wynn. He hadn't cashed it all out.

It was a short distance from the hospital to the airport. It was a short distance between anywhere in Macau. Archie, Davey Boy and the carry-on were in the back of the people carrier. Up front driving and riding shotgun were the two smart hard men who had accompanied them from the New Era. True to his word Archie was not letting his guard down just yet.

"Hell of a few days, Davey".

"Tell me about it. You do know we're getting too old for this shit, don't you?"

"Getting! I'm already there, mate. Look at me."

Davey Boy looked at his friend's plastered leg and smiled.

"Tell you what though, Arch. We're both still here. There's more than a few who would have bet against that back in the day. And isn't that the point? Still being here? It sure beats the crap out of the alternative."

THIRTY

It was Archie's turn to smile.

"So we're all good Davey?"

"What?"

"You know? Huang; the ferry, the whole shit bag. It was all down to me whichever way you cut it."

Davey Boy put hand on his friend's shoulder.

"We're better than good Arch. You were sold a line. It happens. Everything since I couldn't have done without you. So now I'm going to get on this plane, fly off and you're going to finish it. It's more than trust Arch. We're brothers. We've done this together. So no more selling yourself short right?"

Archie put a hand over the hand on his shoulder and clasped it warmly. "Thanks Davey", he said simply.

"Oh, and by the way. Keep back a hundred thou from the lawyer. There's some ginger bell-end in Macau I promised it to. And that's sterling mate. Not Hong Kong dollars.

Archie had booked him first class all the way. Departing on the 18:25 Scoot Air flight into Singapore and then onto the 23:30 SQ A380 flight into London Heathrow. He had insisted the New Era pay.

"You're a big fish now Davey, a proper whale. Officially we hope you'll be laying your money on our tables when you come back. Unofficially it's the bloody least I can do for the screw up mate."

Davey Boy hadn't been shy in accepting and at the departure gates he had embraced the other man like a brother. Archie, unable to reciprocate, had simply stood straight, arms down on his crutches, with a grin as wide as two axe handles.

The Singapore connection had been tight, just an hour, but he only had the carry-on. The flight was direct, all thirteen hours of it, and God willing he would be on the ground before seven am London time.

A double electronic chime disturbed the film playing in his head. Blinking, Davey Boy looked up. The seatbelt sign was illuminated and a warm female voice was flowing from hidden speakers.

"Ladies and gentlemen please ensure your seatbelts are fastened and remain seated until the seatbelt sign is switched off. We anticipate an area of slight turbulence ahead. Thank you."

The anonymous dulcet tones disappeared into silence and Davey Boy shuffled in his seat checking the seat belt buckle. He hoped the word 'slight' was accurate. He took a sip of the remaining champagne. His nose wrinkled. It had become warm and flat. He checked his watch and then the flight map on the digital display monitor on a stalk by his seat. On the screen the little white plane was way off the sea now and somewhere over the 'stans of middle Asia. The stats on the screen said minus sixty outside and six hours to London. They were on schedule.

Job done. Almost.

THIRTY- ONE

The burner looked like it had been smashed with a hammer. Its thin glass screen shattered, crazed with a spider's web of radiating cracks. Split apart, its cheap plastic case lay in bits. The back cracked through like a piece of dark chocolate; the keyboard side ripped away, its rigid plastic, thin as paper, punctured with lines of little holes where the rubberised keys should have been. Freed from the plastic clamshell the phone's exposed innards laid half submerged in a drift of sand a foot-and-a-half deep. But it wasn't sand. It was a dirty mix of milk powder and sawdust. And it wasn't a beach. It was a stone floor deep in the angle of two of the bat cave's thick brick walls. The burner would never connect a voice call again. Chris had seen to that. But it wasn't quite dead. Not yet.

The largest electronic communications monitoring station in the world sprawls not over anonymous American farmland, Russian steppe or Chinese desert but a square mile of the North Yorkshire Dales, near the pretty Georgian Spa town of Harrogate. Codenamed 'Moonpenny', RAF Menwith Hill is a strange installation. It doesn't have runways or aeroplanes or hangars or control towers. But it does have giant golf balls.

Thirty-three at the last count. Massive dimpled white structures, some twenty storeys high, sprouting from the Yorkshire fields like something out of science fiction. Owned by the British Ministry of Defence, this extraordinary facility is administered by USA's National Security Agency and has been for over fifty years. Inside the protective golf balls, the giant geodesic radar domes, are the arrays of powerful radar antennae giving function to this bizarre establishment. For 'Moonpenny' is a satellite uplink station. The biggest on the planet and a crown jewel in the world's most extensive, global mass-surveillance network; the ultra-secret, project ECHELON.

A Cold War baby back in the day, ECHELON started life a simple spy programme developed to intercept transmissions from the early Soviet satellites. Fifty years on, fuelled by oceans of tax dollars, accelerating technology and mountains of paranoia, and baby isn't baby anymore. It's a behemoth; a monstrous cyber-fed arachnid; whose colossal electronic web envelops the globe, capturing indiscriminately virtually every phone conversation, email message and digital data transmission on the planet. But sitting in the SIGINT pit under Menwith Hill's main headquarters building, Technical Sergeant Jackson Schulz, USAF, didn't see it that way. He couldn't have cared less if he tried. Bored out of his mind, he sat hunched over his workstation, watching the bright digits of the signal intelligence packets scroll down his screen. The SIGINT pit was underground. It was like someone had dug a big hole thirty metres down and laid a giant ring doughnut at the bottom of it; a reinforced concrete doughnut five metres high, fifty metres across and hollow. The experts called it a Taurus but to Jackson it was a doughnut. Inside, following the outside wall in a great circle were the individual SIGINT monitoring stations; narrow cubby-holed workstations with monitors attached. Three metres inside this circle was another circle of workstations and inside that another. Altogether there were five concentric circles engaging a maximum of two-hundred-and-fifty personnel in a hermetically sealed, humidity controlled, LED lit doughnut. And Jackson Schultz hated it.

Jackson was a jock; six-foot-three of prime blond Wisconsin manhood. But he was one of the gifted. God had also given him a brain to do more than just keep his ears apart. Both athletic and bright, Jackson was into his third year with the 451st USAF Intelligence Squadron. 'Join the Air force and see the world', the slogan had said. And he had, straight from college. But, apart from his furloughs home, it hadn't said the world would be one of sheep, cows, strange accents, warm beer, and shit ball games.

The glowing digits rolled down the screen, Jackson's eyes following them, but his mind elsewhere. The big game was on Saturday. Baseball, a proper ball game, not that British crap where you could play for five days and still not have a winner. The base had its own diamond and fielded competing teams. He was shortstop for the predictably named 'Harrogate

Hustlers'. The league was tiny but tough with only two other teams; the 'Menwith Muscle' and the 'Satelliters', both made up of civilian contractors. The 'Hustlers' were military men and proud of it. Forget playing five days. Baseball guaranteed a winner in the time it took to take the fast train to London. A win against the 'Muscle' and they would top the tiny league. It would be payback and he was looking forward to it.

There were about a thousand personnel on the base. A little over half were American the rest Brits, mostly in supporting roles from GCHQ. Service personnel were way down though. Only forty with the balance made up of civilians and commercial contractors. The base was pretty much self-contained; decent enough accommodation, a chapel, a fully stocked PX, a fifteen-lane, ten-pin bowling alley, a four-hundred metre running oval, and a sports centre. TV from home was piped in along with movies, papers, magazines and mail. It provided an anodyne life, routine and predictable. The only risks a danger of stepping in ruminant shit or falling foul of a dodgy curry in the town. But it wasn't Milwaukee. It would be Jackson's last summer at Menwith Hill and come fall he would be rotating back to the home of the brave for the last time. He couldn't wait.

The computer pinged. A new line of numbers and text appeared on the monitor. Jackson Schulz stiffened; baseball forgotten.

THIRTY- ONE

Since the beginning ECHELON's weakest link had been analysis. The transcendent technology was indiscriminate. Data was collected en masse; avalanches of it every second. Without analysis it was useless. And that had always been the massive problem. That was until four years ago and the realisation of project CONDOR; the first intelligent speech and optical character recognition filtration system. Now it wasn't people doing the looking and listening, it was the computers. And what they were looking and listening for were 'keys'. The keys could be anything; words, phrases, names, places, things, numbers. They were stored in a programme called PRISM. Most never changed but a small proportion, ordered by topical requirements, regularly did. PRISM ordered the keys with numerical values. The importance of a SIGINT data packet depended on the accumulated value of the 'keys' found in its message. To further make identification easier accumulated values were traffic-lighted into coloured bands. Most SIGINT packets were green; moderate value, moderate interest. High interest was amber and very high interest, flagged red, requiring immediate priority analysis. Occasionally values of specific keys would be programmed so high that a message would be flagged purple. It was rare. Shultz's predecessor had spoken of his predecessor seeing one way back in 2011. It had concerned the confidential location of the terrorist Bin Laden. Schultz never expected he would ever see a purple flag. That was until five seconds ago. Money he could understand. But what was so important about bin-bags and milk powder?

THIRTY- TWO

The SIGINT package was badged purple so it was hustled. The route convoluted. First for verification down the FIBER optic to GCHQ headquarters in Cheltenham then, as prescribed in the message's docket, swiftly on to MI5. They in turn informed the government's Joint Intelligence Committee who liaised with their assessment staff in the Joint Intelligence Organisation before making the call to the Government Cabinet Office. From there, shortly thereafter, another urgent telephone call was initiated. In the office of Raphael G. D'eath, in the financial no-mans' land between the city of London and Canary Wharf, the call connected.

It wasn't just purple flagged messages being hustled that day. Seven hours earlier Davey Boy had landed at Heathrow. The flight was behind schedule, only thirty minutes, but enough for him to hit the back of the queuing masses at immigration. By the time he was in a black cab up onto the M4 it was rush hour turgidity all the way into town. The plan was to make the flat, grab a shower, some shut eye, a change of clothes and get into the office with his sick bed excuses by early afternoon. Resting his arm on the carry-on beside him, he reached for his phone. He made the call and Jason picked up.

"The prodigal has returned," he announced. "Contact our friend and let's meet at the usual place."

He listened for a long moment.

"Well unless he's dead, get him out of his sick bed. He'll want to hear this first-hand. It's *great* news."

Davey Boy listened again.

"Good. Let's say between five and five-thirty. I'll need to leave early anyway, I'm bloody knackered."

He listened a brief moment more.

"Okay. See you guys then."

He pressed disconnect and held the phone idly in his hand. He looked at the drab lines of Tuesday morning cars crawling along on either side. A glacier could move faster. He sighed heavily. It had been a good plan, but something would have to give. He already knew it would be sleep.

D'eath was ushered into a spacious room on the second floor of the Cabinet Office building in Whitehall. The room was at the back of the building overlooking what he supposed would be called a small garden square. A single massive tree filled the space. Two-hundred-and-fifty feet beyond the tree, hidden behind some buildings, was 10 Downing Street, the residence of the British Prime Minister.

Three men were waiting for him.

"Mr Death?"

"Dee-ath," corrected the boss of FIBER.

THIRTY- TWO

"Of course, of course. Please forgive me. Thank you for responding so promptly." Sir Terence Simmenson, Cabinet Secretary, was every inch the tailored Whitehall Mandarin. In his sixties, clean shaven, slim and bespectacled, he exuded a polite 'to the manor born' assuredness befitting of the United Kingdom's most senior civil servant.

D'eath nodded. "I came as quickly as I could."

"Indeed Mr D'eath and be assured it is greatly appreciated. May I introduce Harold Windlass, GCHQ liaison and Roger Everet, MI5, acting DG of their capabilities section."

D'eath regarded the two men. Windlass, boyish, fair-haired and eager. All white teeth and tan in a slim olive suited package. If he ever gave up GCHQ he'd be a shoe-in for pushing trolleys on budget flights to the sun.

Everet, several decades older, looked like he'd be the pilot. Everything about the man was hard; face, eyes, mouth and above it all the skull cap of iron-grey hair. He wore a regimental tie under a double breasted dark blue blazer. Old and worn the blazer still buttoned over a flat midriff as if tailored the week before.

"And this gentlemen," said Simmenson completing the round of introductions, his open hand gesturing towards D'eath, "is Mr Raphael D'eath, head of the Financial Inter-Bank Enforcement and Regulation authority. Mr D'eath has been at the forefront of this investigation since its beginning. It was he who alerted us to, how shall we say, the exceptional elements of this case and it is his team who furnished GCHQ with the list of key words which is why we are here today."

"Gentlemen," said D'eath.

Windlass and Everet nodded back.

"So they've finally surfaced?" said D'eath.

"If we have interpreted the intercept correctly," said Windlass, "of course there's always the chance . . . "

"Can I see the transcript?" D'eath interrupted.

Windlass handed across eight pages of A4, stapled together. The text was bold and double spaced.

D'eath looked up sharply.

"It says this phone conversation took place at 12:45 pm, yesterday?" He looked at his watch. "That's almost twenty-six hours ago."

Windlass didn't blink. "Mr D'eath, it's not good. I know. Believe me. But this isn't Hollywood. With the mass of data we're handling these things can and do happen I'm afraid."

D'eath scanned the transcript rapidly, his forehead furrowing.

"Do you have a voice recording?"

An iPhone was sitting on top of a large paper map half unrolled on Simmenson's desk. Windlass picked it up.

"We were listening to it before your arrival."

He pressed his thumb to the screen and the phone lit up. He put it on loudspeaker, selected a file and pressed play. D'eath narrowed his eyes, concentrating, listening to the voices, to the boyish language; his mind filling with images of trainers, jeans, hoodies and black bin-bags. He knew it immediately. In his bones. They sounded like a pair of bloody idiots; idiots who had outwitted him and his team for months. It was embarrassing. Opening his mouth to confirm it, an image of Frobisher popped in his head. She had snatched at the same glittering prize he was reaching for. She had been equally certain, and she had paid the price, crashing and burning in ignominy. He wasn't about to become another Frobisher.

The recording ended. D'eath changed his focus back to the three men. "It's a possibility," he said guardedly. "They could well be our guys, or it could be coincidence pure and simple."

"Not good enough. We need to be sure," pressed Simmenson, "we can't afford another Ipswich debacle."

"You don't have to convince me of that," said D'eath presenting the three men with his best grimace.

He took his phone from a pocket and held it up.

"Allow me to consult with two of my specialists and I think we have every chance of putting this to bed."

Simmenson looked at Everet who, after a moment's thought, looked back at D'eath and nodded.

"Thank you. Do you have a location?" D'eath asked.

Everet spoke for the first time, the military tones in his clipped voice unmistakeable.

"I'm afraid the phone that initiated the conversation is dead. But we've been luckier with the receiver. It's switched off but the battery is connected, and it still has power. The SIM is pay and go and we've triangulated its position fairly accurately off two cell towers. The carrier's playing ball. They've identified the IMSI number and since we picked up the message they have been pinging the phone for us every fifteen minutes. It hasn't moved in that time. Right now the phone is just about here."

Everet leaned over Simmenson's desk, putting a broad finger on the map. It was a map of Greater London. Everet's fingertip covered an area on the map that could have been the size of a football pitch. D'eath frowned. The location was less than three miles away from FIBER's offices. It wasn't embarrassing anymore, it was humiliating.

"You're planning on mobilising SCO19?"

Everet met D'eath's gaze calmly.

"No. No police this time. Not after Ipswich. In the interests of national security we need to keep a lid on this one. My boys will handle it."

D'eath nodded. It made sense. He prodded numbers on his phone and walked a little way across the room. The call connected and Carter's familiar tones answered.

"Hi Boss Man. How goes it?"

"No time," said D'eath. "Get Bishop on the line and call me back now."

He disconnected and waited. Twenty seconds of uncomfortable silence. His phone sounded. He connected the call and heard Carter's voice again.

"Hi Boss. Bishop's joined on the call. So what's up?"

"I'm in Whitehall with the Secretary to the Cabinet. What I'm about to say is crucial. You both need to listen carefully. Bishop I want you to listen to a recording. I need your feedback on it so pay precise attention, okay? Carter, I need you to plot on a map of London all the ATM theft sites. Reference them to the following location coordinates."

D'eath moved back to Simmenson's desk and slowly read Carter the figures off the map. Carter repeated them back.

"Good. Okay Bishop I'm commencing the recording now."

D'eath gestured to Windlass who fired up his iPhone again and handed it over. D'eath pressed the play arrow and held its speaker to his phone. When the recording was done he handed the iPhone back to Windlass and held his own phone up to his ear again.

"Did you get that Bishop?"

"Affirmative." Bishop's voice was fainter than Carter's.

"You've heard the recording. You've studied FIBER's digital files exhaustively. What do you think?"

"I'm not sure what you want me to say. South London accents, young, male. It could be anyone. There's no way of knowing. But you would know that."

"Good! And you're prepared to stand by that?"

Only hearing D'eath's side of the conversation, Simmenson, Everet and Windlass looked on blankly. D'eath, ignoring Bishop's fumbling reply, waited a moment as if listening, then barked into the phone.

"Outstanding! Thank you, Bishop. Over to you now Carter. Have you got the location data on the ATM sites?"

"Here Boss. The ATM sites are scattered over south east London like a dose of chicken pox. There's a fair few near to the target location but no more than anywhere else."

"I didn't know it would be that obvious," said D'eath, "that's very good news. Are you absolutely sure of that Carter?"

"What?" said Carter.

"So, you are both in agreement? Excellent! That really is most helpful. Thank you both."

D'eath disconnected the call.

A raid on the phone's location was the right move. He was certain of it. This was no farm in a barley field somewhere. But, if things did go wrong at least now he had a measure of plausible deniability. It wouldn't resist serious investigation, but it would put Carter and Bishop in the firing line long enough for him to decide on a plan B. It was a risk. He knew it. They could have been clever. Taken a leaf out of their boss's own devious book and recorded the call. But he doubted it. There were risks then there were risks. Given what he'd heard on Windlass' phone this was one he would take every day of the week.

D'eath looked over to Simmenson.

"Carter and Bishop are two of my best. They are standouts in their respective fields. I asked Bishop to evaluate the voice recording in respect of the data we have on file and Carter to investigate any correlation between the suspect phone's location and the pattern of ATM theft sites. Both concur. They are ninety percent certain these are our guys."

Simmenson looked unsure. Ninety percent still left a hefty ten percent chance of failure. A ten percent chance of a career ending mess like Ipswich. Those were uncomfortable odds for a man in his position. He walked to the tall sash window and looked into the branches of the tree outside. He rubbed the side of his smooth chin with a hand, thinking. Everet and Windlass stood silently, waiting. D'eath could see the Cabinet Secretary teetering.

One final push.

"Sir Terence you more than most understand the need to rely on the expertise of specialists. You have just heard confirmation from two of my very best. They are as convinced as they can be. Their advice is to interdict as a matter of urgency. You have read the reports. We are dealing with something of the highest priority. Something that is entirely unique. Invaluable! We have a window of opportunity, but time is slipping away. We need your decision, sir."

Simmenson suddenly stiffened, turning away from the window.

"Do it," he said.

D'eath suppressed a smile.

"I am turning executive management of the situation over to you Roger," said Simmenson. "The ball's in your court now. The most important thing is to secure the package unharmed and intact. Are we clear on this?"

"Absolutely clear," replied Everet, his phone already in his hand.

"When do you propose to go in?" D'eath asked.

Everet looked at his watch. Windlass was redundant now. He stood silent, to one side.

"The operational commander will need to be briefed then he will need to brief his team, prepare and mobilise," said Everet.

He thought for a moment, silently calculating factors.

"We'll plan for eighteen-hundred hours," he said finally.

"I'd like to go in with the team," said D'eath. "As a rear echelon observer of course. But I've been eight months chasing these bastards and I'd like to be there when you take them down."

Everet looked to Simmenson.

The Cabinet Secretary sighed. He'd just committed to one possibly hazardous decision. What was one more?

"Just make sure adequate precautions are taken," he said.

"Well then Mr Dee-ath," Everet grinned, "you'd better follow me to Thames House. We have work to do and not a lot of time to do it. And by the way I'd count it a favour if you don't go mentioning your name to anyone on the team. They can be a superstitious lot when they want to be.

D'eath had disconnected his end of the call but Carter and Bishop had remained on their respective ends of the line.

"What the hell was all that about?" asked Carter.

"I haven't got a monkey's, mate," lied Bishop.

"This place is turning into looney tunes."

"It's only what I've always said."

"What's that?"

"You don't have to be mad to work here, but it helps."

THIRTY- TWO

Carter laughed briefly "Yeah tell me about it. Anyway have to shoot. Talk later okay?"

"Yeah sure. No problem."

Bishop disconnected one call and immediately pulled the ferret's phone from his pocket and connected another. He had listened to the recording while Carter was pulling up theft locations on the computer. He knew as soon as he'd heard the voices. The milk powder had sold it. It was the perps. It had to be. He was sure of it. GCHQ must have picked up on the phone call using the list of key words he had helped compile. And the map coordinates? They had to be the phone's location. Why else make such a song and dance? And all issuing from the Cabinet Office no less.

The broken nasal whine of ferret's voice sounded in Bishop's right ear. He responded, his voice forced and low.

"We have a location. The information has just come in. There's not much time. But it's close by so you've got a chance, but you have to move fast." Bishop gave the location from the coordinate figures he'd scribbled down and ended the call. Pulling out a soiled handkerchief he patted his face. He was sweating already.

THIRTY-THREE

"Chriseeey! It's Jacey on the phone."

Chris Hutchins got his head off the pillow on the third try. It surprised him. The fact it was still attached. There was only one arm on the clock face. He focused hard. 8:40. It was daylight and bright. Surely he hadn't slept eighteen hours? He sat up. Then he stood up. He felt weak but for the last seventeen years that had been something of an occupational hazard. The fever had sweated itself out. His nose was still blocked and dripping but the headaches had gone.

"Chriseeey!"

"Okay. Okaaay! I'm coming."

His mother had a voice that could strip creosote. Draping a dressing gown over his bony shoulders he went down the narrow stairs and picked the handset off the console table in the hallway.

"Hi Jace."

"Mornin' Chris. How are you feelin', mate? Your mobile's not answering."

"Yeah. Better. Thanks. Phone's likely dead. I think I've been in bed since yesterday afternoon. Can you believe it? Listen Jace I'm really sorry 'bout all that shit yesterday mate. I was feelin' like a pig but there was no call for what I said, no call at all. I was right out of order."

"Forget it, Chris. We've all been there. I've said worse to you before. The important thing is you're feeling better."

"Well thanks mate. I appreciate it. Sometimes I can be a right tosser."

Jason's laugh came down the line.

"No arguments there but listen mate I've got some really good news."

Chris waited.

"Davey's back. He called on his way in from the airport. He wants to see us at the bat cave later and he sounded really chipper. He said it was *great* news Chris. Not good mind but *great!*"

Chris felt his spirits lift.

"What time does he want to meet?"

"Between five and five-thirty. Do you think you'll be able to make it? He really wants to tell us together."

Chris smiled.

"Don't you worry Jace. I'll be there. How 'bout four? We can try to clean the place up before he gets there. This time you on the broom for once."

"Four sounds good, Chrissy. Tell you what though, let's toss a coin for the broom."

Davey Boy had been right. Sleep was the problem but not in the way he'd thought. He'd slept through the alarm or maybe he'd forgotten to set it. Either way it was well past three by the time he'd rushed out of his Chiswick flat, thrown the leather Belstaff over his suit jacket, fastened the helmet strap under his chin and had the Norton out on the Great West Road heading east. Daylight traffic was as light as it was going to get. He knew the route well; up over the Hammersmith Flyover, along the A4 then a long kick south down Earl's Court Road, Redcliffe Gardens and Edith Grove to the river. It was a fine day for the bike. A day that got even finer as he turned on to the embankment and followed the river east. Between the Chelsea house boats, the bridges and majestic avenues of tall London Plane trees, the Thames gleamed like blued gun metal under a high bright sun. With light traffic the bridges came quickly, one on another; Albert, Chelsea, under the Grosvenor and on past Vauxhall until finally he was in under the dark shadow of the Millbank Tower; four-hundred feet of '60s 'Brave New World' glass and steel. Once the tallest building in Britain it marked the end of the ride. He canted the Norton left and then right into Thorney Street and then right again up under the shadow of a massive grey-white Italianate building that looked like a dirty oblong wedding cake. Davey Boy halted the bike against the raised steel 'tank trap' barriers, removed his shades and showed his ID.

"Welcome back, Mr Gilroy, sir. Haven't seen you for a few days. Everything been all right?"

"Couldn't be better, Sam. Just checking in. I needed a few days off to shake the dreaded lurgy."

"You're not the only one, lad. There's been a lot of it about lately. Best thing is hot whiskey and a little honey and lemon. It won't cure you mind, but you'll feel a lot better being sick."

Davey Boy grinned, tucked the shades into a pocket of the Belstaff, waited for the steel barriers to disappear into the ground and then slowly rode the Norton down the wide vehicle ramp into the underground bowels of Thames House, the headquarters of the UK Security Service, commonly known as MI5.

Davey Boy stepped out of the lift, swinging his helmet by the strap like an oversized conker. He frowned. The open plan office was empty. Computer screens glowed; jackets on chair backs, printouts scattered haphazardly on vacant workstations. Where was everyone?

Retracing his steps he paused, knocked lightly on the door of briefing room 'A', opened it a slice and poked his head around. Bingo! They were all there; Reynolds, McLeish, Tarrington, Stephens, the whole team. At the head of the room was a wall mounted screen. Details from a large-scale map were projected on it. Standing next to the screen was his number two, Alex Spring, next to him Everet, head of Capabilities and next to him someone he hadn't seen before, a head taller than Everet, all in black with a shaved head. What the hell was going on?

THIRTY-THREE

"Ah! Gilroy you're back!" Everet exclaimed. "If you were coming in, I would have appreciated you informing resources. As it is Mr Spring here will be team lead for today's soiree."

"Not fully back, I'm afraid, sir. Just checking in prior to a full return to duty tomorrow. A soiree you were saying?"

Davey Boy entered the briefing room closing the door behind him. In front of him were the backs of eight heads. Echo team. His team.

Alex Spring spoke. "Good to see you back boss. Remember the flap about all those ATM raids a while back? Well chances are good GCHQ have located the package behind it all. We've been given a fix." He pointed at an enlarged ringed area on the map projection.

"We're setting up the op now. We're keeping it all in house."

Davey Boy took a closer look at the map and his world shattered like a dropped claret jug. It was impossible. How could they? Even if a dicey conversation had been picked up the burners were always, always, destroyed. He'd drummed it into them. There was just no way. He covered up his expression with a fit of coughing covering the lower part of his face with coupled hands.

"Still a few days needed, I think, Gilroy," said Everet.

"I'll be fine sir," Davey Boy gasped. "Last vestiges is all."

Recovering, he straightened up.

"Good luck lads. Do Echo team proud. What time are you going in, Alex? I'll be raising a glass to you guys."

"Planned for eighteen-hundred Davey."

Davey Boy smiled. It was painful.

"Go get 'em lads," he said.

Davey Boy took the lift back to the vehicle basement. The next steps would be crucial. The obvious action would be to phone and warn the boys off. But he knew a little of GCHQ's capabilities. Jason's potential value to the authorities was off the charts. They would be sparing nothing to get him. Focusing all their ELINT resources on the phone's location and surrounding cell towers. Somehow they had already compromised the boys' phone security. He didn't know how. He didn't know if the boys were already at the bat cave. Making a call blind could prove disastrous. He looked at his watch. Four-fifteen. He would be on the Norton. Echo team would be in a convoy of at least three vehicles. He knew how they would mobilise. They planned to go in at six. He still had an edge, just.

"Heads! I win mate. The broom's all yours."

"Crap! C'mon Jace. I only crawled out my sick bed a few hours ago."

Jason smiled. "Okay, you sad moron, here throw it over. Get the coffee on and I'll make a start."

They had arrived at the bat cave half-an-hour later than planned. Travelling close to 4 p.m. in London on a weekday was never a good idea if you wanted to get anywhere on time. But there'd been no hurry. Davey Boy had said five to five-thirty so there was time to spare.

THIRTY-THREE

The water in the kettle hadn't even boiled when Jason called out again.

"Shit Chris! This powder is bloody everywhere. I thought we'd cleaned it all up before Davey left."

"We! You mean me, you lazy bugger."

Chris crossed the stone floor with a mug in each hand.

"It's the same every mornin', Jace. I think it kind of hangs in the air, invisible, like dust or something. Then at night when nothing's moving around it kind of settles down over everything again."

Jason grunted. He stopped vigorously pushing the broom handle back and forth and stood upright.

"Then this is just plain stupid. There's no point."

"Tell that to Davey. He likes everything clean and ordered. You know that."

"Yeah? Well as soon as he gets here I will." Jason looked at his watch. It was 4:45.

"At least we won't have long to wait."

They didn't. The wicket door set into the closed roller shuttering popped and swung inwards a few inches. A shiver rippled through the linked aluminium planks. Slowly the door kept coming. Moving hesitantly like someone behind it was unsure. Like someone behind it just wanted to check. A quarter along its arc it stopped. From behind it a small, dark head appeared. It looked and withdrew. There were voices, a discussion, then the door was moving again. No hesitancy this time; slamming back hard and fast. A bright summer rectangle into the gloom of the bat cave; a bright summer rectangle through which stepped four men neither Jason nor Chris had ever seen before.

THIRTY- FOUR

Davey Boy rolled the Norton quietly up behind the black Range Rover. It was empty, parked at a camber, half on the narrow lane, half off, in the lee of the old gasometer about a hundred-and-thirty yards from a string of dilapidated buildings skirting the southern railway embankments. The bat cave was one those buildings. Leaving the bike he removed his helmet and holding it by the chin strap moved up alongside the Range Rover. He looked inside. On the back seat were several pairs of steel handcuffs and what appeared to be a bundle of flat black cloth bags. *Hoods?* Quickening his pace he moved towards the buildings.

Jason and Chris froze. The four men didn't. Spreading out across the stone floor they formed a rough arc between the boys and the door. The middle of the arc was filled by an old man. Even stooped he was big. Wild-haired, lined and bulky he stood like an old bear. On either side of him two hulks. Big, like statues hewn from the same block of stone. Black suits, shaved skulls, bodies thick and solid.

Apart from a weighty gold chain around the neck of one they looked identical. The last man, the smallest, crouched out on the far left. His had been the head peering around the door. He held a knife and was smiling.

"So yer man was finally right about something," said the old man, "take 'em and be quick." Then the talking stopped.

Shock can do strange things. Jason didn't move. Chris, stupidly, did. Like a startled rabbit he turned and ran. It was stupid on two counts; first, there was nowhere to run and second, the men expected it.

Chris had almost made the hemmed-in brick corner thirty feet away when the small man with the dancing knife caught up to him. The knife wasn't needed. The kick caught Chris low down in the middle of his back. It wasn't vicious or heavy. It didn't need to be. Chris already had the momentum. It was just a tap; but a tap sufficient to pitch him headlong face first into the brick.

Chris hit the wall, crumpling like an emptied can of Coke-Lite. For a second, he was upright glued to the brick. Then, like a cartoon, he peeled off, toppling backwards full length into deep footings of milk powder and sawdust banked up beneath him. A haze of wood and milk dust billowed up over his prone form, roiling and hazing in the bat cave's still air like smoke. Moaning, legs twitching, Chris lay semi-conscious covered in powder like a poleaxed snowman. The small man pocketed his knife bent over, grabbed an ankle and began dragging him out of the corner. Chris wasn't heavy but the man on his ankle was small and he was pulling a dead weight. The old man motioned and the nearest of the black suited hulks moved in to help.

THIRTY- FOUR

Quietly stepping into the gloom of the bat cave, Davey Boy blinked. The retinal photo was in the lab a quarter second. Then it was in the album; all sharp, high contrasts and vivid. Chrissy, down, damaged, in pain; Jason, motionless, terror in his ashen face, the perpetrators, predatory strangers, four of them, moving in. Davey Boy blinked again. This time he didn't need the lab or the album. Just instinct.

It had been done before. Back then it had been a slingshot of goat skin, a smooth hard stone and a deal of skill. It would still take a deal of skill. Stepping forward Davey Boy started the helmet swinging.

Centrifugal force is strange thing. It's not real. Not in the textbooks anyway. But Davey Boy wasn't interested in textbooks. Three times he whirled the helmet about his head; each revolution quicker than the last. Each building speed, momentum and a force that wasn't real. Midway through the fourth revolution, when he couldn't spin it any faster, he released the canvas strap and let the helmet go. Smooth, round and hard it fizzed along an invisible ten-foot tangent into the back of the nearest hulk's head. A one-and-a-half kilogram projectile of hardened Kevlar and carbon fibre, it impacted the shaved skull with a crack like gunfire. The hulk went down soundlessly, hard into the stone floor. He stayed there, black suited, bulky, on top of an expanding puddle of blood. David had done for Goliath but there were still three more Philistines in the room, and they were moving.

While ferret fumbled for his knife, the old man for the pistol in his coat pocket, the remaining hulk wasn't thinking weapons. His twin was unmoving on the floor. All he needed were hands and teeth. With murder cut into his broad ugly face he lumbered towards Davey Boy.

Finally Jason moved. The eyes of the three men weren't on him anymore. They were focused forward towards the roller shutters; towards the source of danger, towards Davey Boy. Backing off behind them Jason ran into the depths of the bat cave towards Chris. His friend lay sprawled in a bloodied sludge of powder, hands over his face moaning. Kneeling Jason gently prised the fingers apart. Chris' eyes were closed up tight but slowly they opened. His nose was smashed and his mouth full of blood. He spluttered as he tried to speak. Jason saw the grotesquely swollen jaw, split mouth and broken teeth. He saw again the small man's cruel smile, his lazy kick and as he looked down into the broken face of his best friend he was overcome. Not with fear or shock, but with a burning eviscerating anger. And then the shivering started.

The gun and the knife were out and pointing as the hulk, gold pendant swinging, lunged across the last foot of space grasping for Davey Boy's face. Davey Boy was ready. He'd seen it coming, all the way, twenty-five feet across the stone flags, eight loping steps, charging like a freight train. He didn't want to be in the station when the train arrived.

THIRTY- FOUR

The sway to the right wasn't slow but it wasn't fast either. It was an invitation; follow me. And the hulk's hands did just that, momentum pulling the rest of his body's mass along behind. And as the hands, the mass and the momentum went right Davey Boy snapped back left, hard and fast off the right knee. Right elbow primed ready for the passing unprotected right temple. A matador couldn't have done it better, with or without a cape. Then, in an instant, perhaps he could. In the midst of transferring weight for the strike Davey Boy's right shoe suddenly wasn't an anchor anymore. It was a smooth leather puck sliding out from under him on a powder slicked stone rink. Slipping he went down hard, the hulk following all the way.

Jason stood over Chrissy. Eyes closed. Hands loose by his sides. He felt the pressure of the air dropping around him, the shivering increasing, the power growing greater than he'd ever felt it. With every muscle trembling, his senses razored; he smelt iron in the blood on the floor and in the air, sweat, lavender and the stale mustiness of milk and wood dust. He heard sounds loud in his ears; painful moaning, glottal coughing, crude cursing. Everything amplified, crystallised, elemental. The touch paper was lit. Anger had been the match but the fuel was rage, pure, unadulterated. He felt the energy surging within him, both terrifying and intoxicating, and he embraced it.

Jarred back against the stone floor Davey Boy felt like he'd been hit by a meat locker with a year's worth of steak inside. The hulk was on top of him, blacking out light, teeth bared in a snarl, knees on either side, clawing at his forearms, scrabbling for his face, for his eyes. Davey Boy had fists and elbows together high up in front of his head. Like a boxer on the ropes. But the hulk, immensely strong, had the high ground. In a blind rage he wanted blood. And in about six seconds he was going to get it. But six seconds is a long time and rage called blind for a reason. Spiking a knee, Davey Boy drove it upwards hard and fast between the trunk-like thighs straddling him. Leverage wasn't great, but it was enough. The snarl on the hulk's face swallowed itself in a splitting wrench of pain and Davey Boy, knowing what was coming next, tensed. Inevitably the massive hands dropped away clutching at the source of agony and Davey Boy looked up into the exposed face. It wasn't pretty.

Pain, unexpected and excruciating, could do that. Slit welded eyes, a twisted slice of mouth, florid flesh. A rope of gold looped down into Davey Boy's face and he tasted the man's hot, fetid, breath in his mouth. Six seconds were done. Dropping his guard Davey Boy grasped the gold chain; a length of the woven metal in each fist. It felt warm, solid, thick. It would do the job. *This is going to hurt, you a lot more than me.* Chin down into his chest, shoulders bunched, he gripped the chain in both hands and jerked down savage and fast, pulling the hulk's face into the top of his head. The bony dome of his skull becoming the landing pad for the front of the hulk's broad face. He felt, rather than heard, the crunch; the nose giving way, cheek bones fracturing, then his face was wet with blood; the other man's, thick, metallic, hot. Twisting he brought both knees up toppling the bigger man off to one side. Then, taking a lungful of air, he staggered upright into a grey haze and stood transfixed.

The gun and the knife wavered uncertainly in his direction, but their owners were looking elsewhere, over their shoulders back into the bat cave. They were looking at Jason and Davey Boy, breathing heavily, could see why.

Jason was a light show in a swimming pool. Or that's how it seemed. He stood in an ethereal mist of glowing particles, hair floating around his head, dark and thick, as if buoyed in an underwater current. The mist should have been a dirty grey, but it wasn't. It shimmered with a suffusing tracery of blue light. Spidery veins of luminescence rippling, dying and rippling anew through the haze of powdered dust. And the light, all of it, emanated from Jason. He stood, almost silhouetted, within a pulsing, glowing, incandescent corona of energy.

The light show mesmerised Davey Boy but only for a matter of seconds. He was still outnumbered; a gun was in play and Echo team by now would on their way. Life and death were playing out in the bat cave and he needed to move.

The gun and the knife weren't wavering anymore. They had changed about and were now pointing firmly at Jason along with the astonished eyes of their owners. Eyes that didn't know the seventeen-year-old was about to be the last thing they'd see on this earth. The old man's finger may or may not have been tightening on the trigger. Davey Boy would never know. Jason, face hard, implacable, simply raised a glowing arm, pointed, and let loose hell.

Accompanied by a staccato crack a dazzling beam of pure blue-white electrical energy arced from Jason's hand fifteen feet through the misty haze seeking the earth. It found it. Through the gun, through the old man holding it and down into the stone floor. The gun would never shoot anyone again and neither would the old man. Thrown ten feet by the charge he was the forgotten marshmallow left too close to the fire. Hairless, charred, coat still smouldering, he was as dead as it was possible to be.

The ferret, eyes wide in terror, threw his blade across the floor and was pleading when a second arc of pulsing energy hit him. He wasn't as big as the old man and he was thrown much farther; right across the room into the roller shutters. He hit with an impact that put a dish three feet across in the aluminium. But that wasn't what killed him. What killed him was being cooked through like a piece of cheap brisket in the time it took to blink.

Immediately after the second discharge everything stopped. Like a button had been pressed or a switch flicked. The lights went out, all sounds ceased and a kind of numbness filled the space. A strong odour of bleach hung in the haze, now back to a light grey mist, but it was a godsend. It masked the cloying smell of singed hair and scorched flesh. The hulk with the gold chain, the last of the McGimlet four, stirred groaning on the floor by Davey Boy's feet. Davey Boy's head ached enough. He didn't want to go hurting anything else. His black crash helmet was on the floor some feet away. Retrieving it he walked back to the hulk, now on his hands and knees, his face a bloody dripping stalactite. Davey Boy adjusted his stance and teed off like a golfer with a three wood. The swing was more hook than fade, but he wasn't aiming for a distant green. Two birds with one helmet. The hulk collapsed into his own blood and stayed there. Davey Boy looked at the helmet. He could see inner layers through a six-inch crack. The label said good for thirty-five miles per hour into a hard surface. It didn't say anything about two thick skulls. Maybe it should have. He checked his watch. It was past five.

Back in the recesses of the bat cave there was motion and quickly Davey Boy moved towards it. Jason, sitting in two inches of grey powder, looked vacant and bemused, as if he'd just got up after a hard night. Next to him, on his knees, was Chrissy. He was holding a hand over his bleeding mouth and attempting to stand. He wasn't succeeding. Davey Boy hooked an arm around him and looked into his young cousin's eyes. He saw recognition and Chrissy tried to speak. The words were unintelligible, lisping and lumpy through blood and swelling.

"Don't speak Chrissy. Can you stand?"

Chris nodded slowly and Davey Boy carefully helped him up. He propped him up against a brick wall and turned to see Jason gingerly getting himself to his feet.

"Jason." Davey Boy's voice was calm and authoritative. "Are you okay?"

Jason held up his open empty hands in front of him. He looked bewilderingly at them.

"I think so Davey."

"Good. Help me with Chrissy. We haven't much time."

Jason stepped through the powder and put an arm around his friend. He looked into Chris' face wincing.

"Don't worry Chrissy. Hang in there, mate."

Chris didn't reply but leant farther into Jason's shoulder.

Davey Boy paused, frowning, thinking. The he moved quickly. First to the body of the old man; holding his breath he bent over the torched cadaver going through what clothing remained. Nothing. He did the same with hulks one and two and then moved on to the smaller figure lying at the foot of the roll shutters. The keys were low down in a pocket in the left-hand side of the jacket. He was lucky. The entire right side of the body, jacket, shirt, under vest and flesh, was welded together in a seared blistered mess. Relieved, Davey Boy held the keys above his head. "Get Chrissy over to the door. I'll bring up the car," and with that he stepped through the bright summer rectangle in the shuttering and was gone.

Davey Boy was keeping ahead of the curve, just, but it was tough. He'd driven Jason and Chris to the end of the narrow lane, to where it met the road and then a farther half a mile along the main carriageway before dropping them off.

THIRTY- FOUR

His instructions had been simple and direct. Get clear of the immediate vicinity; summon an Uber, Jason to use his personal phone only, get Chris to the nearest A&E and alert the parents. The story; Chris had potholed his bicycle and gone over the handlebars. Any problems claim temporary memory loss. Keep to the story, keep heads down and wait. Davey Boy was family. Let the parents alert him. It would be better that way. Then twenty minutes of hard thinking as he retraced the drive back to the bat cave and the Norton. Twenty minutes of hard thinking with a head that felt like it had been hit with a mallet. Then, thirty yards out on the narrow lane, it had come to him. There was just time. Maybe he should be hit in the head more often.

Impatiently Davey Boy manoeuvred the Range Rover under the stuttering roller shutters up into the rear of the bat cave. He parked near the old white van, switched off and left the keys in the ignition. Using the black cloth bags in the back he did a wipe-over; front, back, steering wheel, door handles and windows. It would have to do.

After the vehicle wipe down, he glanced at his watch. Echo team would be out and well south of the river by now. Bringing the roller shutters back down Davey Boy retreated into the rear of the bat cave. The tables and chairs were against a far wall by the industrial racking. Stacked next to them, the dense shapes of bulkier equipment; the space heater, the safescan counters, boxes of cables and the unused sacks of milk powder. He needed something to cut with. Discarded on top of the second table, by the camping stove, was a Pound Land special; a plastic cutlery tray. Aside from a few spoons, forks and table knives, it held a wavy edged breadknife. That would do. Grabbing the knife he slashed at the topmost polythene sack of milk powder. The plastic was tough, not a loaf of bread, but he was through to the powder in three strokes. Grabbing a chipped mug he dipped, filled, and flung the powder high up into the bat cave where it spread and then fell like snow. Dip, fill, fling. Again and again until the polythene sack was half-empty. Then grabbing the sack, Davey Boy wheeled around shaking out the remaining powder high into the air above his head. There were five more stacked sacks and in quick time they all got the ripper treatment. By the time the sixth empty sack hit the bat cave's floor that was all Davey Boy could see through a swirling gritty fog.

Feeling along the tables, hand over nose and mouth, he picked out the laptops, coffee machine, printer and the dense boxy shape of the microwave and next to it the camping stove. It wasn't the stove he needed but what was on the floor under it; the gas canisters. There were eight, still unused, in a partially shrink-wrapped cardboard tray. Bullet shaped and small they looked like muscled-up coke cans. Lifting the tray, he set it on top of the microwave and twisted out four of the canisters. Popping the microwave's door he filled the space with the four cans. He swung the door shut, spun up the twin dials; maximum time, maximum power and pushed the 'Go' button. Inside the microwave a bulb lit up and the magnetron started with a thrum. On the outside of the microwave a LED panel lit up and digits counted down. Four packed inside, four on top. Hopefully it would be enough. Davey Boy ran through the milky fog for the now pale and opaque summer rectangle in the closed-up shuttering, stooping to snatch up the battered motorcycle helmet he'd left by the door. Stepping through he swung the wicket door shut behind him and gulped clean particle free air. He looked like he'd crawled through a flour bowl but that was the least of his worries. The wind would take most of it when he got the Norton up to speed. Then he ran to the bike; one hundred and thirty yards in twenty sweaty seconds. Squashing the helmet down on his head he hit the ignition, gunned the Norton into first, fish tailed the back wheel through ninety degrees and took off through the gears back down the narrow lane. It was 5:40 p.m.

THIRTY-FIVE

"So much for eighteen-hundred," said Alex Spring, the frustration in his voice palpable. "We're certain the phone's still on location? It hasn't moved?"

"Affirmative," confirmed McLeish.

Sitting in the back seat he held a compact Rohde and Schwarz tactical VHF handset to his ear. The small German radio was excellent. The connection to Thames House was direct and encrypted and McLeish had been plugged into it since they'd been on the road, which by now was getting on for way too long. Next to him sat Tarrington and in front of Tarrington, in the passenger seat next to Spring, was D'eath. The X5 was lead in a convoy of three identical BMW 4x4s, all dark paint and tinted glass. The other two vehicles, driven by Stephens and Reynolds, were in line astern containing the remaining four members of Echo team. Initially progress had been swift. Blues and twos parting the sea of traffic like a latter-day Moses. But a mile out from the target location the sirens had been ditched for a covert approach. Now, with just silent blue lights flashing in the radiator grills, the convoy's speed had dropped off the charts as it wrestled through a congestion of almost oblivious rush hour drivers insulated in drive-time radio cocoons.

D'eath shifted uncomfortably. He was as frustrated as Spring. He'd had an idea in his head that this secret team of ultra-elite specialists would somehow arrow through London like Custer's 7th Cavalry. It was a stupid idea and it had perished quickly in the morass of creeping rush hour traffic. They were behind the clock but at least now the target was close. According to the satnav the derelict development land containing the phone's location was a mere quarter-mile ahead.

Spring glanced across at D'eath and smiled. It was meant to be reassuring. It needed to be. With kneecaps poking above the glove box and creased suit scrunched up tightly inside body armour a size too small, his tall passenger looked as comfortable as a frog on a hotplate.

"Second thoughts?"

"None," replied D'eath tersely. "Glad to be along. But it's difficult to avoid thinking this could have been planned a hell of lot better."

Spring's face was impassive.

"Yeah. Usually we abseil down through the roof, but wouldn't you just know it, today's the pilot's day off."

D'eath focused pointedly on the satnav.

Next left after the approaching junction would be the turn off. Spring saw it too. He glanced back at McLeish.

"Get the lads prepped, Calum"

McLeish nodded. Twisting the knurled nob on the VHF he changed the voice channel.

"Comms and kit check! Sound off lads."

THIRTY-FIVE

The men in Echo team were all uniformed in similar attire; rubber-soled canvas boots, jeans, roll-necks and unmarked ballistic vests that, unlike D'eath's, actually fitted. Each had a semi-automatic holstered on a webbing belt; not the ubiquitous Glock but the Swiss German SIG P226. Additionally, Reynolds and two others carried the Heckler Koch MP-5KA4 submachine gun. At a stubby two kilos and only a foot long the weapon didn't look much, but its curved magazine held thirty rounds and on full auto would empty in two seconds. Both the SIGs and the HKs used the same ammunition; 9mm Luger Parabellum. Spare magazines of additional rounds filled belt holsters for the pistols and webbing pocket harnesses over the vests for the SMGs. Now on top of this, literally, tactical headsets were being strapped on and tested. Wide elasticated Alice bands attached to ear cups, boom mikes, and push-to-talk dongles. And the voices, one after another, clear and audible, started coming through the speaker of McLeish's radio.

"Ready Boss."

"Okay Boss."

"Here Boss."

"Good to go Boss."

And with the voices came the sounds of spring-loaded metal against metal as chambers were checked, bolts cocked and magazines rattled. Spring smiled at D'eath. "Sounds like we're ready," he said and with that he hooked hard left leading the small convoy urgently into the mouth of the narrow-cambered lane.

With the last vehicle off the main drag and well into the lane Spring decelerated to a gradual halt. Donning his own Alice band he looked through the tinted windscreen. Adjusting the mike against his cheek he thumbed the PTT button.

"Heads up lads. Echo leader. Operation remains a go. Objective remains the same. You all know the drill. We go in on my six. Eyes peeled and no playing silly buggers. Let's get this done."

Spring thumbed off the connection and looked sideways at D'eath. "When we go in you stay put in the vehicle. Clear?"

D'eath returned the look, with as much innocence as he could muster. "Absolutely," he murmured.

Spring commenced the car rolling forward again, cautiously, just above walking pace, tyres crunching over loose stone. Reynolds followed six feet behind and Stephens six feet behind him. Peering over the wide bonnet Spring muttered quietly out of the passenger's side of his mouth. "Rear echelon observer my arse. Just don't get in my way."

A hundred-and-fifty metres along the rutted lane and it was a different world. Wooden hoardings curved in off the development land closing in the narrow lane with a twelve-foot-high wall of graffiti tagged blue boarding. On the opposite side of the lane it was wide open, just weedy scrub, rotten brick and dereliction all the way back to the fenced railway embankment drop-offs. Another six-hundred metres of hoardings and dereliction and the lane turned, gradually broadening before petering out in a wide flattened forecourt of hard standing; part weeds, part crumbling potholes and part muddy gravel. Ahead, stark against a flat sky, the rusty frame of an empty Victorian gasometer blocked forward movement. Behind, the wall of wooden hoardings peeled away back on their interminable circuit of the development land while to the south east, a hundred-and-fifty metres across the forecourt, a short low terrace of assorted buildings stood in partial shadow.

Spring stopped his car on the edge of the forecourt. The other two vehicles fanned out ten feet on either side and halted. For a moment all was still. Then eleven doors popped, and the pride of Echo team disgorged; lean, mean and loaded for bear.

McLeish, VHF to his ear, pointed towards the shadowed terrace. "Confirmation's through, Boss. The phone's somewhere in there."

Spring frowned. Apart from Echo team's there were no vehicles to be seen. The site was a half mile off the beaten track. He could hear traffic but it was just a faint hum way back on the dual carriageway. The place was desolate and looked totally deserted. But if no one was here why was the target phone? He looked again at the buildings. They appeared derelict. Uninhabitable. Some didn't even have complete walls let alone roofs. But there was one. At the far end of the terrace, nearest to the gasometer. It had both walls and a roof and a standout door. A roller shuttered security door you could drive a small truck through. The location technology was state of the art. Somewhere in that mess of tiles and crumbling brick a powered-up cell phone was pinging. Odds on it had to be behind that door. There was nowhere else. Motioning to his team Spring unholstered the SIG and in a crouch led eight men slowly towards the bat cave.

D'eath waited until the backs of Echo team were well out across the forecourt before quietly popping the X5's door and stepping out. Relief! Unfolding his tall frame he stood a moment. Spring was a moron; a military automaton, made to follow orders. D'eath wasn't. There was one half-decent building in the collection across the way. The clever bastards that had almost ruined his life; almost had him in prison, were in it and he wasn't going to be a bystander when they were taken down. Moving away from the X5 he started walking after Echo team. This was absolutely something he needed to do. If Spring didn't like it, he could piss up a rope. Then, in an instant, the world turned brighter than the sun and he wasn't thinking anything.

The gas canisters were just simple aerosol cans. Pressurised tinplate tubes of liquid butane. The same colourless liquid found in a billion cheap BIC lighters. But they had been cooking in a thousand watts of microwave energy for almost half-an-hour and they were done. Wedged in the microwave's cavity on their sides, two-upon-two, it was the bottom left that went first. That was all that was needed. Rupturing along a welded seam the aerosol burst open, the vapour of its depressurised liquid sparking instantly into an incandescent fireball. The remaining seven cylinders followed; erupting in searing temperatures of nearly two-thousand degrees, blowing apart the microwave and slicing the hazing air of the bat cave with a vicious cutting shrapnel of glass, plastic and tinplate. And that's where it should have ended; with a big bang, an eviscerated microwave flaming like a medieval torch, a blackened circle of scorched stone and some pock-marked walls. But it didn't. It was just beginning.

The exploding cans were not only aerosols, they were detonators; detonators in a highly flammable fog of powdered milk and wood particles compressed within the oxygen rich confines of a brick box. The bat cave had become a fuel-air bomb and the bomb was doing what it did best, exploding. The chain reaction was light speed quick; a billion floating particles of flaming fuel, an erupting super-heated fireball, a blast wave of burning energy accelerating at ten thousand feet a second, and total utter destruction. For a nanosecond the building held, its brick fusing glassy in a pressurised furnace of incinerating heat, then the walls and roof gave way, blasting apart in a ferocious maelstrom of shattered brick, scorching flames and twisted iron. And there, energy spent, it did end. Under a hot rain of falling debris, floating ash and airborne glowing embers, the evening summer sky stained black with a pall of darkly drifting smoke.

D'eath came to in a silent world that looked like the dark side of the moon. He wanted to move but his body didn't. Bewildered he lay crumpled, uncomprehending, in a mess of dirt and filth. Above him a sagging mattress hung in a tree and snow was falling. He felt the flakes, warm on his upturned face. Wasn't snow meant to be cold? Bemused he lay under the strange sky; charcoals, indigo and inky blacks and low, low, down where the sun lay trapped, peach and slivers of gold. It was beautiful. He tried to hear but his head was an echo chamber, the only sound a plaintive whistling, high and reedy. He needed to move. He tried again. Slowly, like a drunkard, rolling over. He felt crunching beneath him and saw glass gleam in the mud. Feebly turning his head he could see flames; like small campfires flickering amidst blackened scrub, smoke rising from a dozen pyres into the still evening sky. Why weren't the birds singing in the falling snow? It was so beautiful.

Then the mental fog cleared, the whistling died away and the pain came. Abrupt, excruciating, ripping through the left side of his chest and he screamed. Clarity cut like a knife. It wasn't snow falling softly into his face. It was burnt ash. It wasn't a mattress in a tree. It was a roller shuttered door; planks of scorch-welded aluminium, thirty feet up in the mangled remains of an old gasometer. And there were bodies; men, four or five, maybe more, scattered, motionless in mud and filth and the carcasses of burnt out vehicles; charred, still smoking, two on their sides, one incongruously still upright on blackened metal rims. And beyond the vehicles, where the buildings should have been, just smoking rubble pierced with stumps of blackened brick, sheared stone and twisted scorched rebar. And sounds were coming now; men calling out in pain, the spit and crackle of flames, the faint beating blades of a helicopter and in the distance, sirens, multitudes of them, getting closer. He was going to die here in the dirt and the chaos. He knew it. Then pain ripped again and he dropped into darkness.

THIRTY-SIX

D'eath was wrong. He didn't die. Aside from McGimlet and his thugs no one did. But it was close and it wasn't pretty. The difference, cigarette paper thin, had been the emergency services. Medivacked en mass to the major trauma centres of the Royal London in Whitechapel and King's College south of the river, Echo team had presented a triage nightmare from hell; a mess of fractured bones, burst eardrums, ruptured spleens, blast burns and haemorrhaging lungs. But they'd been a distance away from the blast, they were fit and strong and they'd been wearing body armour. That, and the availability of blood banks and surgical teams working around the clock, had proved crucial. For weeks it had been touch-and-go. But with two months on the clock it was now just go. Against the odds and to a man Echo team had survived.

D'eath was healing too. At least his body was. Furthest from the epicentre of the blast his injuries by comparison had been light; a ruptured eardrum, three broken ribs, a fractured knee and some first-degree burns. He'd drawn the winning lottery ticket. He knew it. If the traffic had been lighter, if Spring had parked closer, if he had obeyed the instruction to stay in the vehicle. Any of these and he would be dead. No question.

His tall lean body was still broken but his mind was clear. He knew what had happened but not why. He needed to know. Repeatedly he'd asked the questions but he may as well have been hammering his head against the ward wall. No one was answering. After two weeks he'd attempted to discharge himself, but the door had been locked and the sedatives increased. Now, in moods fluctuating between anger and despondency, he lay impotently between the bars of his hospital bed, the ceiling of his small room pressing down on him. But they couldn't keep him hospitalised forever. He would get out and when he did, he wouldn't be waiting around. He would call in his bullet points, pull up sticks and get as far away from this shit hole as possible. There were greener pastures out there, pastures where one didn't get blown up. Let these incompetent scheming little island bastards clean up their own festering mess. Raphael G. D'eath wasn't going to be a part of it anymore.

The explosion itself had merited just two days of headlines; two days of long-range aerial video, talking heads, police statements and street corner witnesses who'd seen the smoke and heard the bang. The media had demanded a story and slithering into oily action the Government's PR machine had obliged. There could only be one. The emergency services had seen too many weapons and ballistic vests for any other. But it was simple and believable. Heroic security service officers; a Jihadist plot, an isolated bomb factory and terrorists blowing themselves to pieces rather than be captured. Threat levels had been ostentatiously raised and then quietly allowed to drop. No terrorist group had claimed responsibility. The site was derelict, isolated and locked down tight. None of the officers had been killed and apart from some minimal blast damage to a nearby industrial estate and debris closing an adjacent railway line for two days, any octane remaining in the story had been allowed to quietly and naturally evaporate. It hadn't taken long.

But it was a different story driving the authorities. Within a day of the site cooling forensics had been let loose. Another ten days and a highly confidential report had been compiled. It was straightforward and in part brutally simple: three-thousand-degree temperatures, a destructive blast radius approaching two-hundred yards and an airborne particle fuelled thermobaric explosion that anyone within a hundred yards of its volcanic epicentre would have been lucky to survive. And some hadn't. Remains had been found. Organic matter mixed in amongst charred and melt-twisted components that had once been motor vehicles. They thought maybe three bodies but couldn't be sure. Identification of the vehicles would be hard enough. Identifying the human remains, carbonised to the texture of blackened toast, would be nigh near impossible. But some things had been identified. The building at the epicentre of the explosion had housed a business. The Irish owner of the small timber joinery company had been traced. Terrified he admitted an illegal six-month sublet. All cash paid up front. Pressed hard on the identity of his temporary tenant he was useless. Apart from a hat, glasses and ginger hair he hadn't been able to remember a thing.

But in the end, it had all come down to questions. The forensics report had posed more than it had answered. The perpetrators were gone; cooked to extinction in a three-thousand-degree fireball. In their place speculation, conjecture and complete confusion. No phoenixes would be rising from these ashes. The door was shut tight. Any opportunity lost. There was nowhere left to go. Three weeks after the explosion, in the continuing absence of any ATM thefts, in an atmosphere of secrecy and self-interest, in a spacious office above a small garden square, looking out into the dense foliage of a single large tree, the investigation file had been quietly closed.

But it hadn't ended there. It couldn't. Not with other victims out there. Victims the authorities knew nothing about. Chris Hutchins, with a broken nose, a dislocated lower jaw and three sheared teeth in his upper jaw, was one of them. The nose and the jaw had been the easy part; easy but painful as hell. The manipulation, realigning and strapping had been done in the first few days in hospital. The teeth, a trial of extractions, alginate moulds, titanium implants and ceramic crowns, had taken a whole lot longer. But in the end, eight weeks after stumbling into A&E, a bloody battered mess on the arm of his best friend, the temporary teeth had been removed and the permanent replacements fixed. With the grateful thanks of his relieved parents ringing in the medical team's ears, Chris Hutchins had made it back.

But a victim even harder to fix had been Davey Boy. His injuries, hidden deep in the mind, were the invisible wounds of unintended consequence. His team, his friends, were lying close to death, broken and bleeding in hospitals north and south of the river. They were lying there because of him. From the moment the news had broken so had he; overwhelmed with grief and guilt. He'd acted solely to protect the boys but even in the fog of pain and adrenaline how could he have been so recklessly stupid?

The weeks that followed had been a pit of recrimination and bone-aching despair. He'd cursed. He'd howled. He'd swallowed bottles and put fists through walls and he'd prayed. He'd prayed harder than he'd ever prayed. And he hadn't stopped. And then one day, just like that, it had turned. Someone, somewhere, had thrown a lifeline and Davey Boy had grabbed and held on tight. Inch-by-inch his friends had been reeled back from the brink. Chrissy was being put back together and Jason was safe. Slowly the darkness surrounding him had begun to dissolve. The guilt, the remorse, they were still there. He knew they would always be there. But now something else was there too. It was tenuous, it was undeserved, but it was there just the same. It was hope.

THIRTY-SEVEN

Chris stood in front of the wall mirror, running a comb through his newly trimmed hair. With a straight unhooked nose and a Tom Cruise smile, the undertaker's apprentice was an apprentice no more. He looked a new man. He grinned at himself.

"Hell of a way to get a makeover," Jason murmured.

"You wish." Chris gave his image a last smirking sidewise glance then slid the comb into a pocket and sat down.

The small front room at Chris' parents wasn't the most glamorous of settings for the meeting but it was convenient and importantly, with Mr and Mrs H. not expected back until late, totally private.

Barefooted in shorts and 'T's, the boys had an armchair each. Davey Boy, all chinos and short-sleeved linen, had the sofa; the same sofa from behind which Jason had dragged the bin-bag of cash all those months ago. It was late summer, hot, the sun high in a chrome afternoon sky. It hadn't rained in weeks. Inside the small front room the ducks were still flying south on the tired woodchip; the carpet still a mess of well-trodden vibrant swirls. But across the low wide-open window there was a bright new rectangle. Washed and white, the nets hung listless, barely moving in the still air.

"So lads, how are you holding up?"

Jason looked at Chris and then back at Davey Boy.

"Still hangin' on in there Davey. But it's been tough"

"Yeah, I know. I'm sorry lads I wanted to meet sooner but I'm guessing you know things have been pretty difficult."

Jason nodded. If ever there was an understatement that was it. Twelve long weeks had passed since the bat cave had blown apart in a flaming fireball; twelve long weeks since the three of them had last been together and alone. Weeks that had seen Chris hospitalised, Davey Boy a withdrawn despondent shell and the nightmares, his own, night after night, waking him terrified in a bed of sweaty twisted sheets. 'Difficult' didn't cover a tenth of it back then. But today, twelve weeks on, it was different. Sitting on the warm plastic, watching shadows play on the bright nets, Jason was in a better place than he'd been for a long time. Chris, in the best of ways, was back to his comic worst; the long school holidays meandered under summer blue skies and evidenced by today's meeting, Davey too looked to be on the up. But above it all was the sense of anticipation building in the small room. There could be only one reason that Davey Boy had at last called them altogether and that reason had the potential to change their lives forever.

But it was Chris out of the gates first.

"So who the hell were those bastards Davey? They came out of nowhere."

Davey Boy shrugged.

THIRTY-SEVEN

"A call was made. Stuff was said that shouldn't have been said. It was picked up. The burner wasn't destroyed and it was traced. After that I don't know."

Silence.

Chris looked at Jason. Jason looked at Chris. The guilt on their faces said it all.

"Shit!"

"And because of that some bad people died and nearly a lot of good people too."

Oxygen seemed to be sucked from the small room. The air sat hot and still, the nets barely moving in the open window. Laughter drifted in from the end of the street. Light young voices. A shadow quickened across the window and was gone, the popping sound of a two stroke motor receding to the end of the street where it disappeared altogether. Somewhere between the kids and the moped a dog started barking.

"Christ Davey. I..."

Davey Boy held up a hand.

"It doesn't matter Jason. I'm not here to judge. Shit happens. Trust me I know."

"Bad people? Good people?" Chris looked confused.

Davey Boy exhaled a long breath and sat back into the sofa.

"Okay Chrissy. Since you asked, but try and keep up with me okay? The bad people are the ones that launched you headfirst into a wall. No one knows who they are or where they came from. Right now they're in a forensics lab somewhere, or at least what remains of them is. The authorities are trying to extract DNA but given they're working with stuff that looks like it's been scraped off the bottom of a blast furnace, they're not having much luck."

Chris grimaced.

"Ok, so then who are the good people?"

"The good people are the ones that didn't want to launch you into a wall but just wanted to catch you for their masters. The good news is the good people think the bad people are you and Jason and maybe me as well. So because of the bad people the good people aren't looking for us anymore."

Chris' face screwed in confusion.

"So that's... *good* then?"

"It's better than good Chrissy. The whole ATM investigation has been formally closed down."

Jason stared dumbfounded at Davey Boy.

"Really? It's over?" He felt almost lightheaded. "They're not looking for me anymore?"

"Not anymore Jason. Not unless you go and do something stupid."

Davey Boy's voice hardened. "But you do know any of this crazy shit happens again, even if you talk about it, then in all likelihood you will end up gone, gone for good, both of you. There are half-a-dozen government agencies out there, not just ours, who'd give up five years' worth of budget to have you in a laboratory somewhere. You've seen up close and dirty how these guys play. In their game *any* means can justify an end and I do mean *any*."

THIRTY-SEVEN

Chris swallowed hard but Jason, for the first time, appeared almost calm.

"I hear you Davey and you needn't worry. I don't know what this, this…thing in me is? I don't know how it got there or even how it bloody works. But it's there and I guess I just have to live with it. But there's one thing I *do* know," Jason's green eyes narrowed, "there's no way I ever want to go through this again. I don't want to talk about it, think about it or even dream about it. I know what it's like to be hunted Davey and there's no getting away from it, whoever they were, I killed those two people. That's something I'm going to have to live with every day, and I can tell you, hand on heart, never again."

Davey Boy nodded, his voice softening.

"It's for the best Jason but don't be going too hard on yourself. What happened back there was…well…not to be scientific about it…the weirdest, craziest, totally off-the-wall scariest shit, I've ever seen. But whatever it was, it saved our lives mate. No question. Those bastards, whoever they were, attacked you and Chrissy. Not the other way around. It was vicious, unprovoked and you did what you had to do. That's all. So you just keep that thought and keep it strong okay?"

Jason met Davey Boy's eyes.

"Thanks Davey, that means a lot."

Davey Boy nodded reassuringly. "It should Jason. It's the truth."

For a moment there was silence then, breaking the mood, Davey Boy reached for the briefcase he'd brought with him.

Jason had never seen Davey Boy with a briefcase before. It looked expensive; slim, all black leather and gold flip locks. Davey Boy laid it on the sofa beside him.

"And another truth," he said, "the suits can't catch what they can't see and they are going to be operationally blind for a long time with what I've got in here."

Davey Boy popped the locks on the case and withdrew two buff C5 envelopes. He lobbed them on to the carpet between the two armchairs.

"Chrissy your birthday is in November isn't it?"

"Yup! The fifth. Fireworks Night. Dad says Mum was surprised with a big bang."

"That we didn't need to know. What about you Jason?"

"October twentieth."

"Good. That will work; both eighteen in the next few months."

"So?" Chris arched his eyebrows.

"So you will have attained your legal majority dipstick."

"Legal what?"

Davey Boy sighed. "Don't ask me how Chrissy but you'll be classed as an adult and able to sign all the shit you need to sign to get out of this mess."

"I have to sign shit?"

"Yes you do."

"Better get the rubber gloves out then eh?"

Jason sniggered. Davey Boy, wearily, just shook his head.

Chris nodded at the two envelopes on the carpet. "So what are those?"

THIRTY-SEVEN

"You and Jason are going to need legally verifiable identification. Assuming you don't have passports, those are applications. And I also need your signatures on these."

Davey Boy withdrew a sheaf of formal looking typed documents from the briefcase and handed them to Jason.

"These are Trust documents. You'll see where I have marked the pages. They appoint trustees and you and Chrissy as beneficiaries."

"Beni-whats?" Chris' eyebrows were on an upward trajectory again.

"It means we get whatever is in the trusts," said Jason, quickly scanning the documents.

"Thank God!" exclaimed Davey Boy, falling back into the sofa, his hands holding his head. "Finally! Someone with an IQ higher than an aardvark's arse."

"What's an aardvark?" said Chris.

In the end it had all been cleared up. There were two offshore trusts; one in Singapore, one in Luxembourg. Somewhere in between was a shell company in the Seychelles and a bunch of bank accounts in the Arab Gulf. Teflon man had done his job. Once the completed papers were filed the professional trustees, two investment bankers in Singapore and two international lawyers in Luxembourg, would be standing by to advise and act upon instructions received. Davey Boy had provided the boys' details. All that was needed now were the signatures and the identifications. What hadn't been cleared up though was the matter of the money. Deliberately Davey Boy had left this revelation to the end. "The short version lads, we were screwed. The Chinese saw me coming. The bastards increased the commission then thieved the last three shipments off the sea in front of me. I'm sorry lads. There was nothing I could do. It was a total sandbagging."

Jason, his face falling, glanced quickly at Chris.

"How much did they take?"

"Nearly half a million pounds all in."

"Bastards!" Chris stood up. "Absolute bloody arsehole bastards!"

Jason was quieter. "So how much did that leave for the casino?"

Davey Boy shook his head.

"Eleven million Hong Kong in chips, about a million pounds."

"And you still had to pay your mate?"

Davey Boy nodded, "we agreed a hundred thousand."

"Pounds or Hong Kong dollars?"

"Pounds."

Jason's heart plummeted. Chris' followed it down.

"Take away the Tilbury money and that leaves only about half what we started with Davey. *Half!*"

Davey Boy shrugged.

"Look lads, it's still a lump of money. On the upside you could work for years and never see the same."

Jason felt sick.

THIRTY-SEVEN

"It's not just the money Davey. It's what it represented; the expectations, the hope. They were all we had to hang on to after what happened at the bat cave. Now you're telling us half of all that has just gone."

Before Davey Boy could reply, Chris waded in.

"But at least you limited the losses in the casino, right?"

"Well that didn't go to plan either."

"*Davey!*" Jason got up and stood with Chris in the centre of the small room. He looked down at Davey Boy who was sitting on the sofa like a small boy outside the Headmaster's office.

"This was your plan Davey. Your friend fixed it up. No problem you said. All you had to do was collect the chips, gamble a little, lose a little and cash out. How could it go wrong?"

Davey Boy stood up to join Jason and Chris in the middle of the small room. All it needed was a few poles and some straps and they could have been riding a packed six-thirty to Bermondsey.

"I didn't say it went *wrong*. I said it didn't go to *plan*. Look lads, you're right. The idea was to gamble a little and lose a little. But I'm sorry. It just didn't work out. You have to understand, sometimes these things just happen." The beginnings of a smile, just a small one, started at the corner of Davey Boy's mouth, the first hint of a genuine smile for weeks. Chris hadn't noticed. His face looked like it was chewing a lemon.

"So just tell us the damage Davey," he said. "How much did you lose?"

"He *didn't*," said Jason catching on. "That was the *great* news. He only went and bloody *won*."

"You won?" Chris looked at Davey Boy, his mouth open.

Davey Boy sat back down, his legs stretched out in front of him, ankles crossed, hands behind his head.

"Guilty as charged your Honour."

Chris fell onto the sofa beside him, their faces inches apart.

"How much?"

Davey Boy stood up again. He walked towards the window and turned. Behind him the daylight was a bright hard rectangle, his face in shadow. "I went in with the eleven million. I cashed out with over sixty two."

Jason beat Chris to it by a millisecond.

"Sixty two million dollars!"

"Yeah. But don't get too excited lads. It's Hong Kong dollars and I had a stack of fees and expenses. And remember, you both still owed me a chunk too. I reckon three-quarters of a million quid is fair. Anyway, I've drawn up a statement of account with the documents. It's all in there." Davey Boy nodded at the sheaf of papers in Jason's hand.

"But that said, if you two bell-ends pull your fingers out and help me get these papers signed and filed then there's the equivalent of two-and-half-million pounds waiting for you offshore when you turn eighteen…and that's each."

If oxygen had previously been sucked out of the room, now it came rushing back in. Davey Boy stood quietly, a grin on his face, as euphoria erupted around him like champagne in a blender. Whooping and yelping, the boys' kicked off. Chris squealing like a castrated fox, Jason frenziedly hammering the world's worst drum fill into the plastic sofa, then both, embracing, cackling and capering like a couple of looney-tunes. The sudden cork-popping reaction was as much about relief as joy and Davey Boy stood patiently, a human maypole, as the boys cavorted around him.

At last, systems purged, they fell back into their armchairs, spent, partially dazed, wrestling with the sudden implications and strange enormity of it all. For a moment, apart from the heavy breathing, all was quiet in the small room. Then Chris spoke. The look on his face was a picture. Not a pretty one.

"Davey, I don't know shit about trusts and all this stuff. What the *hell* am I meant to do?"

"Right now Chrissy, nothing at all. There's no rush. Your trustees are primed to handle everything. They're specialists and they know their stuff. The more money they make for you, the more they make for themselves so let them do their thing. Even putting the money into a run-of-the-mill bank account will deliver interest around five grand a month, so you'll have plenty of time to decide. And I'm going to be around if you need me. We've come this far together I'm not about to let you fall into the shit now am I?"

Chris' face split into a wide relieved grin. He looked across at Jason.

"I bloody told you Jace. Remember? Arse and sunshine? Me mum wasn't wrong."

Smiling, Jason tapped the side of his nose. "Too bloody right mate."

Davey Boy, puzzled, looked long at both boys. They beamed back. He shook his head.

"So what now Davey?" Jason looked at the man who had pulled them through; who had risked everything for them. Chris' mum was right. The sun didn't just shine, it dazzled.

Placing the open briefcase back on the carpet, Davey Boy sat on the edge of the sofa, back straight, leaning forward ever so slightly.

"Well lads, I'm thinking now might be the time to come clean and bring your parents on board."

Chris started to say something but Davey Boy silenced him with a raised hand.

"Look, I know what you're thinking lads but they're going to find a lot of this out sooner or later. You can't keep five million quid secret. Grasp the nettle now and save your backs the rod later. What's the worst that can happen?"

Chris looked like he'd swallowed a wasp. "You know mum Davey. You tell me?"

Davey Boy shrugged, "A lot of shouting and arm waving never hurt anyone Chrissy. And they are your family. I'm not saying you should open up about all the grisly details but the basics need to be told. Okay, so you cop some flack but in the end do you think it will matter? No it won't. It may take a little time to sink in but when they understand, trust me, they'll just want to make sure you stay protected and safe."

THIRTY-SEVEN

Jason looked across at Chris and then back again to Davey Boy.

"Can you be there with us?"

"Do you want me to be?"

Both Jason and Chris nodded silently.

Davey Boy nodded back.

"I'll speak to your parents and set it up for the weekend. Listen lads, I'm sure it's not going to be as bad as you think. Keep positive and everything will be fine."

Jason got up from the armchair.

"So...is that it then?"

Davey Boy nodded, "I guess it is."

Jason held out a hand. "I've got no words Davey, but… thanks…thanks…for everything."

Davey Boy smiled. "It's a two way street Jason. I wouldn't be here now if it wasn't for you. None of us would. The thing is, you, me, Chrissy, each of us has been put through the grinder but we've also been given a start-over; a clean page. What we write on it now is up to us."

Jason looked down into the carpet swirls.

"I'm not sure I would know what to write?"

"That's for you to decide. It always was. Even before all this started. But you'll figure it out."

Davey Boy bent, picked up the passport applications and put them neatly on a small side table. He pulled a pair of Ray-Bans from the briefcase, closed the lid, snapped the flip-locks shut and stood.

Jason looked up sharply.

"But what about you Davey? What will you do now?"

Davey Boy paused in front of the wide window, the curling edges of his thick dark hair back-lit silver in bright afternoon light.

"The only thing one *can* do on a day like this," he said smiling.

"I'm going for a walk in the park."

THIRTY-EIGHT
EPILOGUE

Falling in a dark green cauliflowering sprawl from the peninsula's limestone and granite spine towards the north-eastern coast of Terengganu, the Malaysian rainforest is ancient; perhaps the oldest on the planet; 130 million years and counting, and it was living up to its name. The noise of water was everywhere. Up in the vast canopy, a hundred and forty feet above the forest floor, it hissed invisibly, a thousand distant finger-cymbals under the monsoon deluge. Below, in dense, dim, cathedrals of leafy green it trickled, dribbled, plinked and gurgled; collecting in mossy pools between buttressed roots, spattering onto the sodden leaf-mulch of the forest floor, running in thick rivulets down dense, damp, hardwood trunks and dripping in fat lens-like drops from the tips of a million quivering leaves.

Sitting on his haunches under the atap, Tengalung listened to the watery susurrations all around him. The pattering rhythms of rain on the fronds above his head were soothing. But the cloudburst would stop soon and then he must move. Poking the greying embers of his small fire with a stick, he looked back into the recesses of the lean-to. Even in sleep he could see the pain etched on his mother's face. But she still had a little strength and they were close now. The small rural clinic at Sungai Berua was less than half-a-day's walk. But with his mother's condition it would still be difficult to reach the kampong by nightfall. The rain had brought an earthy sweetness to the hot humidity of the forest and Tengalung inhaled deeply.

All his young life he had lived in this forest. Two hundred full moons his uncle had told him. It was a place of wonder and sustenance but it was also cruel. His father had been taken by a sickness before he was born. Then the men had come from beyond with fire and machines. They had raised the forest to bare red earth and had taken his people away; away to places of thin brick walls, blue tin roofs and water from iron pipes. Places like Sungai Berua. But his uncle had refused to go. He had taken him and his mother deep into the forested hills where the men couldn't come and there they had lived as the Batek had always lived; hunting, foraging, always moving. His uncle had been a good man. He had protected him, taught him how to hunt, shown him how a man could be rich with just a cooking pot, a digging stick, fishing pole and knife. But two full moons ago the sickness had returned. It had taken his uncle like it had taken his father and now his mother too was sick. The machines of the men from beyond were mighty. Their medicine must be mighty too. Tengalung hoped with all his heart it would be so. All he had left in this world was his mother. He remembered his uncle telling him that happiness was never having a *sumpit* far from one's hand. But his uncle had been wrong. He had

had his father's blowpipe for as long as he could remember. It had never been far from his hand and yet alone under the nipa fronds, listening to his mother's fitful breathing, watching the wisps of grey smoke from his small fire disappear into the rain, he had never been so sad.

Tengalung glanced up. The pattern of rain drops on the lean-to's sloping roof had changed. Cocking an ear, he waited. Soon enough a mournful 'whooping' erupted high in the canopy and he nodded imperceptibly. The rain was stopping. Already the silvered gibbons were calling each other back out into the canopy. It was time to move.

Carrying his mother in his arms, Tengalung came down out of the hills into the spreading oil palm plantations south of Sungai Berua. The plantations surrounded the old hunting grounds. Lands that had been flooded to form the vast lake they called Kenyir. The water glimmered under the setting sun, hard and flat for as far as he could see. Shoeless, in ragged shorts and soiled singlet, he had left most of their meagre possessions behind in the forest. He carried his mother wrapped in her thin sarong. Her feeble pulse barely felt against his chest. His sharp-bladed *weng* hung in its soft-wood sheath at his hip, his *sumpit* slung across his back with its quiver of *damak*. Five of the long needle-pointed darts remained and they rattled softly in the bamboo tube as he moved.

His mother was frail but she still carried weight. Tengalung was slender, dark and short, with a broad nose, a shock of wiry black hair and bright quick eyes. He had been named for the striped civet cat; agile, fast and cunning but not strong. That he'd found the strength within his small frame to carry his mother such distances and over such terrain, shocked him. *How was it possible?* Touching the small amulet on the lace around his neck he prayed it was an omen; a good one.

Stepping out from the last of the plantation rows Tengalung ascended a small rise. Cradling his mother awkwardly he clambered over a low steel Armco barrier and onto the last curve of metalled road before the kampong. Light was failing, the sun already hidden behind the western hills. The monotonous electric shrill of cicadas was building and the shapes in the indigo sky were those of bats now, not birds. The road rasped against the calloused soles of his feet but it was warm from the day's heat and flat. Adjusting the weight of his mother in his arms he picked up pace and, swallowing apprehension, walked on towards the small settlement.

The government kampong had been constructed along one side of the road. Tengalung could see the rows now, almost barracks, of off-white grubby tin-roofed blocks indistinct in the growing darkness. A narrow metallised fillet forked off the main road and he followed it down a low embankment, past a sign on two poles, over a storm drain and into the settlement. Already kerosene lamps were being lit; dim yellow rectangles glowing amidst a ragged cultivation of darkening banana, mangosteen and durian. The metallised lane petered into a path of beaten earth, the warmth dissipating under his feet, and he stopped, uncertain of the way. The sporadic sounds and smells of community, near and distant, drifted in the growing gloom; infants crying, dogs barking, the tinny clattering of cooking pots, the aromas of rice, yam, burning charcoal and the sweet smell of clove tobacco.

"Who are you?"

Tengalung turned. Two men sat on a low step, the coals of their cigarettes glowing. They spoke Batek. It shouldn't have surprised him. Following the land clearances many of what remained of his people lived in government administered kampong-camps such as Sungai Berua. But he hadn't heard the spoken word since his mother had fallen sick. It had been many days.

He shuffled under the weight he was carrying. "I am Tengalung. My mother, she is sick," he said.

No further explanation was necessary. It was the Batek way. The men nodded solemnly. One gestured, a spark flying from his smoke.

"It is late. To find the doctor you must go quickly." He pointed up an intersecting path.

"There will be a sign. A new moon painted red like blood."

Nodding thanks Tengalung moved ahead down the indicated path, between rows of identical dull-bricked huts separated by patches of scrubby vegetation and washing lines heavy with the limp shapes of clothes drying. The night had fully settled now but it wasn't truly dark. Not like the forest. Not like he was used to.

He found the crescent of the new moon on a faded tin sign back up alongside the metalled road at the far end of the kampong. In daylight the crescent may have been as red as fresh blood but now it was as dark as a bat's wing. Behind the sign two shadowy single-storey brick buildings stood on a metalled forecourt behind a low gated chain-link fence. One with a pitched tin roof and a deep veranda, and one set-off behind it at an angle. Both the buildings were small. The front building had windows; dim yellow lamplight gleaming behind horizontal glass slats, opened wide in the forlorn hope of catching a breeze. There were no windows in the building behind, just a closed tightly louvered door. Like the moth, Tengalung followed the lamplight. Since coming down from the rainforested hills the temperature had risen. The humidity was like a blanket and the heat hummed in the plastered brick of the buildings and the metaled surface of the small forecourt. Under the veranda and inside through the open door it was even hotter; like a dim, tin-roofed oven.

Tengalung laid his mother down tenderly across the plastic seats of four metal chairs pushed up against the inside of a whitewashed wall. She was unconscious, sweating heavily, her small face flushed and mottled. He propped his *sumpit* up against the wall by his mother and looked about him.

EPILOGUE

The room was concrete and brick. Smooth floor and plastered whitewashed walls, the ceiling vaulted under the pitched tin roof. A large four-bladed fan flanked by shaded lights on long flexes dangled in the void. Steel window frames filled with horizontal glass slats perforated three of the walls. The fourth wall had a closed door in the middle of it behind a waist-high counter of hardwood. A table-fan and two kerosene lamps stood on the counter top. Under the windows and either side of the open door, lines of metal-framed chairs with hard plastic moulded seats, like the four he'd laid his mother across, were pushed back against the walls. Above the chairs one wall was festooned with cartoon-like coloured medical posters and pinned notices. At knee height in a gap between two chairs, the carcass of an air-conditioning unit protruded through the wall, its plastic grill thick with matted dust. The only light in the dim room came from the two oil lamps on the counter. They threw competing shadows across the posters, chairs, counter and open windows. Nothing else moved, shone, worked or made a sound. The room was empty.

Tengalung called out. He waited and then called again. He called a third time. Behind the hardwood counter the door opened with a smell of food cooking. A man and a young woman emerged from an equally dimly lit room beyond. They were Malay. The man, lean, a thin unbuttoned white coat over brown trousers and a white cotton shirt, rubber flip-flops on his feet. His hair razored so short his brown scalp showed through the black bristles. He looked irritated. The woman, hardly more than a girl Tengalung thought, wore jeans, a long sleeved blouse and white trainers. Her head and shoulders covered in a blue tudung, pinned back around the young oval of her face.

The man took a long look. He saw the blowpipe, the ragged shorts, the dirty singlet, the dark skin and thick frizzy hair. He didn't look at the woman in the sarong laid across the chairs. He didn't need to.

"Orang Asli," he said. It was a statement, not a question.

Tengalung only spoke a few words of Malay but he knew what the man had said. All Batek would know what the man had said. It was the Malay 'catch-all' for people like him; people like his father, his uncle and his mother; for the people who had been forced from the forests to live in places like Sungai Berua, for all the aboriginal peoples. Officially it meant 'original people'; the 'people of the forest'. Unofficially it lent to something else; something demeaning, degrading, something evocative of illiteracy, ignorance, filth, paganism and disease. But Tengalung, pointing at his mother, simply nodded.

"My mother. She is sick. She needs medicine. I have brought her from the forest. Help her please."

The man turned to the young woman. "What did he say?"

The woman spoke quickly, translating the Batek to Malay. She was in the third year of an anthropology degree at the University of Malaysia and for the past two months had been living at Sungai Berua, gathering research for her thesis on Proto-Malay peoples. Her dissertation was almost finished.

The man frowned. "It is impossible. We have no power. Tell him to look around. He can see for himself. Until we have repairs and the batteries replaced we are lucky even to have these lamps." He gestured at the two oil lamps on the hardwood counter. The woman turned to the short, dark boy with the broad nose and shock of wiry black hair. His quick, bright, eyes looked at her expectantly. She spoke to him as kindly as she could.

"I am sorry. We cannot," she explained. She saw the look in his eyes and she understood. They were the original people, the people of the forest. It was a disparaging term for a misunderstood and maligned minority; a minority with less than a thousand individuals that was on the verge of extinction. A simple proud people they had been marginalised, exploited, moved off their land, discriminated against, despised. The bulk made to reside in government kampongs in cheap regimented easily contained and controlled communities. And now this boy's mother was dying. He had come to them in desperation and they were turning him away.

Tengalung turned and walked back to where his mother lay. He knelt by her side, his bamboo quiver and wooden sheath scraping the concrete floor. He could see her life-force leaching into the oppressive humidity of the night. It wouldn't be long now. He stood and turned.

"Please. Help my mother."

The man approached and shone a small torch into his mother's face. He held her wrist and then held two fingers to her neck. He listened with a tube from his ears to her chest. Then he turned to the young woman.

"Tell him there is nothing we can do," he said, "she is burning up with fever. We have no power to cool her, no refrigeration for our antivirals, no bloody power for anything. Our hands are tied. You have to try and make him understand. Tell him to look at the village. Where are the electric lights, radio, TV? Does he think this is how we live, with just oil lamps and mosquito nets?"

"That's exactly how he thinks we live," said the woman.

"Well we don't. So tell him."

Tengalung didn't need to be told.

He'd built the death platform for his uncle himself; as high in the canopy as he could manage. He and his mother had pulled together on the braided vines, hoisting the body of her brother high above the forest floor to rest with the spirits of their' ancestors. And now these people who had destroyed his home; who had come with mighty machines, who had decimated his people and their way of life, were sending him back to do the same for his mother. Anger, failure, desperation and utter despair welled up inside him. They were turning her away to die like his father, like his uncle, leaving him isolated, alone. They were sentencing his mother to death without even trying. He stood at the open door, by the prone body of his mother, shivering in the heat. Clenching his fists he closed his eyes and howled. Startled, the man and woman stepped back. Tengalung spun around; his hair a mane of floating black, his eyes luminous, bright, glowing. Dashing the table-fan into the floor he scrabbled at the wall posters, hurling chairs and smashing window slats. He kicked hard at the air-conditioning unit. The brittle plastic frame cracked through and his foot, hard, calloused like iron-wood, struck the thin metal evaporator coils. A cloud of sparks erupted with a fizzling crack and an unseen bolt of pure energy coursed through the steel of the compressor and condenser coils; through the welded steel contacts; along a finger-thick insulated copper wire, through the brick wall, down into the ground and up into the power-generator building behind the clinic.

The electrification of Sungai Berua had been a miracle; an expensive government-funded miracle. Way out on the edges of deep rainforest, in the middle of nowhere, its power came from the sun. Photovoltaic panels harvested the energy. Banks of heavy lead-acid batteries stored it. Solar invertors, as big as fridge-freezers, transformed it. Cheap renewable electricity fed on demand into a micro-grid of power lines spreading throughout the small settlement.

At least that's how the system manufacturers had touted it. But it hadn't turned out that way. The money had been paid, the kick-backs received and the commissions pocketed. The politicians had moved on. There had been no after-sales support; no maintenance, no training, no education. The power was free. It was magic. The residents had plugged in anything they could; TV, lights, radio, cookers, refrigerators, fans, more lights. Solar panels had been stolen, overgrown with vegetation, broken. The lead-acid batteries drained recharged and drained so many times they had become as useless as stone boulders. But the network of cables and connections was still there; running through Sungai Berua from the generator house like empty veins in a cadaver. But, for an instant, just a micro-moment, they weren't empty anymore.

By-passing the invertors and banks of useless batteries, an explosion of unregulated electrical energy surged from the generator house like water through a hole in a dam. Overloading the network of cables and connections at 1,860 miles a second, Sungai Berua lit up like a lightening flash in a thunderstorm. In the clinic; in the run-down schoolhouse opposite, in the fifty drab tin-roofed houses, between the pathways of beaten earth and washing lines, way out on the margins of the rainforest, in the middle of nowhere, light-bulbs exploded, cables melted, neon tubes shattered and fuses detonated like gunfire.

The lean man unwound from his foetal position on the floor. He sat up. Thin shards of light bulb glass peppered his black bristly hair and white coat. He helped up the girl lying next to him. Her tudung had slipped. Beneath it her dark hair was held loosely in a rubber-banded pony tail. "Be careful," he said, "there is glass in your hair." She nodded thanks, lifting delicate fingers to her scalp. The man smelt ozone in the air; a thin, clean, chemical smell like bleach. It mingled with a stench of burning and melted plastic. Through the door and the open window came noise; loud anxious voices, young and old, dogs barking, lots of them, babies and infants crying. He turned, looking for the boy and his mother; the short dark boy with the glowing eyes and mane of black floating hair. The body of the small frail woman lay where he had examined her, across the four hard plastic seats, unmoving, covered in her thin sarong, the long length of blowpipe still propped against the wall beside her.

The boy was gone.

Coming soon
ATM2 – The Phantom.

About the author

Born into the Mau-Mau uprising on the East African slopes of Mount Kenya, Tom Chaine grew up in rural Malaysia and then Singapore. The son of a military engineer he has developed a forty year career supplying military defence equipment to the governments of South East Asia on behalf of some of the foremost defence equipment manufacturing companies in Europe and the USA. Pursuing a love of writing and classic cars, Tom lives on the edge of two and a half thousand acres of wild parkland near Richmond, West London.

www.tomchaine.com